ROGUE'S MAGIC

EERIE SIDE OF THE TRACKS BOOK 3

ELLIE FERGUSON

ALSO BY THE AUTHOR

Written as Sam Schall

BATTLE FLIGHT

VENGEANCE FROM ASHES

DUTY FROM ASHES

HONOR FROM ASHES

FIRE FROM ASHES

BETRAYAL FROM ASHES

RISEN FROM THE ASHES

Written as Amanda S. Green

NOCTURNAL ORIGINS

NOCTURNAL SERENADE

NOCTURNAL INTERLUDE

NOCTURNAL HAUNTS

NOCTURNAL CHALLENGE

NOCTURNAL REBELLION

NOCTURNAL REVELATIONS

NOCTURNAL PREY

SWORD OF ARELION

DAGGER OF ELANNA

Written as Ellie Ferguson

HUNTED

TRACKED

Prey (coming soon)

MOSSY CREEK/EERIE SIDE OF THE CREEK SERIES

For my Family

"Hey, Doc. Phone!"

I closed my eyes and fought the urge to curse. Instead, I inhaled deeply. The odors of antiseptic, blood and other things best left unsaid assailed me. At least Keelan waited for me to finish repairing the German shepherd's injured hip before interrupting. Still, she knew better than to call me to the phone unless it was an emergency.

My stomach did a flip and then a flop and my heart beat a quick staccato. Keelan did know better than to interrupt me while in surgery. Whoever was calling, it wasn't good. Not good at all.

I opened my eyes and looked over my shoulder, not surprised to see her standing outside the small room the practice euphemistically called the OR. She lifted a hand and pressed the button on the other side of the wall, activating the speaker once again.

"Sorry, Doc. But I think you need to take this. It's Ali O'Donnell."

The world slammed to a halt. Ali. My seven- almost eight-year-old goddaughter. As precocious and precious as she could be. And an *Other*, like her mother and her mother before her.

Her call could mean anything. She might want to tell me about something that happened in school or her latest lesson with Miss

Serena. But I knew better. Ali never called unless she needed help with something. I blew out a breath and looked at Keelan.

"Tell her I'll be there in a minute. I need to finish up here." I didn't wait for Keelan to answer. "Devin, I want him monitored until he comes out from the anesthesia." The vet tech nodded and waited as I dictated instructions for treatment and meds. "I'll check on him later and I'll call Mr. Calloway and let him know Kaiser came through the surgery all right."

And that hadn't been a sure thing. Calloway didn't believe in keeping his dogs fenced in. Because of that, Kaiser paid the price by getting into a fight with several other dogs in the neighborhood. He'd have scars, a torn ear and a probable limp from now on. And Calloway was going to find out what happens when you don't take care of your pets. I'd warned him before that I'd call the county and report him if another of his animals got hurt because of his negligence. Today, he'd learn I was a woman of my word.

No one, absolutely no one, hurts an animal and gets away with it. Not if I can help it. And old man Calloway had hurt Kaiser through his negligence.

I rested a gentle hand on the dog's head and offered up a quick prayer. Then I stepped back, stripping off my gloves and mask. I dropped them into the receptacle by the door. Time to see what my goddaughter wanted.

Keelan met me with a mug of coffee, a bottle of water and two Tylenol. I thanked her before tossing back the pills and washing them down with half the bottle of water. Then I took a grateful sip of coffee, wishing I had time for a shower before dealing with Ali. Unfortunately, that had to come later.

"Here you go, Doc." Keelan handed me my cellphone.

"Thanks." I smiled slightly. One bracing breath later, I took the call off hold. "Hey, Ali. What's up?"

"Auntie Jax, you need to come home. Something's wrong."

I swallowed hard and once again closed my eyes, searching for my center. Once before I'd gotten a call like this from Ali. That time, she'd summoned fire for the first time. She and her mother, one of my oldest and dearest friends, lived in Montana then and I could do little to help from my home south of Austin. But now they lived in Mossy Creek, the small town where Quinn and I grew up. The same town that seemed determined to bring all its wayward children home.

And if there was ever a wayward child, it was me.

"Ali, what is it? Is your mama all right?"

"It's not Mama, Auntie Jax. Something's wrong with Aunt Annie."

My heart skipped a beat and I dropped onto the chair behind my desk. After switching the cellphone to speaker and setting it on the desktop, I reached for my laptop. My fingers flew across the keyboard as I began searching for flights to Dallas. If something really had happened to Annie Grissom Caldwell, another of our inner circle going all the way back to elementary school, I needed to get to Mossy Creek as quickly as possible.

"What's wrong with Aunt Annie, sweetie?" I did my best to keep my voice calm even as I screamed mentally in frustration and fear. Then it hit me. My goddaughter had called me. Not her mother. Not Annie and not Sam, Annie's husband. Maybe it wasn't too late. Maybe Ali had another talent manifesting and she'd *seen* something that hadn't happened yet.

"I don't know."

I heard the tears in her voice and wanted to reach out and hold her. But I couldn't. Instead, I inhaled deeply and prayed I found the right words to reassure her.

"It's okay, Ali. I promise we're going to find out what's wrong." I thought for a moment. "Is your mama home?" I knew the answer before Ali replied. She'd called from Quinn's phone. That meant Quinn hadn't yet left for work.

I hoped.

"Ali, let me talk to your mama. You aren't in trouble, I promise. But if something is wrong with Aunt Annie, your mom can help until I get there."

I hoped.

"But you're coming?"

"I'll be there just as soon as I can. Promise."

I shouldn't. I was the junior vet at the clinic and my bosses made it clear from the beginning that they expected me there, no matter what. I needed the job to pay off my college loans, not to mention rent and other bills. But I heard the fear in Ali's voice and her conviction that only I could help. I'd never turned my back on the little girl before and I wasn't about to start now. Hopefully, by the time I got to Mossy Creek, whatever had Ali upset would be dealt with. Then I could spend the night with my friends and get back to New Braunfels and work.

"Jax? What is it? Is something wrong?"

Quinn's voice broke into my thoughts and I shook my head. Ali clearly hadn't told her mother about calling me. Great.

"Quinn, listen and don't interrupt. Ali called me, telling me I need to come home. She said something's wrong with Annie, but she doesn't know what." I waited, praying Quinn had an answer. Instead, she cursed almost as inventively as I can and that's saying a great deal. The fact she was doing it where her daughter could hear wasn't good. Not good at all.

"Hang on. Let me see if I can reach her."

As I waited for Quinn to come back on the line, I turned my attention back to finding a flight out. Now it was my time to curse. I could fly standby or book a seat on the one o-clock flight. Neither option appealed to me. But what choice did I have? I needed to get to Mossy Creek and flying was faster than driving, at least if I stuck to the speed limit.

I slid an earbud into my left ear and made sure it synced with the cellphone. With that done, I drafted out care instructions for Kaiser and my other patients. I'd give that to Teegan on my way out. Then I called old man Calloway on the office phone. He sputtered and cursed before promising he'd keep Kaiser in the yard or on a leash from now on. Still waiting for Quinn to get back to me, I wrote up my notes on the call and added them to Kaiser's file.

Why hadn't Quinn gotten back to me?

"Jax, you still there?" The barely controlled anger in her voice told me all I needed to know. Something was very wrong.

"What's happened?" I grabbed the backpack I carried instead of a purse whenever at work and shoved first my laptop and then my wallet inside.

"I don't know the details, but Annie's been hurt. Robbie found her in the laundry room when he came home from playing across the street. Lucas is on his way there. As soon as Mom gets back from the store, I'm heading over there as well. Where are you?"

"At the clinic and heading out."

"What's your flight information? I'll pick you up."

I shook my head and then remembered she couldn't see me. "I'm driving. No flights available until this afternoon."

"Jax."

I heard the warning in her voice and understood. But what choice did I have?

"You just tell whoever you need to that I'm coming up I-35 and I'm not going to be doing speed limits."

She growled and I smiled slightly. Quinn might think of herself as a rebel but, at heart, she believed in the rules and did her best to follow them. That's what made her such a good DEA agent. Me, on the other hand, earned my childhood nickname of Rogue. Rules were meant to be broken, especially if they were rules set down by my parents.

"You just be careful," she warned.

"I will." I pushed back from the desk. "Quinn, find out what the hell is going on and keep me in the loop. I'll be there as soon as I can."

"I will." She paused and I listened as she told someone she'd be right there. "Sorry, Mom's home and Ali's trying to tell her about her feeling that something's wrong with Annie."

At least Mrs. O'Donnell was there. One of her gifts was foresight. Maybe she'd be able to explain why Ali knew something happened to Annie when no one else seemed to know anything was wrong.

"Tell Ali I'm on my way. Then get over to Annie's. Find out what the hell is going on. Call me as soon as you know anything. I'll let you know when I reach town."

"Be careful, Jax." Worry, for Annie and for me, thickened her voice.

"You, too." Now it was my turn to tell her to hang on for a moment. I needed to take care of a couple of things before heading out.

I drew a bracing breath and slung the backpack over my shoulder. A moment later, I dropped my notes on Teegan's desk. She wasn't there, fortunately. I wasn't up to explaining. Then I slid a sealed envelope under the closed door for the practice's senior vet. It was better to quit than be fired. At least that's what I told myself. On my way out, I stopped at one of the treatment rooms and let Coby Campion, the practice's newest vet, know I had an emergency and needed to leave. Fortunately, it was Saturday and most of our patients for the day could be handled by the techs. Coby would call in help if she needed it.

"Quinn," I continued as I slid in behind the steering wheel of my 2018 Chevy Camaro. The engine roared to life and I carefully backed out of my parking space. "I'm on my way. You keep Annie safe. And tell Miss Serena I'm heading home and want to see her, tonight if possible."

"I will. Don't take any chances."

I promised to be careful and ended the call. Almost instantly, my phone rang. I knew without checking the display who it was. I tapped my earbud and answered.

"Jax," the soft drawl I knew so well began.

"I know, Aunt Bitsy, and I'm on my way home. I should be there in a couple of hours." No need to tell her I was driving. She'd only worry. Or, knowing Bitsy, cheer me on. Like me, she knew rules were made to be broken, at least when it meant helping someone you loved.

"How?" she started to ask and then stopped. "Quinn?"

"No." I actually laughed. "Ali." I quickly related the basics of my conversation with the little girl.

"That little girl might just take your place as Mossy Creek's rogue, Jax."

Bitsy chuckled and I joined in. What could I say? Especially since I had a feeling she was right. We spoke for another few minutes. Unlike Quinn, Bitsy didn't try to dissuade me from driving. Instead, she said not to take time stopping by my apartment. I had clothes at her house, and we'd get anything else I might need once I got there.

That was Bitsy and just one of the many reasons I loved her. She understood how I thought and what was important to me. Unlike my parents, she never tried to make me into something I wasn't. When things got bad with them when I was in high school, she stood up for me, offering me a place in her home and making sure I graduated and got into college. She'd been more of a parent to me—even before that happened—than her brother and sister-in-law ever had been.

And it was why I wouldn't be staying with her. I couldn't. My parents, once they knew I was back in town, would make her life miserable if they knew she was putting me up. But that was something to worry about later, after I knew how Annie was.

Still, I wanted to make a statement when I "officially" arrived in town and Bitsy was just the person to help make it happen. I explained what I had in mind and grinned when she laughed gaily, her worry for Annie momentarily forgotten. I imagined her sitting in her sunroom, rubbing her hands together gleefully as she considered what she could do to "improve" on my plans.

Heaven help Mossy Creek. The rogue was coming home and was being aided and abetted by the aunt everyone continued to underestimate.

2

I didn't need to see the green and white sign welcoming me to Mossy Creek. I felt the change the moment I crossed the city limit line. The energies of the land reached up to welcome me. If I stopped the car and rolled down the window, I'd hear "You're home, you're home, you're home", or some variation of it, whispering on the wind. I had a connection with the town, one living more than a hundred miles way had not severed. Now the town itself, and the land it sat on, welcomed me home.

Home.

To an outsider, Mossy Creek looked like any number of other small towns. It was but it was also so much more. More than a century ago, Mossy Creek became one of the first towns in Texas—not to mention the nation—where *Others* were welcomed. From the beginning, we lived in peace with the normals. We went to the same schools and churches. We were neighbors and friends, lovers and more. Sure, there are still those who look at us as abominations, no matter how much we do for the town or our neighbors. Fear and envy are ugly things and so long as there are humans on the Earth, those two emotions will exist. That's something I learned first-hand from my parents.

Of course, the fact I hadn't made any real effort to be the "good" daughter they wanted didn't help matters any. Not that I cared. I wasn't going to change for them or for anyone else. Thankfully, Bitsy understood and encouraged me to be my own person.

As I drove through the center of town, I fought the urge to go directly to the hospital to check on Annie. Quinn's last call had been short and to the point. Evidence pointed to someone having attacked Annie inside the house. No, the twins hadn't been hurt and Robbie, other than being worried about his mother, was fine. As for Annie, all Quinn knew was she'd been taken by ambulance to the hospital and she was being treated.

Good news and yet not enough to ease my worry. Nothing would until I saw for myself that Annie was going to be all right.

Before I did that, I needed to see Quinn who, at least as far as I knew, was still at Annie's house. But there was something I needed to do first. If the rogue was back, I needed to look the part.

Ten minutes later, I stood in the bedroom of the apartment over the garage at my aunt's house. Bitsy set it up for me when I was a teenager, knowing I needed a safe space away from my parents. In the years since, she'd kept it for me, updating it as needed. For not the first time, I silently thanked her.

Then I turned and smiled. Elizabeth "Bitsy" Powell-Gunnerson was my champion and always had been. Small and sleek, the image she presented to much of the world was that of a flighty woman with too much money, too much time on her hands and not enough common sense. Hard drinking and harder loving, those who bought into the image thought she had fluff for brains. That failure on their part helped build her rather impressive business portfolio because, beneath the ditzy exterior, lived an astute businesswoman with the heart of a tigress when it came to protecting those she loved.

I was fortunate enough to fall into that category.

"I'm going to the hospital to sit with the family," she said from where she stood just inside my bedroom. "Do you want me to say anything to them about your arrival?"

I shook my head and then turned my attention to the clothes she'd laid out on the bed. A smile lifted one corner of my mouth. She'd taken me at my word when I told her "Rogue" was coming home.

Thank God.

"I'll be there as soon as I talk with Quinn. Hopefully, she'll know what the hell happened and who hurt Annie."

Anger spiked along with frustration. With it came a tingling in my palms. Bitsy merely arched one finely shaped brow as the ground did a slow roll we felt even though we were above the garage. Frowning, I closed my eyes and concentrated, letting go of my anger. Of all the gifts, as an Earth elemental, mine was one of the most dangerous. The last thing we needed was me calling an earthquake or something worse because I didn't keep my temper in check.

"Let me know if she does. In the meantime, I'll try to keep Catherine calm."

I couldn't help my grin. Keeping Annie's mom, Catherine Eugenia Metzger Grissom Dinsmore Carlisle, calm would take a miracle. She loved Annie and Drew, Annie's twin brother, but to say Catherine was self-centered and immature was putting it mildly. She was trying, however.

Sometimes she was trying in more ways than one.

"Thanks, Aunt Bitsy."

I quickly stripped out of the scrubs I'd worn on the drive up. Soon I wore black jeans and a black tank top. Black boots replaced my tennis shoes. My fingers worked quickly to French braid my auburn hair. I completed the image with black leather cuffs on both wrists. Satisfied, I studied my reflection in the full-sized mirror. Even without the tattoo sleeve with its animals that seemed alive covering my left arm, I presented the image of potential troublemaker.

Good.

"New ink?" Bitsy moved to stand next to me. She took my left arm and gently ran a finger down the tattoo of a bobcat perched on a tree limb, expression intent, ears seeming to twitch as it studied its prey.

"Yeah."

I didn't say anything more. I didn't need to. Bitsy understood the importance of my tats. She'd never questioned why I wanted them and had, in fact, paid for my first one, a wolf sitting in the shadows of a tree.

"Take these." She dropped two keyrings onto my upraised palm. "The first is to the black Porsche in the garage. Title, insurance, everything you might need are in the glovebox. Tank is full. It took some doing but I managed to get one without dealer's plates." Before I could say anything, she grinned and mischief gleamed in her eyes. She was having fun. "The other keys are to a Ducati Panigale V4. It's parked next to the Porsche. I figured a kick ass rogue like you ought to have an equally kickass car and motorcycle."

I looked from the keys to my aunt and dropped onto the edge of the mattress. That was so like Bitsy. She didn't care how much either the car or the bike cost. She thought about why I might need them, especially if I was dusting off my persona as the town rogue. She was a smart enough investor to know she'd be able to sell both of them and not lose much, if any, of her initial investment if she played her cards right. In the meantime, she'd be hurt if I didn't take advantage of the gifts she offered.

Besides, who in their right mind would give up either a Porsche or a Ducati?

"Thanks." I stood and leaned over to kiss her cheek. "You didn't happen to think about a riding jacket and helmet by any chance?"

"With the bike." She grinned and mischief sparkled in her eyes. "Jax, I'm glad you're home. The girls are going to need you, especially if anything serious happens to Annie."

I swallowed hard and nodded, not wanting to think of what Quinn and I would do if Annie had been seriously hurt. Without Annie to talk us down, we would cut a swath of destruction through the town until we found whoever was responsible for hurting her. As if reading my mind, Bitsy took my hands in hers and gave them a gentle squeeze, waiting until she had my attention.

"Jax, I know how much Annie means to you. I also know you will do everything you can to protect her and to find out who hurt her. But, and I want you to remember this, you aren't the rogue. And certainly not in the way your parents and their friends meant when they called you that. You don't do anything just to buck authority. You are a protector, even a fighter when you have to be. Most of all, you are a caring young woman who would never misuse her talents."

I sniffled once and pulled her into a hug. She had always known exactly who and what I was—even when I didn't. "You go make sure Catherine didn't try to take her *babies* to the hospital."

Bitsy groaned and I laughed, my first real laugh since Ali's call.

"If she did, I may take them and drown them and tell her they ran off," my aunt threatened

Still grinning, I shook my head. Much as she might be tempted, Bitsy wouldn't do it. She was a sucker for animals, even if those two geriatric poodles barely qualified as living, much less as animals. Demons was more like it. They were the meanest things I'd ever seen on two or four feet. The fact they'd taken one look at Annie when we were younger and instantly hated her didn't endear them one bit to me.

"Aunt Bitsy?"

She paused in the doorway and turned to look at me.

"Thank you. I'll figure out a way to repay you for everything you've done."

Her expression softened. A moment later, she once again stood before me. She reached up and gently touched my cheek.

"Jax, you don't owe me anything and you know it." The look she gave me spoke volumes and I ducked my head, not wanting to get into it just now. "But we can discuss it later. I'm going to the hospital and you need to go find Quinn."

"Yes, ma'am."

"Let me know what Quinn says."

I nodded and watched her leave the room. Then I turned back to the mirror, taking one last look at my reflection before following.

How easy it was to slip back into the role I left behind when I left town. Now to find out if Mossy Creek was ready for the rogue to return.

3

Fifteen minutes later, I turned onto the street where Annie lived. The tree lined street with its stately homes that evoked visions of Mossy Creek in its early days brought a smile to my lips. Annie lived in the house that had once belonged to her great-grandparents. She'd inherited it, unbeknownst to her, upon her grandfather's death. It wasn't until almost five years later—and her mother being charged with murder—that she'd returned home to Mossy Creek and discovered she'd inherited not only the house but the building where her grandfather had his law office. Two years later and she still complained, albeit with more good humor than she once did, about him reaching out from the grave to manipulate her life.

But now the peace of the neighborhood had been broken by the presence of a number of police and media vehicles. The former worked feverishly to find out what happened to one of their own. Annie might be a defense attorney, but her brother was a sheriff's deputy. Her father-in-law was a judge. Since returning home, she'd become an integral part of the town. No one would rest until her attacker was brought to justice.

I carefully guided the Ducati down the street toward Annie's house. Cop cars and media vans lined both sides of the wide roadway.

Neighbors stood in their yards, talking among themselves but not to the reporters. That didn't surprise me. Mossy Creek was protective of its own and Annie's family had been here since the town's founding. As the Ducati neared, heads turned in my direction. A few of the faces registered recognition and I smiled to myself. It wouldn't be long before the grapevine went to work and word spread that the rogue had returned.

As I parked behind a black SUV, I grinned. Right on time, Quinn appeared from around the corner of Annie's house. Two beautifully matched Belgium Malinois walked on each side of her, their leads in her left hand. She paused and lifted her head. If I didn't know better, I'd think she was scenting the air. Then she turned and looked in my direction. Just like when we were kids, she seemed to know not only I was there but where I waited.

Some things never change and, for once, I was glad of it.

I swung my leg over the Ducati and removed my helmet. After placing it on the bike's seat, I looked around and inhaled deeply. For a moment, I stood there, my hands at my side, palms toward the ground. Energy seemed to flow upward toward me, filling me even as it welcomed me home. I needed to take time to reconnect with the land, but that had to wait until I knew more about what happened to Annie.

"Jax." Quinn reached out and pulled me close. Then she stepped back, her hands holding mine. Her eyes took in my appearance and the tattoos covering my arm. A smile touched her lips as she lightly ran a finger over the coyote moving through the trees above my wrist. She knew without asking why I'd chosen to be the rogue once again. "Are you sure you want to play it this way?" she asked softly, her expression troubled.

I nodded. "Tell me what happened?"

She led me around SUV, the Mals at her heels. "I don't know much. Robbie was across the street playing. When he came home, he found the front door open. The twins were upstairs crying. He called out for Annie, but she didn't answer. He didn't know what to do so he called Sam who told him to go upstairs and lock himself in the nursery with

16

the twins. He wasn't to come out until either Sam or Annie told him it was okay."

I nodded. That sounded exactly like what Sam would tell his son. Hell, it's what I'd tell my own child if I had one. "But?" I knew there was more. Otherwise, Quinn wouldn't look so worried.

"He didn't do what Sam said. After making sure the twins were all right, he went looking for Annie. He found her in the laundry room. She was unconscious and bleeding from a head wound. He called 9-1-1 then, telling them his mother had been hurt. He was still with her, doing what he could to stop the bleeding when Lucas and Drew arrived just ahead of the EMTs."

My lips peeled back, and a growl sounded deep in my throat. Quinn nodded, anger and fear darkening her eyes.

"How bad?"

"I don't know." She shook her head to keep me from interrupting. "My mother, not to mention Annie's mother and grandmother, are at the hospital with Sam and his parents. Ali and Robbie are with Miss Peggy at my place. Sam promised to call as soon as he knew something. But he wanted me here, finding out what I could about who hurt her."

I nodded again. Sam knew one of Quinn's gifts was the ability to sometimes see a crime from the viewpoint of the victim or prep. It was something she'd been doing for years as a DEA agent in Montana without realizing it. Until she and Ali returned to Mossy Creek a year and a half ago and she called fire and wind for the first time, she thought she was a normal. She still had trouble from time to time accepting the fact she was an *Other*.

"Have the neighbors been able to tell you anything?"

She shook her head.

Damn it, why couldn't this be easy?

I knelt on one knee and touched my right palm to the grass. Eyes closed, I opened my senses, letting the energy of the earth flow over and through me. In the back of my mind, I felt something, not quite a consciousness but an awareness that wasn't quite awake. Even so, it felt worried, angry and I followed it toward the house. I chuckled softly as realization dawned. If I was right, I really needed to have a chat with Miss Serena before the day was over.

"What?"

I looked up and saw Quinn watching me, her brow knitted with concern.

"Nothing." When she arched one brow, I stood and brushed my hand on my jeans. "Okay, nothing that helps explain what happened. But something I want to talk to Miss Serena about before I say anything else."

Serena Duchamp.

She was, without a doubt, the most powerful *Other* I'd ever met. Her family had been one of the very first to settle here and they never left. Now she helped protect the town and train new *Others* in the use of their talents. Part grandmother, part mentor and all someone I could rely on, no matter what. If anyone knew why I felt what I did, she would.

"Jax." Quinn drawled it out and I relented, at least a little.

"Think about your house. Now think about what it might feel like if the house was asleep instead of aware like it is now."

Quinn looked at me for a moment as if she wasn't sure what to think. Then a slow smile spread across her face. I understood. Like me, she'd always believed Annie was an *Other* even though she showed no overt talents. Could this be an indication we'd been right? That was a question for later, after we knew Annie would recover and after we found the person responsible for hurting her.

"Any chance I can get inside?" I knew the answer before she shook her head. But I had to ask. The part of me that made me "the rogue" needed access to the area where Annie had been attacked. I might be able to pick up the scent of the attacker.

"Not like this." She waved a hand at me. "Or in any other way."

I grinned and looked at the Mal. Quinn caught the look and just shook her head. Then she grabbed my arm and pulled me to the back of the SUV.

"Jax, I'd give my right arm to get you inside, shifted or not, but I can't. This isn't my scene and we can't do anything that might jeopardize the case if Lucas and the others make an arrest. You know that."

I did, but that didn't make it any easier to accept. The fact I'm an Earth elemental as well as a skinwalker made me an oddity even among *Others*. Not that many knew the walker side of me. Quinn did, as did Annie and a few others, including Aunt Bitsy. Right now, the urge to shift into a coyote, my preferred form, was strong. Anyone looking closely at my tattoos would see them moving. Unlike the ancient myths about skinwalkers, I didn't need a piece of pelt or fur to shift. Their magical likenesses on my skin were the only talismans I needed.

"How about walking the perimeter instead?" she suggested.

I nodded. It was better than nothing. Maybe we'd get lucky and between my walker abilities and my Earth magic, I'd pick up something that would help identify Annie's attacker.

"Well?" she asked a few minutes later as we rounded the house and crossed the lawn toward the street.

I ducked back under the police tape and led her back to her SUV. As I did, I shook my head. There were too many people around the house. Too many scents and sounds. Worse, too much time had passed. I needed to get inside, or I needed a moment with what Annie wore when she was attacked. Then I might hit on something. When I said as much, Quinn nodded, her expression grim.

"C'mon. Let's get out of here. Sam texted and Annie's been taken to a room finally."

"The dogs?" I nodded to where they sat on either side of Quinn. Even though they were working dogs, they didn't belong at the hospital.

"I'll drop them at the house."

I thought for a moment. Then I shook my head. Much as I wanted to discuss the situation with Quinn, I wanted to get to the hospital more. I'd get there quicker on the Ducati and without making a stop at the house.

"I'll meet you at the hospital."

She cocked her head to one side and didn't—quite—roll her eyes.

"I have a better idea. Follow me home. We can leave your bike there and we'll go to the hospital together."

For a moment, I simply looked at her, wondering what she had in mind. Then, figuring she wanted to talk as much as I did, I nodded. Besides, the thought of leaving the Ducati on one of the hospital lots where it could be damaged—or stolen—or a bird could dive bomb it convinced me to leave it where I knew it would be safe.

Fifteen minutes later, Quinn and I stepped off the elevator and walked down the corridor toward the ICU unit where Annie had been taken from the Emergency Department. Outside the double doors was the entrance to the waiting room. A uniformed sheriff's deputy stood guard. As we approached, he stood straighter and his hand dropped to the butt of his gun. Annie chuckled and pulled out her badge case.

"Stand easy, Chip. She's family." The deputy gave me a long look and then relaxed. "Deputy Chip Inuye, this is Dr. Jax Powell. She should be on the approved visitors list."

"She is," he confirmed and then extended his hand. "Good to meet you, doctor."

"And you, deputy."

I shook his hand before following Quinn into the waiting room.

"Auntie Jax!"

I dropped to one knee as Quinn's daughter ran to me. As I held my goddaughter close, I looked over her shoulder. Robbie, her best friend and Annie's and Sam's son, sat in his father's lap, his expression telling me everything I needed to know. Peggy Russell, owner of the local café, stood nearby, her eyes on locking with mine. I didn't need her to explain. She'd brought the kids to the hospital because not knowing what was going on with Annie was worse for them than being here with family as they waited would ever be.

Even so, they were too young to be here and be exposed to what was happening. It didn't matter that this wasn't the first time for Ali. Her biological father had abused Quinn, sending her to the hospital once that I knew of and possibly more before Quinn divorced him. After Quinn moved them back to Mossy Creek, Ali saw that son-of-a-bitch kidnap her mother. He damn near killed Quinn before Lucas and Ciara, Quinn's older sister, found them. I knew without asking that Annie and Sam, as well as Robbie, had been here for Quinn and Ali just as they were now here for Annie and her family.

Never again. Never again would those dear to me be hurt. I didn't care what I had to do to insure it.

"Robbie, come here."

I held out a hand to him and waited. A moment later, he slid off Sam's lap and hurried to me. As I pulled him close, I noted how he slipped an arm around Ali. Almost instantly, the girl's aura expanded, enveloping him, calming him. Oh my, Annie and Quinn were going to have their hands full with these two as they grew up. But, for now, Ali was exactly what Robbie needed until we knew for sure Annie was going to be all right.

"Auntie Jax, are you going to find the bad man who hurt Aunt Annie?" Ali asked when she finally broke my embrace.

I sat back on my heels and ran a gentle hand over first her head and then Robbie's. "That's your daddy's job, Ali." I nodded over her shoulder to where Lucas Moore, Quinn's husband and Mossy Creek's sheriff, stood talking softly with Annie's twin brother Drew.

"But you're going to help, aren't you, Dr. Jax?" Robbie looked at me with such hope my heart melted.

He and Ali clung to me like a lifeline. They recognized me as a protector, just as their mothers had when we were younger. I knew what I needed to do. I might not be a cop like Quinn or Lucas or former military like Sam, but I had my own talents and I would use them in whatever way was necessary to protect my friend and her family

"Robbie, I love your mother. She and Quinn are my sisters by choice. You'd better believe I'm going to help. I'll tell you something else. I'm not going to let anything else happen to her or to you and the rest of the family." When Lucas looked at me, I shrugged. What else could I say? I wasn't going to lie to the little boy. Besides, I had every intention of finding the person responsible for attacking Annie. When I did, they'd learn just how foolish it is to hurt someone I care for.

"Jax, thank you for coming." Mary Kate Metzger, Annie's grandmother, moved to where I knelt and helped me to my feet. Then she pulled me into a hug. "She's going to be all right, but she's going to need you. I know I don't have any right to ask, but can you stay?" She spoke softly and I doubted anyone else heard.

I leaned back and smiled gently. Then I took her hands. "I'm here as long as I'm needed."

"Jax?" Quinn looked at me, her brows knitted in concern.

I shook my head. This wasn't the time to get into it. But, seeing the determination reflected in her eyes, I knew I didn't have a choice. But I could try to postpone it for a bit.

"Ali, Robbie, why don't you take everyone down to the cafeteria for some ice cream? I need to talk with your daddies for a few minutes." I dug in my pocket and pulled out a couple of twenties, handing one to each of the kids.

Before they could object, Annie's mother, in a show of common sense that surprised me, said she thought that was an excellent idea. Then she reached for Robbie's hand and promised they wouldn't be long.

"Dr. Jax?" He looked at me, uncertain.

"I promise I'll send for you if the doctor says you can see your mama."

Ali assured him I really would, reminding him that I never broke my promises. I waited as the two of them led everyone but Quinn, Lucas, Drew and Sam from the waiting room. As they stepped into the corridor, Quinn moved to the door. She softly told the deputy to go with them. Then she turned back to the rest of us, her expression worried.

"Jax, thank you." Sam pulled me into a hug and held on. His body gave one long shudder as he fought to control his emotions. Then he stepped back, his eyes dark with concern. "You didn't have to promise Robbie you'd stay. I know you need to get back."

I shook my head and held his hand. He needed as much reassurance as his son. "Sam, I'm not going anywhere until we know Annie's going to be all right and the person responsible for hurting her has been caught."

"Your job?" Drew asked, running a hand over his short-cut red hair.

"Let's just say I'll be looking for a new place to open my practice." Fortunately, people had pets and show animals all over the state. Not to mention the cattle and horse ranches. I could set up my vet practice wherever I wanted and, for the first time, I'd be my own boss.

"Jax, are you sure?"

"I am. We can talk about it later." I turned my attention back to Sam. "What have the doctors said?"

"Not much." Sam dropped his head in his hands. Lucas rested a hand on his shoulder as Quinn moved to Drew's side and slid her arm around his waist, nudging him with her hip as if telling him she was there for him.

"It looks like she was hit from behind." Lucas' soft voice did nothing to hide his anger. "I have deputies looking for the weapon. When she fell, she hit her head on the corner of the dryer. She has a couple of head lacerations and you know how much they bleed."

I nodded, my expression grim.

"We're waiting on the results of the MRI, but the doc guesses a serious concussion is the best case scenario with the possibility of a skull fracture and bleeds."

I swallowed hard against the fear trying to claw its way up my throat. "Has she been conscious?"

Sam looked up and shook his head. My heart aching, I moved to crouch in front of him and reached for his hands.

"Sam, I promise we're going to keep her safe." When I looked at the others, they nodded in agreement. "Drew, where's Meg?"

The redhead almost winced before answering. "She's in DC to argue a case before the Supreme Court. When I called her to tell her about Annie, she was ready to fly home. Me reminding her my sister wouldn't thank her—or that their client wouldn't—wasn't what she wanted to hear."

Now I winced. I didn't know Meg Sheridan Grissom well. But I knew her well enough to know she would want to be here with her law partner and sister-in-law. Nor did I have any doubt she'd be on the first flight home once she finished in DC.

"Miss Olivia and Beth are running the office," Sam said.

"Then we'll be able to reassure Annie everything's in good hands." I smiled and leaned in to give him a quick hug before climbing to my feet. While Quinn and Drew did their best to reassure him, I moved to where Lucas stood. With a jerk of my head, I led him into the corridor outside the waiting room. "What haven't you told him?"

And Quinn for that matter.

He rubbed a hand over his face. As he did, I waited. He looked haggard, drawn. I understood. No sheriff liked cases like this. Mossy Creek was supposed to be safe and Annie had been attacked in the safety of her own home. Worse, Annie was "family". Lucas had to walk the very fine line of running an unbiased investigation and getting justice for his friend and her family.

"Annie was targeted, Jax. Sam hasn't figured it out yet, but he will. Nothing was taken from the house. So robbery wasn't a motive. Someone wanted to hurt Annie, maybe kill her."

I closed my eyes and blew out a breath. Then I nodded. I'd suspected as much.

"What can I do?" When he simply arched a brow in my direction, I smiled slightly. "Lucas, I'm not a cop. I know my limitations and the last thing I want is to fuck up any case you try to build against whoever hurt Annie. But there are ways I can help. You know that. So tell me what I can do."

"Keep an eye on Annie." He glanced over my shoulder in the direction of the waiting room. "And keep my wife from doing anything foolish."

I nodded, mentally shaking my head at the idea of me keeping Quinn or anyone else from doing anything foolish when all I wanted to do was tear through town, leaving destruction in my wake until I found the bastard responsible for hurting Annie.

4

S everal hours later, Mary Kate and Quinn's mother, Judith, took Ali and Robbie home. I knew they'd wind up at Quinn's. They'd be safe there if the person responsible for hurting Annie tried to get to Robbie. To say Quinn's house was different was putting it mildly. The house was at the least semi-sentient. The front gate wouldn't let anyone in the family didn't approve of. The house itself could be downright scary the way it adapted to danger. I didn't doubt it would eat, or at least try to, anyone who managed to get into the yard and who was then foolish enough to try to get inside.

In fact, there was only one other place in town was safer than Quinn's house. If necessary, they would retreat there. But, for now, they'd be safe enough in the semi-sentient house that had already proven it would—and could—protect its own.

"Sam, she's going to be all right." I handed him a bottle of water and sat next to him.

He nodded, his eyes on the bottle as it dangled from his hands between his knees. When he looked up, anger burned in his eyes. "Lucas, any news?"

Lucas shook his head. I knew he wouldn't tell Sam if he knew something. Right now, we all wanted Sam focused on Annie and nothing else. Besides, Lucas didn't want to risk Sam trying to take justice into his own hands. Not that we'd ever know if he did. I had no doubt Sam learned enough in the Army to make sure no one ever found any trace of Annie's attacker if he managed to get his hands on the bastard.

"Not yet. But it's still early in the investigation." He crouched in front of his friend, putting himself at Sam's eye level. "I promise we're going to find who did this to her. All you need to do is be here for your wife. I will keep you in the loop. I'm also putting a guard on Annie. As long as she's here, no one's getting to her that you haven't vetted."

"Thanks." He set the bottle to one side and rubbed his face with both hands. As he did, his mother slid onto the seat to his other side and slipped her arm around him. "Can Robbie stay with you and Quinn?" He glanced at his parents before continuing. "I know you would die protecting him, Mom, Dad. But I want whoever did this to Annie to know they can't get to our son and I want them to know there is no reason to possibly hurt you."

Camille gave her son a gentle smile and hugged him. As she did, his father, Judge Robert Caldwell, reached behind her and squeezed their son's shoulder.

"We understand, Sam. Don't worry. I think we will all rest easier knowing Robbie is safe," the judge said.

"You can all stay at the house if you want," Quinn said. "You know that."

"Thank you. Right now, I think we'll go make sure Robbie's settled in."

Judge Caldwell climbed to his feet and extended a hand to his wife. Neither one really wanted to leave, that much was clear from their expressions. But it was the smart thing to do just then. They could get some rest and spell Sam later. It also kept the judge from hearing anything he shouldn't as an officer of the court. Besides, I knew they were both anxious to check on the twins, who were currently with Annie's mother—something I didn't blame them for one bit.

"Thanks, Dad." Sam stood and embraced first his mother and then his father. "I'll call you if there's any change in Annie's condition."

"You'll keep an eye on him?" Camille looked from Quinn to me to Lucas.

"We will," I promised and Quinn nodded in agreement.

"Tell Annie we love her."

Lucas walked with them into the corridor. I listened as he told the deputy on duty to escort them to their car. Once they were on the elevator, Lucas radioed Dispatch and ordered an escort for them and a guard for the house. Until this was over, he was taking no chances.

"Sam, has Annie said anything about anyone threatening her?" Quinn asked.

He shook his head. "I've wracked my brain and she's said nothing about anyone wanting to hurt her."

"How about Beth and Miss Olivia?" I asked Drew. "Have you checked with them?"

If anyone knew about any threatening calls or notes, it would be those two. Miss Olivia worked for Annie's grandfather, managing the law office until his retirement. When Annie returned to town, Miss Olivia returned to work part-time and her daughter, Beth, took over as office manager. Not that it fooled any of us. Miss Olivia was there to make sure Annie and Beth did things to her standard—and neither minded.

"They don't know of any threats and neither noticed Annie acting differently," Drew said.

He cellphone buzzed and he glanced at the display before excusing himself. Quinn looked at me and grinned before mouthing "Meg". I nodded and watched as he moved across the room before answering, speaking softly enough we couldn't overhear. But his body language screamed how worried he was just then.

"Sam, look at me." With a hand on his arm, I waited until he did. "You're going to have to trust us, especially Lucas and Drew, to get to the bottom of what happened. I promise I'm not going to let anything else happen to Annie. But I need something from you. We all do."

"What?"

"We need you to stay here with your wife. Reassure her everything is going to be all right. But let your folks and Annie's grandma spell you some because your kids are need you too. Quinn and I will do everything we can to help with them." I glanced at Quinn who nodded in agreement. "But they need you, especially Robbie."

"I know." He closed his eyes and we waited, giving him time to try to process everything that happened. When he opened them again, he reached for my left hand, his eyes on my tattoos. "Jax, you don't have to do this. I won't ask you to sacrifice your job."

Crap! I hoped he hadn't realized I'd done exactly that.

"I don't believe you have," I said simply and covered his hand with mine. "I have vacation time coming. If my bosses don't see it that way, I don't want to work for them. Annie's family. Like I told Robbie, she's my sister by choice, just like Quinn here."

He leaned forward and pulled me close, burying his face in the crook of my neck. I held him, letting him give in to his emotions. He'd always been the rock for the rest of us growing up. It was time we returned the favor.

"Thank you," he whispered.

The clock moved slowly, too slowly, as we waited. Every time the doors to the unit opened, we looked up, hoping it was Annie's doctor. An hour after the judge and Camille left, Lucas said he needed to get back on duty. Drew remained, too worried about his sister to work. So we waited, alternating between praying and talking on the phone to family and friends, reassuring them Annie would be all right and we'd let them know if there was any change.

"Sam."

We looked up as a small, compact woman in scrubs stepped into the waiting room. As one, we stood and waited for Dr. Patricia Reyes to join us. Her short cropped dark hair had a few more strands of silver in them than the last time I saw her and exhaustion etched deep lines from the bridge of her nose to the corners of her mouth. But there was nothing in her expression to worry me. In fact, I'd lay money on her having good news.

At least I hoped so.

Dr. Pat looked at me, letting me see how she took in my clothing and tats before she grinned. "I heard the rogue was back. Good. You'll be able to keep everyone from doing anything foolish."

I shook my head, smiling. "Have you seen Annie?"

She nodded. "I just checked on her." She turned to Sam and I recognized the shift as she went from family friend to dedicated physician. "A nurse will be out shortly to take you to see her, Sam. Her doctor's making arrangements for you to stay in the room with her. The rest of you will be able to see her for a few minutes but that's all. Right now, she needs to rest and stay calm."

"But she's going to be all right?" Sam spoke softly, hope and fear heavy in his voice.

"Assuming nothing unforeseen happens, she will." She motioned for us to be seated. "I know Dr. Kennison told you she suffered a severe concussion in the attack."

Sam nodded and reached for Quinn's hand.

"We're going to keep her here for several days at least to keep an eye on her, make sure she doesn't suffer any complications. Once she goes home, she's going to have to take it easy for a while. That's where you're going to have to be firm with her. No going in to work and no bringing work home. Most of all, we need her to stay calm and not worry about anything until she's well on her way to recovery."

"We'll make sure of it, Dr. Pat," Drew promised and Sam added his assurances.

"I called Maddy and let her know what happened."

Quinn groaned and Dr. Pat simply inclined her head, the look on her face telling me Quinn—and probably me—were in trouble with our friend for not calling her ourselves.

"I knew she couldn't come home right now, Dr. Pat, and didn't want to worry her," Quinn said. When I looked at her in question, she continued. "Maddy's in the middle of a major project at work. Last time we talked, she was in London and said she'd be there another month or more."

Impressed, I agreed Quinn did the right thing by not calling her right away. Even so, I knew there would be hell to pay once Maddy returned to Mossy Creek. With luck, I'd already be gone and wouldn't have to face her.

"We'll call her tonight. I promise," I said and Dr. Pat waited until I crossed my heart.

Before she could say anything else, a nurse appeared from inside the unit. Sam and Drew stood and, when she motioned them forward, they followed her back inside the unit. Dr. Pat watched as the doors slid shut behind them before turning her attention to Quinn and me.

"Girls, I'm not going to lie. Annie was lucky. If she'd fallen at a slightly different angle, she could have fractured her skull. There's still the possibility she could develop a bleeder. That's why her doctor wants to keep her here for several days. So, while it looks like she'll make a full recovery, she's not out of the woods yet."

"What can we do?" Quinn asked.

"Talk to Amy and Miss Serena. See if they will come and do a healing session."

"I'll talk to them," I promised. After all, I planned on talking to Miss Serena about what happened anyway. Besides, I knew why Dr. Pat was hesitant to do a healing session herself. As a physician, she needed to maintain appearances, if for no other reason than to keep her malpractice carrier happy. Not that it would stop her once Annie was released.

"Thanks." She smiled and hugged first Quinn and then me. "It's good you're here, Jax, even if you are going to give more than a few folks a heart attack. Meg may have ridden in looking like a leather clad biker babe but you look like trouble walking."

"Good." I grinned and let my inner wolf, my preferred animal, shine through my eyes.

Dr. Pat laughed, patted my cheek and walked off, leaving Quinn and me to wait our time to see Annie.

Five minutes later, Drew appeared in the doorway. As he did, Quinn and I stood and hurried to him. He drew us in and held us close for a moment. Then he released us. His expression said it all. Annie might be better, but she was still hurt and he wouldn't rest until he caught the person responsible.

"You can see her for a few minutes. She's groggy from the meds and the hit to her head and she doesn't remember anything. Right now, she's more worried about the kids than anything else."

"Go throw some cold water on your face, Drew. Then call Meg." I patted his arm, wishing I could do more to reassure him. "We'll do our best to reassure her and then we'll go check on the kids."

"Thanks. You might call Meg when you leave. She's worried I'm not telling her the truth about Annie."

Quinn grinned. Her chuckle was a touch evil. "What you mean is your wife's not happy you told her to stay in DC?"

Drew rolled his eyes. "What do you think? I'm probably going to be sleeping on the couch for the next month."

"Don't worry, Drew. I won't let her be too mean to you," I teased.

He shook his head and, laughing softly, motioned for us to go see his sister. Glad we'd been able to cheer him at least a little, I hit the button on the wall to open the doors and stepped inside. As I did, I wondered what we should expect when we saw Annie.

"Rogue."

Annie smiled. At least I think she smiled. Her eyes were black and swollen. An angry looking bruise colored one side of her face. A thick bandage was secured over a cut at her left temple. With her red hair pulled back in a loose tail, every bruise and all the swelling seemed magnified. But she was awake and aware.

She called me Rogue, which meant she recognized the persona I'd dusted off when I arrived in town and, at least for now, approved.

Of course, that would probably change once she was no longer under the influence of painkillers.

"Hey, Annie." I crossed to the bed and bent to gently kiss her cheek. "How are you feeling?"

"I'm flying." She grinned a loopy grin and Sam shook his head, amusement sparkling in his eyes.

Quinn patted her foot and waited as Annie focused on her. "You keep tripping, Annie. Sam and Drew are going to stay here while we go play with the kids. Do you want us to bring you anything when we come back?"

She shook her head and her eye lids drooped. We stood there and watched as she drifted off. Even though Quinn had wanted to ask her about what happened, I knew this was best. Annie needed to rest to recover. Maybe then she'd remember what happened and identify her attacker. Until then, Dr. Pat was right. We needed to keep her calm.

"They said she'd do this for a while," Sam said softly as he stood and led us to the door. "Just make sure our kids are all right. It would kill Annie if anything happened to them."

"I promise to keep them safe, Sam."

Quinn echoed my reassurances. "You just worry about Annie," she added.

Not long after that, we climbed into her SUV. Once the doors were closed and locked, she started the engine. Then she sat here, her hands tightly gripping the steering wheel. The anger radiating off of her matched my own. The sight of Annie had rocked me, firming my determination to find the person responsible for hurting her.

And when I did. . . .

But that was later. For now, we had to make sure we kept Annie safe. Maybe by morning, she'd remember what happened. If not, well, we'd cross that bridge when we came to it.

"Jax, are you staying with Bitsy?" Quinn asked as she pulled away from the hospital.

I shook my head. "No. You know what my folks are like. They know by now that I'm back in town. If they think I'm staying with Bitsy, they'll make her life hell."

Quinn nodded. She knew all too well. More than once growing up, I took refuge at her house after a fight with my folks when Bitsy was out of town.

"So where are you staying?" When I didn't answer, she glanced at me, her expression speaking volumes. "Let me guess. You plan on checking out Annie's and Sam's place and then going back to the hospital."

Since that's exactly what I planned, I didn't say anything.

"Jax." She shook her head. "You'll stay with us. You know as well as

I do that your folks won't dare show up there. They're scared of the house, not to mention my mother."

I smiled, remembering an incident back in junior high when Judith O'Donnell let my mother and father know exactly what she thought about their parenting skills. Things had been tense at home, to put it mildly, and I started acting out at school. It was around the time my gifts started manifesting and my parents were anything but pleased to find out I was an *Other*.

And they made no secret of it, especially to me.

After school that day, a couple of the local bullies decided it would be fun to pick on Annie and Quinn. Back then, Annie went by Jules, a shortened version of her first name. Not that I blamed her. What mother in her right mind named her red haired, blue eyed twins Anne and Andrew and not expect them to be called Raggedy Ann and Andy? As for Quinn, she always felt like an outsider. Everyone in her family was an *Other* except her. Or so she thought. That left her open to taunts that maybe she wasn't really an O'Donnell and worse.

That afternoon, Joe Bob Sawyer and some of his friends thought it would be fun to go after my friends. When I came upon them, Quinn stood in front of Annie, trying to protect her from the taunts being shouted at them. Already on edge, that was the last straw. I ran forward, dropped my shoulder and sent Caleb Willis, the first string quarterback, flying. Before he could get to his feet and rally the troops, I slid to a halt next to Quinn. She took up a fighting stance while I dropped to one knee and pushed my palms against the ground. I didn't—quite—call an earthquake but it was close. Several school windows broke and alarms went off, activated by the motion created as I pulled energy from the ground.

I'm not sure what I would have done if Mrs. O'Donnell hadn't appeared then. Without a word, she placed herself between the three of us and the bullies. A look from her was all it took to send the six racing away. Then she turned to us and extended a hand to help me to my feet. Before Quinn could explain, Mrs. O'Donnell shushed her and asked Annie what happened.

Seeing the look on the principal's face as she neared a few minutes later had me wanting to hide behind Mrs. O'Donnell. Instead, she slipped her arm around my shoulders and kept me at her side. Before Mrs. Wingate could start in on me, Mrs. O'Donnell told her in no uncertain terms that I'd prevented both Quinn and Annie from being attacked by Sawyer and his gang. She went on to tell Wingate that she'd take it straight to the school board if the woman tried to do anything to me. After all, did Wingate really want to answer why she was letting a group of bullies run roughshod over a couple of girls?

Later, when my mother showed up at the O'Donnells to collect me, Mrs. O'Donnell let her know in no uncertain terms what she thought of the way she'd been tearing down my self-confidence. No, I hadn't said anything to her. I didn't need to. She could see it in how I held myself and in the way I was acting out. According to her, my parents didn't know what a gift they had in me. They might not appreciate me and the gifts that made me special, but she and her family did as did others in town.

Then she'd done the same thing Bitsy had. She offered me a place to stay whenever I needed it. When she did, I felt the house for the first time. I know that sounds strange, but the house is alive. It might not be sentient, but it is damned close to it and that day it let me know I would always be welcome.

"Thanks, Quinn. I'll stay the night. Tomorrow, I'll figure out where to stay until this is over." Bitsy probably knew of an apartment for rent short term.

"We'll discuss it in the morning. Tonight, we're going to make sure the kids are all right and then I think the two of us need to have a talk with my daughter to find out how she knew something happened to Annie."

Assuming Quinn's mother hadn't already done so.

"As long as food is involved somewhere along the line, I won't argue. I haven't eaten today." As if to punctuate my comment, my stomach growled loudly.

"Idiot," Quinn turned down the street leading to her house and frowned at me. "Why didn't you say something sooner?"

"Other things on my mind?"

Which was the truth.

"Mom will have dinner ready soon, if it isn't already. Afterwards, we both have calls to make, including to Miss Serena. Then you need to get some rest. Tomorrow, we'll discuss exactly why you can stay as long as you're needed here."

The look she gave me spoke volumes. She knew, even without me telling her, that I didn't have any reason to hurry back to New Braunfels. The question was what she'd do with that knowledge. I had no doubt she'd try to use it to convince me to move back permanently. After all, she and Annie had moved home. Wasn't it time for me to do the same?

To which the answer was a resounding "Hell no!"

5

"Care to tell me what's been eating at you since we left the hospital?"

I leaned back in my chair and watched as Quinn glanced into the hall to make sure no little ears were around to overhear what she had to say. Apparently satisfied, she closed the door. Almost instantly, I felt the subtle change in the room and knew the house had done. . . something. I doubted anyone could overhear what we might say, no matter how hard they tried. The house was taking its own precautions and that worried me.

For a moment, she stood there, one hand on the door, her head bent. When she turned, I sat up. I was right. Something was wrong. So why hadn't she said something before now?

"Quinn?"

She dropped onto the chair next to mine and dangled her hands between her knees. I waited, giving her time to gather her thoughts. Not that I liked waiting. But I knew her and I knew she would tell me when she was ready. I just hoped that was soon, before I lost patience.

"First of all," she began, still looking down at her hands. "I want to throttle Annie. I've been worried about her for some time now. She's put up a good front, but she's been worried about something. When

I've asked her about it, she's laughed it off and said I was imagining things."

I turned slightly in my seat to see her better. When I did, my mouth drew tight. Quinn looked miserable. She was blaming herself for what happened.

"Quinn, don't." I lightly touched her arm, waiting until she looked at me. "Annie told you nothing was wrong. If there was, it's on her for not telling you and not asking for help."

Still looking miserable, she shook her head. "I should have pressed harder, Jax. Every instinct I have was telling me something was going on. But I took her at her word and now she's been hurt."

"Again, not your fault." I was beginning to understand now. One of Quinn's gifts was seeing patterns and being able to follow them, often using that talent to help her visualize what happened during a crime. "You're her friend, right?" She nodded. "You respect her and she respects you. Right?" Another nod. "And you trust her."

She didn't say anything for a moment and then she cursed softly. "Yeah, I trust her and she played on that trust to keep me from digging any deeper."

"Maybe." I shook my head when she opened her mouth to interrupt. "Or she might not have realized there was a problem and didn't know you were picking up indications because of your gifts."

She cursed again and this time I knew it was because she hadn't followed her gut and pushed Annie. But we both knew—well, I knew and Quinn would once she calmed down—Annie didn't think the way we did. She was the one of our group of friends who saw the good in everyone. She was also independent almost to a fault and for me to say that is something. She didn't like asking for help and wouldn't unless it was the last resort.

And that was something she and I would have a long talk about, but later. After she was back home and well on the way to a full recovery. For now, Quinn was my concern. I needed to know why she felt there was something wrong and then we needed to figure out what we could do about it without jeopardizing any case Lucas might be building.

"She doesn't talk to me much about her work," I began and Quinn nodded. Apparently, Annie followed the same rules with her she did with me. "But you're here. You see her regularly and you hear the gossip. What does your gut tell you?"

"Other than it's time to take her out behind the proverbial shed and beat her for being so stubborn that she didn't tell me something was wrong?"

I bit back my grin. Angry Quinn was better than a Quinn blaming herself for something she had no control over. Now I needed to guide her into thinking Quinn.

"Yeah, Sam might not appreciate it if we beat her up after all she's been through."

Quinn glared at me for a moment before relaxing. A soft chuckle escaped her lips a moment later. Good. That was good. At least I hoped it was.

"Tell me what's been going on, what the grapevine has to say."

Instead of answering right away, Quinn pushed out of her chair. I watched as she crossed the room. In the far corner stood what Aunt Bitsy called a butler's table. Bottles of whiskey, Scotch, Irish whiskey and vodka rested on the top along with several high ball glasses. Without asking, Quinn poured healthy doses of Irish into two glasses. I thanked her when she handed me one before she returned to her chair.

"Remember when we used to play down here?" she asked instead of getting to the point.

I looked around the room. These days, it served as Quinn's home office. Floor to ceiling bookshelves lined one wall. A cherry wood desk and judge's chair stood in front of the window. The comfortable chairs we sat in were across the room in what I'd call a conversation arrangement. Okay, interior design isn't my forte by any means. But these chairs, the small table between them, and a small sofa were arranged to make conversation easier. It was a far cry from the play-room and then media room it had been when we were kids.

"How could I forget? We spent a lot of time up here when we were kids."

Those had been some of the best days of my life back then. Not once did I feel like Quinn's family judged me. I was different, even by the standard of the *Others*. But the O'Donnells, not to mention Annie's grandparents and Maddy's family, accepted me for who and what I was. They encouraged me in ways no one else besides Bitsy ever did. In so many ways, they were my family more than my parents ever had been or could be.

"Even then, Annie tried to protect us by not telling us when something was bothering her," Quinn said.

I nodded. Even as kids, Annie knew Quinn and I would stand up for her, whether she wanted it or not. Hell, we'd do it even if it meant we'd get in trouble.

"Do you think that's what she was doing this time?" I sipped the Irish.

"I don't know." She knocked back her Irish and placed her glass on the table between our chairs. "I'm not even sure there was anything wrong. But I'd been worried about her because she seemed pre-occupied and wasn't talking about it."

"Could it be a case she's working on?"

Quinn shook her head. "Not according to Meg."

"But?"

"There's been one thing she won't talk about." She shook her head. "That she hasn't talked about," she corrected.

"Quinn, I'm not going to know unless you tell me."

"According to the grapevine—"

Which meant it was pretty damned reliable. The grapevine in Mossy Creek was more accurate than any media report and had its heart at Miss Peggy's café. At least that gave me a place to start if Quinn didn't get to the point.

"—Jason Alvarez is not going to run for reelection."

It took me a moment to place the name. Alvarez had been the county's elected district attorney for the last eight years or so. From what Annie told me, he'd been excellent in the position—even if he'd been foolish enough not to fire Joe Bob Sawyer until after the bastard filed murder charges against Annie's mom.

"Word is also that he's been talking to Annie, trying to convince her to run."

I blew out a long breath. Annie would be excellent as the county's DA. She'd missed being a prosecutor once she moved back to Mossy Creek. Besides, it would be another way she followed in her grandfather's footsteps. Mr. Metzger had been an attorney, did a couple of terms as DA and even sat on the bench for a while. But I knew Annie. She'd be torn. She had a thriving law practice. Meg had joined the firm a year or so ago when she moved to Mossy Creek. They were even talking about bringing in a third attorney to help with the case load. That's enough to distract Annie but it didn't explain why someone would want to attack her.

Or did it?

"Does the grapevine say anything about anyone else who might be running."

Quinn's expression hardened and I knew the answer before she said anything.

"Sawyer."

I downed my Irish and pushed out of my chair. I didn't see Sawyer actually attacking Annie. He was too much of a coward. Even when we were kids, he would instigate trouble but do his best to keep his hands clean. Could that be the case here?

Perhaps the rogue would go have a little chat with good ole Joe Bob come morning. But there was something I needed to do first.

"That gives us a starting place." I stopped and shook my head. "It gives me a starting place. You can't get involved."

Quinn's eyes flashed and the temperature in the room rose slightly as her anger flared. "Pardon me?" she drawled.

"Quinn, you are a cop." Her eyes flashed again. "Okay, an agent," I corrected with a grin. She was rightly proud of her position as an agent with the Drug Enforcement Agency. "That means you can't be around during my *chat* with our former classmate. I don't want to put you in the position where you might have to arrest me."

"Jax."

"Don't worry. I won't lay a hand on him. But he might not like

41

what I have to say and might try to make a case of me threatening him. You can't be involved."

She stared at me for a moment and I waited, watching as she got her temper under control. Then she nodded and I relaxed slightly as the room's temperature returned to normal. One thing about a fire elemental: you knew when they were mad at you.

"And now I think I'm going to get some rest. I've been up since five."

"Same here." Quinn stood and linked arms with me. "Don't expect to be able to sleep in. I guarantee the kids will be up early and Ali is going to want Auntie Jax to have breakfast with them."

I grinned. "Auntie Jax thinks that is a wonderful idea." I bumped my hip against hers and grinned. "Quit beating yourself up. We'll figure out what happened, and we'll make sure Annie's not hurt again."

"That's the plan." She slid an arm around my shoulders and gave me a one-armed hug. "I'm glad you're here, even if you still haven't explained why you said you can stay as long as needed."

"In the morning." I yawned. "Now I need to find my bed."

She said good night and moved to her desk as I crossed to the door. Seeing me looking at her, she explained she had some paperwork to deal with. Nodding, I stepped into the corridor, closing the door behind me. I wanted a shower and time to think. There was one more thing I wanted to do. I just wasn't sure this was the time or place to do it.

The house quieted as I stepped out of the shower and I felt it going on guard. I pulled on a pair of loose sweatpants and tank top. A few minutes later, I padded through the darkened house. As I did, I remembered doing so as a kid. This time, however, the house didn't try to stop me from opening the back door and stepping out onto the deck that had been added after Quinn and Ali moved in.

Come back, come back, come back home, it whispered in the back of my mind.

I smiled slightly and lightly patted the doorframe. "I will," I promised. "Keep them safe."

Safe, safe, safe.

I soundlessly walked across the deck to the steps leading down to the yard. Without taking time to think what I was about to do, I dropped to my knees. For a moment, I looked at the full moon and smiled. I didn't need this phase of the moon for what I was going to do but it did make it easier. Now to remind myself—and the rest of the town—why I am the rogue.

I glanced at my left arm, one finger of my right hand lightly tracing the coyote tattoo. Heat radiated from my finger to the inking and then up my arm. Pain followed. Dropping to hands and knees, I threw my head back and fought the urge, the need, to cry out. My back arched and I growled as pain raced through my like fire through dry brush. Bones twisted, broke and reformed. If I wasn't so focused on remembering to breathe, I'd see hands turn to paws, arms to forelegs. Would that shifting be as easy as all the Hollywood films of late made it seem.

A few minutes or a lifetime later, I lay on the grass, snout on my paws, panting. Shifting always hurt but some times were worse than others. This was one of the worse. I hadn't been able to prepare for the shift because I didn't want Quinn to know what I planned. More than that, I didn't dare risk letting Ali know. I didn't want her to ever think of me as a monster, something too many normals and *Others* already did.

"Going somewhere?"

My ears flicked back against my skull and I covered my eyes with my paws. So much for doing this without Quinn knowing. Damned house probably tattled on me.

Safe, safe, safe.

I pushed to my feet, all four of them, and padded to where Quinn stood by the door. She'd changed into jeans and a black tee. Instead of lecturing me, she knelt down and smiled, one hand scratching under my chin. My tail thumped the deck and, just to make her laugh, I let my tongue loll out the corner of my mouth.

"You don't fool me." She chuckled and climbed to her feet. "It's been a while since I've seen you as a coyote, but it's a good choice. I assume you're heading to Annie's."

I dipped my head once.

"All right, but you're going to take this with you." She showed me something that looked suspiciously like a fanny pack. It's got your cellphone, some cash and your ID inside. There's also a thin tank and running shorts. That way, you can shift and not worry about being arrested for indecent exposure."

I sat still as she carefully fastened the pack around my neck, making sure it wasn't too tight.

"You know, you're lucky. It takes Lexie's uncle so much longer to shift and I've never been convinced he's really in control of his wolf once he's in that form."

I growled softly and shook my head. Lexie's uncle, a troublemaker from the day he was born if Quinn's mother was to be believed, was a were. Like all his kind, he was more animal than human when in his animal form. Fortunately—or not—for Mossy Creek, he was a joker and so was his wolf. Honestly, he should have been a coyote, he's that much of a trickster.

I'm many things, but a were I'm not. I'm what is best described as a skinwalker. Unlike many of the myths surrounding my kind, I don't need a pelt or piece of fur to change into an animal. My tats are my connection to my animal side. They are as alive as I am. I got the first one when I was sixteen, when Miss Serena finally figured out what was happening to me. She'd arranged for me to meet with a Cherokee tattooist. Bitsy took me and paid for the magical tat that freed the animal part of me.

Quinn chuckled again. Then she gently grabbed my snout and turned my face so we were eye to eye.

"You listen to me. Don't do anything foolish and don't get yourself caught. Understand?"

I twisted my snout out of her hold and nodded. Then I turned and, with a flick of my tail, ran around the corner of the house. By the time I reached the front gate, it swung open. Whether the house was letting me out or Quinn, I didn't know nor did I care. The only thing that mattered was getting to Annie's and seeing what my canine nose could tell me.

I trotted down the street, sticking to the shadows. Most folks wouldn't recognize the difference between me and a dog, but I didn't want to run the risk. All I needed was some Nosy Nora calling Animal Control or, worse, popping me in the ass with buckshot. I'd had that happen once and had no desire for a repeat performance.

My ears twitched as the sound of an engine neared. I veered deeper into the shadows and dropped to my belly. A moment later, a dark SUV pulled into sight. If I could have laughed, or more likely cursed, I would have.

The SUV slowed and the driver's window rolled down. From my vantage point deep in the shadows under Mrs. Manning's trees, I watched as Quinn scanned the area. I should have realized she wouldn't be satisfied letting me go off on my own. I probably wouldn't be either if our positions were reversed. But I didn't need her following me. I needed her home, keeping an eye on the kids.

Let's see how good she was at find the coyote. Doing my best canine grin, I shimmied further back into the shadows, keeping low to the ground. As she continued to scan the nearby yards, I moved carefully, silently through the darkness. If she could keep track of me, fine. Otherwise, I'd do what I needed to. When I got back to her house, we'd have an overdue conversation, one she wouldn't like.

I trusted Quinn with my life. Because of that, I didn't want her in a position where she felt torn about what to do. She had a job she loved, one that required her to enforce the law. What I planned to do was technically trespassing and could even be called tampering with evidence. Okay, that would be a stretch but I could see a prosecutor trying. I didn't want her in the middle if it came to that.

But there was something else. Quinn might be a fire elemental, but she hadn't come into her powers until recently and she was still learning how to use them—not to mention getting used to not being a "normal". Those powers saved her life when her ex tried to kill her. That helped her realize they were a gift. But if push came to shove, I knew she'd go for her gun first and that might not be the best route, especially since we didn't know what was going on.

And that was the real problem. You see, I wasn't as sanguine about what had been happening in Mossy Creek over the last several years as my friends were. They saw the events—Annie's mom being accused of murder, Quinn's ex coming to town and kidnapping her mother before trying to kill Quinn. Then there was Meg, whose mother grew up here and who ran away and never told Meg about Mossy Creek. Meg whose maternal relations still in town tried to defraud her of her inheritance and who tried to kill her—as being separate incidents. Events that simply happened and had no connection beyond the town. But I wasn't so sure. Why had each of them—First Annie then Quinn and lastly Meg—been drawn back to Mossy Creek and then placed in life threatening situations? My sixth sense, if there is such a thing, told me there was more going on than they knew. That meant I needed to find out what. And that meant a trip to see Miss Serena. If anyone knew—or suspected—what was going on, it was she.

But that was for tomorrow. Tonight, I wanted to have a closer look at Annie's house. Who knows, maybe I'd get lucky.

As I neared the house, I put my nose to the ground and began the search. I crossed back and forth across the front lawn, searching for something, anything that might help us identify who attacked her. All I found were too many scents, some I knew and others I didn't. Not that it surprised me. There had been so many people there, between the cops, the EMTs, the techs and even the neighbors.

Growling softly in frustration, I padded around the corner of the house and searched for entry into the backyard. Annie and Sam kept the fence in good condition. There wasn't so much as a loose board or low spot under the slats. For a moment, I considered digging under the fence. If I did and one of the dogs got out, Annie would kill me. What I really needed were hands to open the gate.

As if the thought called her, Quinn seemed to materialize at my side. She looked down at me and grinned. Then she opened the gate. For a moment, I stood just inside the backyard, expecting her to follow. Instead she shook her head and said she'd meet me at the

SUV. I dipped my head in the canine version of a nod, relieved. This way, she could honestly tell Lucas she hadn't done anything that might muck with his case. Besides, she could warn me if anyone neared.

A few minutes later, I trotted back around the house. Seeing the SUV parked at the curb, I cut across the lawn in its direction. As I neared, Quinn reached back and opened the rear passenger door. I jumped in and she closed the door. As she did, she muttered something about how her dogs would never forgive her. I grinned at her and leaned forward to lick her neck.

"Stop that!" she laughed as she pushed my head away. "I guess I should be thankful you shifted into a coyote instead of a cat of some sort. Then the Mals really would never forgive me."

She started the engine and pulled away from the curb. "Sweats and tee are back there along with water. Go ahead and shift. We need to talk."

Worried something else had happened, I lay on the bench seat and thought about my human form. Pain had me whimpering and wanting to claw through the upholstery. Later, I lay there, knees drawn up to my chest, gulping in air. Slowly, feeling a hundred years old after shifting twice in little more than an hour, I sat up and dragged on my sweats and tee shirt. Proving she could think of everything, Quinn even included underwear and shoes. I ignored the former but slid my feet into my running shoes before crawling over the seat to join her in the front of the SUV.

"You okay?" she asked as she turned onto Main Street.

"Yeah." I fastened my seatbelt and leaned back, closing my eyes. God, I was tired. "And, no, I didn't learn anything. Too many people have traipsed through the yard and around the house. But I do have a question."

She glanced at me before returning her attention to the road. "What?"

"Where were the dogs? They've got two, three dogs?"

Quinn nodded. Her hands tightened around the steering wheel. I watched her profile as she considered my question.

"My guess is Robbie had his with him. He takes them with him whenever he can."

"And Annie's?" I knew Quinn basically bullied her into getting a German shepherd bitch at the same time she helped Meg get her Mals. I had no doubt that if I didn't watch out, Quinn would try to do the same with me.

"A very good question and one we'll need to ask her in the morning." All conversation stopped as she pulled into the only fast food restaurant still open. A few minutes later, she dropped a bag of burgers in my lap before handing me a large Coke. "Back to Annie's dog. My guess is that she left Brigid with the twins. Robbie will be able to tell us for sure. He can also tell us if the door was closed when he went to check on them."

I nodded and dug into the first burger, moaning softly as I did. I needed the calories after the two shifts.

"We also need to know why her security system, or at least the outside cameras, weren't on." I'd noticed the cameras as I circled the house.

Quinn sighed heavily and I waited. She said so much and yet so little with that sigh. And all of it worried me.

"I may break her legs this time," she muttered.

"This time?" I turned in my seat to look at her, my burgers forgotten.

"Long story short, Annie's been licensed to carry concealed since before she moved back to town. There have been a couple of times when she needed her gun—or at least the threat of it—and she hasn't had it. That's one of the reasons I insisted she get Brigid. Sam put in the security system after she was attacked at the house right after she moved back home. She only sets it when they go to bed at night. That includes the cameras. Our Annie not only thinks nothing will happen but that she is indestructible."

That didn't surprise me. But it was something I'd be talking with her about. Even if she didn't want to take precautions where she was concerned, she had the twins and Robbie to think about. I wasn't above using them to guilt her into being careful. If that didn't work, I'd help Quinn break her legs.

I finished the first burger and reached for the second. "Let's talk to her about it tomorrow. But before we do, I need to see Miss Serena."

And I hoped she had some answers for me. Otherwise, I'd be doing more than looking like the rogue. I'd become the rogue and Mossy Creek wasn't ready for a grown-up Jax on the warpath.

6

"Jax, you didn't need to come."

Annie lay in bed, the head of the mattress slightly raised. She looked better than she had last night but not by much. Her eyes were still black and swollen, as was her nose. But the other facial swelling had gone down now. Better yet, she'd been able to cut back on the pain meds and was more alert. I knew it might only be temporary, but I'd take it.

"Of course, I did." I bent and kissed her cheek. "How do you feel?"

She shifted slightly and winced. Sam instantly stood and helped her get settled again.

"Like I lost the fight."

I nodded and moved to stand on the opposite side of the bed from Sam. I rested a hand on Annie's and watched as she turned it over, her fingers curling around mine.

"You just worry about getting well. Robbie stayed at Quinn's last night and your in-laws have the twins."

"They're all right?" She looked from me to Sam, fear reflected in her eyes.

"They're fine, love. I told you." Sam glanced at me and I didn't need him to tell me to do my best to reassure her.

"Annie, you know we wouldn't lie about the kids. They're fine. I promise." I gave her hand a reassuring squeeze. "When I left Quinn's this morning, Ali and Robbie were eating breakfast and planning how to spend their day."

She relaxed and I glanced at Sam.

"She's done nothing but worry about the kids since she woke up this morning."

"You're a good mother, Annie." I smiled and lightly brushed a lock of red hair from her forehead. When she didn't respond, I held my breath, fear rising. Then I realized she'd fallen asleep again. I carefully eased my hand from her loose grasp and motioned for Sam to join me at the door. "Has she said anything about what happened?" I spoke softly to keep from disturbing her.

He shook his head, his gaze never leaving the bed. "She doesn't remember anything about the attack."

I shouldn't be disappointed, but I was. That meant we needed to leave the investigation to Lucas and the Sheriff's Department. Of course, we should anyway, but I wanted to know who hurt my friend. Then I wanted to make sure they knew never to even think about hurting her ever again.

"Sam, where were the dogs when this happened?"

He looked at me, his brows pulling down as if he couldn't quite understand what I was asking. The understanding dawned on him. He cursed softly and one hand clenched at his side. I doubted he'd thought about the dogs until I asked and was kicking himself for it.

"Robbie took his across the street with him. He told me Brigid was with the twins."

I nodded. That answered one question.

"Don't worry, Sam. You know Lucas and Drew won't stop until they find the bastard who did this to her."

He nodded.

"And you know Quinn and I will make sure she and the kids stay safe."

Another nod.

"You don't worry about anything except being with her. Understand?"

He didn't answer. Instead, he reached for one of my hands. As he held it between his, he studied me. I fought the urge to fidget. Something about his gaze seemed to bore deep inside of me, almost as if he was looking into my very soul.

"What did it cost you to come home?"

I had a feeling he wasn't asking about the cost of gas between New Braunfels and Mossy Creek.

"Don't worry about it, Sam." I smiled at him, hoping he'd let it drop.

Instead, he shook his head and drew me into the corridor. "I mean it, Jax. What did it cost you to come home right now?"

I closed my eyes and blew out a breath. He wasn't going to let it go. I could hedge, but I wouldn't. Not when he'd worry about it. Not when he needed to focus only on Annie's recovery.

"If I tell you, I want you to understand something. I made the decision to come here knowing the cost. Annie, not to mention you and the kids, mean more to me than just about anyone and anything else."

"You think we don't know that?" He ran a hand over his face and, for the first time that morning, I realized how tired he was. "Jax, you've been there for us all our lives. You stood up for Annie, Quinn and Maddy when we were kids. You've dropped everything whenever one of us has asked. You've always put us before yourself. So tell me. What did you give up this time?"

I gave him a gentle smile and looked down at my hand still in his. "I don't want Annie to know."

He started to say something and then stopped. Without a word, he dropped my hand and stalked several feet down the corridor before turning back. One look at him and I knew he'd put it together and he was pissed. Pissed at me and pissed at my bosses.

"Don't." I leveled a look at him that dared him to disobey. "Sam, I don't regret what I did. I'd do it again without a second thought. There's something else you need to consider before you decide whether you're going to belt me or drive to New Braunfels to belt my bosses. I loved my job but not all the restrictions put on me by the practice. I was basically low man on the proverbial totem pole. I was expected to cover for everyone. I hadn't had a weekend off since joining the practice more than a year ago. The fact I quit to come up here doesn't mean I'm staying in Mossy Creek. All it means is once I'm sure Annie's all right, I'll be looking for a job, something I'd already decided to do before I found out she'd been hurt."

Not exactly, but it was something I'd figured out during the night.

He didn't say anything for a moment. Then he nodded. "I won't tell Annie," he promised.

"Do either of you need anything?"

"The head of the bastard who hurt her?"

I chuckled softly. "I'm working on that."

I glanced over my shoulder toward the sound of someone walking toward us. A dark-haired man who carried himself like a soldier neared. In each hand he held coffee cups from the cafeteria. He nodded at Sam. Then he turned his attention to me. I had no doubt he took in everything about my appearance, making sure I presented no threat to Sam or Annie.

"Here you go, Sam." He held out one of the cups as he joined us.

"Thanks, Rafe." Sam took a sip and grimaced slightly. "Rafe Sabatini, Dr. Jacqueline Powell. Jax, Rafe Sabatini."

Sabatini extended a hand. I took it, my gaze going from him to Sam and back. Then I caught the glint of a silver chain that reminded me of the sort of chain soldiers wore their dog tags on under the open collar of his polo shirt marking him as one of Sam's employees at the construction company he'd inherited from his grandfather. I also saw a hint of a tattoo on his left bicep.

"Rafe's an old friend, Jax. We served together in the Army and I wouldn't be here if it wasn't for him."

I took another look at Sabatini, remembering the story of how Sam had been seriously injured in Afghanistan while on patrol. He rarely talked about what happened. But Annie told me not long before they married a couple of years ago how he would have bled out if one of his squadmates hadn't disobeyed orders and gone back for him.

"You saved my ass more than once, Sam." A look passed between the men, something I figured only another combat veteran would understand. "Pleased to meet you, Doc. Annie and Sam talk about you a lot."

"All lies, I promise."

"Of course." He grinned and then turned his attention back to Sam. "You go check on the twins. I'll sit with Annie until you get back."

"That's sounds like a good idea, Sam," I said before he could hesitate. "Annie is going to worry if she wakes and realizes you're still wearing the same clothes you had on yesterday."

"You won't leave her?"

"I promise nothing will pry me from the room before you get back," Rafe said.

"All right." He patted his pockets and then returned to Annie's room, probably to get his car keys.

"Thanks, Doc."

"Thank you for staying with her." I pulled a business card from my phone case. "My cellphone's on there. Call me if Annie needs anything."

He glanced at the card and then slipped it into his pocket. "I will." We watched as Sam collected his wallet and keys from the table next to Annie's bed before bending to kiss her cheek. "Trust me, Doc. No one's getting near her again."

I did. Something about him reassured me. I could see not only his loyalty to Sam but the deep friendship he held for both Sam and Annie. I'd still check him out with Quinn, but I had a feeling she'd agree with my gut and tell me I didn't have anything to worry about where Rafe Sabatini was concerned.

My next stop was Miss Peggy's Café. It was the heart of the town and the headquarters for gossip central. As I pushed open the doors, I braced myself for the onslaught of questions about why I was home, if I'd seen my parents, how long I was going to be in town. . . if I was married yet. Then there'd be the inevitable lecture from Miss Peggy herself, all five foot nothing of her, because I hadn't been in before now. Instead, the café fell silent. Everyone waited as Janny, Miss Peggy's daughter, poured me a mug of coffee and motioned for me to take a seat at the counter.

"Mom said she saw you at the hospital yesterday, Jax. How's Annie?" she asked as she placed a menu on the counter in front of me.

The odd silence continued as everyone waited for me to answer.

"She's still in the ICU. Her doctor is optimistic but he's being realistic. Head injuries are tricky. So they're going to keep an eye on her, make sure she doesn't suffer any complications."

"Do they know who hurt her?" Angie Wallace asked.

"Was it a robbery?" Mrs. Younger, our third grade teacher, asked. Damn, she must be a hundred years old.

More questions came. I waited until everyone seemed to pause for a breath before responding.

"Sheriff Moore is doing all he can to find out what happened. Since it is an on-going investigation, he hasn't said much." I sipped my coffee and shook my head when Janny asked if I wanted anything else. Then I swiveled around to look at everyone. "I know you all care for Annie as much as I do." Heads nodded. "If you've seen or heard anything you think might help the sheriff figure out what happened and why, let him know. If you see any strangers in town, let him know. Mossy Creek takes care of its own and Annie Caldwell is most definitely one of ours."

Ours?

What the hell did I just say?

I saw how several of the other patrons looked at me, obviously wondering if that meant I was moving back. Part of me wanted to run for the hills. Another part, the rogue who resented like hell the way I'd been treated by my folks—not to mention one or two sitting not far away—reveled in their reactions. It wouldn't be long before the grapevine started speculating about it. If that kept the gossips busy and out of Lucas' investigation, I wouldn't complain.

"So, are you moving back?" Janny asked softly as she refilled my mug.

"Right now, I'm not thinking about anything more than making sure Annie's safe and recovers." Which was the truth. "Where's your mother?"

"She stopped by Quinn's house with some treats for the kids. She should be here soon."

I glanced at my watch. If I didn't get on my way soon, I'd be late for my meeting with Miss Serena.

"Will you ask her to keep her ear to the ground and let me know if she hears anything that might help me figure out who hurt Annie?"

Janny nodded. Then she looked over as the bell over the door rang. She waved as another customer entered and said she'd have his coffee in a minute.

"I will. You stop back by here later today or she'll have both our hides."

I laughed and nodded. Miss Peggy might be retired—at least she kept telling everyone she was. Not that she'd cut back her hours by much from what Annie and Quinn told me—but she still expected each of us to check in with her.

"Tell her I'll be back." I tossed a ten onto the counter and waved aside Janny's protests.

Before I reached the door, Janny was there, a to-go cup in her hand. I thanked her, glad to have it. The café brewed the best coffee I'd ever had and tired as I was, I needed the boost. But now I needed to hurry if I was going to get to Miss Serena's on time.

Except, this being Mossy Creek, surprises were bound to happen. I'd barely stepped onto the sidewalk when my cellphone rang. I tapped the earbud in my right ear. At the same time, I spotted two people I'd hoped to avoid coming down the sidewalk in my direction.

"Jax?" Bitsy's voice carried both concern and anger.

"I'm here and I see them."

And wished I was anywhere else.

"Watch yourself, Jax, and remember you don't owe them anything."

"Thanks, Aunt Bitsy."

"Call me later. I'm heading over to Catherine's now. We'll head over to the hospital once I get there."

I thanked her again and then ended the call. As I did, I considered my options. I could play this one of two ways. I could let my parents know I had no desire to speak with them. Or I could throw them off their stride and have some fun without causing a scene. At least not the sort of scene my parents wanted.

I waited as they neared. Dad hadn't changed much over the years. He might be a little thicker around the waist and his brown hair more gray than brown. His tan probably came from a spray gun instead of a tanning booth. But he carried himself like he owned the town, something most folks around here resented. Especially since he had done nothing to earn their trust or their friendship over the years. Dante (originally Daniel but he thought Dante sounded more cosmopolitan) Powell was more interested in living the high life than in actually working or contributing to the community.

Then there was my mother. Small, thin to the point of being gaunt, the once beautiful Emma Powell had fallen a victim to her own vanity. Too much plastic surgery, too many Botox injections and who knows what else had turned her into a walking advertisement for cosmetic surgery gone wrong.

"Jaqueline," my father drawled as they stopped in front of me.

I fought down the spike of anger at his use of my given name. They both knew how much I hated it. I've always thought that's why they've insisted on using it. Why else would a parent do so?

"Daddy, Mama." I grinned and reached out as if to hug them.

They stepped back almost in unison, their expressions matching looks of horror. It was almost as if I'd sprouted a second head. I stood there, hands extended to them, letting the café crowd get a good look. For once, I was the one trying to make peace, at least that was the impression I gave. And it did exactly what I expected. It showed my parents for the bigots they were. I was different. I didn't bend to their will. So I wasn't worthy of their love or affection.

Fuck 'em.

"Jacqueline, how dare you!" my mother hissed. Her lips curled back in distaste as she looked at my sleeve of tattoos, my tank top and jeans. "If you're trying to embarrass us, you're doing a good job of it. What will everyone think?"

Before I could answer, I felt someone slide an arm around my waist and pull me to him. It was most definitely a him. A him with rock hard muscles that quivered with barely controlled rage. Looking up, it took all I had not to gasp to see Rafe Sabatini. He smiled down at me, a smile that didn't reach his eyes, before he turned his attention to my parents.

"Hey, Jax. I hoped I'd catch up with you," he said. "Sam wound up staying at the hospital after talking to his folks. They were on their way over with a change of clothes for him."

"Thanks, Rafe." I wasn't sure how I should react. But, from the look on my father's face, he liked Rafe no more than he liked me. Interesting. "Daddy, Mama, do you know Rafe Sabatini?"

"I've had the pleasure."

From Rafe's tone, it had been anything but a pleasure.

"I guess we shouldn't be surprised, Jacqueline." Mother's voice dripped with derision. "It's not enough you embarrass and disrespect us by walking around town looking like some biker's whore. You certainly didn't waste any time jumping into bed with the likes of him." She nodded to Rafe. "I told Judge Caldwell he needed to get his son to fire this *person*. But would he listen to me? No. I suppose I should be thankful you haven't married him yet. Or don't you believe in marriage anymore?"

Rafe's arm tightened around my shoulders as he fought to keep from responding to my mother's taunts. I, however, had no such compunction.

"Despite everything you and my father showed me, I do still believe in marriage. Just not the sort the two of you enjoy—if that's what you call it." I reached up and patted Rafe's hand and took a step forward. "If you want to get into everything out here, in the middle of town, I'll be glad to oblige. As for Rafe, I'll tell you this. I trust him a hell of a lot more than I do either of you. I'm guessing you hired Sam's company to do some work for you, tried to stiff him on the bill and Rafe here stood up to you. If that's the case, good on him. It's time folks around here quit letting you get away with shit other folks would go to jail for simply because your last name is Powell."

"How dare you!" My father took a step forward, stopping when Rafe matched him.

"The truth hurts, doesn't it?" I motioned Rafe back. He nodded, his gaze never leaving my parents. "One more thing, don't try to bully Aunt Bitsy either. I'm not staying at her place and, no, I'm not telling you where I'm bunking."

"You ungrateful—"

"Dr. Powell, everything all right?" Deputy Inuye asked as he emerged from inside the café.

I barked out a laugh at my mother's shocked expression. "What is it, Mother? Didn't know your only daughter can legitimately call herself doctor?" No need to tell them it was as a doctor of veterinary medicine.

"C'mon, Doc. They don't deserve any more of your time or attention." Rafe once again slid an arm around my shoulders and steered me away. As we passed Inuye, Rafe asked him to make sure my parents found their way anywhere but after us.

"Are you all right?" he asked as we walked around the corner.

"Yeah. That was pretty mild where my parents are concerned." I stopped and looked up at him. "And thanks. But what are you doing here? I thought you were staying with Annie."

"Drew showed up and spelled me so I could take care of a couple of things at work. I'd just parked when I saw them bearing down on you."

"I appreciate the save and I most definitely want to hear what happened between you and them. But not now. I'm running late already."

"Sam told me you were meeting with Miss Serena. Tell her I said hi."

"I will." I glanced around the corner, relieved to see Inuye escorting my folks in the opposite direction. "How about letting me buy you a cup of coffee or a drink tomorrow? I owe you for stopping me from doing something foolish."

"Sounds good." He glanced at his phone. "I'll probably see you at the hospital later."

"See you later. And thanks again."

As I made my way back to the Ducati, I wondered if I should run by Bitsy's to switch to the Porsche. I wasn't really comfortable driving the Ducati after dark, and it looked like this was going to be a very long day. But swapping the bike for the car would make me even later. Common sense won out and I sent a quick text to Miss Serena, apologizing and telling her I'd be there soon. Hopefully, she'd understand.

Thankfully, Mossy Creek isn't that big. Twenty minutes after texting Miss Serena, I drove the Porsche down the long, tree lined drive leading to her house. At the end of the drive stood her three-story plantation style home. The front doors opened as I parked. By the time I climbed out, Miss Serena stood on the porch waiting for me.

"Sorry I'm late." I bent and kissed her cheek.

Serena Duchamp smiled up at me. Her hazel eyes sparkled and a wrinkled hand reached up to lightly pat my cheek. To the casual observer, she looked like someone's beloved grandmother, which she was. But she was also the most powerful *Other* I knew. When my talents began manifesting, she became my teacher, just as she taught almost every other *Other* in town. She was mentor, friend and confidante and so much more.

"Is Annie all right?"

I nodded as I linked my arm with hers. "Dr. Pat suggested yesterday that it might help if you and Amy visited and gave her a healing treatment."

"I'll talk with Pat and make sure she's let the staff know. Once she does, Amy and I will be there." We walked inside and through to the kitchen.

"Thank you." I sat at the ancient oak table and watched as she poured coffee for us both.

"I spoke with Mary Kate earlier. She said Annie doesn't remember what happened." Miss Serena placed a china cup and saucer on the table in front of me. A moment later, she joined me at the table.

"She doesn't. Her doctor said that's not surprising." It didn't surprise me that Annie's grandmother had been talking with Miss Serena. They were close friends, much like Annie, Quinn and me— and Maddy when she was home. "I saw her this morning. She looks like hell, but she is better. Worried about the kids."

Miss Serena sipped her coffee and nodded. Then she reached across the table and grasped my hand. "And you?" She nodded to my clothes and then my ink.

I told her about the call from Ali and not thinking twice about quitting my job to come home. She smiled and shook her head to hear how Bitsy conspired with me to make sure "the rogue" made an appropriate entrance. Then, hearing how my parents tried to ambush me—and there was no other word for it—and how Rafe came to my rescue, she smiled again.

"He's a good man, Jackie, and he needed Mossy Creek after his discharge."

I smiled and sipped my coffee. Miss Serena was the only one I let get away with calling me Jackie. Not that she did it all that often. She knew what I thought about my given name and most nicknames associated with it. I'd learned that when she did use it, she had a point to make. And, for whatever reason, this time it had to do with Rafe Sabatini.

"Sam told me Rafe saved his life in Afghanistan."

"He did, just as he saved Rafe's earlier. After Sam's discharge, Rafe served another four years or so before deciding not to re-enlist. From what Mary Kate's said, he wandered around for a while, trying to cope with his demons. He finally ended up here. Seems Sam talked about the town a great deal and Rafe fell in love with it. Once he got here, Sam helped him first by making sure he got the treatment he needed for his PTSD. Then he hired him. Camille told me the last time we had lunch that Rafe's now acting as Sam's right hand man with the firm."

That sounded like Sam. He took care of his friends, whether we wanted him to or not. Of course, those same friends had accused me of doing the same thing more than once.

"Miss Serena." I looked at my now empty coffee cup and gently pushed it away. I was stalling and, from the look on her face, she knew it.

"What's bothering you, Jax?"

What wasn't bothering me was more the question. I blew out a breath and leaned back, trying to order my thoughts.

"I've been by Annie's a couple of times since hitting town."

She nodded, her expression telling me she knew. Not that it surprised me. She was so connected with the town she probably felt the moment I crossed the city limit line.

"Just say it, child. What's bothering you?"

I told her how I connected with the earth energies at Annie's. Her lips twitched slightly and a very definite gleam lit her eyes when I described what I'd sensed. Without commenting, she stood and left the kitchen. I waited, wondering what was going on. When she returned a short time later, she carried a bottle of very fine and very rare bourbon in one hand and a thick, leather bound book I recognized. She placed the book on the table. When she returned to her seat, she handed me both the bourbon and two highball glasses and told me to pour a drink for both of us.

"Why do I get the idea I'm not going to like this?" I asked as I carefully poured amber liquid into the first glass.

"Because you are a suspicious young woman?" she teased.

I laughed and nodded once. She had me there. At least I sensed no tension or worry in her, at least not about what I'd said. That ought to reassure me, but it didn't. She knew something, or at least suspected something. Hopefully, she'd tell me what and together we'd figure out how to deal with it.

"You know the town's history probably better than most of your generation, Jax."

She rested one hand on the worn leather cover of the book in front of her. I nodded, remembering all her lessons when I was younger. I'd enjoyed them almost as much as I'd enjoyed the lessons teaching me how to control and then master my earth gifts. Young as I was, I'd responded to Miss Serena's love for our town and its place in history. Many afternoons were spent going over the information in the book, the family histories and news articles and all the other wonders inside.

"You remember the founding families."

It wasn't quite a question, nor did it require an answer. I gave one anyway.

"Your family, the O'Donnells, the Mathisons, the Russells, and the Delmars representing the *Others*. The Youngs, Brewers, Kings, and Lees were also among the first to settle here."

"Do you remember the family trees?"

I nodded after thinking back to those long ago lessons. "Some of them are easy. Your family, both sides, Quinn's mother's family, Dr. Pat's maternal line, Miss Peggy's paternal line and." I stopped and a grin lifted the corners of my mouth. Oh my. "Annie's grandmother's maternal and paternal lines. All of them are descended from the original *Others*."

"That's right. What I didn't tell you back then was that the original Others bound their land to their families. Over time, that binding has weakened and, in some cases, it's been broken. Time does that if the bindings aren't renewed, especially if the family moves or dies out."

I nodded, putting it together in my mind.

"That house Annie inherited from her grandfather sits on the location of the original family homestead. The dates are all in here and it would do you good to study them, but the important part is his grandfather bought the land from the Delmars. Because the families were so close, Mariah Delmar expanded the binding to include the Metzgers. It has weakened over the years because most of the Metzgers were normals. When Annie moved in, the binding awakened. But it is a pale shadow of what it once was."

I sipped the bourbon, considering what she said. More importantly, I considered what she didn't say.

"Is this your way of telling me Annie's an *Other*?"

"What do you think?"

"I think she is. I've always felt that way." Miss Serena said nothing as she waited for me to explain. I blew out a breath and then took another sip of the very fine bourbon. "Miss Serena, even as a kid, I knew she wasn't like the other normals we ran with. It went beyond her accepting me for what I am. She always seemed to be where she was needed, even before the person knew Annie was necessary to whatever the situation was. Most folks might call it intuition, but I've always felt it was something more. Perhaps a touch of precog."

Now Miss Serena smiled. When she did, pride filled me.

"Her grandmother and I have always felt the same way. Annie denies it, even after seeing Quinn's gifts manifest. But Annie exhibits many of the same talents her grandmother possesses. The fact the land awakened even a little when she moved in proves it."

I considered what she said.

"Miss Serena, is this binding what makes your house and Quinn's so—" So what? Special? Different? Terrifying?

She poured me another shot of bourbon and nodded. "It is. The stronger the binding and the more powerful the *Other* in residence, the more aware the land and buildings seem to be. And, yes, before you ask, it does pick up echoes of the personality of the strongest *Other* in residence."

My eyes went wide. I gulped once and then I burst out laughing. Oh, my. That explained so much. So very much.

"So, if I'm understanding right, all the things the house did to Quinn when we were growing up was because it recognized her as an *Other* and was picking on her because she wouldn't come out and play?"

"I wouldn't put it quite that way, Jax, but yes." Her eyes twinkled as if she knew I couldn't wait to tell my friend. "And it is why my house is more sedate."

I wouldn't exactly call it sedate. But it was definitely more subtle than Quinn's place.

"Does all this mean there's some way to awaken the binding at Annie's place and, if there is, would it help protect her and the kids?"

"There is."

"Can it be done without her involvement?"

Annie wasn't ready to admit she was an *Other*. Hell, she might never be. Besides, it would be best if the binding could be strengthened before she was released from the hospital. I know Sam would rest easier and so would the rest of us.

"I believe so, but I'll need to do some research to confirm what needs to be done."

I reached for her hand and squeezed it. "Please. I'll do whatever I can to help."

"You're a good girl, Jackie." She looked at the book and then, to my surprise, pushed it across the table to me. "Take this and study it. You may see something I've missed. We'll meet again later to discuss what we can do to make sure our Annie is kept safe."

"Thank you. I won't let anything happen to it." I rested my right hand on it, much like I would on a Bible before swearing to tell the truth in court.

"Something else is bothering you, child. What?"

I shook my head, a bemused smile lifting one corner of my mouth. Like Bitsy, she knew me so much better than my parents ever had.

"A couple of things, to be honest."

I told her about my concern that everything that happened from Annie's mother being charged with murder to Quinn's ex and even Meg's problems with her mother's family were interconnected. Add in Annie being attacked, and I couldn't shake the feeling there was more going on in sleepy Mossy Creek than anyone else realized.

Part of me wanted her to tell me I was seeing shadows that weren't there. Instead, she reached for the bourbon and poured herself a healthy shot and downed it. That, by itself, was enough to send my concern soaring through the roof. I could count on one finger the number of times I'd seen her do something similar. She was a sipper, especially of a fine bourbon like this. Not someone to shoot it back without taking time to enjoy it.

"Miss Serena?"

"This is something else we need to discuss but others need to be here when we do." She stopped me before I could interrupt. "Jackie, this is something we've worried about as well. Now that you're home, we need to discuss it and figure out the best way to proceed."

I nodded, my heart pounding and my stomach feeling like it might climb out my throat at any moment. I'd so wanted her to tell me I was imagining things.

"Who?"

Maybe that would tell me something. It sure couldn't hurt.

I hoped.

"Pat and Mary Kate."

I opened my mouth and slammed it shut when she shook her head. "I—we'll explain when we're all together. I promise."

I nodded again. I trusted her. I could wait a little while—I hoped.

She stared at her hands wrapped around her glass for a moment and then looked up at me. Her expression was still troubled, but I had a feeling it was because of more than what we'd been discussing.

"Miss Serena, are you all right?" Fear licked at me. I couldn't imagine Mossy Creek without her. Hell, I couldn't imagine my life without her in it.

"Just worried." She smiled and reached over to lightly pat my hand.

"About? I take it that it's more than what we've been talking about."

Now it was her turn to nod. I waited, wondering what had her so hesitant to say anything. One thing I knew about Serena Duchamp, she was rarely at a loss for words.

"Jackie, I won't break confidence."

"I would never ask you to."

"But I will say this. You need to have a serious discussion with your aunt. Things between her and your parents have deteriorated even more than I think you're aware of."

I closed my eyes and did a slow count to ten. I'd been afraid of that but, coward that I am, I hadn't asked. It was also another reason I'd not hesitated to turn in my resignation. My subconscious, at least, wanted me to come home and deal with things I'd left unsettled for much too long.

"That's part of why I'm here, Miss Serena." I could admit it to her even if I wasn't so sure about it myself.

"Your job?"

Ah, now she was getting to the heart of what bothered her. As well as I knew her, she knew me better. She knew I didn't like asking for help. She knew I'd taken on my entire college and vet school debt even though Bitsy offered to help. I had loans to pay and now no job that would allow me to do so.

"Let's say I'll be looking for a place to work as soon as we find out who hurt Annie." Even now I wouldn't ask for help.

Her expression said it all. I was being stubborn. I was being foolish. She was more than willing to help me if I'd just let her. But instead of lecturing me, she sat in silence. I could almost hear the wheels turning as she considered said the situation. Then she surprised me by changing the subject.

"Where are you staying?"

Obviously, she knew I wasn't staying with Bitsy. Interesting.

"I spent last night at Quinn's but after the run-in with my parents, I need to find somewhere else to stay." Except I'm not sure even finding a hotel in Dallas or Denton would be far enough away to keep them from trying to bother me.

"The caretaker's house is empty. Meg and Drew moved out last week. You'll stay there."

I arched one brow at the mandate, but she continued as if she hadn't seen.

"You know your parents won't come out here." Her smile betrayed her contempt for them. "Even if they do, they won't be allowed past the main gate. Not without you or me allowing them in."

In other words, the land and the house would keep them out. Damn, but I'd have killed to have that sort of protection for my bedroom growing up.

"It will also give you the room to shift and hunt without having to worry about someone seeing you."

Which was a very good point.

"And there is a benefit for me."

I tilted my head and waited, wondering what she had up her sleeve.

"Dr. Oliver isn't handling large animals anymore. If it can't be brought to his office, he won't see it. That means I've been having to bring in a vet from Denton County to check the horses and cattle. I'd rather hire you and have you looking after them, at least until you find a full-time job."

Tempting as it was, I couldn't do it. I didn't have a clinic. I didn't have the tools except for what I carried with me on a regular basis. I'd be no better than her farm manager and farm hands and I told her so.

"We've got a decent set up here, Jax. Take a look and see. Just tell Jimmy what else you need and he'll get it ordered."

It was tempting, too tempting. I remembered Annie and Quinn telling me how they felt the trap closing about them when they first returned to town. With Annie it was the house and law practice—not to mention Sam. With Quinn, it had been the need to protect Ali and Mrs. O'Donnell. Then there was the sudden awakening of her talents. Was this the town's way of keeping me here?

Still, it wasn't a lifelong commitment. I could do it—assuming Miss Serena and I agreed on terms—and leave when all this was over.

Besides, I had a feeling I'd be spending time with Miss Serena figuring out why we both thought there was more going on in town than everyone else believed.

"Thank you." I stood and moved around the table to kiss her cheek. "I can move in tonight, if that's all right."

"That's perfect. The keys to the house are on the hook by the back door." She watched as I collected them. By the time I returned to the table, she had a small remote control in her hand. "This will open the front gate." She pushed it across the table in my direction.

"Thanks."

She glanced at her watch. "Amy will be home soon. As soon as she is, we'll go see Annie."

I slipped my arms around her and gave her a hug. "I know I don't need to say it but thank you."

She patted my arm and looked up at me. "Leave the book here. You can pick it up tonight when you move in."

Since I felt better doing that than leaving it in my car, I agreed.

Five minutes later, I slid behind the Porsche's steering wheel, feeling like I'd been run over by a train. I'd been in town less than twenty-four hours and already my life had taken twists and turns I hadn't anticipated. I so did not want to know what else Mossy Creek had in store for me.

7

Before heading back to the hospital, I stopped by Annie's office. As I parked behind the building, I looked longingly at the café's rear door. As if knowing where I was, my stomach rumbled, reminding me it had been a long time since breakfast. Unfortunately, I didn't have time to stop. I wanted to see what Beth Soukis, a friend from school and Annie's office manager, could tell me about what happened. Then it was on to the hospital before going by Aunt Bitsy's to grab some clothes.

I strolled around the building. A bell chimed somewhere in the back of the office as I opened the door. The firm's receptionist, Carli Sanderson, looked up from her computer and smiled. Then she winced slightly as raised voices from behind the door leading to the private part of the office filtered toward us. I couldn't understand what was being said, but the tone was unmistakable. Someone was seriously pissed and Beth was doing all she could to calm them down.

Carly motioned to the door next to her desk.

"See if you can talk any sense into her, Dr. Powell."

"Who?"

"Mrs. Grissom."

"She's back already?"

Carly nodded and glanced at the door as Meg once against said something that had Beth trying to calm her down. "Caught the red eye last night and was here when I got in."

"Buzz me through."

The young woman didn't hesitate. Not that I blamed her as I stepped into the back area. Beth stood in front of her desk. From her jeans and red blouse, I guessed nothing had been on the court docket today. Even with her back to me, I saw her tension. Her back ramrod straight, her feet shoulder width apart and one hand fisted at her side all spoke volumes.

But it was the sight of Meg that brought me up short. We didn't know one another well. I'd met her the first time when I came home for the party Miss Serena and Mary Kate Metzger threw to celebrate Meg's marriage to Drew. We'd gotten together, along with Annie and Quinn, a couple of times since then. To my surprise, I liked her a great deal and I understood why Quinn and Annie so quickly accepted her as part of the inner circle.

At the moment, however, she was a very angry air elemental. Anger and worry darkened her expression. From where I stood, I felt the air beginning to stir. Small wisps of her hair danced around her face as her power built. The air felt almost electric. This wasn't good. Not good at all. Especially since Beth was a normal and had no way to protect herself if Meg lost control.

Praying I wasn't about to make things worse, I stepped up to Beth's side. She relaxed almost instantly as I rested a hand on her shoulder. Then, as I gave a quick jerk of my head, telling her to step back, she nodded. Not that she moved far away. But at least she was out of the direct line of fire if I didn't manage to calm Meg down.

"Ease down, Meg." I pointed to her hands and the lightning dancing around them.

She glanced down and then cursed softly. I watched, not sure what to expect, as she closed her eyes. She drew in one deep breath, then another and another. Slowly, the air around us stilled and the tension in the room dropped. I waited, not ready to drop my guard yet.

"Beth, care to tell me what's going on here?" I asked without taking my eyes off Meg.

"Nothing to worry about." When I glanced back at her, she repeated her reassurance. "She's just worried about Annie."

Well, that made two of us.

When I glanced back at Meg, she leaned against Miss Olivia's desk. Her shoulders slumped and she looked over my shoulder to where Beth stood.

"Sorry."

"No need." Beth ran a hand down my back and then gave my right hand a quick squeeze. "Have you seen Annie today? They won't let us in yet."

I nodded, noticing that she had no doubt I'd found a way to see our friend. Not that it surprised me. She'd known me as long as Annie had and knew the lengths I'd go to protect not only Annie but any of our circle, including Beth herself.

"She's going to be all right." I glanced between the two of them. "The doctors are talking about moving her out of the unit later today or tomorrow if she continues to improve. But head injuries are tricky. Trust me, it's for the best that they are being careful and not rushing her right now."

"Did she tell you who did this to her?" Meg's eyes flashed, an unnecessary reminder that she could easily call lighting.

"No. So far, she doesn't remember what happened." I glanced around and motioned toward the small breakroom off the work area. Once we all had coffee and had settled around the only table in the room, I continued. "Sam can't think of anyone who'd want to hurt Annie. As far as he knows, she hasn't received any threats. Quinn told me she's been worried because Annie's seemed pre-occupied. But when she asked about it, Annie told her nothing was wrong."

I left the question unasked as Meg and Beth looked at one another. Then they both shook their heads, their expressions telling me they knew nothing more than Sam did.

Damn.

"I've gone through all her correspondence, looking for anything that might explain what happened. There are a couple of former clients who aren't happy with what she told them. That's why they are former clients. I gave Lucas their names."

Which is exactly what I figured Beth would do.

"Could it be someone she prosecuted before she moved back here?"

Meg shrugged. "That's another possibility he's looking into."

"But?" I prompted. "And what were the two of you arguing about?"

Instead of answering, Beth sat back and watched Meg fiddle with her mug.

"I don't do well when people I care for have been hurt," Meg said without looking up. "And I'm pissed at Annie. I've known something was bothering her and has been for the last month or more. But I didn't push, even when my gut told me I should."

"Neither of us did, Meg," Beth waited until she looked up. "I've known her a lot long than you and she wouldn't let me in either. Whatever it is, she didn't want us to know."

"I don't mean to sound like your mother, Beth, but find out." I grinned when she rolled her eyes. "After all, isn't it better to beg forgiveness than ask permission in a case like this?"

A slow smile spread across Meg's expression. "I knew I liked you for a reason." She turned her attention to Beth. "Annie uses her office laptop to check email. Hack into her personal account. If she says anything about it, I'll take the heat."

"Oh, we'll both take the heat. Trust me." Beth probably should have at least tried to sound like she didn't agree with the action, but she didn't. Not that I expected her to.

"Call your mother in. See if she'll help," Meg said.

I chuckled softly. If I knew Miss Olivia, and I did, she was already digging into everything she could think of to explain what happened to Annie and why. Now she had permission from one of the law firm's partners to dig even deeper. She'd love it and by the time she and Beth finished, Annie would have no secrets—at least not from the two of them. It might be a violation of her privacy but if it helped keep her safe, she'd could just learn to live with it.

"Are you heading back to the hospital?" Meg asked while Beth called her mother.

"Yeah." Meg didn't need to know I had two reasons for going. Not only did I want to check on Annie, but I wanted a few minutes with Sam. Something told me I needed to know the story behind the bad blood between my parents and Rafe. "Want to ride over with me?"

"Please."

Five minutes later, I grinned as she stood next to the Porsche, one hand reverently caressing the front fender.

"Sweet, isn't she?"

"She's a beauty and not what I expected from you."

Fair enough. She didn't know me as Mossy Creek's rogue. I'm sure the others had told her some of the stories, but that was different from actually living them.

"Then you should see the Ducati I rode yesterday." I laughed as lust lit her expression. Quinn and Annie told me she was a biker. In fact, she'd first ridden into town on a Harley. "And, before you say anything, my usual mode of transportation is either a Camaro or a beat up work truck. But Aunt Bitsy decided I needed something a bit more in your face if I was resurrecting the rogue."

Meg looked at me in open speculation. But, instead of asking any of the questions I knew had to be running through her brain, she watched as I unlocked the car. She waited until we were pulling away from the office before she said anything.

"Rogue, huh?"

"Let's say I had a bit of a problem with acting out and standing up for my friends growing up."

"And following the rules from what Annie and Quinn, not to mention their husbands and mine, have said." She grinned, showing approval for my actions when I was younger.

"That is still pretty much the case." I grinned at her.

"Is that why Lucas and Drew aren't raising hell because you're poking around in what happened?"

"Probably. They both know it wouldn't do any good. Hopefully, they also know I'm not going to do anything to jeopardize their case if they do manage to ID Annie's attacker."

"Mind if I butt in? I want a piece of the SOB who hurt her."

I grinned and nodded. She'd have access to information I couldn't get, at least not easily.

"Afternoon, Doc," Deputy Inuye said as we approached the doors to the intensive care unit.

"Afternoon, Deputy." I shook his hand. "Thanks for the help earlier."

"My pleasure. Believe me, it was all my pleasure."

From the way he said it, I had no doubt he'd had run-ins with my parents before. I swallowed the urge to apologize. No one should have to deal with them.

He reached behind him and pressed the button to open the doors. "Mrs. Grissom."

"Meg," she corrected before following me inside.

I paused at the door to Annie's small room, Meg at my side. Dr. Pat and Dr. Kennison stood on either side of the bed. Sam stood at the foot of the bed. Even though I couldn't see his face, I felt his worry. The three of us waited in silence as the doctors finished their examination. Dr. Kennison assured Annie she was doing well and that she'd get to move into a regular room soon. When she asked about going home, he patted her leg and told her one step at a time. The rebellious look on her face told me all I needed to know. She was not going to be patient much longer.

Sam thanked Dr. Kennison. The he turned and saw Meg and me in the doorway. Before he could say anything, Annie smiled and waved us inside.

"You can't stay long. She still needs to rest," Dr. Pat told us. "I'll make sure she gets moved to a private room as soon as one's ready." She turned back to Annie. "And you, young lady, will do exactly as the doctor tells you or I'll let your grandmother know and ask your mother to come sit with you. Maybe even suggest she bring her babies."

I tried not to laugh as Annie paled at the threat. As threats went, it was a good one. Catherine by herself was enough of a trial. Add in her two geriatric poodles from hell and no one in their right mind would want to deal with the three while recovering from a head injury.

"I'll walk you out, Dr. Pat," Sam said. Before leaving the room, he looked at me. He didn't need to say anything. I was to make sure nothing happened until he got back.

"Hey, partner. How you feeling?" Meg asked as she hurried to the bed.

"Like someone hit me with a sledgehammer." Annie tried to smile but failed. "How did the argument go?"

"All right. Now we wait." When Annie reached for the plastic cup on the tray next to the bed, Meg grabbed it and helped her sit up some. Then she held the cup while Annie drank her fill. "You're not to worry about the case or the office. Beth and I have things well in hand." Now she grinned. "And, if we don't, Miss Olivia will. You know she's not going to let us do anything too foolish."

Annie's grin this time was real. Then she turned serious again. "My kids?"

"They're fine. I promise." I moved to stand opposite Meg on the other side of the bed. "I—we're—not going to let anything happen to them or to you. I promise."

She looked from Meg to me. When she reached out to me, I took her hand and held it between both of mine. As I did, I felt the call of my tattoos. The need to shift because I could protect her better with fang and claw than without. Except I could. I'd learned a great deal about how to control my gifts and use them without causing unintended harm over the years.

"Have you remembered anything else?" Meg asked gently.

She shook her head. "I was doing a load of laundry. I heard something behind me and thought it was Robby, home from playing. I started to turn. There was pain. I don't remember anything else."

"You're doing good, Annie. Really good. That's more than you remembered this morning." I brushed a lock of red hair from her brow. "Rest now or Dr. Pat will throw us out."

We watched as her eyes drooped. A few minutes later, she slept.

Leaving her to rest, Meg and I moved into the corridor outside her room. We could keep an eye on her from there and still talk without disturbing her.

Not that Meg had much to say. Anger radiated off of her. Her right toe tapped an impatient rhythm against the tiled floor. Sparks of lightning danced around her hands where they clenched and unclenched at her sides.

"Look at me." I waited until she did. "We will find out who did this to her, and we will make sure they never hurt her or anyone else again. You have to believe that."

"I do." She tilted her head back and studied the ceiling for a long moment. When she looked at me, I had a feeling she'd come to a decision. But what?

"We don't know one another well but we both love Annie and Quinn."

I nodded.

"And, for whatever reason, Drew." She grinned mischievously at the mention of her husband. "The way I see it, that makes us family. If you're okay with that."

I didn't need to think about it. I was very okay with it and told her as much.

"Then let's make a pact. We'll work together to find out what happened and, if you need me in my professional persona, I'll be there for you. Just try not to go too much of the rogue."

I grinned and agreed. As I did, Sam walked down the corridor toward us, Drew at his side. "I've some things I need to do this afternoon, Meg. I assume you can grab a ride back to town with Drew."

"I think I probably can." She winked and I laughed gaily, suddenly realizing my childhood friend had his hands full with his wife.

I told her I'd talk to her later and slipped my arm through Sam's leading him back toward the entrance. Before he could object, I stopped and watched as Drew and Meg disappeared inside Annie's room. Then I turned my attention back to Sam.

"I know you want to get back to Annie and I promise this won't take long. But I need to ask something about Rafe."

He rocked back on his heels, his expression telling me that was the last thing he expected. "What about him?" A hint of suspicion roughened his voice.

"I don't know if he told you, but I had a run-in with my parents earlier. He saw it and came over to make sure everything was all right. It was clear from what they said—and didn't say—that there's a history between them. Is it anything I need to worry about?"

I very carefully didn't ask him what that history was. I didn't want to put him in the position of having to either betray a trust or lie to me if my suspicions were wrong. Now I waited, giving him time to consider what I asked and how to answer. If he answered at all.

"I'll let him tell you all the dirty details, but your folks tried pulling the same shit with him over a job they contracted for that they have with so many others. He gave them every change to pay up. When they didn't, he told me and we filed a lien against the house." He shoved his hands into his pockets, suddenly looking very uncomfortable. "Jax, they're in deep and not just with us. There are at least half a dozen liens filed against them right now. And that's just the ones I know about."

I closed my eyes and cursed softly. No wonder they'd been after Aunt Bitsy. She'd never tell me, but I knew my parents. They wanted her to bail them out, just like my grandfather used to do until Grandma died. After that, Granddad told my father to grow up. Unfortunately, he never did.

"Did Rafe get his money?"

"Well, technically, it's the company's money and not yet. They appealed the default decision we received. Said there wasn't proper service."

I closed my eyes and counted to ten. Not that it was enough to still my anger. How many times had my parents pulled this sort of thing? More importantly, why did anyone in town continue to do business with them?

"How much?" I asked. "And was it for work to their personal property or the family business?"

The family business that my father was part of only because my grandfather hadn't seen fit to completely cut him off. Almost a century ago, my great-great grandfather opened Powell Real Estate. Under my grandfather's leadership, the company went from selling houses in this county and in Denton County to investing in real estate and brokering major commercial land deals across the Southwest. An astute businessman with the talent for knowing what areas would be the next to build up, Granddad doubled the company's worth. By the time he died at the ripe old age of eighty-seven, he'd made enough for the family to live comfortably on for at least a couple of generations and insured the company was strong enough to withstand almost anything.

He was also a very wise man, even in his old age. He revised his will after Grandma died. He divided the business between Bitsy and me, with my father receiving a small portion and a job with the company as long as he followed certain rules set out by my grandfather. Bitsy was the executrix of the will. She was also the trustee for the portion of the estate set aside for my father. Granddad surprised us all by setting up a trust, making sure my father couldn't get his hands on the bulk of his inheritance.

If things had been bad between us before, they went to hell after that. My parents blamed me for Granddad pretty much cutting them out of the will. It didn't matter that my inheritance was tied up in a trust until my thirty-fifth birthday. Not that I wanted any of it. I signed a power of attorney the day after the will was read, giving Bitsy the authority to vote my shares in the company and to handle all legal and financial aspects of my part of the estate that wasn't tied up in the trust. Then I'd headed back to Texas A&M to finish vet school.

Now, however, I'd ask for enough money to pay Sam and Rafe what they were owed. It was the least I could do. Not that I planned on letting my parents off the hook. But they were my problem, not Sam's and certainly not Rafe's.

Instead of telling me how much they owed, Sam shook his head. "Nope. I've already told Meg I didn't care how much it cost. We will hold them accountable."

"Sam." I ground it out.

"No, Jax." He folded his arms across his chest. He was the very image of stubborn as he stood before me.

"We will discuss this later." After I talked with Bitsy. I had a sinking feeling Sam was only one of many businessmen my parents had taken advantage of.

"You can try." He gave me a cocky grin.

"Go check on your wife. I have errands to run. Tell her I'll be back in the morning." I reached out and stopped him before he could do more than turn toward Annie's room. "Sam, call me if you need anything."

"I will." He gave me a quick hug. "You don't do anything foolish."

"Who? Me?"

He laughed and shook his head. I kissed his cheek, reminded him to call if he or Annie needed anything and left the hospital. I wanted to stop by the café to see if Janny or Miss Peggy had learned anything. Then I needed to have a long talk with Bitsy about my parents. Sam might not want to tell me how much he was out because of them but I had no doubt Bitsy knew or could find out. And all that needed to be done before I headed back to Miss Serena's.

8

"All right, what's going on?"

I finished rinsing the last of the dinner dishes and watched as Amy loaded them into the dishwasher. Miss Serena's granddaughter was two years older than me. Blonde, green eyed, she looked like she could grace the cover of any beauty magazine. Not that she'd ever want to. Like her grandmother, she was grounded, powerful and someone I had always admired.

"Your guess is as good as mine." She cocked her head, listening, as the sounds of Miss Serena and the others talking in the family room once again reached us. Then she smiled at me, her expression filled with understanding. "You know my grandma. She never does anything without a reason."

I nodded, not that it answered any of my questions.

"Don't worry, Jax." She dried her hands before patting my arm. "My guess is they simply want to make sure you're all right." Now she chuckled and my stomach did a slow roll. "They've been making bets since Annie came back about how long before you, Quinn and Maddy joined her here."

"What?" My voice broke as I stared at her in surprise. Oh hell no. I was not, most definitely not, moving back to Mossy Creek. Not now, not ever, at least not as long as my parents lived here.

She grinned and, taking my hand, led me to the kitchen table. While I sat, she moved to the fridge. When she joined me a moment later, she handed me one of the two beers she held. I twisted off the top and took a long draw. Then I waited, not sure I wanted her to explain.

"The four of you—but especially you, Annie and Quinn—have always held a special place in my grandma's heart." She smiled and gave a slight shrug. "In all our hearts. Everyone who matters understood why each of you needed to get away after high school. But we all hoped you'd return."

I ducked my head, my cheeks burning. When I looked up, Amy simply sat there. I felt no demands, no expectation that I respond. Only love and support if I'd accept them. In other words, exactly what she, her grandmother and so many others had offered all my life. They were all more than happy to welcome me home if I wanted to take that step. But there was more. They wouldn't condemn me if I chose not to return. All they wanted was what was best for me at the moment.

God, I loved them. Why couldn't my parents be even a little like these wonderful people?

"Thanks." I tilted my bottle in her direction. "And thank you for going to see Annie this afternoon. When I talked with Sam before dinner, he said she was resting easier after you and your grandmother worked with her."

"We didn't do much. Head injuries are tricky."

"And Dr. Pat didn't want much done while she's still in the hospital." Which made a great deal of sense. Even those medical professionals who were also *Others*, like Dr. Pat, had to worry about things like malpractice lawsuits and hospital guidelines. Fortunately, once Annie was home, such concerns would take a backseat to doing everything possible to help her heal.

Amy glanced at her watch. "I've got to run. Brian will be home soon."

I nodded. She and Brian McNally planned to marry over the Memorial Day Weekend. They'd bought their first house and moved into it less than a month ago.

"Go. Give Brian my love." He'd been a geek in high school, tall and skinny and, well, geeky. Now he was taller, had filled out after discovering the joys of working out regularly and he owned a small tech company.

"I will, but I've got a question first."

I recognized the look on her face. It was the same one her grandmother wore when she was about to ask me something I probably didn't want to answer. Instead of asking what she wanted, I arched a brow and waited.

Instead of saying anything right away, she rested her hand on top of mine where it rested on the table. "Jax, I know you came home only because Annie was hurt. Grandma told me you quit your job to do so and that she's asked you to take care of our horses and cattle while you're here."

I nodded, not sure where she was heading with this.

"I'd appreciate it if you'd take her up on it. Jimmy is getting old and the other hands don't know animals the way he does. Grandma's not worried about paying a vet to come out whenever needed. Even if it's only temporary, we need someone to keep the stock healthy and to take some of the pressure off of Jimmy who refuses to admit he can't still do it all."

I blew out a breath. Then I jumped in with both feet.

"What about Jimmy? How will he react to her hiring me?" I knew the old man and respected him. He taught me how to ride and helped foster my love of large animals. I was a vet in large part because of him.

She chuckled softly. "Hiring you was his idea."

I felt the trap Annie and Quinn warned me about tightening around me. Not that I was going to fight it—yet. I needed to be in Mossy Creek until we knew what happened to Annie and why. Not to mention finding out who was responsible. That meant I needed a job and this fit the bill. All I had to do was make sure everyone else understood this didn't mean I was committing to staying here permanently.

"Don't worry. I'll be here for the near future and I'll do whatever I can to help out." Now it was my turn to pat her hand. "Now go home. Tell Brian I said he owes you a night out for working late." I grinned as she blushed to the roots of her hair.

"Come join us, Jackie," Miss Serena said as I entered the living room a short time later.

I didn't cringe but it was as close thing. She called me Jackie. That meant she had something on her mind, something I had a feeling I wasn't going to like. At least I knew it was important. Unlike when my parents called me by my given name or the more common nickname, there had been no censor in her voice, no condemnation.

Not that it made me feel much better.

I nodded and slipped down to sit on the floor next to Miss Serena's chair. It was the same position I'd taken for as long as I could remember. It wasn't a sign of submission. My animal side wouldn't permit it. But it was one of respect, that of student to teacher or child to adopted and much beloved grandmother. Which was exactly how I felt about her. The thought brought a smile to my lips. Each of these women were special and had always been there for me, no matter what.

"I sort of feel like I did in high school when the four of your got together to talk to me about how I'd been acting out."

That afternoon, they'd met me as I left school. Judith explained that Quinn was worried about me. Before I could try to reassure her, as if a fifteen-year-old in trouble at home and school could do so, Mary Kate added that Annie was worried as well. So, Dr. Pat said, was Maddy. But it was the concern and lack of condemnation in Miss Serena's expression that almost did me in. Without another word, I hugged each of them and piled into Miss Serena's Lincoln Town Car.

It didn't' take long for them to get the truth out of me. A week earlier, my parents forbade me to see Miss Serena again. No more lessons, no more "being turned against them" they told me. Then, two days before, they told me I couldn't see my friends except in class. I was to go to school and come straight home. Whether I liked it or not, I was no longer an *Other*—as if I could just turn it off to suit them.

I'd reacted badly, to put it mildly. The day before, seeing Sawyer and his "friends" picking on Annie, I'd let out all my frustrations. Oh, I was smart enough not to use my Earth magic. Instead, I called on my skinwalker abilities and the added strength and speed they gave me. I beat two of the starting football lineup to a pulp before turning my attention to Sawyer. He yelped, pissed himself and ran away.

And I'd been placed in in-school suspension yet again. The only reason I hadn't been tossed out was because I had been protecting Annie.

These four women talked to me that day and assured me they would always be there for me. I'm not sure what they did afterwards, but my parents never again tried to force me to give up my gifts. Oh, their attacks on who and what I am continued, but not as overt as they once had been. More importantly, they were such I could basically ignore them, knowing I had only a year and a half before I could head off to college.

"Not quite, but we do need to talk to you." Miss Serena lightly stroked my hair. "But first, have you decided if you're going to take me up on my job offer?"

I craned my neck so I could look up at her. "I have." Feeling a little strange talking business sitting of the floor while everyone else sat on chairs or the sofa like adults, I climbed to my feet. As I took the chair across from Miss Serena, she waited for my answer. "Amy told me Jimmy Reardon is all right with me helping out." It wasn't quite a question, but it did require an answer.

"He is."

"Then I will accept your offer. We can talk money tomorrow."

When the others looked between us in question, Miss Serena explained. "While she's here, she's going to stay in the caretaker's house and act as our vet."

Judith gave me a speculative look. For a moment, I considered running for the hills. She was up to something. Hell, who was I kidding. They were all up to something.

"Would you be interested in taking care of our various menageries?" she asked. "I know Quinn's not happy with Dr. Oliver. He doesn't understand the difference between working dogs and pets and he most certainly isn't up on the changes in the profession."

"I'm not opening a clinic." I shook my head, wanting them to understand this was not a permanent position.

"But while you're here," Mary Kate pressed. "I know I'd feel better if you were taking care of my dog."

I couldn't say no. But, instead of actually saying "yes", I dipped my chin in agreement.

The four looked at one another and then back to me.

"Jackie, I spoke with them about our earlier conversation, about how you feel what's been happening the last few years may all be connected," Miss Serena began. "What I didn't tell you then because I wanted the chance to talk with them first, is that it is something we've been worried about since Meg came to town."

"I don't understand."

And I didn't. I knew Meg's background. Annie and Quinn gave me the basics not long after Meg's arrival. Later, after Meg and I met and realized we were starting to form a friendship, she told me more. But what did that have to do with everything?

Miss Serena and the others took turns explaining their concerns. It was almost as if they'd rehearsed it. They hadn't. I knew that. It wasn't how they worked. But it was obviously something they'd been worried about. In one way, that made me feel better. After all, it meant I wasn't overreacting. But, in another, it worried me. I much preferred this to be a product of my overactive imagination.

"It's clear you think this goes back further than Annie's return home," I commented half an hour later. "Why?"

"Quinn's told me you know Meg's history, at least in general terms," Judith said and I nodded. "Her mother, Pat and I grew up together. We were all in the same class and we were as close as you, Annie, Quinn and Maddy are. Because of that, we knew something was wrong. She'd come to school with a black eye or bruises on her arms. She did her best not to go home any sooner than absolutely necessary. But, like you, she was also the protector. Never did she hesitate to step up and step in if she thought someone needed help."

My anger rose as I listened to them describe Faith Donnelly's life in Mossy Creek. Of course, Donnelly hadn't been her name then. As soon as she was old enough, she petitioned the court for a name change. Annie's grandfather was her attorney. Miss Serena her mentor and protector. She took Faith in when her family kicked her out for having the poor taste to be an *Other*.

My stomach roiled dangerously to hear how her own brothers and a family friend tracked her down around the time she graduated from college. They beat her and the so-called friend raped her. If she wouldn't come home with them, they'd make sure she never darkened their door again. What Faith didn't know at the time was the family wanted her home only because she'd inherited her great-grandmother's estate. Her parents wanted the money and land, not their daughter.

I didn't need Dr. Pat to tell me Meg was the product of that rape. Instead of giving her up, Faith moved to some small town I've never heard of in Kansas and raised Meg on her own. Not once did she tell Meg what happened. Nor did she tell her about Mossy Creek. In fact, Meg didn't know the town existed until her mother died a little more than a year ago from cancer. After her death, Faith's attorney delivered a letter to Meg. In it, Faith asked her to come to Mossy Creek and find Miss Serena.

I thought about what they said. As I did, the pieces began to fall into place. But I was missing something, something important. Hopefully, Miss Serena and the others could fill it in.

"Serena told us she gave you the book earlier and suggested you study it," Dr. Pat said.

"She did. I left it here and haven't had a chance to really look at it yet."

"Before you do, there's something else we need to talk with you about." Judith sounded serious enough it worried me.

"I'm listening."

And ready to run for the hills if necessary.

"We spoke earlier about how the original Others in town bound their land to them and vice versa." Miss Serena waited until I nodded. "What I didn't tell you is that they represented each of the elements. One of them was also a walker like you. Earth, Air, Fire and Water were represented along with what we'll call Life for now. They became the protectors for the town. Special wards were set up to warn of trouble. Without abusing their gifts, they did everything they could to help the town grow and thrive. And, for the most part, they did just that.

"They realized as they grew older that they needed to pass their positions down to a new generation. My great-grandmother was the youngest of that generation. So, she became mentor to the new generation of guardians. She taught them and guided them. Then, when it was time, they stepped up and took over from their predecessor."

"We've had trouble each generation. There are those who would like to see our kind wiped from existence," Mary Kate took up. "But nothing like what happened to Faith and nothing like what has happened to Annie, Quinn and Meg."

I swallowed hard as my brain started putting two and two together. Then I shook my head. Whatever they were leading up to, I did not want to hear it. Not now and quite possibly not ever. So, to prevent Mary Kate from saying anything else, I interrupted.

"So we make sure this is the last attack against us." I suddenly grinned. "Does this mean Annie's an *Other*?" It certainly seemed to confirm it, as if I still needed confirmation after my earlier conversation with Miss Serena.

"Don't tell her." Mary Kate's grin matched my own. "My granddaughter is even more stubborn than Quinn about this one aspect of her life."

Before anyone could say anything else, the grandfather clock in Miss Serena's study chimed nine times. That seemed to be a signal. Dr. Pat and Judith climbed to their feet. The rest of us followed suit. Goodbyes were exchanged and soon the two left. Miss Serena excused herself, saying she wanted to call the hospital and check on Annie. As she disappeared deeper into the house, Mary Kate motioned for me to join her on the sofa.

"Ma'am?"

"Jax, Serena told me what you've given up to be here. I want to say you didn't need to but I can't. I'm selfish. Annie's so very important to me. I thank you for being here for her. She's going to need you until this is over and we know who hurt her and why."

"Mrs. Metzger, I wouldn't be anywhere else."

She smiled affectionately and reached for my hand. "You are an adult now. You can call me by my name."

All I could do was promise to try. That seemed to satisfy her.

"I don't mean to pry, but are you planning on returning to Annie's tonight?"

I nodded, not telling her I intended to do so in one of my animal forms. Instead of arguing, she seemed to relax. Seeing it, I cocked my head to one side, looking at her in concern.

"What's wrong?" I took one of her hands and held it between both of mine. For the first time that I could remember, she looked old, almost frail. Worried, I wanted, wondering what had her so upset.

"I'm sorry. Talking about Faith on top of what's happened to Annie has me unsettled." She lightly patted my hands with her free one. "But I'll be honest. I'm worried this isn't over. Every instinct I have tells me more trouble is to come and I'm terrified whoever hurt Annie might try for the children next."

I bared my teeth and growled. Then I shook myself. If it was the last thing I did, I'd protect those kids.

"No one's getting to them. I promise." I leaned forward and rested my cheek against her. "You should head home and get some rest. Annie's going to need you tomorrow if they move her into a regular room."

"Why don't you come with me?" she suggested. "You can change at my house and then head to her place. It's only two blocks."

I considered the offer for a moment. I had no doubt she meant I could shift at her house. She knew I was a skinwalker. Not once had she treated me differently because I'm a hybrid, a rarity for *Others*.

Now she offered me a measure of safety, both when it came to a place to shift and a shorter distance to travel before reaching Annie's.

"All right." I gave her hands a quick, reassuring squeeze. "I'll meet you there. I want to grab a change of clothes and tell Miss Serena." And give Quinn a call to let her know as well.

"Thank you." She smiled gently and I smiled in return. "Don't be long."

"I won't."

Five minutes later, after telling Miss Serena what I planned, she walked outside with me. As we stood on the front porch, the full moon shining down on us, she linked her arm with mine and leaned against me. We stood that way for a moment, enjoying being together and letting the worries of the outside world slide away, if only for a brief time.

"I'll see you for breakfast, Jax," she said as we slowly walked down the steps to the drive. "If you need me before then, call. It doesn't matter what the time."

I promised I would. Then I climbed into the Porsche and drove off, wondering what the rest of the night would hold.

9

I leaned against the doorframe and smiled. First thing this morning, Annie was moved to a private room. That not only meant she was doing better but that she could have company beyond the few of us Dr. Pat assured the staff were "family". It also made things easier for Miss Serena and Amy. Sam told me I'd just missed them. They'd been there when Annie changed rooms and helped get her settled, including giving her another healing session. Better yet, Amy and Lexie, her best friend and another *Other*, would be back later so Sam could run home for a while.

"What happened to the rogue?" Annie looked at me, a grin on her lips.

I pushed away from the doorframe and approached the bed. As I did, I took in her appearance. Her temple was still bandaged. The bruises on her face were fading and her eyes and nose were no longer so swollen. Better yet, her words didn't slur and her eyes weren't dull from painkillers. She was healing and now it was up to us to keep her calm and find out who hurt her.

When I didn't answer, she waved a hand at me. What could I do? I shrugged. I'd come straight from Miss Serena's after talking with her farm manager and checking the stock. Instead of looking like the tattooed troublemaker, I wore a pair of fade blue jeans, a red polo I'd borrowed from Amy, and scuffed cowboy boots. I held a well-worn baseball cap in one hand. I looked more like a ranch hand than the rogue who came into town two days earlier.

Instead of answering right away, I glanced around the room. A collection of mylar balloons in almost every color imaginable floated up from the foot of the bed. Flowers, some cut and others in pots she could replant when she returned home, lined the windowsill and almost every surface in the room. But it was the sight of Rafe Sabatini seated in a chair by the window that drew my attention. His posture might say he was relaxed but the way his eyes checked out every sound told me otherwise. He was on duty and I, for one, was glad.

"Well?" Curiosity and frustration filled her voice and I fought the urge to grin. After all, it wasn't nice to pick on her when she was hurt. But it was tempting.

"I'm surprised Miss Serena didn't tell you." Okay, I'm not a nice person all the time. Fortunately for me, Annie loves me anyway.

"I swear if you don't tell me what's going on, I'm climbing out of this beat and beating it out of you, Jax."

Now I did grin, cocky and confident. Annie did exactly as I expected. She scowled, wincing slightly and then stuck her tongue out at me. I laughed and bent to kiss her cheek.

"Seriously, I did expect her to tell you." I rested my hand against her cheek for a moment and then carefully sat on the edge of the bed.

"Tell me what?"

I'd thought long and hard how to explain it to her. The last thing I wanted was for her to jump to the conclusion that I'd come back for good. That decision wasn't one I was ready to make and probably never would be. On the drive in, it dawned on me that all I could do was tell her the truth.

"Long as I'm here, I'm going to be taking care of Miss Serena's stock and her dog. We worked a deal out so I can do that in exchange for living in the caretaker's house." I made a show of glancing over my shoulder in Rafe's direction, hoping she assumed that meant I didn't want to say anything more in front of him.

"Your job?"

I smiled and told her not to worry.

"Jax." She reached for my hand, holding it just as she held my gaze. Then she gasped softly before a smile turned up the corners of her mouth.

"Don't start getting ideas, Annie. I'm only here as long as you need me."

The smile turned into an almost wicked grin and I shook my head. "Don't start getting ideas. I'm not here for good." At least I didn't think so. "Can I bring you anything the next time I come?"

"A ride home?" she asked hopefully.

"Not until your doctors say so." I couldn't help laughing softly as she pouted in response. "You scared us, Annie."

"I scared myself," she admitted softly. She reached for my hand once again, holding onto it tightly. "Jax, I'm still scared. I don't remember what happened and whoever hurt me is still out there. What if he tries for Robbie or the babies?"

I smiled slightly, understanding. "I might not look like the rogue right now, but you know she's never far below the surface. I'm not leaving until the bastard responsible for hurting you has been arrested. Promise."

"Still taking care of me." Affection lit her expression even as her eyes began to droop as her meds kicked in.

"You're my best friend, my sister by choice. Of course, I'm going to take care of you." I gently brushed away a tear from her cheek and then leaned close so only she could hear. "You've always been there for me, Annie. All I'm doing is returning the favor."

Before anything more could be said, a knock sounded at the door. I coughed to hide my laugh as Annie paled to see her mother all but bound into the room. Catherine wore a hot pink jogging suit. With here were two of her three best friends, all members of what Annie and drew called "The Terrible Trio". The only one missing was Aunt Bitsy. Since I really didn't want to see her in a matching hot pink jogging suit, I decided this was my chance to slip away.

"My baby!" Catherine practically cooed as she rushed to the bed and threw her arms around Annie.

Rafe looked up. His eyes sparkled and he quickly jerked his head toward the door. I didn't need any further encouragement. I slipped out of the room while Annie, her eyes all but wheeling as Catherine, along with Danielle Underwood and Margie Beckett, assured her they were there to keep her company so Rafe could grab some coffee and stretch his legs.

"Have time for a coffee?" he asked as we stepped onto the elevator.

"Sure." Hopefully, he had some answers for me. I had no doubt he'd been digging into what happened. He didn't strike me as the sort of man who sat on the sidelines while others did the dirty work.

"Has Lucas been by this morning?" I glanced at my watch. Almost noon. Where had the morning gone?

He nodded and sipped, grimacing at the taste of hospital coffee. Not that I blamed him. "He was in before eight and, before you ask, he didn't tell us anything of import."

I frowned. So much for it being easy. To my surprise, he looked as frustrated as I felt. Curious, I tilted my head to the side and decided to jump in with both feet.

"Rafe, I know Sam and Annie trust you not only with her life but the lives of the kids. That tells me a great deal."

"Sam and I went through hell together and learned to rely on one another." His eyes darkened briefly. Since I knew at least part of the story, I didn't press. There would be time for that later. "D'you know, I fell in love with this town in the Afghan desert?" Now he smiled. "Sam told me about the town and growing up here. I heard all about Miss Peggy and the café, Miss Serena, Catherine and the Terrible Trio, his family, even you."

My brows winged up in surprise and he nodded. "He told me how the rogue was always there to protect and stand up for her friends, even if they didn't think they needed it. He knew as long as you were around Annie would be safe. Then, you, Annie, Quinn and Maddy left after high school. He joined the Army, married the bitch Mia. The only good thing to come out of his marriage to her was Robbie. When

I found out Annie returned here and the two of them got back together, I knew things were finally looking up for Sam. Then, when she adopted Robbie, I realized everything he'd told me about Mossy Creek was true."

"Those two always belonged together." I sipped my coffee, considering what to say next. "What finally brought you here?"

He didn't answer for a moment. Instead, he looked over my shoulder and I had a feeling he was seeing something far different from the hospital cafeteria. I waited, not wanting to push. I remembered Sam after his discharge. Between being seriously wounded and then having Mia walk out on him and Robbie on Christmas Day of all days, he was as close to being broken as possible. It took him time and the love and support of his family and friends to pull out of the depression that held him. I'm not sure what would have happened if he hadn't had Robbie. Knowing the little boy needed him was his lifeline. Now he put his own experiences to use helping other vets deal with returning to civilian life. Part of that included hiring them at the construction firm and giving them a stable job.

"Sorry. My demons are still pretty close to the surface." He closed his eyes and pulled himself together. "But to answer your question, Sam. I'd been out about six months when he showed up at my door. At the time, I was living in one of those long-term motels, bouncing from job to job. He told me he'd given me enough to time feel sorry for myself. I was to pack up. We were coming here. I had a job with his company and it was up to me to decide what I wanted to do with it. As I threw my few things into my duffel, I realized coming here was exactly what I wanted.

"He put me up in his old house and told me my rent consisted of doing some updates to the place. He'd supply the materials and help on weekends. I was also to help with updates at his parents' place as well as Annie's grandmother's. Once I showed I still knew how to read plans and use a hammer and nails, I'd start with his company."

"He's a good man." I smiled when Rafe nodded. "I know he's asked you to keep an eye on Annie while she's here. I have a feeling you're doing more than that."

He leaned back in his chair. For a long moment, he studied me. I sat there, waiting, figuring he was trying to reconcile the image I presented today with what he'd seen earlier.

"Who are you, really?" he asked instead of answering my unasked question. "Are you still the rogue?"

Instead of answering, I lifted my right hand, letting him see it. Then I lowered it, palm down, toward the ground. I held his gaze as I concentrated on the earth beneath the foundation of the building. As the energies responded, I pictured the hospital in my mind. I needed to do this carefully.

Sweat pricked out on my brow as the energies rose up through the building. If I closed my eyes, I would see them racing along conduits and rebar reinforcements, electrical lines and through the water lines. They converged on our table. Slowly, carefully, I moved my fingers toward my thumb, drawing the energy up through the floor to the table base. Rafe's eyes went wide and he quickly looked around as the table began to shake. Coffee sloshed from our cups.

I closed my fist and then my eyes. Concentrating, I sent the energies back into the earth. Satisfaction filled me to know I'd managed this little show of power without causing any damage. Now to see if he accepted it or if ran for the hills.

"Impressive." Respect shown in his eyes as he mopped up the spilled coffee. "But that doesn't answer my question. Quinn is a fire elemental. Meg air. You just proved you are an earth elemental. But that doesn't make you a rogue, much less *the* rogue."

Suddenly uncomfortable, I considered how to respond. Then, realizing he wasn't judging me, I made a decision.

"Do you know why they called me the rogue when we were growing up?"

He shook his head.

"I'm assuming you're comfortable being around *Others* since you moved here."

A nod this time.

"Then you know there are different kinds of *Others*. Some of us are elementals, some are what are best called kitchen witches, some have special talents when it comes to things mechanical, others have foresight or can read patterns in actions. There are some who shift into one animal or another. And that's just to name a few of the various gifts we might have."

"I served with several *Others*," he said. "They used their gifts to keep us alive more than once. I didn't realize it growing up but my mom was a kitchen witch. She ran one of the most successful restaurants in St. Louis. She sold it last year when she and my dad decided it was time to retire. They sold the restaurant, their house and bought a place in Utah."

"Have you ever met anyone who has two very different gifts?"

His brow furrowed. He didn't understand.

"You know how Quinn, even though she is a fire elemental, can call the wind."

He nodded.

"That is because they are complimentary talents. It also makes her very dangerous if she should ever lose control. Fire burns and wind spreads the fire. Fortunately, she is about as scrupulous and honest as they come." And that was putting it mildly. "Where she differs from a lot of Others is that she has another gift, one she didn't realize she had, until she and Ali moved back here. She reads patterns in actions, much like Lucas does. They can look at a crime scene and sometimes picture exactly what happened. That is not something usually seen in an elemental. Even so, that sort of thing isn't unheard of."

"I take it you have an additional gift, one that makes you different?"

Now it was my turn to nod. It was also my turn to take the conversation down a different path, at least for a moment.

"Rafe, you've had the *pleasure* of meeting my parents and seeing what they are like."

"Not exactly how I'd put it."

"Me neither, to tell the truth." I managed a soft chuckle. "So you can guess how they felt to realize that I not only was an *Other* but I wasn't going to let them mold me into the perfect daughter. They wanted someone they could trot out at business and social occasions, an accessory to further their ambitions. When my gifts started manifesting, I was forbidden from using them. They even forbade me from studying with Miss Serena and seeing Annie, Quinn and Maddy except in class."

He winced and then grinned almost evilly. "I assume that went over like a ton of bricks."

"To say the least. I began acting out. Fortunately, Aunt Bitsy and Miss Serena intervened. Bitsy gave me a safe haven to escape to and stood up for me with my parents. Miss Serena made sure our lessons continued. I'll tell you more over drinks one day. But none of that made me the rogue. Nor did me standing up for Annie and the others when the school bullies picked on them. It enhanced the reputation, but it wasn't the cause of it."

"I don't understand."

Hoping I wasn't about to make a very big mistake, I looked down at my left arm and the tattoos that covered it from wrist to shoulder. As I did, I wondered if he saw them moving. He'd have to look close but it was there to see.

"Rafe, shapeshifters come in many shapes and sizes."

"Yeah. We had two with the unit, a jaguar and another was an Asian black bear."

Good. He had personal experience with shapeshifters. Hopefully, that made this easier.

"Did anyone have tattoos like I do?" I nodded to my arm and its tattoo sleeve.

He shook his head. Whether he knew he'd answered another question or not, I didn't know. But I'd find out soon enough.

"Quick lesson. Shapeshifters are *Others* who have a single animal they shift into. They aren't limited to only shifting on nights of the full moon. That's something books and then Hollywood promoted. That said, it is easier for them on those nights. Also something those stories almost got right is that when these *Others* shift, they lose much of their humanity, becoming their animal selves. That's what can make them dangerous. If they stay in their animal form too long, they lose their humanity. That is where the legends about werewolves and the like began."

"But? I have a feeling there's a but in there."

I grinned. "There is. That's why I asked about the tats."

"I don't understand."

"I am an earth elemental. I am also a walker. I don't call myself a skinwalker because, unlike Native American mythos, I don't need a skin or pelt of an animal to change shapes. My tattoos are my link to my animal aspects. Also, unlike shapeshifters, I maintain my humanity in my animal form. Walkers are very rare. To have one who is also an elemental is all but unheard of. That makes me different, even among *Others*. And that is where the rogue came from. So, all that is a very long-winded way of telling you that, yes, I am still the rogue."

Instead of being appalled or afraid, he nodded and smiled. Then he lifted his now empty cup in salute.

"Then, between the two of us, we might be able to not only keep Annie safe but find the bastard who hurt her."

I grinned, relieved he shared my priorities.

He glanced at his watch and climbed to his feet. "I'd better go rescue Annie from her mother and the others. Let me buy you dinner tonight and we can figure out where to go from here, especially since it's clear Lucas is not going to share intel with us."

"Sounds good." I pushed away from the table and climbed to my feet. "Let me call you later though. I need to make rounds again at Miss Serena's and see the rest of the stock I missed this morning. I don't know how long that will take."

He pulled out a business card and scribbled a number on the back. "That's my cell. Call me when you know what time you'll be free. I promise we won't make it a late night."

I watched as he left the cafeteria. That went better than expected. But now I needed to get out of there. I wanted to run by the law office and see if Beth and her mother had found anything to help identify Annie's attacker. Then I needed to run into either Dallas or Denton to buy some clothes. And, like it or not, I needed to return a call to Drake at the clinic. My boss had left three voicemails that morning, each one more demanding than the last, telling me we needed to talk.

Well, he could wait until everything else had been dealt with. The last thing I needed just then was being told I'd acted irresponsibly and hear him threaten, yet again, to file a complaint with the state licensing board.

10

It was a little after five by the time I returned to Miss Serena's. All I wanted was a hot shower, some food, maybe a drink and then bed. Unfortunately, it looked like that had to wait. Parked in front of the main house were Quinn's SUV and Sam's Aggie maroon pickup. There were several other cars I didn't recognize. Remembering my promise to meet Rafe for dinner, I pulled out my phone and texted him that something had come up. Almost instantly, he responded that he knew and to text him later. Even as I agreed, I wondered what he knew that I didn't.

I switched off the Porsche's engine and climbed out. I hadn't taken two steps when the front door opened. Ali raced outside and threw herself at me. I grinned and lifted her, hugging her close. Then I set her down and repeated the process with Robbie. As I did, I took note of the concern in his eyes, the way he hung back a little. Silently cursing the person responsible for scaring him and hurting Annie, I set him down and reached for his hand. He was my first project of the evening.

"Ali, go tell your mama and the others we'll be inside in a few minutes."

She looked at me for a moment and then, as if realizing I was going to try to help her best friend, she nodded. As she hurried back up the steps to the porch, I slipped an arm around Robbie's shoulders. When I did, he leaned into me. A few moments later, I slid to sit on the grass in the shade of an ancient oak tree in back of the house and he dropped down at my side.

We sat in silence for several minutes. Much as I wanted to talk to him, to make sure he was all right, I knew better. Just then, he was like a wounded animal. He needed to know he was safe. With my arm around his shoulders, his head resting against my side, I let him get used to my presence. Finally, I felt him beginning to relax.

"It's hard, isn't it?" I looked out into the pasture beyond the yard, watching as a couple of yearlings galloped by.

He didn't ask what I meant. He just nodded.

"Robbie, it's never easy when someone we love is hurt. I have a feeling you're a lot like me and you wish you'd been there to protect your mom."

Another nod before he pulled his knees up and wrapped his arms around them.

"You know something?" I waited until he looked up at me. "As much as you wish you'd been there to protect her, your mom is glad you weren't. She's scared about what might have happened to you if you'd been there."

His little face scrunched up as he considered what I said.

"And she is awfully proud of you. So are the rest of us, especially your dad."

"Why? I let her get hurt. I wasn't there to protect her." Tears pooled in his eyes.

"But you were, Robbie. You were there when she most needed you." I drew him close, hoping it helped comfort him. "I want you to listen to me, okay?"

He nodded.

"You realized something was wrong when you got home. You made sure your little brother and sister were all right and then you called your daddy to let him know. Then you went looking for your mom and found her. Instead of running away like a lot of folks would do, you stayed with her. You called 9-1-1. You called Quinn and your dad. More than that, you did everything you could to help your mom until your dad and the others got there." I lifted his chin so he looked up at me. "Do you know what that makes you?"

Another shake of his head.

"It makes you a hero. You were very brave and you helped protect your mom by calling for help. We all know that. Now you need to believe it. Okay?"

"I don't feel like a hero."

I smiled and pulled him onto my lap. "Because you've been scared?"

"Yeah."

"Robbie, it's okay to be scared. Being scared actually means we're paying attention to our instincts and to what's going on around us. That feeling sometimes helps us stay alive. It also means we care about other people, like you care about your mom. You're scared because you don't want anything else to happen to her. Right?"

"Right." He put his arms around me and held tight.

"Want to know a secret?" I looked down and waited until his head moved up and down against my chest.

"I was so scared when Quinn told me your mom had been hurt. I was scared because I didn't know how badly she'd been hurt. I was also scared because I didn't want anything to have happened to you or the twins.

"I was angry too. Angry at the person who hurt her and scared you and your dad. But I was angry at myself too because I hadn't been here to stop it from happening. Even though I know that's foolish, it's how I felt. So I understand what you're feeling right now."

"Did you really blame yourself?"

I nodded. "And I cried because I was so scared."

As if those were the words he needed to hear, he broke down. He sobbed and I held him close, one hand gently stroking his back. That's when I realized Sam had joined us. He silently thanked me as he settled in the grass next to me. Carefully, gently, I transferred Robbie to his father's arms. Leaving them to talk, I stood and made my way to the house.

I found everyone else in the dining room and kitchen. Miss Serena, Judith and Mary Kate were in the kitchen, preparing dinner for everyone. In the dining room, Meg and Quinn stood with Drew and Lucas and I had no doubt they were talking about what happened to Annie and what the investigation had found so far. Dr. Pat was on the phone with the hospital, leaving instructions concerning one of her patients. Amy was setting the table with Ali's help. If this wasn't a war council, I didn't know what was. The only thing that surprised me was the fact Maddy hadn't come home yet. That bothered me because I knew her mother had told her about what happened to Annie.

"Any word from Maddie?" I asked as Dr. Pat joined me by the front window.

"She still overseas and pissed she can't be here. But this assignment is time sensitive and she said she figured you have everything in hand." She grinned and then her expression sobered. "I'm not going to lie, Jax, but I don't want to say anything to the others right now. I'm worried. This isn't like her."

That was an understatement. But this wasn't the time to discuss it, not if she wanted to keep everyone else in the dark.

"Let's talk about it later," I said softly. "Care to give me a hint about what's going on?"

"Serena decided it was time for us to put our heads together and try to figure out what's going on." She looked toward the kitchen as Miss Serena and Mary Kate appeared, Judith just behind them. "Looks like dinner's ready."

The large table was crowded by the time everyone found their places. Miss Serena sat at the head of the table, Amy at the opposite end. The rest of us ranged around the table, one big family by choice if not by blood. I found myself sitting to Miss Serena's right, Judith next to me. Dr. Pat sat across from me, Mary Kate next to her. Everyone else found their places and, after Miss Serena said grace, we dug in.

Over chicken fried chicken, salads, garlic mashed potatoes and gravy, we talked. From where he sat next to Ali, Robbie told us about the twins who were with Sam's parents. I smiled when I caught his eye and gave him a wink. A blush colored his cheeks before he grinned. Over his head, Sam mouthed another silent "thank you". I nodded and then turned my attention to one of the best meals I'd had in a long time.

When we were done, Quinn and Meg cleared the table. As they did, the rest of us made our way into the living room. Amy handed out cups of coffee to those who wanted it while her grandmother poured bourbon for the rest. Figuring I needed a clear head because something was up, I took a cup of coffee. Then, when Mary Kate suggested the kids take the dogs and go play, I knew I was right. At least we didn't have to worry about anything happening to Ali and Robbie. Between Quinn's two dogs, Ali's lab, Meg's dog, Miss Serena's and Robbie's dogs—Annie's was at the Caldwells with the twins—the kids were well protected.

And that was if whatever danger had already touched our circle of friends managed to get through Miss Serena's protections.

"Someone want to tell me what's going on?" I asked as Quinn and Meg joined us.

"We need to talk, all of us," Miss Serena began. "Sam, how's Annie?"

He smiled, relief lighting his expression. "She's better. Starting to chafe at having to stay in the hospital. She says she'll heal better at home."

All eyes turned to Dr. Pat where she sat on the stone hearth. She might not be Annie's doctor, but Dr. Kennison brought her in at Sam's request.

"Honestly, she could come home." She held up a hand before anyone could interrupt. "We're keeping her in the hospital until we know for sure she isn't going to suffer any complications from her injuries and until certain steps can be taken to secure the house."

Sam's brow, not to mention most everyone else's, furrowed as they tried to figure out what Dr. Pat meant.

Instead of answering, Miss Serena looked at me. For some reason, she seemed to think I needed to be the one to talk to Sam about this little twist. Wonderful.

"Sam, would you object if the same sort of protections in place here and at Quinn's were put in place at your house?"

For a moment, he looked at me like I'd grown a second head. Then he shook his head. "Not at all." He looked from me to Miss Serena and then to his wife's grandmother. "Can you really do that?"

Miss Serena nodded. "It won't be easy, but it can be done."

"But how?" Quinn wanted to know.

"I don't care how. Just tell me what I need to do." Sam's comment had Quinn closing her mouth with a snap.

"Quinn asked a good question. I'd like to know how you plan to do this." Meg sounded like an attorney arguing a case before judge and jury. Not that I blamed her. If they hadn't explained at least the basics of it all earlier, I'd want to know as well.

Miss Serena explained, much as she had with me. Occasionally, Dr. Pat or Mary Kate added a comment. No one else said anything. Even so, from time to time, I caught Quinn glancing in my direction, a speculative look to her eye. Finally, I arched one brow in question. She smiled and shrugged. Even so, I had a feeling she'd be cornering me for more information the first chance she got.

"Miss Serena, I meant it. I don't care what needs to be done. Just do it," Sam said when she finished. "I've already talked with Lucas and Drew, not to mention Rafe. We'll be updating the security system over the weekend."

"It will take us a day or so to prepare." Miss Serena looked at Dr. Pat.

"We'll keep her in the hospital."

"Rafe or I will stay with her. I don't want her left alone." Sam's voice hardened and I knew he was thinking about seeing her unconscious on the floor of the laundry room.

"And I'll keep an eye on your place at night." As I had since arriving back in town.

"Each of you need to remember this is my department's case. I

108

don't want you doing anything to jeopardize the prosecution when we find the bastard who hurt Annie."

Quinn laid a hand on her husband's thigh, almost as if to settle him. "They know, love."

"Sam, we'll discuss this with you some more once we're ready to activate the protections," Miss Serena said, cutting off any further discussion. "For now, there's something else we need to discuss, something that involves all of you." She looked at each of us, her expression serious.

"Miss Serena?" Quinn leaned forward, concerned. When Miss Serena didn't reply right away, she looked at Judith. "Mom?"

Over the next fifteen minutes or so, Miss Serena, Mary Kate, Judith and Dr. Pat gave the rest of us a Mossy Creek history lesson. Since I knew most of it thanks to our earlier conversation, I only half-listened. Until Miss Serena said the one word I'd been praying not to hear ever again. I sat up, not sure I liked the direction the conversation was taking.

"I really don't understand, Miss Serena." Quinn looked like she might join me when I ran for the hills.

"Quiet. Let her finish." Judith waited until Quinn, her expression mutinous, nodded once.

"Jax already knows some of this." As one, Quinn and Meg, not to mention Sam and their husbands, looked at me. I shrugged, still not sure where all this was going. "And, with all that has happened, it is time for you to know as well."

The only sound in the house as Miss Serena wove her tale was that of the grandfather clock in the other room striking the quarter and then the half hour. Outside, an occasional laugh from one of the kids or bark from a dog failed to break the spell. Miss Serena, the ancient leather bound book now in her lap, took us back to the town's founding and the roles our ancestors played.

Quinn and Meg moved to sit on either side of me as Miss Serena spoke about my family. I knew my grandfather had been a walker like me. But his mother, who died before I was born, had been an earth elemental. The family throughout the generations had been mainly

Others. My father was the exception. Even Bitsy, although she downplayed it, was an *Other.* Her gift a subtle one that allowed her to see financial patterns. Because she had a strong ethical sense, she didn't abuse the ability. Still, it helped her keep the family business afloat and I'd never begrudge her that.

Then the other shoe dropped. Miss Serena described how the town had been protected by the four guardians from its founding. When she explained how Quinn, Meg and I were descended from the original guardians, Quinn begin shaking her head. She practically vibrated with the need to escape. Not that I blamed her. I'd been eyeing the front door for the last few minutes, wondering if I should make a break for it.

"My wife may be surprised by all this, Miss Serena," Lucas began. Amusement and a dawning understanding shone on his face. "But I doubt any of the rest of us are. Quinn, Meg and Jax are three of the most powerful I we know. Present company excepted."

"He is so going to die," Quinn grumbled. When Lucas only grinned, she bared her teeth. "See if we have sex anytime in the next decade," she threatened.

Unabashed, he simply grinned broader and then sobered as Judith picked up the tale.

"Serena, Pat and I are the current guardians." Before anyone could interrupt, she continued. "There was a fourth, but she never took her place as one of us. We know the reasons now and understand. To be honest, if we'd known what was happening, we'd have insisted she take the action she did. After all, we didn't think there was any problem with going on with just the three of us protecting the town."

"My mom?" Meg asked softly, the color draining from her face.

Dr. Pat nodded. "Yes. Faith would have been our fourth. But you all need to understand something. She did what she needed to for herself and for Meg. That is all that matters."

"But?" I knew there was a "but" coming. There had to be.

"We were wrong, at least on one thing. And we've been lucky," Judith said. "Mary Kate might not advertise her abilities, but she is stronger than most people realize. She has done all she can to help fill the gap left by not having the fourth guardian here in town." Now she looked at me and I swallowed hard. I so did not like where this was going. "Every set of guardians has had one or two *Others* who act as sounding boards. People who won't hesitate to tell them if they are wrong and who act as their eyes and ears when needed. Mary Kate has always been there for us, just as Amy will be for you."

For a moment, I considered bolting from the house and running for the hills. Glancing at Quinn, so new to her powers, I had no doubt she'd beat me there. Her chair slid across the hardwood floor and she started to rise. She paused, halfway to standing, when Amy placed a light hand on her arm. Compassion and understanding were reflected in Amy's eyes as she asked Quinn to hear everyone out. Only Quinn's love for Miss Serena—and the look Judith sent her—kept her from fleeing into the night.

"As I was saying, Mary Kate, and Amy for the next generation, assist the guardians. They are a most necessary support system and they keep the current guardians grounded." Judith glared at her youngest child, all but daring her to interrupt. "They are often healers, either of the mind or body."

"W-why are you telling us all this?" Quinn asked.

"Because Jax brought up a concern earlier, one we share," Miss Serena said.

All eyes turned to me. When no one said anything, I realized they waited for me to explain. Why the hell hadn't I decided to meet Rafe after finishing my errands instead of coming back here?

"You guys know me. I'm the cynic of the group." I gave a small smile and a shrug. "On the drive here after learning Annie had been hurt, I started thinking." For once no one made a joke about how dangerous that could be. "Annie's been back in town about two years. Think about everything that's happened, starting with why she returned."

It didn't take more than a moment or two. Lucas cursed and Quinn looked ready to go to war as they started putting it together. Pushing to his feet, Lucas paced the room, muttering angrily, wondering how he missed it. Understanding, I gave him time to process what he was figuring out before continuing.

"Catherine was found standing over the body of Spud Buchanan, bloody knife in hand. I doubt I'm the only one who wondered if she didn't kill him. After all, they'd been enemies for years and now, suddenly, they're lovers and the first night she spends at his house, he's murdered?"

Sam inhaled sharply.

"That brought Annie home. Before managing to prove her mother's innocence, she's attacked at the house and then in her office. Now, without warning, she's attacked again?" I stood, needing to pace as badly as Lucas had a moment before. "I didn't buy it on the drive up and I don't buy it now."

"But that got me thinking about everything else has happened. Judith was kidnapped, beaten and drugged by Quinn's ex in an attempt to get her to tell him how he could get onto the property without the house eating him or something." I managed a slight smile. "Then he kidnapped Quinn and damn near killed her. Faith died, sending Meg here, to a place she'd never heard of before. That led her into direct conflict with her mother's family and the bastard who raped Faith. She, too, was almost killed the day she arrived in town.

"Mossy Creek isn't perfect. But to have all that happen in a relatively short period of time?" I shook my head. "Something's going on and I want to know what."

"Judith, Pat, Mary Kate and I have worried about the same thing for a while now," Miss Serena took up. "When Annie was attacked this time, we realized what had been troubling us. It is almost as if the next generation is being targeted. But by whom and why? Those are the questions we need answered."

Next generation?

Quinn, Meg and I looked at one another and grinned. So much for the question of whether or not Annie was an *Other*. She might not want to admit it but that didn't appear to be the case with Sam. When I glanced at him, he gave a small smile and shrugged.

"I've always known she was special. Since everyone started

returning to town, I figured she has some sort of innate talent that's just waiting to burst out."

"She does," Mary Kate said. "Like Quinn here with her first talent, Annie's is subtle. She's been using it to help the rest of you all along. She simply hasn't realized it."

"And that brings us to the problems facing us." Miss Serena inclined her head slightly, motioning for me to return to my seat. "We don't know what we are facing. More than that, we are minus one guardian and the next generation—most likely you three—aren't prepared to take over for us. We need to correct that right now."

In the silence that followed, I heard Meg and Quinn swallow just as hard as I did.

"If you're including me in all this, you're forgetting something. I haven't moved back." And, after hearing all they had said, I was seriously considering leaving town and never returning. I didn't like the idea of my life being mapped out by my ancestors, fate or whatever.

"Jax, we know this isn't what you signed on for." Mary Kate looked as if she understood exactly what I felt just then. "None of us did. But there's one thing we all know about you. You stand up for those you care for. You didn't hesitate to come home when you heard Annie had been hurt. You would have been here for Quinn if we'd taken time to call you."

I nodded, my expression grim. I'd reamed Annie, Sam, Lucas and pretty much everyone else after learning what happened to first Judith and Quinn. They hadn't called me because I'd just joined the practice and they knew I'd drop everything to come home—just as I did this time. But knowing they were trying to protect me didn't make it any easier to accept. I was supposed to protect them. . . .

Shit!

"I think she's finally figured it out," Dr. Pat said, amusement lighting her eyes.

But Mary Kate wasn't satisfied to leave it there. "Jax, I don't have any right to ask you to stay. None of us do. But I'm going to do just that. You love Annie and she needs you right now. We need you. If you stay, we will stand for you just as you have always stood for us."

As they always stood for me.

I needed to remember that. These men and women had always been there for me, especially when things were bad with my parents.

"What do I have to do?"

Quinn looked at me, startled by my quick acquiescence.

"The three of you need to start working with each of us every evening. We'll hone our gifts and determine the best way to protect our loved ones and our town."

"All right," I answered for not only myself but for Quinn and Meg as well. "When do we start?"

Please don't let it be tonight.

I needed to shift and run. I needed to get away and think about what I'd just agreed to do. More than that, I needed to make sure nothing else happened to Annie or anyone else I cared for.

"Tomorrow," Miss Serena said as the back door slammed and the sounds of the kids and dogs racing inside reached us. "We'll put this away until then. I'm sure Ali and Robbie are ready for dessert."

As we began drifting toward the kitchen, Sam stopped me. Worried, I led him to the far end of the living room. It wasn't exactly privacy, but it gave the appearance of it.

"Are you okay?" I searched his face for some indication of what he felt.

"I am." He glanced over his shoulder and smiled as the sounds of Ali and Robbie cheering for ice cream filled the air. "I just wanted to thank you. Robbie hasn't wanted to talk about what happened to Annie. I was worried because he was keeping everything bottled up and I couldn't get him to tell me what he was feeling."

"Sometimes kids need someone other than a parent to talk to." That was a lesson I learned long ago. For me, it had been Aunt Bitsy, Judith and Miss Serena. Of course, I hadn't wanted to talk to my parents about anything by the time I entered middle school. Even then, I knew they thought I was a disappointment. Probably even a failure. "I'm just glad I could help."

"You did more than help." He bent and kissed my cheek. "I know you're not convinced we need you here, but we do. Don't let the rest of it send you running for the hills."

"How did you know?"

"You got the same look in your eyes Annie did when she realized how her grandfather was still pulling strings from the grave. Think about it. She suddenly had a house and a law office. There were other things as well, all set up by her grandfather before he died and dropped in her lap by my father. Who, I'm ashamed to admit, enjoyed the hell out of it." He chuckled softly.

Remembering Annie telling me about it as it happened, I could picture not only her reaction but Judge Caldwell's enjoyment.

"It's just a lot to take in." And then some. How the hell was I supposed to pay off my student loans if I moved back here? The town had a vet, one I doubted would be happy to suddenly have competition. "But, for the time being, I'm here for all of you—and that means you as well."

"I know." He paused as Quinn appeared from the kitchen. "Thank you."

"Go on. I'll be there in a minute."

I turned and looked out the front window. Darkness had fallen. Outside, the world looked so peaceful. Yet, somewhere in the darkness, danger waited. The problem was I didn't know from where or from whom. Until I did, and until it had been dealt with, I couldn't leave. These people were my family. I would not abandon them. I wouldn't be able to live with myself if anything happened and I did nothing to stop it.

As the rogue, I'd always been a protector.

Some things never change.

11

"Thanks for meeting me."

I slid into the booth opposite Rafe. As I did, I smiled in appreciation. When I texted earlier to see if he still wanted to get together, he asked me to join him at The Roundhouse. The small bar on the northside of town had been around as long as I could remember. Little more than a dive bar, it served cold beer, local music and not much more. At least not that I'd been brave enough to try.

Better yet, he'd asked what I wanted to drink and, as I walked inside, I saw Darcy, one of the two bartenders, bring over two beers. Thank goodness. After the last couple of hours, I needed a drink badly.

"Bad day?" He nodded to my beer.

That was all the encouragement I needed. I lifted the frosted mug and took a long draw. I savored the hoppy flavor and then nodded, taking another sip before answering.

"Let's just say it's been a day."

Much to my surprise, I wanted to tell him about it. But not here. There were too many ears and a few faces I didn't recognize. As if understanding, he didn't press. Instead, he sipped his beer and waited. Leaving it up to me to break the silence.

"Tell me about your day. I'll bet good money it was more interesting than mine." Well, maybe not more interesting but certainly less earthshattering.

He laughed and the sound of it acted like a soother. Maybe I told myself it was the beer but, if I was honest, it wasn't. It felt good to be with someone who didn't expect anything from me. Even my friends, those I was closest to, had expectations. They wouldn't hold me to them. That's what real friends were for. But they knew me and knew I'd hold myself to them and, in some ways, that was even worse. But Rafe accepted me for who I was. Better yet, he didn't know me well enough or long enough to know how I'd react to any given situation.

That was sort of freeing.

"Trust me, that's a bet you'd lose. I spent the day trying to keep Annie from killing her mother—or me for not finding a way to get Catherine out of her room."

I laughed, picturing the scene. Annie loved her mother, but Catherine drove her crazy. Long ago, about the time we entered middle school, Annie realized she and Drew were more mature than their mother ever would be. The fact the two of them managed to grow up and be successful in their careers and find spouses they loved and respected was a miracle considering the example Catherine set for them. I'm not sure how many times she'd been married. She wanted security and position, confusing them with happiness. Now that Annie and Drew were grown and she was, at least for the moment, unmarried, she'd turned her attention to them. Between wanting to be there every day for Annie's and Sam's twins and pressuring Drew and Meg about how they needed to give her a grandbaby, she was driving both couples crazy.

"You laugh." He finished his beer and signaled for another round. "If your aunt hadn't been there most of the day, I would have found a reason to toss Catherine out. Preferably out a very high window. At least Bitsy kept her in line for the most part."

"I swear, she's the only one who can manage Catherine and not want to kill her." I paused as Darcy arrived with fresh beers for us. She took our mugs and returned to the bar after telling us to let her know if we needed anything else. "Annie okay otherwise?"

He nodded. "Ready to go home and starting to wonder if we're not keeping her in the hospital for some reason other than her injuries."

I winced. Sooner or later, Annie was bound to start putting two and two together. I'd hoped for later. Now we needed to figure out how to keep her from doing something foolish like checking herself out of the hospital. Maybe Dr. Pat could help with that. Smiling in apology, I pulled my phone and sent a quick text to her, adding Miss Serena, Judith and Mary Kate to the text as well.

"I let Dr. Pat and Annie's grandma know," I explained as I slid my phone back into my pocket.

"Good idea." He studied me over the rim of his mug. "Your aunt said you're going to take care of Miss Serena's stock and her dog. Moving home?"

I drew circles on the tabletop with my mug. Wasn't that the million dollar question? And didn't I already know the answer, like it or not?

"That's what it looks like." Saying it made it real and I wasn't sure I was ready for real.

"Jax, I know we don't know one another well." He chuckled softly. "Hell, we don't know one another at all, not really. But I know you love Annie and the others and would do whatever it took to keep the safe. I know they have always trusted you to have their backs and to stand for them, even when they wouldn't stand for themselves. I've got a pretty good idea of what your relationship with your parents is and I know your aunt adores you. That much became clear today as she talked about all you've accomplished and how proud she is of you."

I ducked my head and blushed. Bitsy always has been my biggest cheerleader.

"I can also tell you love this town. So what's holding you back?"

A reasonable question, one I should probably ask myself. But, now that he'd asked, I needed to answer. Or did I?

"Rafe, you hit on part of the problem already."

"Your parents?"

I nodded. "Trust me, what you saw is minor compared to what they would have said and done had we been somewhere private. You see, I'm their biggest failure and disappointment. It doesn't matter that I am one of the youngest to graduate from A&M's vet school in years. It doesn't matter that I never once asked them for a dime when I went to undergrad and then to vet school. I worked and I took out loans in my name, loans I have to pay. All they see is the daughter who wouldn't let them mold her into the perfect accessory they could trot out to prove what wonderful parents they were and then shove back into the shadows until the next time they needed me."

"Then they are bigger idiots than I thought."

Now it was my turn to chuckle. "They're not really idiots," I corrected. "But they are self-centered and believe the world exists to do what they want."

He nodded.

Before he could say anything else, the noise level in the bar suddenly dropped. Our conversation forgotten, I glanced toward the door. My lips peeled back and a growl sounded deep in my throat. Joe Bob Sawyer stood just inside the door, looking completely out of place. Where most everyone, Rafe and me included, wore jeans and tee shirts or casual shirts, he wore black slacks that looked like they were part of a cheap suit and a rumpled white shirt. His red tie was knotted at his throat. His hair, what little he had left, was slicked over a growing bald spot. He looked like one of those used car salesmen who used to run commercials on late night TV or, more appropriately, an ambulance chasing lawyer.

He was also Annie's opponent should she actually decide to run for DA.

Rafe followed my gaze. The moment he spotted Sawyer walking toward the bar, his body tensed. Interesting. Whether it meant he saw the former assistant district attorney as a threat or simply a pimple on the face of humanity that needed to be squished, I didn't know. To be honest, I didn't much care. Not as long as he didn't suddenly reveal himself to be Sawyer's best friend.

"What's he doing?" I asked softly as Sawyer, beer now in hand, stopped at one of the tables, spoke for a moment and then moved on.

"Campaigning." Disgust filled Rafe's voice.

"You've got to be kidding me."

I continued to watch. As I did, it became easy to see which tables told him to move on and which ones gave him at least the courtesy of listening. The former far outnumbered the latter. Then, seeing him moving in our direction, I made a quick decision. I stripped off the shirt I wore, revealing a black tank top under it. Rafe grinned. He either approved of what he saw or what he assumed I had in mind.

We sipped our beers and watched Sawyer slowly make his way to our table. The Smokehouse was a typical Texas bar, dark and smoke-filled. Because of that, Sawyer didn't notice me right away. He was about to find out how foolish it was not to pay attention to his surroundings.

"Rafe old buddy, how ya' doing?" He slapped Rafe's shoulder and laughed like an idiot instead of running for the hills at the warning look in Rafe's face. "I'm hoping I can count on your vote this November."

"Keep hoping, Sawyer. Hell might yet freeze over."

Disdain filled Rafe's voice and I shivered slightly. It amazed me Sawyer didn't notice. Annie and Quinn told me he'd gotten worse since graduation and now I saw they weren't kidding. Much like my parents, he seemed to think the world revolved around him. It was time to dissuade him of that notion

"And who do we have here? Can't say I've seen you with a date before." He leered at me from across the table.

"Hello, Sawyer."

He blanched and gulped as he finally recognized me. His gaze went from my face to my left arm with its tattoos. One foot stepped back from the table, as if trying to force his body to move. Then he drew himself up to his full height of barely five five and did his best to glare down at me.

"What the fuck—"

Sawyer didn't finish his comment. Rafe pushed back his chair and stood. To say he towered over the weasel would be an insult to weasels. But it did the trick. Sawyer glared even as the last of the color drained from his face. Then he turned his attention back to me, something very close to hatred filling his eyes.

"We'll be talking soon. I promise you."

He turned and moved as far away from our table as he could and still be inside the bar. I kept an eye on him as he stopped at a table. He said something, jerking his head in our direction. I grinned as Larry Barnett and Kim Nguyen told him to move on.

"How about the two of you come in every night?" Darcy said as she stopped at our table a few minutes later. She placed fresh beers and a basket of chili fries on the table between us. "That's on the house as a thanks for getting that asshole to leave. He comes in three, four times a week, trying to convince our customers to vote for him. Deke threatened to ban him just last week when he caught Sawyer planting at least a dozen campaign signs around the parking lot."

"We'll be back. I promise," Rafe said and I nodded. "Anything else you can tell us about him?"

She looked at him and I saw when she put two and two together. "You think he might have something to do with what happened to Annie?"

By now the entire town knew someone had attacked Annie in her home. Instead of answering, Rafe gave a slight shrug. It said little but it said a lot. He wasn't going to accuse Sawyer but he knew there was bad blood between Sawyer and Annie. Hell, the whole town knew it. So he planted the seed of doubt, undoubtedly hoping Darcy would spread the word. Smart.

I needed to make sure I didn't get on his bad side. He thought too much like me.

"I think I'll talk to Meg in the morning and suggest she have a talk with Darcy and Deke about Sawyer," I said softly once Darcy returned to the bar.

"That's a good idea." He glanced around. "I recognize some of our crew. I'll have a word with them."

"Thanks." I leaned back and thought for a moment. "I'll admit that

I've wondered if Sawyer might be involved in what happened, but I've never really put any credence in it. He was always a coward in school. But he was a sneak and mean as hell too. And, like so many bullies, he didn't do the dirty work himself. He had *friends* do it for him."

Could he have done the same this time?

We finished our drinks and the chili fries. As we stood, Rafe threw several bills on the table, more than enough to cover our tab and tip. I opened my mouth to protest. Before I could say anything, he reminded me that he'd asked me out. I could return the favor whenever I wanted. Then he grasped my right hand in his left and led me toward the door.

"Bitsy said you're staying at Miss Serena's."

We stood next to the Porsche. I nodded, suddenly regretting having the second, not to mention, the third beer. I wasn't drunk. Far from it actually, thanks to my walker metabolism. But that wasn't something I wanted to try to explain to a cop if I happened to be pulled over. So I made a quick decision.

"I think I'll bunk at Bitsy's tonight." At least Rafe didn't ask me to explain.

But he did hesitate a moment.

"Why don't you bunk at my place. No strings attached. I have a spare bedroom you can use, and you can leave the Porsche in the garage overnight." He continued before I could interrupt. "I live less than a mile away. This way, we can discuss what you didn't want to talk about inside and we can check on Annie's place, make sure everything's okay there."

I'll admit part of me was disappointed about the no strings part, but I understood. Even if he felt the attraction I did, we didn't need the distraction right now. Later, if I stayed in town—and it looked like I was going to, it was something we could explore.

Wait! Where did that come from? I wasn't sure I was going to stay in town. Okay, I wasn't sure if I wanted to stay in town. And I sure as hell didn't need to be thinking about starting a relationship with Rafe. That was the surest way to let Mossy Creek get its hooks into me. Nope, nope and hell nope.

As I followed him to his place, I realized how easy it would be to keep an eye on Annie's house. He lived less than six blocks from Sam and Annie. Better yet, his house backed onto the creek that ran through town. There was a heavy wooded area just beyond his back fence. All I needed to do was jump the fence and then I could shift and check out the area.

Which is exactly what I did an hour after Rafe and I said goodnight. I slipped outside and into the night, melting into deep shadows of the trees. With the house behind me, I stood still. Eyes closed, I listened. A light breeze stirred the leaves above me. Crickets sang their song. In the distance, a dog barked and others answered. Closer, an opossum scuttled across the path in front of me, pausing to hiss in my direction. I smelled freshly mowed grass, the remnants of someone's barbeque and the faint aroma of burning leaves. Hopefully, someone called the fire department before things got out of hand.

I undressed and carefully folded my clothes, placing them in the crook of a nearby tree. Then I dropped to hands and knees, picturing my coyote form. It had been a long time since I'd been able to shift so often in such a short period of time and I reveled in it. That part of me, the animal part, needed the outlet. Not that the human part of me ever went away. But it was good to have the freedom of the coyote, to run and hunt without having to worry about the constraints of proper human behavior.

It didn't take long to make my way to Annie's house. As I neared, I gave a canine laugh. Without conscious thought, I'd approached the house from a different direction each night. Good. Not having a pattern meant less of a possibility of someone realizing what I was doing.

I paused at the edge of the property and dropped to my belly, snout on my paws. My ears twitched as night sounds filled the air. The grass was long enough to tickle my nose and I sneezed, startling a racoon under a nearby bush. For several long minutes, I lay there, doing my best to fade into the shadows as I watched the house.

The wind shifted and I growled as an unmistakable scent rolled over me. Blood and other bodily fluids hung thick in the air. My muscles tensed and it suddenly felt as if every hair on my body stood on end. Let me tell you, that's a hell of a lot on a coyote my size. Warily, belly almost touching the ground, I inched forward. A kill was close, too close, and I growled softly. Had the attacker returned and hurt Sam or one of the kids?

Click, click, click. My claws sounded unnaturally loud in the night air as I climbed the steps to the front porch. Even as I growled louder, relief raced through me. Something—or someone—left a very pointed message on the front mat: a pair of gutted cats, on the front mat. As a coyote, I might not have much use for cats, but they didn't deserve this. It didn't matter whether they were someone's pet or feral. They'd been killed not for food and not for sport but to terrorize my friends.

Much as I wanted to shift and check it out, I couldn't. I knew that. I didn't like it, but I knew it. Hell, I couldn't even allow myself to move closer because I might leave forensic evidence that could contaminate the scene. Instead, I checked the perimeter and then raced off. I needed to get back to Rafe's and call this in and that wasn't going to happen as long as I was still a coyote.

Panting, I slid to a halt a few minutes later near the tree where I'd left my clothes. I dropped to my belly and hid my eyes behind my paws, groaning in my mind as I caught an unmistakable scent. I moved one paw and yipped in surprise. Rafe stood under the tree, my clothes in his hands. So much for sneaking out and back in without his knowing.

"I saw you sneak out and followed. Figured you were going to check on the house. I'll admit, I didn't expect to see a coyote disappearing into the trees by the time I got out here. You shift faster than anyone I've ever seen." Admiration and humor filled her voice.

He placed my clothes on the ground in front of me. To my surprise, he reached over and scratched my ears. Then he straightened and turned around. Interesting, most people, especially most guys, would at least joke about wanting to watch me shift back. Instead, he was giving me a modicum of privacy.

He might think I shifted quickly but, to me, it seemed to take forever. Pain washed over me as bones broke and muscles twisted.

Pores burned as fur receded and skin replaced pelt. By the time it was over, I knelt there, one knee pulled up against my chest, head bent, drenched in sweat. My chest heaved as I drew first one breath and then another. With a shaky hand, I reached for the pile of clothes and slowly pulled them on.

"Thanks." My voice sounded rough, as it often did after a shift. I coughed and tried again. "I need to borrow your phone."

He didn't ask any of the questions I saw reflected in his eyes. Instead, he pulled his cellphone from a hip pocket. I watched as he thumbed it before he handed it over. Thanking him, I quickly input Lucas' number and waited., knowing Quinn would not be happy I called her husband instead of her. But this was his jurisdiction. She'd be my next call, assuming she wasn't with him when he answered.

"Jax?" He sounded as if I'd awakened him.

"Jax? What's wrong?" Quinn asked from somewhere close by. I had a feeling they'd both been in bed. At least it saved me a call.

"Lucas, you need to get to Sam's and Annie's." I nodded to Rafe as he motioned toward his house. When he reached for my hand, I didn't object. I was too tired and too focused on telling Lucas what I could before I fell on my face.

"What's wrong?" I heard him softly tell Quinn to go back to sleep as he climbed out of bed.

"Someone left a couple of gutted cats on the front porch."

"What?" Well, that woke him up. Quinn too judging from the way she told him not to dare think about leaving the room. "Tell me what you can."

Quickly, I explained how I'd shifted and gone back to the house to make sure everything was all right. He didn't interrupt until I finished. Then he took me over it again, this time asking questions.

"Lucas, stop." I was tired and didn't feel like putting up with what Quinn called "officious Lucas". "I didn't touch anything. Once I scented the blood and confirmed what had been killed and where, I left. And no, your techs won't find any of my fur on the cats unless it blew there from where I stood at the top of the steps. Give me a little credit."

"Sorry. It's just this hits too close to home."

I nodded even though he couldn't see it. I understood.

"I'll get a car over there right away. I'll be there as soon as I get dressed."

"We'll be there," Quinn corrected and I chuckled softly.

"I assume you're with Rafe since you're using his phone."

"Yeah. I'm at his place. He suggested it since it's closer to Annie's than Miss Serena's."

"Have him drive you home. You sound exhausted." Officious Lucas had been replaced by big brother Lucas. "I'll touch base in the morning to let you know what we found. And, Jax, thanks."

Before I could say anything, he ended the call. At the same time, Rafe opened the back gate. I handed him his phone and thanked him. Then I crossed the backyard and climbed the three steps to the deck, collapsing on one of the lounge chairs. Lucas was right about one thing. I was exhausted.

"Are you okay?"

I opened my eyes and turned my head. A slight smile touched my lips to see Rafe on one knee next to my chair. A line of worry creased his forehead between his brows. Then he handed me a bottle of water and watched as I twisted off the cap before downing most of it.

"Thanks, just tired. I've been shifting and watching the house every night. It's starting to take a toll." I sat up some and thanked him as he took the bottle, setting it on the deck within easy reach. "Why didn't seeing me shift freak you out? The others have known me all my life and they still have a hard time seeing the actual shift."

He grinned and nudged my hip so I'd move over a little and let him sit down. "You told me you're a walker. The one I knew in the service could shift almost as quickly as you do. I learned to rely on him just as he did me. And as we all rely on you." Another smile, this one gentler than before. "Now you need to get some rest. You're exhausted."

I nodded and let him help me to my feet. With his arm around my waist, we went inside. I'd have been happy sleeping on the chaise, but a bed sounded much more inviting. If only I could stay awake long enough to get there.

12

By seven the next morning, I sat on the back patio at my aunt's house enjoying what I hoped was my first of many cups of coffee for the day. I certainly needed it after being awakened by a call from Quinn an hour earlier. While I wanted to know what Lucas had discovered at Annie's and Sam's, Quinn wanted to know if I'd spent the night "with" Rafe. I didn't need to ask to know what she meant. Nor could I mistake her disappointment to learn I hadn't slept with him. No way was I going to admit to being disappointed myself. Not when it would give her even more ammunition to use to convince me to stay in town permanently.

Bitsy settled on the chaise next to mine and smiled in affection. "It's been too long since we've started the day together." She sipped her coffee, her expression peaceful, a rarity. She usually had so much going on in her head that peace was the last thing you saw if you bothered looking beyond the ditsy exterior she so often presented to keep people from really knowing her.

"It has." I glanced across the lawn and smiled as several squirrels played tag as they ran from tree to tree. "I know you've got a lot on your plate right now, but I was hoping you might be able to help me with something."

"Of course, especially if it has to do with keeping you in town." Amusement colored her voice and I shook my head. I should have guessed she knew about at last some of the changes that happened in the last twenty-four hours.

"It does." I sat up and turned to face her. "I'm guessing you know I agreed to take care of Miss Serena's stock and her dog."

Bitsy smiled, obviously pleased with the news. "And she's letting you stay in the caretaker's house." I nodded. "Jax, you know you always have a home with me, whether it's here in the house or above the garage. That will never change. But you need your own place, somewhere your parents won't bother you. Besides, you'll have the freedom there to shift and hunt without fear of anyone seeing you and deciding you're some wild animal to be shot—or worse."

I reached for her hand. She'd always worried something might happen to me while I was in one of my animal forms.

"Believe me, I took both of your concerns into consideration when I accepted Miss Serena's offer." No need to let her know the other reasons, not yet. Maybe not ever. "Now I need to find someone to pack up my apartment and either store my things or bring them here. I also need to get my truck up here." My pickup was much better suited for work than the Porsche or the Ducati. And that reminded me. I needed to switch the Porsche out for my Camaro. Bitsy could store the Porsche in the extra wide garage here if she wanted to keep it. Maybe she'd even let me borrow it from time to time.

"I have a company I use when one of my renters needs someone. Let me contact them. If they can do the job, I'll put you in contact with them."

"Thanks." I smiled in relief. If she trusted them, I knew I could as well. "Then I guess that brings me to the next thing I need your help with."

"Finding a place to open your clinic?" she asked hopefully.

I shook my head. That was definitely moving ahead faster than I was ready for. "I'm not ready for that. Hell, Aunt Bitsy, I'm not sure I'm going to stay in town once this is all over. I know everyone seems to take it for granted that I will, but my situation is different from

Annie's and Quinn's. Mossy Creek doesn't need another vet. It has Dr. Oliver. Besides, I do not want to have to look over my shoulder every time I leave the house in case my parents decide to ambush me with more complaints about how I'm an ungrateful and unloving daughter."

I hadn't meant to say it. I sure hadn't meant to let her hear how much my parents' attitudes still hurt. But it was out before I could stop it. And, as always, Bitsy was there for me. She was off her chaise and pulling me to my feet before I knew it. A moment later, she pulled me into an embrace, doing her best to comfort me for a lifetime of hurt no child should ever feel at the hands of her parents.

"Jax, my brother—and I use that term loosely—and his wife don't deserve you and never have." She lightly patted my cheek and then took my hand, leading me inside. Once in the kitchen, she motioned for me to take a seat at the table. Then she collected our mugs and refilled them before joining me. "And we need to have a serious discussion about them, but not this morning. Tell me how I can help you instead."

That was Bitsy. Cutting to the chase. . .when she wasn't playing the ditz.

"I need your help with Annie." Of all the things I could have said, the way she suddenly sat back and looked at me in surprise told me that was the last thing she expected. "She's getting tired of being in the hospital. Part of that is she's feeling better. Part of it is she wants to be home, making sure Robbie and the twins are safe."

"That's our Annie."

"It is, and it is a problem right now."

"I don't understand."

"You were there most of the day yesterday from what Rafe said." She nodded. "So you know she really is getting better. The problem is we—Sam, Rafe, Quinn, Meg and me and a few others—want to make sure the house is as safe as possible for her and the rest of the family before she goes home. She didn't have the security system on when she was attacked. Not that I blame her. It was daytime and Robbie was across the street playing. But she had also turned off the cameras on the doors. The guys want to update the system so the cameras are running all the time. There are a few things the girls and I want to do as well. But we want it done before she comes home because we know she will object."

Bitsy grinned, her eyes sparkling with approval. "You're protecting her just like you did when you were kids."

Which meant we'd ask forgiveness when she found out instead of permission ahead of time.

"Yeah. Pretty much."

"What do you want me to do?"

"I need her distracted for another day or two. Can you figure out a way to make sure Catherine doesn't make her take a bolt?"

Bitsy threw her head back and laughed. It wasn't a ladylike titter but a full-belly laugh. Clearly the thought of keeping Catherine from driving her daughter insane struck my aunt's funny bone. When she sobered, she glanced at me and I swallowed hard. I knew the look in her eyes. It almost always meant she had something up her sleeve that I wasn't going to like.

"I think I can figure something out. Let me talk to the girls—"

I groaned. "The girls" were the other members of what Annie and Drew called the Terrible Trio. Bitsy, Catherine and the two of them grew up together. When it came time for college, they headed down to the University of Texas at Austin, pledged the same sorority and became indoctrinated in all things longhorn. They still hadn't forgiven me for going to Texas A&M. To them, I was an Aggie and to me they were tea sippers. At least the rivalry was held at bay now that the schools no longer played football against one another.

"Bitsy." I couldn't keep the warning from my voice.

"Don't worry. We can manage both Catherine and Annie. I think I'll suggest that we head over to her house to clean it and get it ready for her return. I'm sure it will take at least two days. Will that give you long enough to do what needs to be done?"

Oh, she was good. I had no doubt she'd make the suggestion in front of Annie. My friend, smart woman that she was, would do anything to keep from being present as the four of them took over her house. Hell, she'd probably beg Sam to change the locks, buy attack dogs and put the house on the market. Aunt Bitsy and the others could be formidable—and scary—when they wanted.

"That would be perfect. Thanks." I leaned over and gave her a hug.

She sipped her coffee and looked thoughtfully at me. "Jax, I won't push, but are you thinking about staying after the SOB who hurt Annie is caught?"

"I don't know." She opened her mouth to say something and then closed it when I arched one brow. "Honestly, Aunt Bitsy, I don't know. At least not for sure. Part of me wants to stay. Something's going on none of us understands yet. Something that has hurt not only Annie but Meg and Quinn. Even Catherine if you think about it."

For a moment she studied me. Then her eyes went wide as she realized what I meant. "You think all that's related?"

I nodded. When she didn't say anything, I continued. "Think about it, Bitsy. In the last two years or so, more trouble has visited Mossy Creek than I remember in the last twenty. Much of it has centered on Annie. I want to know why, and I want to make sure we put an end to it."

"Which means you need to be here, at least for the immediate future."

"Yeah." And I felt the Mossy Creek trap tightening. If I wasn't careful, I'd never get out of here. But did I want to? Did I dare after hearing all Miss Serena and the others said last night?

Like it or not, it looked like I was home—if not for good, then for a good while. That meant I needed to start putting down a few roots. Something I'd been doing without consciously realizing it.

"Then it's time we have a serious discussion about a number of things, including your parents."

"Yeah, but not right now. I need to run by the hospital and then I have some things to take care of. But you're right. We do need to talk."

She nodded. Instead of pushing, she pulled out her cellphone. I watched as she activated the screen. She studied something on it and then nodded, as if to herself, before looking up.

"How about meeting for breakfast tomorrow? It will have to be early. I have an eight-thirty meeting with my attorneys in Dallas."

"That would be great." I quickly added it to my digital calendar, wondering if Meg would have time to meet with me today. There were some things I needed to do if I planned on staying in town for long, things I needed legal advice on. With Annie still laid up, that fell to Meg—if she agreed.

"Is there anything else I can do?" Aunt Bitsy asked.

I shook my head. "Not right now. Just get me the information on the movers—and let me know if they can't get my truck up here for me. If I need to fly down to drive it back, I want to do it in the next day or two."

"I'll make the call as soon as we're done here. If they can't do it, I'll find someone who can."

"You're the best, Aunt Bitsy."

And she was.

"Is there anything you need right away that would make your life easier?"

"For my parents to move to Rome and the bastard who hurt Annie to walk into the sheriff's office and confess?" I asked hopefully.

"That would be nice."

More than nice, but I didn't have to say it.

"But seriously, Jax, I know you left town without so much as stopping at your apartment. What do you need until your things are shipped here?"

I thought for a moment, considering the few items I'd brought with me and the few clothes I kept here and that I'd purchased the day before. Clothes could wait. I had jeans, shirts and tanks, running shoes and boots. I even had one good outfit in the closet of the apartment over the garage. What I needed was more in the way of professional needs: equipment I wanted so I could treat Miss Serena's animals the way I wanted, something other than my travel laptop, a truck.

None of which I'd mention to Bitsy.

"Jax," she prompted when I didn't say anything.

"Nothing for you to worry about, Aunt Bitsy."

She narrowed her eyes at me, and I swallowed hard. That had been the absolutely wrong thing to say.

"Jax."

"Aunt Bitsy, there are a few things. Some of them Miss Serena will pay for because they will help me work with her stock and the dog. The rest?" I gave a small shrug. "Let's just say my finances are a bit compromised right now and will be until I find a job."

The look she gave me then spoke volumes. Not only did she think I was wrong but that I was also exceedingly foolish. Damn it, I kept digging that hole deeper and deeper. Now I wasn't sure how to get out of it.

"You are as stubborn as your father is needy," she muttered, and I felt my back go up. "You know better than that, Jacqueline Powell."

Oh man, I was in trouble. She never called me by my full name.

"My father, your grandfather, made sure you would never want for anything. Yes, it is still held in trust for you, mainly to keep your father from getting his hands on it. But I'm the damned trustee, as you well know. Unless you plan on giving the money to your parents, you know I'll sign a check for almost anything you want. If it is something that will make your life easier, I'll do so without question. So tell me what you need."

I dropped my head to the tabletop and slowly pounded it against the wooden surface. We'd had this discussion before. Hell, we had it almost every time we saw one another. And she was right. I was stubborn, especially where my inheritance was concerned. Part of it was because I knew she was a better custodian for the trust than I'd ever be. But a large part of it was my father. I didn't want to be remotely like him. So, I vowed not to touch the trust before it came to me on my thirty-fifth birthday. Then I'd set up another trust, basically making it so I couldn't give in to temptation.

"Bitsy—"

"No." Voice firm, looking like a mother about to lecture a recalcitrant child, she shoved to her feet. "Your parents did all they could to screw you up and, on the whole, they failed. But this insistence you have not to touch money that is yours is unhealthy. Do not let them deny you something that's yours simply because you're afraid of suddenly turning into one of them."

"Bitsy—"

"No," she repeated. "For once, you're going to listen to me. You are a strong, capable young woman any parent should be proud of. You aren't to blame for your parents' failings. That falls directly on my parents, my mother in particular. She babied your father, giving him everything he wanted until he learned to expect it. Nothing our father did ever changed that about him. You aren't your father and you certainly aren't your mother, who is one of the most vapid people I've ever had the unfortunate luck of meeting." She paused and grinned almost wickedly. "Look at it this way, Jax. She makes Catherine look stable and responsible."

I couldn't help it. I laughed. She was right, at least about Catherine. It would take time for me to accept the rest of it—if I ever did.

"Now tell me what you need." Her look warned me not to hesitate.

Knowing I had no choice, I carefully laid out what I was looking at for Miss Serena's stock as well as what I needed. It didn't surprise me when her thumbs began typing in something on her phone. Bitsy had always been one for making lists. Apparently, she was now making a list of what I rattled off. When I finished, she put her phone on the table and looked at me.

"What else?" she prompted. "You're not telling me everything. Almost all that is what Serena will order as soon as you tell her you need it."

"Everything else will be here once I get my apartment packed up and moved up here."

"Jax, don't make me go to the apartment and then out to Serena's to go through your things. I'll do it and you know I will."

I threw my hands in the air in surrender. Bitsy in this mood would steamroller over me until I gave in.

"I don't know why anyone thinks you're a soft touch," I muttered.

"Because I know how to play them so they underestimate me." She grinned unrepentantly.

I didn't underestimate her, but I knew when to throw in the towel. Still, I needed it to be on my terms.

"If I tell you, it is with the understanding that I will repay anything spent." I waited until she nodded. "Then it's simple. I need a work truck and I'd like not having to wait until someone can drive mine up here. I need a new laptop. I brought my travel laptop with me, but it is not enough for what I need if I'm going to play vet even if only for Miss Serena. I'll need to pay licensing fees for certain software, but I can wait on most of it. I can use paper files and notes to start. And I'd like to keep the Ducati. It's too sweet to give up."

Bitsy grinned at the last. Then she nodded. A moment later, she excused herself. As she left the kitchen, I wondered what she was up to. Waiting for her to return, I called the hospital to check on Annie and then Lucas to see if he knew anything else about what happened last night or who attacked Annie.

"I talked with Serena and she said to give her the list of what you need for work and she'll see to it," Bitsy said as she returned to the kitchen. "I told her you'd get it to her today."

I frowned. She'd boxed me in, and I should have expected it. Like everyone else, she wanted me to stay in town. That trap Annie warned me about tightened even more.

"And you are to use this to order whatever else you need." She slid a credit card across the tabletop and waited until I took it. "This is yours and it goes to the trust. So don't go crazy. I'd hate to box your ears."

I laughed. She wouldn't box my ears. At least I didn't think she would.

"Now, for your work truck. What do you want?"

"A Dodge Ram or Ford F-150."

The only reason I answered was to keep her from going out and buying something without any input from me. I had visions of a top of the line truck built more for luxury than work and I needed something I could take off-road when necessary.

"All right. I'll see what I can find." She reached over and covered my hand with hers. "Jax, I know this makes you uncomfortable. Think of it this way. It will be a jab at your father, reminding him that he failed to prove to our father that he would protect the family legacy while you, just a teen, managed to show Dad something he wanted nurtured. I've done my best to do just that."

"You've been the best parent I could have asked for, Aunt Bitsy." I slid an arm around her shoulders and hugged her. Then I stood, slipping the credit card into my pocket. As I did, I promised myself I'd use it only for the few things I'd named and then put it away. I didn't want to get into the habit of relying on the trust for things I could buy myself. "What time tomorrow?" I asked as I stood.

"Six?" Even as she suggested it, she winced. She was not a morning person and that was very early for her.

"See you then." I kissed her cheek and left before she could wheedle even more information out of me.

Back in my familiar Camaro, I headed toward the hospital. I'd check in on Annie, maybe stay with her until Bitsy, Catherine and the others arrived. A quick call to the law office and I had an appointment with Meg right after lunch. That left me time to go back to Miss Serena's, meet with Jerry and see any of the stock that needed my services.

The top floor of the hospital was visible in the distance when my cellphone rang. I reached up, tapping the earbud in my right ear. "Hello?"

"Dr. Powell? Dr. Jaqueline Powell?" a woman asked.

Frowning, I flipped on my turn indicator. "Yes. Who's this?" One hundred feet later, I pulled into the parking lot outside the local dollar store.

"Dr. Powell, this is Marta Ruiz. I'm principal at Mossy Creek Elementary."

"Yes, ma'am. What can I do for you?" And why the hell was she calling me?

"I'm sorry to bother you, but Annie and Sam Caldwell listed you as an emergency contact for their son Robbie."

My heart raced and my mouth went dry. If something had happened to Robbie. . . . .

"Is he all right?"

"He is, but there's been something happen we need to discuss, something I'd prefer not bothering them with right now."

"Mrs. Reyes, perhaps it would be best if you just spelled it out." Before I reached through the phone to shake her.

"One moment."

I listened as she told someone to sit with Robbie and keep him in the office. Then the sound of heels clicking on tile followed. I waited, picturing her hurrying to someplace where she could speak without interruption—or perhaps without being overheard.

"I'm sorry to keep you waiting, Dr. Powell," she said a few moments later. "Robbie's fine, upset is all. But we have a situation I don't think either of his parents need to deal with right now. When I asked Robbie who he wanted me to call, he said you."

Oh this did not bode well.

"I'm five, ten minutes from the school." I pulled out of the lot and headed away from the hospital. "What happened?" I repeated.

"Robbie's class was outside for phys ed. His teacher noticed a woman loitering near the fence closest to where they were playing t-ball. When Miss Granger went over and asked who she was, she identified herself as Robbie's mother. Before Miss Granger could ask anything else, the woman excused herself and walked toward the building. Miss Granger contacted me just as the woman entered the office and tried to sign Robbie out."

My hands tightened around the steering wheel and I was all I could do not to press the accelerator down to the floorboard. "I'm assuming you didn't release him to her."

"Of course not!" She sounded affronted that I'd even suggest such a thing. "The office clerk on duty followed protocol and checked his file, saw this woman wasn't listed and explained she couldn't do as asked."

"And?" Okay, maybe I did increase my speed, wanting to get to the school as quickly as possible.

"She's still here. She's on her phone, says she's talking to her attorney."

"All right. I'm almost there." The Camaro's tires squealed as I took the corner at Main and First. "Don't let her near Robbie."

"Trust me, I won't."

Three minutes later, I parked in front of the school and raced up the walk to the main entrance. I hadn't been in the school in more than a decade, but it didn't matter. The office was still located directly across from the double doors. I paused before the office door and drew a deep breath. Then I opened the door and stepped inside. Instantly, memories of my time as a student here washed over me. The memories disappeared a moment later as a petite woman with a dark bob and concerned expression appeared from an office off the main area.

Her eyes cut to my right and the blonde standing near the wall. I glanced over, noting the curves only a doctor could give her and an equally enhanced tan. From her designer clothes to the purse hanging off her shoulder that cost two week's salary—or more—she was everything I detested. I had no doubt she was a younger version of my mother. She was also someone I recognized from a picture Annie showed me not long after she and Sam married.

Mia Caldwell. Sam's ex-wife and Robbie's biological mother. The woman who walked out on the two of them one Christmas morning without a backwards glance.

What the hell was she doing here now?

"Dr. Powell, I'm Marta Ruiz." The principal extended her hand and I shook it. "Why don't we go into my office?" Something about her expression told me not to argue.

"Of course. Thanks for calling me." I gave Mia one last look and then followed Ms. Ruiz into her office.

She closed the door and instantly Robbie launched himself into my arms. I held him, softly reassuring him that everything was going to be all right. When I looked up, Ms. Ruiz watched us with undisguised approval.

"Thanks for calling me," I said again. I lifted Robbie and, as he wrapped his legs around my waist, settled him on my hip. "And thank you for protecting Robbie." He buried his face in the crook of my neck. As he did, I felt the shudders running through him.

She simply nodded, her expression worried as she watched Robbie and me.

I carefully shifted Robbie so I could see his face. "Hey there." I smiled at him, letting him see not only that I was worried but that I was proud of him for having the school call me. "Before I go deal with her, I need you to tell me something. Okay?"

He nodded.

"Has she tried to talk to you before today?"

Another nod before he buried his face against my neck again. I closed my eyes and counted to ten. When I opened them again, I ran a gentle hand down Robbie's back. I started to hand him over to Ms. Ruiz and then stopped. I needed her to not only witness what I said to Mia but to make sure the bitch understood she wasn't to come onto school property again.

"Robbie, I need you to stay in here until either Ms. Ruiz or I come for you. Can you do that for me?" I held my breath, hoping he agreed.

"Okay. Can I call my daddy?"

"Tell you what. Let's call him together, okay?" I smiled and pulled my phone. "Ms. Ruiz, would you make sure she doesn't leave before I have a chance to speak with her?"

"Of course, Dr. Powell. I believe I'll have our security officer keep her company for a few minutes." She slipped out of the office then.

With Robbie watching, I dialed Sam's cellphone. He answered on the second ring. Hearing the sounds of Bitsy and others laughing in the background, I knew he was at the hospital.

"Hey, Jax. What's up? Annie was wondering when you're coming to see her."

"Tell her I'll be there as soon as I can," I said. "Sam, I need you to step out of her room. Please."

He didn't say anything and I waited, listening as the background noise from the Terrible Trio and Catherine faded to silence.

"What's wrong?" Worry thickened his voice.

"Sam, when's the last time you saw or spoke to Mia?"

Dead silence stretched between us for several long moments. "Not since she walked out on us. Why?"

"First of all, I want you to stay calm and stay at the hospital. Second, you need to trust me to handle this. All right?"

"Jax, what the fuck are you talking about?" Then he gasped. "Robbie?" Fear replaced frustration.

"He's fine, Sam, and wants to talk to you. But you and I need to talk first." I waited until he agreed. "Now answer my question. When was the last time you saw or spoke to Mia?"

"Like I said, the day she walked out on us. Why? What's happened?"

"Remember what I said. Robbie's safe." I gave him a moment to accept that before continuing. "She showed up at the school. His teacher saw her hanging around the playground. A few minutes later, she tried to check Robbie out of school."

"She did what?" He spoke slowly, softly and I knew he'd kill Mia if she'd hurt his son.

"Don't worry. The school staff did exactly what they were supposed to. They refused to release Robbie to her. Ms. Ruiz asked Robbie who he wanted them to call. Fortunately, Annie had me listed as an emergency contact. I'm with Robbie now."

"And Mia?"

"Let's just say she's about to meet the rogue." I smiled down at Robbie, praying this was the last time he ever had to deal with the woman who gave birth to him. "Now talk to your son. Once we're done here, I'm going to check him and Ali out. I'll take them to either Quinn's or Miss Serena's. I'll let you know where."

"Thank you."

I knew he meant for more than just taking Robbie out of school.

"Here's your dad." I handed my phone to Robbie. "I'll be back soon."

I waited until I was sure he and Sam were talking. Then I left the office. A slight smile touched my lips to see a uniformed deputy standing in front of the exit, preventing Mia from leaving. He must be the security officer Ms. Ruiz mentioned. The principal stood at the counter, filling out a form I guessed was a trespassing warning. As for Mia, she looked like a recruiting poster for righteous indignation.

And I was about to make her day much worse.

"Where's my son?" Mia demanded right on cue.

"My godson." Okay, he wasn't technically my godson, but I didn't think anyone was going to argue just then. "Is talking to his father. As for whose son he happens to be, he certainly isn't yours. You walked out on him and his father when Robbie was just a baby. You couldn't be bothered to appear to fight for your parental rights. Robbie's mother is Annie Grissom Caldwell both by choice and by law. You have no right to him and no right to call him your son."

"Who the fuck are you?" Her eyes blazed as she turned to me.

"Language," the deputy warned. "Or I'll write you up for disorderly conduct."

She bared her teeth but wisely didn't curse again. "I asked you a question."

"I'm your worst nightmare," I said simply, leaning against the counter. "I'm one of many who will stand between you and that little boy. Believe me, you do not want to try me. You won't like the results." I called on my wolf aspect, letting my eyes glow a deep green.

"What the hell are you?" She gasped and took a step back, right up against the deputy.

"I warned you." He moved away from her and pulled his citation book. I swear his eyes gleamed with satisfaction as he began writing out a ticket.

"Dr. Jax Powell." I waited, watching to see if she showed any sign of recognizing my name. Nothing, not that it meant much. I had no idea how good of an actress she might be. "I answered your question. Now you answer mine. Why were you trying to get Robbie released from school?"

"He's my son."

"The son you threw away along with his father." I looked over her shoulder to where the deputy stood. "Correct me if I'm wrong, but couldn't she be charged with attempted kidnapping, deputy?"

He gave a crooked smile. "I believe she could. Of course, it would

143

be up to the DA's Office to decide whether to present it to the grand jury or not."

"You wouldn't dare!" Mia gasped.

"Trust me, I'd dare much more than that to keep Robbie safe from you." I straightened and took a step closer to the woman. "This is your only warning. Do not try to contact Robbie again. Don't try to take him out of school or get him to go with you anywhere without first getting his father's and mother's permission. Is that clear?"

"I'm his mother!"

"Not in the eyes of the law." I glanced back at Ms. Ruiz. "Thank you again for contacting me. I'm going to check on Robbie."

"And Deputy Restall and I will make sure she finds her way off school property."

I didn't dare say anything, but I hoped the school had surveillance equipment that would let Lucas see what kind of car Mia got into. Better yet would be if it showed the license plate. Her sudden appearance in town set off all my warning bells. Could she be responsible for what happened to Annie? I needed to talk to Quinn and Meg about it and soon. But first I needed to check on Robbie.

"Here's Dr. Jax, Daddy." He held the cellphone out to me.

"Thanks." I rumpled his hair. "It's taken care of," I said simply.

"We need to talk."

"Agreed." And then some. "Let me take care of a couple of things and then I'll head to the hospital."

"Judith will meet you at her house. I texted her and asked."

"All right." And that meant I needed to talk to Quinn sooner, rather than later. "Get back to Annie and tell her I'll be in soon."

"Take care of my son."

"I will." I slid the phone into my pocket and smiled down at Robbie. "How about we get Ali and head over to her house? You can wait there for your daddy to come get you."

"Are you going to stay?"

"I will if you want me to." What else could I say? "We'll talk about it when we get there. Okay?"

He nodded as a soft tap sounded and the door opened a moment later. Ms. Ruiz stepped inside, smiling in reassurance as she did. "It's taken care of, Dr. Powell."

"Thank you." I considered what to say. "Ms. Ruiz, I know I'm asking you to break the rules, but would it be all right if we got Ali Moore and I took them home?"

"That's not breaking the rules at all," she assured me. "You're authorized to pick Ali up just as you are Robbie." She held her hand out to Robbie. He looked at me and when I nodded, he slid his hand into hers. "Why don't you and Ms. French go get your backpack and your homework assignments, Robbie? Then you can get Ali. Dr. Powell will be ready to leave by the time you're back."

I watched as she escorted him to the outer office and handed him over to a woman I assumed was the assistant principal. Then she turned back to me, her expression grim.

"The deputy made sure she left school property and she's been officially warned not to return. I thought it best to file a report with the sheriff's office."

"I agree." I glanced out the door, knowing enough time hadn't elapsed for the kids to be there but wanting to make sure. "If you have any surveillance of her or of her vehicle, I'd appreciate it if it made its way to Sheriff Moore. If for no other reason than to make sure she isn't involved with what happened to Annie Caldwell."

"I'll see to it." Now it was her turn to check the outer office. "I'll be in contact with the sheriff about putting extra patrols for a while."

"I'll talk to him as well." And I'd be talking to Rafe as well. But, before that, I needed to talk to Meg. There might be something she could do in court to keep Mia from causing any more problems. Even if she couldn't, she'd know an investigator we could hire to trace Mia's whereabouts for the last few months. "I need to make one more call before I head out with the kids."

"Use the office." She moved to the door. "Dr. Powell, I'm glad you're back. Both Robbie and Ali have been full of tales about their Auntie Jax. The fact their parents trust you with them speaks volumes and it is clear you love them and will do everything you can to keep them safe."

"I will," I assured her. She nodded once and left the office, closing the door behind her. I wasted no time calling Meg. "It's Jax," I said the moment she answered.

"Sam already called. I'm pulling the termination papers and adoption papers now," she said. "Where are you?"

"Still at the school. I'm checking Robbie and Ali out of class and taking them to Quinn's."

"Come to the office once you drop them off."

"There might be a problem. Robbie asked if I could stay with them. This, on top of what happened to Annie, has shaken him."

She didn't respond right away. Instead, I heard a soft tap, tap, tap and figured it was the end of her pen against the desktop. "All right. Call me if you need to stay with them and I'll come to you. Otherwise, come to the office."

"All right." Ms. Ruiz opened the door and let me know the kids were there. "Got to go. Talk to you soon."

I took a moment to calm my anger and put away my phone. Then I stepped into the outer office to greet the kids, unsurprised to find Ali standing protectively at her best friend's side. Good. He needed her just then.

"C'mon, kids. Let's get out of here."

I held out my hands and, as they took them, thanked Ms. Ruiz and the others in the office. As we left, I made a mental note to send them something to say thank you.

But that needed to wait. For now, all I cared about was getting Robbie somewhere I knew Mia couldn't get to him.

13

"Will you hit me if I tell you that you look like you ought to be in bed instead of here?"

Rafe looked at me, his expression worried, as I slid into the booth opposite him. After leaving the kids with Judith, meeting with Meg and then going to the hospital and having to go over everything with Sam, I felt like a horse that had been rode hard and put up wet. Sitting in my car afterwards, I called Rafe on impulse and asked if he'd join me for dinner at the café. He agreed and asked what I wanted, saying he was just down the street and would grab us a table and place our orders.

Before I could answer, Miss Peggy stopped at our table. I groaned, actually groaned, in relief as she placed a large Irish coffee in front of me. I would have preferred she just bring the bottle of Irish whiskey, but this would do. At least for a start.

I took a careful sip, licked the fresh whipped cream off my upper lip and gave Rafe a weary smile. "Not when I know it's the truth. It's been a hell of a day."

"But it could have been a lot worse."

I nodded. I kept telling myself that. So much could have gone wrong, starting with Robbie's teacher not being vigilant and seeing

Mia watching the little boy and his classmates. I shivered slightly as the possibilities struck. What would she have done if she'd gotten her hands on him?

And why in the hell had she suddenly shown up here?

"I know."

I took another sip of my drink. Miss Peggy probably shouldn't be serving the Irish coffees. I didn't think she had a liquor license. But no one was going to turn her in. For one, she never charged for the Irish coffees. For another, she rarely made them, only when one of us really needed a drink.

And I really needed a drink.

"You said you were not far from here when I called." It hadn't struck me at the time that it meant he wasn't at the hospital. Maybe Sam needed him on a jobsite.

"I was just leaving Meg's office. I had some business to talk with her about."

I leaned back and eyed him. He'd been just a little too nonchalant with his answer. I wasn't sure what it meant, but I had a feeling it had to do with one of two things. Either he'd been there talking about the problems he and Sam had with my parents or they were talking about Mia and how to protect Robbie. Either way, I needed to know.

"You can tell me to butt out, but why?"

"Three guesses and the first two don't count."

Something about his expression caused me to glance around. Seeing too many sets of eyes on us, I fought the urge to bang my head against the tabletop. All those curious eyes meant even more curious ears. He was right. We probably shouldn't be talking about what happened here.

"What did my parents do this time?" I asked, figuring that was a safer topic. It also had the benefit of being something most the town already knew.

He chuckled. "Same ole same ole."

Before he could explain, one of the part-time waitresses arrived with our meals. We thanked her and dug in. As we did, I realized I hadn't eaten more than a candy bar out of the hospital vending machine—than God Mossy Creek had not succumbed to the health fad gripping much of the nation—since breakfast. No wonder I was starving. I'd blame my headache on it as well, but I knew better. That rested solely on Mia's shoulders.

"Seriously, are you having more trouble with them?"

"It's nothing, really." He waved it off.

"Rafe, my parents are not easy people. Trust me, no one knows that better than me."

A few of those close enough to overhear without being overt about trying to listen in, nodded in agreement.

"Let's just say they are trying again to avoid paying us for work we did for them." When I motioned for him to continue, he arched one brow.

"Rafe, please." I leaned in and lowered me voice. "It will distract me, at least for a few minutes."

He reached over and ran one finger gently down my cheek. "All right." He lifted his fork and used it to motion for me to eat. "You knew we got a judgment against them for failing to pay for work we did at their house."

I nodded.

"They appealed and I was served this morning before I left for the hospital. Normally, I'd have met with Annie about it but." He shrugged and I nodded again. Annie wasn't exactly in a position to do anything about it right now.

"If you don't mine me asking, what did Meg say?"

And what could I do to help?

I didn't say it, but I would help. I was past being tired of this sort of behavior from my parents.

"All we know so far is they've filed notice of intent to appeal. Meg's already requested the court records and now we wait to see what the appellate brief says. In the meantime, she's put Miss Olivia on checking out their litigation history." He smiled and I almost choked. There was a gleam in his eyes that told me he looked forward not only to the fight but to finding out what Miss Olive would find out.

"If there's anything to find, she'll find it."

We spent the rest of the meal talking sports, the latest gossip in town, about anything except what we wanted to discuss. When we were ready to leave, I tossed a couple of twenties on the table, more than enough to pay for our meals and leave a hefty tip. Before Rafe could protest, I reminded him that we agreed I'd pay this time. Instead of arguing, he simply said the next meal was on him.

Ten minutes later, I led him into the caretaker's house at Miss Serena's. I hadn't done much to move it. After all, there wasn't much I could do until my things arrived from New Braunfels. That reminded me I needed to check with Bitsy to see what she found out. That had all been knocked from my mind with the events at the school. The furniture might not be what I'd choose, but it was comfortable. There was food in the fridge and I'd stopped by the liquor store earlier, so I had beer and a bottle of good whiskey.

"You really should get some rest," he said as I handed him a whiskey a few minutes later.

I curled up on one end of the sofa and smiled as he sat at the opposite end. He stretched his long legs out before him and angled his body so we faced one another.

"I will soon. But I want to hear what you didn't want to talk about at the café."

"It's nothing earth-shattering."

I arched one brow, waiting for him to continue.

"You know Sam's got his PI's license, right? That he'd been with CID in the Army?"

I nodded.

"Normally, in a situation like this, Annie would have him look into the parties involved. But with her laid up and with Mia being involved, Meg asked me to fill in."

"I don't understand."

"Sam had me get my license when I moved here. That was part of the deal. He'd get me a job at the construction firm and I'd help him with investigations when Annie needed an extra set of eyes or something."

"And Lucas is all right with this?"

"Let's say what he doesn't know won't upset him."

I laughed softly, appreciating the way they were approaching this.

"What can I do?"

"Exactly what you have been. Keep an eye on Annie and be there when any of them need you." He leaned forward and reached for my hand. "But now, you need to get some rest. You've been pushing yourself since you got here. I bet you've not gotten more than a couple of hours sleep a night. Right?"

I shrugged. I didn't want to admit he was right, but I also couldn't argue. Except there was a problem. I didn't want to be alone. After everything that happened, I wanted to know someone was there for me. It was silly. I'd never felt this way before.

"This is going to come out all sorts of wrong," I began, looking at our joined hands. "But would you mind staying until I fall asleep?"

"I don't mind at all." He smiled and stood, pulling me to my feet. "Why don't you go shower and get ready for bed? I'll finish my drink. Then I want to check in with Sam."

I nodded. Then I stepped closer. My arms went around his waist and I rested my head against his shoulder. He stroked one hand down my hair to my shoulders and then my back. As he did, I inhaled the scent of him, masculine and safe.

And, just then, I needed safe. I needed to be able to drop my defenses and not be the protector. That was something my closest friends didn't realize, mainly because I never told them. They didn't know the toll of always being the one to step up and act as defender took on me. Somehow, I had a feeling Rafe understood.

"Go on." He pressed a light kiss on the top of my head.

"Thanks." I smiled up at him. "Make yourself at home."

Ten minutes later, I slipped on an oversized tee shirt. I probably should have been embarrassed but Rafe had already seen me naked. He'd been a gentleman about it, turning his back so I could dress after shifting, but he'd seen more skin then than I showed now.

I padded barefoot down the hall to the den. Rafe lounged on the sofa. The TV was on, a football game playing, the sound turned down. He held his cellphone to his left ear. Expression serious, he listened to whoever was on the other end. Then, seeing me, he smiled and sat up, motioning me forward to let me know I wasn't interrupting.

"Sam, I be careful. Lucas is right. Whoever hurt Annie is still in the area. The cats on the porch last night proved that. Mia's presence might be connected, or it might just be a really bad coincidence." He fell silent and I heard the murmur of Sam's voice. "Yes, I'll keep an eye on Jax. . . Yes, we had dinner at the café."

He rolled his eyes and I stifled a giggle. I had no doubt Annie was prompting this particular line of questioning.

"Sam, tell your wife to find someone else to act as matchmaker for. If she doesn't, I'll tell Jax what she's trying to do."

He winked and I almost lost it. He was very definitely enjoying himself. Not only did his comment tell me he knew Annie well, it also confirmed he wasn't afraid to tell her when she needed to back off. But it was the look in his eyes as he watched me cross the room in the direction of the kitchen that brought a blush to my cheeks. After all, what woman doesn't appreciate a man who appreciates her?

Down, girl. That's not why you asked him to stay.

"Can I get you anything?" I asked as he ended the call.

"No, thanks." He smiled and shook his head. "It seems Annie heard about us having dinner together."

"And, this being Mossy Creek, she's decided a dinner at the café means we're involved." I shook my head. I should have anticipated that development.

"Basically." He waited until I returned from the kitchen, a bottle of water in each hand, before continuing. "And I'm sorry. I didn't think about what having dinner there would mean to folks in town.'

I shrugged. "Neither did I." I handed him one of the bottles and sat next to him. "To be honest, even if I had thought of it, it wouldn't have mattered."

He gave me a small grin and leaned forward.

I smiled as his lips found mine in a gentle kiss. As he placed one hand behind my head, holding me close, I sighed. This was a much better way to get ready for bed than trying to read.

Much, much better.

"Jax, where the hell are you?"

"Quinn, it is too early for this even if I've been up since five."

Breakfast with Bitsy had not been what I expected. Or, more accurately, it had been much more of what I did expect. She'd done exactly what I told her I didn't want. She'd bought a Dodge Ram with all the bells and whistles and arranged for it to be delivered tomorrow. The moving company she recommended for her tenants when they needed help would be packing up my things and they should be here the middle of next week. She apologized for the delay, but they were fully booked until then. But, if I wanted, she'd be glad to offer them an incentive for getting it done sooner. Even though I knew in the back of my mind that she'd do all that, at six in the morning, it was hard to accept.

Now I had Quinn sounding worried and more than a bit pissed, demanding to know where I was. Maybe the smart thing to do was hang up, go back to the house, climb into bed and pull the covers over my head. Not that I would. Quinn wouldn't sound like that unless she had good reason and those possible reasons worried me.

"What's happened?" I pressed the key fob and the Camaro beeped as the door unlocked.

"Where are you?" she repeated.

"I'm about to leave Bitsy's." I slid in behind the steering wheel and started the engine. "What has you so pissed off?"

Silence.

I slid an earbud into place and activated it. Then I pulled away from the house. The safe bet was to head toward town. Of course, if Quinn didn't tell me what was going on and soon, I'd head to her place. I wasn't in the mood for games.

"Quinn?"

"Sorry." She sounded a bit calmer. "No excuse except for lack of sleep and pique at my husband."

I grinned, guessing what that pique was about. "Let me guess. He isn't telling you anything about the investigation."

"Not a word, even when I remind him I'm a reserve deputy. Something about me being too close to the case." Disbelief and affront filled her voice and I knew better than to tell her he was right. "But that's not why I called. Meg called earlier. She's been trying to reach you."

I frowned and pulled to a halt at the stop sign at the end of Bitsy's street. Taking a moment, glad no one was behind me, I reached for my cellphone where it rested on the passenger seat. The display showed two texts from Meg. Their time codes showed they came in during breakfast. I hadn't heard them come in so I assumed it was when I'd helped my aunt carry breakfast out to the patio where we'd been sitting.

"I see the texts now. What's up? Is Annie all right?"

God, please let her be all right.

"Damn it, I'm an idiot."

I smiled slightly and started off again. As I did, I pictured Quinn beating her head against the wall in frustration. Hopefully, it was with herself and not something or someone else.

"Not arguing. Tell me what's going on."

"Bitch." She laughed softly. "Meg filed a motion for a restraining order against Mia. Lucas put the word out, unofficially, to the surrounding agencies asking for help locating her. He got a hit back an hour or so ago. Meg's having her served as we speak. Judge Tamika

Washington will hear the motion later this morning. She agreed with Meg that this is a matter of urgency."

"Thank God." Relieved, I signaled a right turn and guided the car onto Main Street. "So why did she want to talk to me?"

"She didn't go into detail, but I think she wants you at the hearing since you were there when Mia tried to take Robbie from school."

"All right. I'm not far from the office. I'll check in. Then I'll need to run back out to Miss Serena's and change clothes. I'm not exactly dressed appropriately for court."

"Run by my place if you need something to wear. I know you didn't bring much with you."

"Thanks." I thought for a moment. "Annie?"

"She knows and is pissed. Sam's threatened to have Dr. Pat sedate her if she doesn't calm down." Quinn's tone made it clear she approved of the threat. Not that I blamed her. I did as well.

"Who the hell told her?"

"Three guesses." Disgust filled her voice now and that was all I needed to know the answer. Catherine. Damn the woman. For once, why couldn't she have the common sense God gave a flea?

'Damn it." I forced my fingers to ease their grip on the steering wheel. "I'll talk to Bitsy again. She promised to keep Catherine in check."

"Don't blame her. She wasn't there."

Well, that made it a little better. Not much, but a little.

"All right. I'm going to head to your place to raid your closet. Will you let your mom know?"

"I'm still home. I'll see you when you get here."

Half an hour later, I stood in Quinn's bedroom wondering if I'd made a mistake in coming. She considered the contents of her closet. As she did, she assured me her mother was looking after not only Ali and Robbie but the twins as well. Camille would be joining them after the hearing. But she and Judge Caldwell wanted to be in court for their son. More than that, Camille had promised Annie she'd go and report back to her. I knew it was Camille's way of trying to keep Annie in bed, but I also knew Annie. That wouldn't stop her.

So I did the only thing I could think of short of me skipping the hearing and sitting on her.

"It's me," I said as soon as Rafe answered the phone.

"Hey." His voice deepened and I heard the smile in it. Thankfully, Quinn still had her back to me and didn't see my own grin. "What's up?"

"I need you to do me a favor."

"Of course."

Most guys would ask what. Not Rafe. Whether he knew about the hearing and guessed what I wanted or something else, I didn't know and I didn't care.

"Thanks." Now I turned my back. I so did not want Quinn to see my expression. If she did, she'd know immediately we'd slept together. And that would bring questions and good-natured teasing, neither of which I was ready for. "Is there any way you can sit with Annie this morning? Maybe even sit on her?"

He chuckled and then sobered. "I'm at the hospital now and about to go up to her room. Sam called and filled me in." He fell silent for a moment and I wondered if the connection had dropped. Then he was back. "Sorry. I stepped outside. Figured I'd lose the signal in the elevator."

"Did Sam tell you Annie knows about the hearing and about what happened yesterday?" He cursed inventively and I nodded even though he couldn't see. "That's about how I feel. I take it he didn't say anything to you about it."

"He did not."

Oh man, he was not happy. I had a feeling he'd be talking with Sam about that little oversight.

"And don't worry. Annie won't get out of her room."

"Thanks." I glanced over my shoulder and found Quinn watching me, a grin on her lips. Oops. Busted. Shit. "I'll call once the hearing's over. Let me know if anything happens on your end." I slid the phone into my hip pocket, schooled my expression and turned.

"So." She drawled it out, her eyes twinkling with equal parts amusement and speculation.

"Don't." I shook my head. "Quinn, I swear I'll get in my car and drive straight back home if you start in on me."

She tilted her head to one side and studied me. Then she sobered and nodded. Without a word, she placed several pairs of slacks, blouses and tops as well as a couple of light weight jackets on the bed. When she straightened, she held a hand out to me.

"I promise to be good." When I snorted, she had the good grace to laugh. "Okay, as good as I can be."

"And?"

"I forgot for a moment what it's like to suddenly be thrust back into life here, especially when it is doing its best to beat you down." She rested a hand on my arm. "You are always strong for the rest of us. I can't think of the last time you put your wants or your needs ahead of us. That's why it's so good to see you doing for yourself. I'm not going to tease and I'm not going to pry. At least I'll try not to. But I want to say one thing. Rafe is a good man, almost good enough for you."

"Thanks. He's turning into a good friend."

I wasn't about to say anything more than that. Instead, I studied the clothes she'd laid out and chose a pair of black slacks and red silk blouse. My cowboy boots would be a little out of place with them but not much. Besides, I'd never really cared about fashion rules before and this wasn't the time to start.

"Has Lucas said anything about the *gift* someone left at Annie's?" I pulled my tee shirt over my head and reached for the silk blouse.

Quinn frowned and shook her head. "Not much. The vet examined the carcasses and said the cats were dead before they were gutted."

I nodded. That explained where there was so little blood when I found them.

"But it will be several days before he gets Lucas anything more." Frustration filled her voice. Pausing as I stepped out of my jeans, I looked at her in question. "Sorry. This is one of those things we all promised not to hit you with."

I had a feeling I wasn't going to like the answer, but I had to ask. "Hit me with what?"

She shook her head. "Forget I said anything."

"Yeah, right. That's not going to happen." I frowned, worried. This wasn't like Quinn. "C'mon, what's going on?

She blew out a breath and dropped onto the edge of the mattress. For a long moment, she stared at her hands where they hung between her knees. When she looked up, her expression said it all. She wanted to kick herself for saying too much. But, somehow, I knew it had nothing to do with Annie or with today's hearing.

At least I didn't think it did.

"Tell me." I spoke softly and sat next to her, reaching for one of her hands.

"Meg and I, not to mention our husbands and a few others, have been talking. You always give up so much for the rest of us. We don't need to ask you to do it. Hell, we'd beg you not to if we just stopped and thought. But you do. You are our friend, our protector and so much more. You've already given up too much be here now."

I opened my mouth. Then, seeing the look on her face, snapped it shut.

"We made a promise that we wouldn't ask you to do anything more than you are already."

"What does this have to do with the vet and his report?"

She shook her head. I rolled my eyes and blew out a breath. She wasn't going to make this easy. I loved her because I had a feeling she was trying to protect me in some warped way. But they needed to understand I was a grown woman and I made my own decisions—and I accepted the consequences for those decisions.

"Jax."

Understanding, or at least a hint of it, struck. "Quinn, is he not doing the job?"

That also explained a lot of what Miss Serena didn't say when we discussed me taking over care of her stock. I'd assumed Dr. Oliver simply preferred being a small animal vet. Lots do. But he was getting older, close to retirement age. Could that be part of it as well?

"When the hell am I going to learn to keep my damned mouth shut?" she muttered.

I reached over and tilted her head until she looked at me. "Moira Quinn O'Donnell Moore, tell me the truth. Is there a problem with Dr. Oliver, one you have all been hiding from me because you decided it was your turn to play the protector?"

Looking almost miserable, she nodded. I blew out a breath. My mouth then tightened into a thin line. I got it. They loved me and they were doing their best to make sure I didn't return here unless I wanted to. The last thing they wanted was for some sense of duty to tie me to the town, especially if it made me miserable. I loved them for it even as I wanted to knock their heads together.

"Listen to me." I waited until she nodded once. "I'm a big girl and I make my own decisions. But the only way I can do that is if I know everything. You and the others don't need to protect me." I grinned as inspiration hit. "Or are you trying to make the rogue mad at you?"

She grinned a little sheepishly. "Nope."

"Then quit trying to keep things from me." I slid an arm around her and she leaned her head against my shoulder, much as she used to when we were kids and I finally convinced her to tell me what was bothering her. "What about Dr. Oliver?"

"Let's just say he's not doing the job he once did. I don't know if he's tired and ready to retire or if he simply doesn't want to put in the hours he used to or if it's something else. But he told Lucas he'd get the results when he got them."

I winced slightly as I imagined how well that had gone over.

"Is that why Miss Serena no longer uses him?" I explained how I didn't completely buy Miss Serena's explanation for suddenly using a vet from out of county not only for the stock but for her dog, Athena, as well.

"Yeah." She nodded and sat up, turning to face me. "It's why I don't use him for our pack of dogs either."

"I'm not making any promises, but I will think about it. If I decide I'm not staying permanently, I'll find you all a vet you can trust. Promise."

She gave me a slight smile and pushed off the mattress. "You need to finish dressing. We're due at the courthouse in half an hour."

Twenty-five minutes later, we slid into seats directly behind Meg where she sat at counsel table. I didn't surprise me one bit to see Miss Olivia sitting next to her. After all, she thought of Annie as one of her own kids. Beyond that, she knew more when it came to the town and the legal community than all the rest of us, except maybe Miss Peggy, combined. She'd make sure Meg missed nothing during the hearing.

Only a minute or two after Quinn and I arrived, the doors behind us opened again and Judge Caldwell, Camille and Sam entered. The judge and Camille walked with him to the rail and then gave him a hug. He nodded to Quinn and me and then took his place at the table with Meg and Miss Olivia. As he did, my heart went out to him. Dark shadows bruised the skin under his eyes. He looked as if he'd aged a decade in the last few years. Annie being hurt had been hard enough on him. Having Mia show up out of nowhere and try to take his son came close to pushing him over the edge.

Just before the bailiff called the case, the doors opened once again. When I glanced over my shoulder to see who it was, my lips pulled back and I bared my teeth in a low growl. Mia, wearing a designer dress that had to cost a small fortune, gold chains around her neck and gold hoops on her ears, entered on Joe Bob Sawyer's arm. He looked like the geeky guy living in his mother's basement who won a date with a starlet. But there was a gleam in his eye that set off all my alarms.

Once they took their places at the other counsel table, the bailiff called the case to order. Judge Washington recapped Meg's motion and asked if the parties were ready to proceed. Meg stood and said she was. Then Sawyer climbed to his feet.

"Your honor, we object to these proceedings. Not only is there no basis for the motion but my client and I have not had a chance to prepare a defense to the motion. I request a two week continuance to allow us to prepare an informed response to the petitioner's motion."

Judge Washington's expression never changed. Instead of ruling, she turned her attention to Meg. "Mrs. Grissom?"

"Your Honor, we respectfully object to this attempt to unreasonably delay this motion. The facts are not in dispute. My client is the minor child's biological father. He was granted sole custody of the child when the respondent abandoned not only her marriage but her child as well. Mr. Caldwell filed to have her parental rights terminated after she failed to have any contact with the child after she walked out on them. As you can see from the documentation attached to our motion, all reasonable and required methods of locating the respondent and serving her with notice of the intent to terminate her rights were made. There is also a certified copy of the judgment in the court's file. The fact that she comes in now, seven years after abandoning the minor child and after having her rights terminated, and tried to remove him from his school makes this matter urgent. We ask the court to hear the evidence and rule today. It is our belief that the safety of the minor child rests on it."

"I agree, Mrs. Grissom. Motion for continuance denied."

The court reporter, head bent, took it all down. Sawyer dropped onto his chair, his eyes shooting daggers at Meg. Interesting. He used to be better at hiding his feelings, at least if none of his bully friends weren't around to protect him.

"Call your first witness, Mrs. Grissom."

Over the course of the next two hours, Meg built her case. She called Ms. Ruiz, Deputy Restall and Robbie's teacher, Miss Granger. Each of them described their interactions with Mia. Miss Granger described not only her suspicions about Mia but how upset Robbie became after Mia spoke to him. No, he didn't want to see her, much less go anywhere with her. As far as he was concerned, his mother was Annie. He didn't know the woman. He'd never seen her before, only pictures, and he knew she'd hurt him and his daddy.

Then it was my turn. Meg carefully guided me through why I was back in town, making sure she didn't come right out and accuse Mia of possibly being involved in the attack on Annie but laying out enough that the judge had to wonder. I described what I'd seen and heard at the school and my concerns about Robbie. Then it was Sawyer's turn to question me.

While he hadn't done much to question the others, he looked almost gleeful as he stood and approached the witness stand. I leaned back and crossed my legs. This was going to be fun. Obviously, he'd forgotten how foolish it was to underestimate me. Meg saw something in my expression and tilted her head, one brow arched. I smirked slightly, letting her know I had this under control.

"You've never met my client, have you?" Sawyer began without preamble.

"I have not."

"So you really can't tell this court anything about what sort of mother she is or what she feels for her son, can you?"

Oh, he was even more cock sure of himself than when we were kids and just as dumb. I tried not to let me contempt show as I glanced at the judge, making sure she would allow my answer. She nodded, interest brightening her eyes. If I didn't know better, I'd say she wanted to see how long it took for me to demolish Sawyer.

"Actually, I can," I corrected. "I've known Sam Caldwell as long as I've known you, Mr. Sawyer. I also know what kind of man he is. I was here when he moved back to Mossy Creek after being medically discharged from the Army and after your client abandoned him and their infant son.

"I also know that Annie Grissom Caldwell legally adopted Robbie once she and Sam married. Even though your client's parental rights had been terminated some years before, they made a good faith attempt to locate her and let her know. Except they couldn't because it was as if your client had dropped off the face of the Earth. That tells me something important. If she really cared about Robbie, she'd not have made it impossible for his father to find her. She'd have sent Robbie cards and remembered things like his birthday and Christmas."

"Your Honor, I move to strike the witness' testimony as being unresponsive!"

Judge Washington shook her head. "Denied. You asked the question and she answered it. I suggest you remember the adage about not asking a question if you don't know the answer. Now continue or dismiss the witness."

A muscle in Sawyer's jaw twitched and he nodded curtly.

"Isn't it true you're close friends with Annie Caldwell, Miss Powell?"

"It's Dr. Powell," I corrected. "And yes, I am. I've known Mrs. Caldwell since we were children, just as I've known you." A none-too-subtle reminder, at least for him, not to push. But was he smart enough to pick up on it?

"It would be fair to say you're best friends, wouldn't it?"

One corner of my mouth lifted. He'd missed the warning. Good. I had no problem embarrassing him in front of the judge. If it helped dismantle his case for Mia, all the better.

"It is."

"And you'd do just about anything to protect your friends and make sure they got what they wanted, wouldn't you?"

I shook my head, my expression matching that of Mrs. Haverstock, our first grade teacher, when one of us said something particularly stupid. Meg pressed her lips together and humor danced in her eyes. Sam's expression went from stormy to speculative, as if he realized I was about to demolish Sawyer without breaking a sweat.

"Dr. Powell?" the judge prompted.

"Your Honor, Mr. Sawyer knows the answer to that. Yes, I will do whatever I can, within the bounds of the law, to protect Annie and her family. That is why I didn't hesitate to rush to the school when they called me and said his client was trying to take Robbie. You see, I love my godson very much and I am very well aware of the history with his birth mother.

"Mr. Sawyer knows something else. Mrs. Caldwell would have my skin, figuratively if not literally, if I committed perjury or otherwise broke the law in an attempt to protect her or her family. I'm afraid he is letting his long-standing dislike for Mrs. Caldwell color his judgment regarding this case."

"Your Honor!"

"Quiet, Mr. Sawyer." She spoke almost gently but her eyes glinted in warning. "Would you care to explain, Dr. Powell?"

"Of course, Your Honor."

I quickly explained Annie's history with Sawyer without going into too much detail. Then I came to the charges he'd filed against Catherine. Charges Annie not only proved were baseless but that led to Sawyer being fired and sanctioned by the Bar. He'd failed to turn over discovery and exculpatory evidence. He'd instructed local law enforcement personnel not to talk with Annie or anyone from her office. In short, he'd done all he could to convict Catherine, not giving a damn whether she'd actually done it or not.

"Your Honor." He once more stood, his face an interesting shade of purple. "My relationship with Annie Caldwell has nothing to do with the matter currently before the court. My duty is to my client, Mia Caldwell, and representing her best interests. And those interests are letting her see her son."

"Do you have any further questions for Dr. Powell?"

"One or two." He sneered at me. "Isn't it true you haven't lived in Mossy Creek in more than ten years?"

"It is."

"So any information you have about the town and its citizens, including Sam Caldwell, comes from hearsay."

I grinned and leaned forward, my forearms on the rail in front of me. "Not at all. I might have left town to pursue my education and work, but I have not been a stranger here. I come back every few months to visit family and friends. They come visit me. Trust me, I probably know more about the town and the people living here than you do."

"But it still remains that you aren't living here any longer and you don't see the petitioners on a regular basis."

He simply never learned.

"And there you are wrong again, Mr. Sawyer. I have returned to Mossy Creek and am establishing my residence here." As I spoke, silence fell over the courtroom. I saw a couple of those in the gallery pulling out their phones, their fingers flying as they sent texts. By the time I left the stand, word would be out that I was back. "I am currently living in the caretaker's house on Miss Serena Duchamp's property and she has hired me as vet for her stock and personal pets."

It was all I could do not to laugh as Sawyer's mouth opened and closed without him making a sound. With his eyes bugging out, he looked a lot like a fish pulled from the creek, gasping for air.

"Pass the witness." He ground out the words as he dropped onto his chair, defeated.

"Then let me be the first to welcome you back home, Dr. Powell. Mrs. Grissom, do you have any other questions for the witness?"

"No, Your Honor." Meg smiled as I stood and, as I walked by the counsel table, winked.

"Do you have any other witnesses?"

"Samuel Caldwell, Your Honor."

Sam stood and then stopped as the judge motioned for him to stay where he was. "Mr. Caldwell, I think we can cut straight to the heart of the matter. Have you had any contact with your ex-wife since she left your domicile?"

"No, Your Honor."

"To the best of your knowledge, has she had any contact with your son?"

Sam didn't answer for a moment. Then, his expression hard, he nodded once. "She attempted to stop and talk to him the day before she showed up at his school. He didn't recognize her and told her he wasn't allowed to talk to strangers. Then he did exactly what his mother and I have taught him. He went inside Connie's Bookstore because it was the closest to where he was and waited until Mia left."

"That is the sole extent of his contact with the respondent?"

"Yes, Your Honor."

"How can you be sure?"

"Because Robbie would have told me." He glanced across the courtroom to where Mia sat next to Sawyer. When he did, his expression actually showed pity for the woman. "Robbie used to ask about her when he was younger. He didn't understand why his friends all had mothers and he didn't. He was afraid he'd done something to drive her away. My parents helped me reassure him it was nothing he did. I also made sure he received counseling to help him accept it.

"He quit asking after Annie moved back to town and became part of our lives. She became his mother in every way that matters. She loved him as a mother should. When I offered to sign a prenuptial agreement to protect her assets, she told me that wasn't necessary. She loved me and Robbie and she would never leave either of us. Instead, she asked if she could adopt my son. But she didn't just ask me. She asked Robbie if he would let her be his mother and he didn't hesitate one moment. He said yes. The day I proposed, Robbie did too. He formally asked her to be his mother."

"One more question, Mr. Caldwell. Would you consider letting your ex-wife see Robbie?"

"No, ma'am." He shook his head when Meg placed a hand on his arm. Whether she wanted him to stop talking or what, I didn't know. But I tensed, wondering what might happen next. "My son has suffered more than any child should because of Mia. I don't want her seeing him and making him thing things are better only to have her walk out on him again. She had the chance to fight my motion to terminate her rights and she chose not to."

Mia leapt to her feet, a perfect picture of outrage. "I didn't know!"

"You did," Sam corrected, and I looked at him in surprise. "We didn't get service on her, but I made sure copies of the motion along with notice of court dates were delivered to her parents, her brother and what friends of hers I could think of. I spoke to her brother afterwards. He told me he gave her the paperwork well before the hearing. She chose not to fight for Robbie. She gave up any right she had to my son. So, to answer your question, I don't want her within shouting distance of my son."

"Objection!" Now it was Sawyer climbing to his feet. "Hearsay!"

"I'll allow it for the purposes of this hearing." Judge Washington leaned back and studied the parties. "I think I've heard enough."

"Your Honor, my client would like to address the court." Sawyer looked as if he couldn't belief the turn the hearing had taken.

"She can do so at the final hearing." She quickly checked the court calendar. "Mrs. Grissom, I'm granting your motion for a temporary restraining order against the respondent. Mia Caldwell, you are hereby prohibited from having any contact with the minor child, Robert Samuel Caldwell, until we reconvene for the final hearing.

That includes phone or digital messaging. No calls, no texts and no e-mail. You are further ordered to stay at least one hundred yards from him. You are not allowed on property owned by or occupied by his parents or grandparents. Do you understand?"

"I just want to see my son."

"You will have a chance to prove your right to do so at the final hearing," Judge Washington said. "Now, do you understand the restrictions of the TRO?"

Mia nodded and then said she did when prompted yet again by the judge.

"Mr. Sawyer, I expect you to make sure she does." Then she turned her attention to Meg. "Mrs. Grissom, draft the preliminary order. I expect it on my desk by end of day."

"I have it here, Your Honor." She accepted several sheets of paper from Miss Olivia. After receiving permission from the judge, she approached the bench and handed them over.

"Very good. I will review these and, assuming there are no problems, sign them. Check with my clerk after three."

"Yes, Your Honor. Thank you."

The judge stood. "Then we are adjourned. The clerk will inform you of the time and date for the final hearing on the restraining order."

Sam and Meg thanked everyone for their support and, with his parents at their sides, left the courthouse. Quinn and I watched as they made their way toward the law office. When I turned, I found Quinn watching me, her expression softer than in the courtroom, affection reflected in her eyes. Without a word, she reached for my hand and gave it a squeeze.

"Are you sure?" she asked softly.

I didn't need to ask what she meant. I had kind of dropped a bombshell.

"Yeah." There would be time later to tell her about my conversation with Miss Serena and the others. A conversation I'd been thinking about more than I realized. "We'll talk about it later."

"Oh, you'd better believe we will." She grinned and lightly slapped me on the shoulder. "I'm going to head over to the hospital to fill in Annie and make sure she hasn't tried to do a bolt. You coming?"

I shook my head. Much as I wanted to, there was something I needed to do first. "No. Give her my love and tell her I'll be by later."

With that, I took the steps down to the street two at a time. After my announcement in court and the way texts went flying out in response, there were some people I needed to talk to before I did anything else.

As I pulled up to Miss Serena's house, I chuckled softly to see three cars I recognized parked out front. Relieved I didn't have to send for them, I parked the Camaro next to Judith's Cadillac. By the time I climbed out, the front door opened. Miss Serena stood there, her expression a mix of concern, relief and welcome. I smiled, not wanting her to worry, and hurried up the steps.

"Are you sure?" she asked softly as I hugged her.

I nodded, still smiling. "I am. Let's go inside. I need to talk to all of you."

Miss Serena led me into the den. The others stood as we entered. Mary Kate hurried to me, pulling me in for a hug as she thanked me for helping keep Robbie away from Mia. I nodded and promised I'd do everything I could to keep him safe. Then I thanked Miss Serena as she handed me a glass of iced sweet tea.

"Before we get started, let me answer the one question I know you each want to ask." I sipped my tea, realizing how thirsty I was. "I am staying in town. Not just until this is over. Mossy Creek's home and the events of the last few days." Not to mention the last few years. "Have convinced me this is where I want and where I need to be."

"We don't want you to feel you have to do this out of some sense of duty," Miss Serena said.

"I know." And I did. It dawned on me while I was on the stand that this really was my decision. "But it means I have some decisions to make about things like a job and where to live."

"You're welcome to stay where you are as long as you want," Miss Serena said. "Meg and Drew will tell you I'm a hands-off landlord."

"I appreciate it, Miss Serena, and I will take you up on it for the near future." But I wanted my own place. "I will continue looking after your stock, if you'd like, but I'm going to need to open a clinic or see if Dr. Oliver won't give me a job."

"If you are asking our opinions," Dr. Pat began. "Open your own practice. Old Oliver is slowing down and I'm hearing murmurs that his wife wants him to retire. He's not ready for that yet, but he isn't seeing as many patients as he used to."

"Thanks." I nodded once. I'd need to talk with Dr. Oliver. I didn't want to start out by making an enemy. "Now, for the rest of it." I sipped my tea and tried to order my thoughts. "I'm assuming Sam or Meg called and told you the outcome of the hearing."

They nodded, their expressions varying degrees of relief.

"Let me add a few things they might not have told you. Sawyer was Mia's attorney and he made it very clear this is as much about his rivalry with Annie as it is anything else, at least where he's concerned."

"Did you find out anything about why Mia is here or where she's staying?" Mary Kate asked.

I shook my head. "The judge didn't hear from her. But don't worry. You know Meg is going to do everything possible to not only find out what Mia's been doing since she walked out on Sam and Robbie but to find out where she is staying and why she chose now to suddenly show up."

"What now?" Judith asked.

"We make Annie's place safe. I don't want her coming home and finding anything like I did on their front porch night before last."

Four sets of eyes stared at me and I frowned. How did they not know? Had the grapevine finally missed a piece of gossip?

For once I wish the grapevine worked like it usually did. Telling them, especially Mary Kate, about finding the two dead cats, was one of the hardest things I've ever done. They listened, never interrupting.

"To be honest, I'd prefer it if Annie could go to either your place, Judith, or here when she's discharged. I know she'd be safe either place. Safer than anywhere else in town."

"But?" Miss Serena asked. "You know she and her family are more than welcome here."

"Unfortunately, my granddaughter is as stubborn as my husband was." Mary Kate sounded both wistful and frustrated. "She's going to break out of the hospital if she isn't released tomorrow. When that happens, she's going to insist on going home."

"And we don't have any reason to keep her as an in-patient any longer. We're going to have to discharge her tomorrow unless I think of something to keep her." From Dr. Pat's tone of voice, that chances of that happening were slim to none.

"Then we have no choice. We have to set the protections on her house."

Except something was wrong. They looked at one another and then at me. My heart skipped a beat and my stomach did a slow roll. They knew something and I had a feeling it was something I needed to know. Carefully, I set my glass down on the table at my elbow and looked at Miss Serena, trusting her to tell me the truth.

"What is it? Something's bothering you."

"When we talked earlier about the protections, I didn't tell you one thing, Jax," she said.

I didn't want to ask, but I had to. "What?"

"It will take all four guardians to activate the protections."

I closed my eyes and cursed silently. We were screwed then. The fourth guardian, Meg's mother had she stayed in town, was dead. Miss Serena already told me how the lack of that fourth might have something to do with the troubles that had come to town the last few years.

But there had to be something we could do. We couldn't just give up.

An idea came to me, one I wasn't sure I wanted to think about, much less say out loud. However, I didn't have a choice, not if we were going to do everything we could to protect Annie and her family not to mention the rest of the town.

"How are guardians chosen?" I asked, trying to remember everything Miss Serena said the other night and wishing I'd had time to study the old book I'd left here instead of taking with me.

"They have to be an elemental and they have to accept the position," Judith said. As she did, they all watched me, waiting to see if I understood. I didn't need them to tell me that, not when it was written on their faces.

"Each element has to be represented, right?"

"Yes." Miss Serena stood. A moment later, she sat next to me on the sofa. "Jax, I know what you are thinking. But you have to be sure. If you do this, you will be forever tied to the town. Are you ready for that?"

If she'd asked me that twenty-four hours ago, I'd have said no. But something changed overnight. I wanted to stay and not just because I felt duty bound, maybe even honor bound, to do so. This was home. I wanted to be close to my friends, the closest thing to sisters I had. I wanted to be able to go have breakfast or a drink after work with Aunt Bitsy. Hell, and this scared me more than I'd ever admit, I wanted to see if anything happened between Rafe and me.

"I am. This is where I want to be. It's where I belong."

"Jax, think about it. I'll find a reason to keep Annie in the hospital," Dr. Pat said.

I patted Miss Serena's hand and then made eye contact with each of the others. "I am sure about this, Dr. Pat. I think part of me has always known this day would come. If the four of you feel I am the right person to step up and fill the role, I will do it. Mossy Creek might not be ready for me to come home for good, but I think I'm ready."

What else explained the way I'd kept myself tied to the town? If I wasn't, I wouldn't still be subscribed to the local paper. I wouldn't keep pumping Bitsy for all the gossip when we talked once a week. I certainly wouldn't have come running, giving up a job I loved, when Quinn called to tell me about Annie. This was where I was supposed to be.

Like it or not, I'd come home.

"Of course, we agree." Judith hurried to where I sat and pulled me into a hug.

"That means you're going to have to tell me what I need to do."

Hell, who was I trying to fool? There were going to have to teach me what I needed to know and do. Oh God, what were we going to tell Annie when she realized her house had come alive? I laughed a bit hysterically and hoped that was one conversation I could leave to her grandmother.

"I have a feeling you're going to be teaching us as much as we teach you." Miss Serena slid an arm around my waist and smiled up at me. "For now, let's go to the workroom. We may as well get started."

15

"You didn't have to come."

I looked across the car at Rafe. I'd called him earlier to let him know about the hearing and to tell him I wouldn't be able to join him for dinner after all. After a few minutes that included him telling me how he'd been sorely tempted to either tie Annie to her bed or ask her nurses to sedate her, I told him he wouldn't have to worry about her making a bolt for it after tomorrow. Without missing a beat, he asked why. I didn't go into detail, simply saying we were taking care of a couple of things tonight that would let her come home and would reassure the rest of us she was safe.

When he asked if he could do anything to help, I hadn't hesitated. I asked if he'd join us at her house. Judith had already talked with Sam, so I knew he would be there. Maybe Rafe could keep him occupied, or at least distracted, while we did what Quinn would call our "woo-woo" thing. He agreed and said he'd pick me up.

The clock on the dash of his pickup showed it was almost eleven as we parked in front of Annie's house. Sam's pickup was in the driveway. Judith had parked behind it. As I unbuckled my seatbelt, other vehicles joined us. Headlights briefly illuminated the gathering before they switched off. Soon, people and dogs crossed the yard toward the front door where Sam waited.

"Before we get started, I want to say two things." Sam closed the front door and watched as everyone found places to sit. We ranged around the great room, some on sofas and chairs, others on the floor or hearth. "First, thank you. I can't tell you how much it means to me to know you love Annie enough to do this for her and for us. Second, which of you is going to tell Annie you've turned the house into a version of Quinn's?" He grinned and I relaxed. If he could see the humor it in, hopefully Annie would as well. It might take a decade or two, but she'd come to accept it.

I hoped.

"Sorry, son. That's your job." Judith grinned and he held his hands up, as if to ward off a blow.

"Nope. No way am I telling my wife our house is now alive. Of course, she'll probably just blame her grandfather."

We laughed, remembering how she'd blamed him for reaching out from his grave with things like the house and the law office when she came home to defend Catherine against the charge of murdering Spud Buchanan. Then we sobered. The protections we would soon activate might keep the family safe here, but they wouldn't protect Annie away from home.

"What do you want us to do, Miss Serena?" Quinn asked as we fell silent.

"You, Meg, Amy and Mary Kate will assist the four of us. Sam, you are our connection with the house and land."

"All right, but I don't understand," he said.

"Don't worry." Mary Kate reached for his hand from where she sat next to him. "You will be in the circle with Serena and the others and you will give them permission for what they do. That's all."

He looked uncertain but he nodded.

"Rafe, you'll remain outside the circle with Lucas. The dogs will be with you. I don't think there will be any trouble, but you are our first line of defense if something does happen."

As if picking up on my concern, Lucas grinned. "Yeah, I can see a couple of neighbors calling the department to complain about the party Sam's throwing."

His comment did as he hoped—at least I think it's what he hoped for. We laughed and some of our tension eased. After all, he had a point. Everyone in the neighborhood knew Annie was still in the hospital. If anyone happened to look outside, they'd see the half dozen or so cars, trucks and SUVs parked out front and wonder what was going on. I doubted any of them would think Sam was holding a party, but someone might get the wrong idea and come over to see what was wrong.

"And us?" Meg asked.

"You, Quinn, Amy and Mary Kate will cast the outer circle under our guidance. Then you will stand between the cardinal points, our next line of defense," Miss Serena said. "When we start awakening the connections here and temporarily tying them to ourselves, we will be vulnerable. You stand as protectors of the land and of the people here during that time."

"And Jax?" Quinn looked between us, something very much akin to suspicion darkening her eyes.

"She is one of our four," Judith replied. As she did, she held a hand out to me. "The guardians are complete again. That is the only way we're able to do this now."

"I don't understand." Meg looked between us, clearly confused.

My fellow guardians—and it felt strange to think of them and myself that way—looked at me. It was my tale to tell.

"Miss Serena told us some of this the other night. You know there have always been guardians protecting the town." Quinn, Meg and Amy nodded. Of the three, Amy had already put it together, judging by her smile. Either that or her grandmother had clued her in on the drive over. "After the hearing today, I met with Miss Serena, Judith and Dr. Pat. I told them, needlessly because of the grapevine, that I am staying in Mossy Creek. This is home and I've never been able to cut ties with it, no matter how hard I tried. Then I asked how we activated the wards around this house so it could be as safe as yours, Quinn, or as Miss Serena's."

"That is when we told her it required the guardians but that we couldn't do it. We have been short one member. As long as Faith was alive, we kept the position open, hoping she would move home." Judith smiled at Meg, telling her without words how glad they were she'd come to Mossy Creek and settled down.

Meg's eyes went wide and she shook her head. Hands in front of her, she stepped back until she stood against Drew who looked as much like a deer caught in the headlights as his wife did.

Miss Serena chuckled. "Don't worry, Meg. We aren't asking you to take her place—yet. But you had best be prepared for the day to come. We've already discussed it."

Meg swallowed hard. Then she grinned and looked at Quinn.

"Don't." I spoke softly, but the command was there. "I accepted my place as guardian. Yes, it scares me to death. But it also feels right. Even so, I have a lot to learn and so, my friends, do you. We are the next generation of protectors, even if you aren't guardians now or later. Something is coming to Mossy Creek. Hell, it might already be here. Something dark and dangerous. Something that wants to destroy our loved ones and our town. Will you stand with us now to protect our sister and will you stand with us going forward to protect the town and those who live here?"

Quinn stepped forward and nodded. She might be a little pale, but she would do what she saw as her duty, just as she did when it came to her job as a DEA agent. A moment later, Meg joined her. Both still looked like they might bolt for the hills. Amy, on the other hand, hugged me and then her grandmother before looping arms with Meg and Quinn and leading them back to where they'd been standing.

"Just tell us what to do." Quinn looked at the others and they nodded in agreement.

"Miss Serena?"

"Let's get started. It will take time to get everything prepared."

Unlike what the movies and too many books, there wasn't any cleansing bath or naked ritual. Thank goodness. Instead, Miss Serena explained how she wanted Quinn, Meg, Mary Kate and Amy to cast the first circle. This one encircled the house. The rest of us waited inside, watching as they carefully walked around the house, calling on their elements and pulling power from air, earth, fire and water. I closed my eyes and watched the energies rise up and pull down, flowing over them and forming the first protective circle.

Once they were done, they took up their places. Quinn, as Fire, stood to the north. Meg, as Air, took East. Mary Kate, as Water stood in the West with Amy in the South as Earth. They raised their hands skyward and their energies flowed upward, stretching high before arcing back down, intertwining, joining and strengthening until a shimmering dome I was amazed no one outside the circle could see. Power radiated from it, alive and searching.

"Our turn," Miss Serena said.

I nodded and took my place in the center of what would be the inner circle with Sam. I watched as Miss Serena, Judith and Dr. Pat began to softly chant, calling on their elements as they cast the circle. The air around us turned electric. Their auras came to life as they pulled energy from earth and air, fire and water.

"Jackie." Miss Serena nodded to me.

I drew a deep, calming breath and sank to my knees. I pressed the palm of my left hand to the floor, focusing on what I needed to do. Eyes closed, I opened my mind and reached for the essence of what made me an Earth elemental. Down my arm and out my palm, through the floor and basement. The soil beneath, warm, moist, teeming with life. Nearby, the warm and electric feel of a ley line. It would be so easy to get lost in it.

Control. Focus.

I collected tendril after tendril of power from the Earth and from the ley line. I tied them into the first the inner circle and then the outer. I pictured stitching a line and then doubling it, tripling it. The stitches turned into woven strands I carefully turned into layers, like the skin of an onion. They rose above and below the surface, enveloping the house and the land surrounding it in a protective coat.

The power flowing through me was intoxicating. I knew the danger of giving in to it. The temptation beat against me. I could have anything I wanted, do anything I wanted. All I had to do was accept the power of the ley line and all it could give me.

This was the danger of being an Earth elemental. So much power that was so easily abused.

No!

This wasn't me. I wasn't here for personal power. I was here to help protect my friends, my sister-by-choice.

Inhale, hold it, relax, focus, exhale.

I repeated it half a dozen time until I felt temptation fade. Then I returned to the task. With the house protected, I focused on the surrounding yard. I felt the land and its energies slowly awake, as if from a long sleep. Even inside the house, I saw the flare as long dormant wards snapped into place. They might not be as strong—or as alive and loud—as the wards at Quinn's or as masterfully woven as Miss Serena's, but they were once again online, for lack of a better word.

"Very good, Jackie." Miss Serena rested a hand on my shoulder, and I felt revitalizing energies flow through her hand into me. "One more step and you're through for tonight."

I nodded and closed my eyes. When I opened them again, I could see the energies from my fellow guardians: red for Fire, blue for Water, white for Air and green for Earth. I reached out with my right hand. Concentrating for all I was worth, I wove my green energies first with Miss Serena's white. Opposite to opposite. Red interwoven with blue. Earth and Air, Fire and Water. Then I wove the four together. One last thing, the final bit until Annie was home and we linked her to the wards. I joined our four energies with the protective energies I'd woven around, through and into the Earth.

I'd never have believed it if I hadn't been there, but the moment the energies joined, there was a *snap* and then a sound very much like the sweet pealing of a bell. As if that was the signal, the connection I held with the ley line snapped and I dropped onto my ass, exhausted. Sam knelt next to me, his arms going around me, supporting me so I didn't hit my head on the floor.

"We're almost done, but your part's over," Miss Serena said softly.

I relaxed, glad I didn't have to do anything else for a while. Then I nodded to Sam that I was all right. I didn't want him worrying about me. But it was the look of worry on Rafe's face as he stood just beyond the edge of the circle that forced me to try to sit up. I didn't try standing. Not yet. Not when I had a feeling I'd fall flat on my face if I did.

So I sat there, watching as Miss Serena, Judith and Dr. Pat finished the ritual. Once they had, they looked to me. They didn't say anything. They didn't have to. I knew they wondered if I felt strong enough to help banish the circle. I nodded and let Sam help me to my feet.

We weren't quite done—not yet.

With the circle banished, we walked outside. Quinn, Meg, Amy and Mary Kate still manned their cardinal points. To the normal eye, they looked like four women, possibly who had drunk too much, standing around the house, arms extended above their heads, fingers splayed. But to me, they shimmered with energy, anchoring the outer protections. But it was the looks on Quinn's and Meg's faces that caused me to bark out a quick laugh. Awe and denial, excitement and fear, I saw and smelled it on them. Not that I blamed them. This was so far out of the realm of normal, even for us, that it wasn't funny.

And now it was my turn again.

I knelt and reached down with both hands. The grass was cool beneath my palms. My fingers dug through the blades of grass and roots, into the cool, damp earth. I breathed in the fresh smell of soil. I sensed all the life in it, nutrients that fed the worms and other living creatures that made the ground their home. Grass, tree and plant roots, all carrying nutrients to the living things above the soil. The term Mother Earth was more accurate than most people realized and now I needed her to grant me the right to tap into her energies to help keep Annie and her family safe.

Much as I had done inside, I gathered the lines of energy from Quinn, Meg, Amy and Mary Kate, binding them, element to element. Then I tied them into the wards they'd raised. I wove those protections to the wards we'd put in place for the house. That connected it all to us. Finally, praying I didn't do anything wrong and fry my ass, I tied everything back to the earth, drawing on the power pool I'd sensed the other day.

For a moment, nothing happened. Then, suddenly, the entire property came alive. The land's awareness slammed into me, knocking me on my ass yet again. It was on alert. Something was wrong.

Wrong, wrong, wrong. Danger!

Even though we were outside, I couldn't locate the source of danger.

"Inside!" I snapped as I climbed to my feet. "Everyone inside!"

No one argued. Sam slid an arm around his wife's grandmother and all but carried her up the steps and inside the safety of the house. Rafe did much the same with Miss Serena. The others followed and I brought up the rear, Quinn at my side.

The moment we were inside, the door closed behind us, Miss Serena went to work. She pulled on her new connection with the house and the land around it. At the same time, Mary Kate, Dr. Pat and Judith cast a new circle. Before they got to me, I stepped out of it, shaking my head. Judith looked me in the eye and nodded once.

"Be careful," she said softly.

I nodded and then gave in to my instincts. I shifted without stripping. After all, there were others present who didn't need to see me naked. I dropped to hands and knees. My back arched and I threw my head back and cried out as pain washed over me. Damn it, I'd really like it if shifting was as quick and painless as Hollywood made it seem.

"Easy, Jax," Rafe soothed as he knelt next to my four-footed form.

I growled and rolled, trying to rid myself of my clothes. Back paws clawed at pants and I bit at my shirt, trying to wrestle out of them. Then Rafe rested a gentling hand on my shoulder. I stilled, sniffing only concern, no fear. I lay there, panting, as he cut away my clothes. Once he had, I climbed to my feet—paws—and head butted him, rubbing against him and scent marking him.

"I didn't know you could turn into a cougar." He ran a light hand down my head. Then he stood and opened the door. "Go. I'll be right behind you."

I ran outside, using my new connection to the land to find who— or what—was setting off all the alarms.

I raced through the night, intent only on catching the person. If I did, the danger to Annie might finally be over. Nothing else mattered.

I ran through the night, keeping to the shadows. I paused, opened my mouth and inhaled, taking in all the scents around me. Mrs. Benton's yappy little dog out doing his business in the backyard. Nocturnal creatures—opossums and raccoons and others—scurried away, recognizing me as the bigger and much more deadly predator. Oil and other mechanical smells so prevalent in this form and usually ignored when human.

Snap!

I swung my head, lips pulling back to show teeth that would terrify most people. I scented again. Human. Not Rafe. Not that he'd be foolish enough to make a sound when he knew I was hunting. Besides, the scent was familiar. I simply couldn't place it. I wouldn't have that issue with Rafe. Not after last night.

Crouching, belly almost touching the ground, I moved slowly toward the scent. I was a very large cat tracking the proverbial mouse. The hunt was on.

There!

Someone stood in the shadows of the trees across the street. I knew it wasn't a neighbor. They wouldn't be out this late for one thing. For another, they would not feel the need to hide their presence. This person, whoever it was, used the tree trunk to hide, peeking out ever few moments to look in the direction of Annie's house.

They thought they were so smart. Well, they'd soon find out who was the biggest, baddest alpha around.

Growling softly, I moved a bit faster in their direction. Even though I wanted to stand and run full out, I didn't. This was still the hunt. I needed to catch them, not give them time to get away. Stealth over speed and muscle. Catch them and make them pay for hurting Annie.

The silence of the night was broken by the sudden yapping of a dog. Stupid dog. Scared dog. It had picked up my scent and wanted inside *NOW!*. I swung my head in the direction of the sound and then back. Just in time to see the shadow of the person I'd been hunting turn and run in the opposite direction.

Foolish, so foolish. I was faster than they were. I was stronger than they were. All they were doing was prolonging the inevitable. My paws hit the pavement almost soundlessly as I raced across the street and after them. Now the hunt was getting interesting.

Two front yards, more yapping little dogs. Why couldn't Annie live out in the country?

The man, it had to be a man. Everything about the way he ran and what I could see of him shouted male. An out of shape male, but one doing a good impression of a long-distance runner. Funny what you can do when you're scared.

I chuffed a laugh and gathered my muscles. In one moment was I running after him. In the next, I leapt through the air, my front paws catching him in the back. I rode him down. As I did, he squealed in fear. Yes, definitely a man.

He struggled, rolling this way and that in an attempt to shake me off. As tempting as it was to close my jaws around his neck and hold him, I didn't dare. With my luck, he'd break his neck and I'd get the blame. What I really needed to do was pin his arms behind his back but that's pretty damned impossible with paws. It was even harder with him doing his best imitation of a wet snake, slithering and sliding.

His toes dug into the turf. His elbow caught me in the side, once and then twice. Not wanting to hurt him, at least not too badly, I snarled, hoping he took the warning. Instead, he fought harder. Cloth ripped under my claws and he flopped onto his back. His hands clawed at my head, my face. Then they disappeared.

The night erupted into an explosion of sound and pain. I screamed in pain. At least I think I did. I could hear nothing over the sound of the gunshot and the ringing in my ears. The man wriggled out from under me and gained his feet. He was running, disappearing around the corner one house down before I recovered enough to try to stand.

"Jax!" Rafe dropped to his knees next to me as collapsed.

Pain washed over me. I snarled and wanted to curl into a ball as Rafe gently patted my flanks and sides, checking for injuries.

"Lie still, Jax. I've got you." He ran a hand over my head and wisely waited for me to do as he said.

"Rafe?"

I lifted my head, hissing in pain.

"He went around the corner, Lucas!"

Almost instantly, a car engine gunned. Tires squealed. Lucas cursed and ran past us, his boots sounding loudly as his heels struck the sidewalk. I rested my head against the grass. I could leave this to Lucas. I had to leave it to Lucas.

"This is going to hurt, but I don't want you trying to walk," Rafe warned.

Since I couldn't exactly ask him what he meant, I did the feline version of gritting my teeth. He slid his hands under me. Carefully, he lifted me. He staggered slightly as he stood. After all, I was one hundred twenty or so pounds of cougar. Not exactly dead weight but certainly not what he'd be used to lifting. My center of gravity was different in this form than as a human and certainly different from any weights he might lift. But once on his feet, he settled me and began the slow walk back to Annie's.

"Shh," he soothed as I whimpered. "I'm not going to let anything else happen to you."

I rested my snout on Rafe's shoulder and closed my eyes, hoping I hurt the bastard who shot me as much as he'd hurt me.

16

When I woke, I was back in my own skin. Well, my human skin. My questing fingers found the bandage someone had secured over the wound in my shoulder. if that wasn't enough to convince me it hadn't all been some sort of bad dream, the way the wound throbbed with each beat of my heart was. Damn it, I'd gotten careless, trusting that my animal form, especially my cougar form, could handle anything we came across. Foolish, so foolish.

And not something I planned on repeating any time soon.

I opened my eyes and glanced around. At some point, they'd brought me to Quinn's house. It bothered me I couldn't remember anything after Rafe picked me up and started carrying me back to Annie's. Even so, I wasn't going to object. There's only one place I felt safer and that was Miss Serena's.

Turning my head on the pillow, I recognized the room as the one I slept in whenever I stayed the night. Lifting the sheet that covered me, I relaxed to see someone, probably whoever had treated my wound, had dressed me in an oversized tee shirt much like what I'd seen Quinn sleep in. That meant I didn't need to hunt up something to wear before finding a bathroom—something I needed to do soon, judging by the pressure on my bladder.

My brow furrowed slightly to see a sliver of light coming in through a crack in the drapes. It must be morning, which meant I'd been unconscious for several hours at least. So what time was it? I didn't have my watch on. I vaguely remembered the band snapping when I shifted. Who knew where my cellphone was and there was no clock in the room.

One thing was certain. I couldn't put off the bathroom much longer. Maybe by the time I came out, someone would be kind enough to bring me a mug of the coffee I smelled in the air. Then they could answer my questions. I needed to know what had happened since I passed out.

Carefully, gritting my teeth as my shoulder screamed its objection to moving, I sat up. Then I smiled slightly. Rafe sat across the room, his head bent. His chest rose and fell in slow, shallow breaths. In that unguarded moment, I wondered if he might be sleeping. Then he glanced up, catching my gaze. Without a word, he stood and moved to the door. After calling downstairs that I was awake, he hurried to the bed.

"Lie still." He tried to ease me back and I shook my head.

"Bathroom."

He looked at me and chuckled softly. Then he bent and slid an arm around my waist. He helped me to the adjoining bath and stepped back into the bedroom, giving me some privacy. Part of me wanted to laugh. He'd seen me naked. Hell, he'd made love to me. Still, this was part of what drew me to him. He considered what I might want and feel and, so far at least, he hadn't made any demands.

"Get back to bed, young lady," Dr. Pat said firmly from the doorway when I reappeared a few minutes later. She watched with critical eyes as Rafe helped me cross the room. "We'll take it from here, Rafe. Why don't you let Peggy know Jax is awake and probably desperate for a cup of coffee and something to eat?"

As if to punctuate her words, my stomach growled loudly. He chuckled softly and then bent and pressed a light kiss on the top of my head. He didn't say anything. He didn't need to. His expression said it all. He would stay if I wanted him to.

186

"Go on. She's right. I'd kill for a cup of coffee." And then I wanted answers, starting with whether Lucas managed to catch the bastard who hurt me.

"I'll be back soon."

I watched as he left the room. Then I groaned as not only Dr. Pat but Judith and Quinn entered the bedroom. I didn't know whether to be worried I was hurt worse than I first thought or worried about how they were about to read me the riot act. Neither was a very enticing option.

"Don't look so scared, Jax." Dr. Pat set her medical bag next to me on the mattress and helped me sit up some more. "While I might wish you'd chosen to let Lucas and his deputies handle the situation, you did what you felt was necessary."

"And you proved yet again why you are a guardian," Judith said. "You didn't think about the cost to you personally. You simply acted when you sensed danger and a chance to identify the person responsible for hurting Annie."

"Thank you." I smiled and reached for her hand with my uninjured right hand. Then I looked at Quinn who had yet to say anything.

Quinn leaned against the wall by the door. Arms folded under her breasts, her expression closed, she was clearly trying to hold her temper in check. I swallowed hard and eased my hand from her mother's grasp. As if understanding, Judith stepped back and looked from me to her youngest child.

"Quinn?"

"Don't you Quinn me."

Oh, she was pissed. Well too bad. Maybe if she hadn't fought so hard against being an *Other* and had realized shew as coming into her gifts sooner, she'd be the guardian and not me. Besides, I knew her. She would have reacted the same way—okay, she wouldn't have shifted but only because she couldn't—if she'd had the chance.

"Moira Quinn." Judith's eyes flashed as she warned her daughter to behave with just those two words.

"It's all right." I smiled at her and once again held my hand out to

Quinn. "I did what I felt was necessary, trusting you and Lucas to keep everyone else safe."

Quinn frowned. Then she sighed and nodded. I relaxed, glad she wasn't going to hold it against me. I couldn't take that right now.

"Dr. Pat?"

She smiled and rested a hand on my thigh. "You can call me Pat, you know."

"I'll try." Not that I expected it to happen any time soon. She'd been "Dr. Pat" all my life. "How bad?" I nodded toward my injured shoulder.

"You're going to be all right. But you need to take it easy for the next couple of days. That means no shifting. I want everything to start mending before you put that kind of stress on your system."

"All right." Even as I said it, I wished the movies and books were right. It would be so much easier if I could shift into one of my animal forms and then shift back and be healed. But walker physiology didn't work that way. Hell, I wasn't sure were physiology worked that way. "Please tell me I don't have to wear this sling." There was no way I'd be able to explain it to Annie and she'd be suspicious as hell if I didn't go to the hospital to check on her.

"Sorry. You're going to be in the immobilizer for a couple of days."

"Dr. Pat."

I'll admit it. I whined.

"I mean it, Jax. You were lucky the bullet didn't do more damage than it did." She pinned me with a firm look but that had nothing on her tone. It was the same tone of voice every child learned to dread from her mother. "The bullet didn't hit bone, which is the only reason you're here and not in the hospital. But it tore through the muscles of your shoulder and upper arm. As a cougar, that was bad enough. As a human, it means your rotator cuff was damaged. Serena, Judith and I have done what we can—both mundane and arcane—to speed your healing and we'll give you another session later today. For now, however, you will do as I say or I swear I will not only admit you to the hospital but put you in the same room as Annie and turn her loose on you."

I gaped at her and glared when Quinn chuckled evilly. Then I nodded. I'd do as she said, for the moment at least. Especially if it meant they'd answer my questions.

"How long was I out?" Might as well start with the easy question.

"Twelve hours."

I couldn't say anything. There were simply no words. Instead, I gaped at Dr. Pat before looking to Quinn, who nodded grimly.

"I'll be honest, Jax. I'm surprised you're awake. You were exhausted before you shifted. Add the strain of shifting so quickly and without any preparation and then being injured." Dr. Pat paused, swallowing hard against emotion she normally wouldn't let a patient see.

"That's the only reason I've been out so long?"

"For the most part." Judith rested the back of her hand against my forehead, checking for a fever. "We *helped* initially so Pat could treat you."

"Thank you." I looked at Quinn, still scowling at me. "Even you, sour puss."

She did the mature thing and stuck her tongue out at me. But it did what I hoped for. It broke the tension and all of us, even Dr. Pat, laughed. Unfortunately, it couldn't last. I still had questions that needed to be answered.

"Did Lucas find the bastard?" I asked as Dr. Pat carefully adjusted the immobilizer.

"No. He saw a sedan of some sort speeding away, but the light over the license plate was out and it was too far away for him to get more than a sense of what the car was. He's sending a couple of deputies out today to talk to the neighbors and see if anyone's security system caught video that might help us." Quinn's frustration roughened her voice.

"And Annie?"

"Bitching." Quinn chuckled. "She wants out and is threatening to climb out the window if she isn't released soon."

"Dr. Pat?"

"Let's say we're using you as an excuse to keep her in the hospital until tomorrow."

"What?" Surely they hadn't told her what happened.

"That's mean, Dr. Pat, and I love it." Quinn chuckled. "Too bad I didn't video her reaction."

This time I was the one to stick out my tongue.

"I'm serious. Please tell me you didn't let her know what happened."

"Not at all." Quinn was enjoying this way too much for my liking. "We're simply letting the grapevine do what it does so well."

"Don't pay any attention to them, Jax." Judith shook her head at the two like they were recalcitrant children. "Annie, through the grapevine, knows you plan to stay in town. She's thrilled, like the rest of us. More than that, she has been led to believe the reason you aren't coming to see her today is because you're dealing with certain little details like figuring out where to live, where to open your new vet clinic, arranging to have your things sent here. Oh, and I have it on good authority that she is more than a little upset that you didn't tell her yourself."

I rolled my eyes.

"We can discuss how much trouble you're in later." Dr. Pat grinned and patted my uninjured shoulder almost sympathetically. "Right now, I want you to eat and then you're to get some more rest. If you do, you can come downstairs for dinner. But you have to take it easy and no shifting."

"We'll make sure she does as you say." Judith pinned me with a look that had me nodding in agreement even though I wanted to protest. "Go get some rest."

"I will after I make my afternoon rounds." She turned her attention back to me. "Judith has pain pills for you if you need them. Call me if you need me for anything."

"I will." I grasped her hand. "Thank you."

"No, Jax. Thank you." When I looked at her in question, she continued. "You felt the warning before any of the rest of us did. Probably because you were still so attuned to the land. That let us get inside and get the wards there sealed up while you shifted and did what you needed to do. And, before you ask, Lucas has already sent out notice to all area doctors, hospitals, clinics and even vet clinics to contact him if anyone comes in looking like they'd been in a fight with a large animal."

"I'll walk you out," Judith said. She stopped at the door and looked back at me. "After you eat, you're to rest. I mean it."

"Yes, ma'am."

"Now, while we wait for Rafe to get back with your lunch, you want to tell me what the hell you thought you were doing last night?" Quinn arched one brow, letting me know she wasn't going to be put off this time.

I sighed and patted the mattress. "Quinn, I fucked up. All I could think about was making sure everyone was safe. Then I realized I had the chance to possibly identify the bastard who hurt Annie. I trusted you to keep everyone safe. I knew you wouldn't let anything happen to them. That left me to go after the SOB." I lifted my uninjured shoulder in a shrug.

"All right. But don't do it again. You scared the hell out of me."

"Me too." I admitted as Rafe entered, carrying a tray. I smelled eggs, bacon and, more importantly, coffee. "Thanks," I said as he placed the tray across my legs.

Two hours later, I woke from a nap I hadn't realized I needed. My shoulder still hurt but I no longer felt like shifting and gnawing my arm off. Which was probably for the best since I had a feeling Dr. Pat would carry through with her threat to admit me to the hospital and make me room with Annie. I so did not want to have to explain to her how I'd been shot and what I'd been doing before then. Besides, I needed to have a very long talk with Miss Serena and the others about what happened. Never before had I felt a sense of warning, or fore-knowledge, like I had last night.

Most of all, I wanted to know if Annie had remembered anything about the attack since I last saw her.

"Easy," Rafe said as I leaned up on my good arm and tried to lever into a sitting position.

He hurried to the bed. His hands were gentle as he helped me sit up. Then, miracles of miracles, he handed me a mug of hot coffee. I blew across the rim before sipping.

"Thanks."

"You may not thank me in a minute."

I frowned, worried.

"Sorry. My poor attempt at a joke." He sat on the edge of the mattress. "Miss Serena, Judith and Dr. Pat want to see you. But, before I let them know you're awake, you and I need to talk."

I ground my teeth, trying not to groan. I had no doubt what he wanted to say—how could I have been so foolish? Why didn't I wait for him? I could have been hurt worse. Typical macho male, protect the little female sort of thing.

"Jax, don't." He reached over and slid a finger under my chin, lifting my face so he could look at me. "Don't assume you know what I'm going to say."

I snorted. Not exactly ladylike, but it said everything without having to actually say the words.

"I mean it."

"Sorry. Quinn's already chewed my ass. Guess I assumed you wanted to as well."

"Believe me, chewing your ass is not on the menu of things I'd like to do to—and with—you." He grinned and a blush crept across my cheeks. "What I wanted to say is thank you."

I blinked, not sure I heard him correctly. "Huh?"

"Yeah." He reached for my good hand and linked his fingers through mine. "You were the only one of us who acted right away. You reacted before even Miss Serena. Then you made sure everyone was safely inside not only the house but the protections you and the others erected. Once you had, you shifted and went out there, willing to risk yourself in the attempt to find the person responsible for hurting Annie. I'm sorry I wasn't faster and wasn't there to protect you from that bastard."

I gently freed my hand from his and reached up to cup his cheek. "You were there. I knew I could go after him because I knew you were right behind me. I trusted you to have my back and you did. More than that, you kept him from shooting me a second time."

"Jax."

"Rafe, it's your turn to listen to me." I waited, wondering if he'd agree. Then he nodded. "There's a reason I earned the nickname of Rogue when I was growing up. There are times, especially when people I care about are involved, when I act without thinking about the personal cost. If I think those I love are in danger, the personal cost doesn't matter. That makes me very different from my parents and, by their standards, a rogue and a failure. It doesn't matter how successful I am with the rest of my life. They will always see me that way.

"There was a time when I cared how they felt. That stopped a long time ago. But the rogue is still very much a part of me and always will be."

"I'd never ask you to change. That kind of loyalty is something to cherish." Somehow, I knew he meant it. "And I want you to know something. You can count on me to always have your back."

Before I could respond, a knock sounded at the door. It opened and Judith stepped inside. She asked Rafe to go downstairs to let Quinn know we'd be down for dinner in a few minutes. Then she took his place on the bed. He glanced at me and I nodded. Judith might have a few things to say about how reckless I'd been, but she'd wait until I was feeling better.

At least I hoped she would.

"He hasn't left this room except when we've made him," she said softly once we were alone.

"He's a good friend." Damn it, my cheeks heated and, judging by her grin, she saw my blush. I looked down at my lap for a moment, trying to get my emotions under control. "Did we get everything done last night?" If we hadn't. . . .

"We did. At least as much as we can until Annie is home and we key the wards to her and the rest of the family. But the heavy lifting, so to speak, is done." Now she smiled and her eyes sparkled with affection. "And you did a wonderful job, Jax. You made it very easy for the rest of us to do what we needed to."

"Annie?"

"She's fine. Pat and Dr. Kennison said they'd let her come home tomorrow if she behaves. Mary Kate and Sam then explained how Sam's still upgrading their security system and how they would feel better if she stayed where she was until everything was ready. Between that and knowing you're staying in town, she promised to be good."

I grinned. "I bet Sam didn't tell her how he was upgrading the system."

Her grin matched mine. "Of course not. He's probably hoping one of us will explain."

"Tell you one thing, it's not going to be me."

"I think we can leave that to Sam and Mary Kate." Since I was more than happy to let them tell Annie what we'd done and why, I agreed. "Now, how about letting me help you get dressed so you can come downstairs? Peggy dropped off dinner a few minutes ago and said she'd made all your favorites."

"That sounds wonderful."

Judith smiled and helped me freshen up some and then dress. With my arm in the immobilizer, I ended up wearing jeans and another oversized tee shirt that easily slipped over my head and arm. I was still barefoot when Judith slid an arm around my waist and helped me out of the room and down the stairs.

"Auntie Jax!" Ali bounced to her feet as we entered the kitchen and ran to me. Before her grandmother could warn her to be careful, the little girl stopped. She tilted her head to one side and studied me. Her brow furrowed and she took a hesitant step forward. "Auntie Jax, you look different."

Figuring she meant because I had one arm strapped to my side and hidden under the tee shirt, I looked down at her, trying to figure out how to explain. Before I could say anything, her grandmother spoke.

"What do you mean, Ali?"

"Her—" She paused for a moment and I wondered if she was

searching for the right word. "Her aura is different. It's usually green with little sparks of white. But it isn't now."

My brows winged up toward my hairline as Judith turned to me. Her eyes lost focus for a moment as she *looked* at me. Then she smiled and held a hand out to her granddaughter. Ali slipped her hand into her grandmother's and moved to stand next to her.

"Grandma?"

"Auntie Jax's aura is different, but it's nothing to worry about. It just means that she's growing in her talents."

"Cool." She looked at me with wide eyes. "Can you do something new, Auntie Jax?"

I grinned, relieved she looked at the change as something exciting and not something to fear. "I don't know, Ali. It's one of the reasons why I'm going to stay in town and work with Miss Serena, your grandma and Dr. Pat."

For a moment, she didn't say anything. Then she threw herself at me and wrapped her arms around my waist. Judith opened her mouth to say something and I shook my head. It was worth a little pain to see Ali's smile and know she looked forward to me staying in town.

"Are you going to be one of my teachers like Miss Serena and Grandma?"

"Would you like me to be?" I wasn't sure what I could teach her.

She nodded and then hurried back to her grandmother's side. "Can she, Grandma?"

"I think we need to talk with your mother and Miss Serena, but I don't see why not." Judith lightly ran her fingers through Ali's hair, her love for the little girl shining in her eyes.

"Can you teach me how to shift into a tiger, Auntie Jax?" Ali all but bounced with excitement. "I bet if you do, Mom and Daddy would let me get a tiger tattoo."

Quinn stopped in the doorway to the kitchen. Her jaw dropped and she glared at me over her daughter's head. I shook my head. If she thought I'd put that idea in her daughter's head . . . .

"Ali, that's one of my gifts. It isn't something you can just learn to do. Sort of like your mama trying to call water. She's a fire elemental with a touch of air talent. But, unless something's changed in the last few months, she can't call the water or earth. No matter how much she might want to call one of the other elements, she can't because that's not a talent she has. It's the same with being a walker. You have to be born with the ability and it is a very rare talent." Quinn's glare relented a little. I wasn't out of the woods yet. "As for my tattoos, they are part of my talent. These aren't tats like I'd get if I went to Dodger's Tattoos outside of town. He does regular tattoos. They wouldn't do anything to help me shift into one of my animal aspects."

Ali considered what I said. "Then where do you get them and why?"

"I think that's a lesson for another day, young lady. Aunt Jax was hurt last night and she needs to sit down."

"Are you going to be all right?" She reached for my hand and all but dragged me into the kitchen. Thankfully, Quinn anticipated her and got out of the way.

"I am. I hurt my shoulder and have to wear an immobilizer for a few days. But Dr. Pat's checked it out and said I'll be just fine."

"C'mon, Ali, help me fix a plate for Jax. Miss Peggy brought dinner for all of us a few minutes ago."

Ali gave me a quick hug and then hurried to do as her mother said. Relieved for the redirection, I took a seat at the kitchen table. As I did, I had a feeling this sort of conversation was something I needed to get used to if I stayed in Mossy Creek. Not that I minded. It was part of family and the O'Donnells had been and always would be my family by choice.

17

I stared at Quinn's tablet, not sure I trusted my eyes. She'd pulled up security video from the school, taken when Mia tried to get them to release Robbie to her. The video wasn't clear, the car too far away for that. But it was obvious Mia had gotten into the passenger side of a sedan. Someone drove her to the school and unless she'd used a ride share program, it meant she had help from someone local.

And my money was on Sawyer.

But that didn't make any sense.

Or did it?

I leaned back and considered the possibility. When we were kids, Sawyer did everything he could to make Annie's life miserable. Two years ago, he violated his oaths as an attorney and as a member of the DA's Office in an attempt to convict Catherine of a murder she didn't commit. He'd sworn vengeance when Annie made his actions public. He lost his job and the Bar sanctioned him.

But was that enough to make him seek out Mia and bring her to town to cause trouble?

"You're thinking awfully hard," Quinn spoke softly, as if afraid we might be overheard, even though Ali had gone to bed an hour ago.

Judith excused herself shortly after that and Lucas was downstairs in the basement media room watching football.

"Trying to put the pieces together." I paused the video and set it to playback once again. "I don't believe for one moment it's just coincidence that brings Mia to town right after Annie's hurt. The fact Sawyer showed up as her attorney at the hearing makes me wonder if he's not the one who took her to the school. But why? He has to know that's a dangerous game to play, especially if Annie puts it together. She will take him back before the Bar's disciplinary committee."

"I may have the answer." Quinn gently took the tablet from my hand and placed it screen down on the table. "You know Jason Alvarez isn't running for re-election. That's why Sawyer thinks he can be elected. But there's been a hitch in his plans, one I doubt he anticipated. According to the grapevine, Alvarez asked Annie to run and he promised to endorse her if she does."

I leaned back and blew out a breath. If Quinn was right. . . .

"What's Annie said?"

"Not much. Whenever I've brought it up, she redirected." Quinn sat back and stared into space for a moment. "Come to think of it, it's possible this is what she's been distracted by the last few weeks. What she wouldn't talk to me about."

I cursed softly. I knew what it meant and so did Quinn, even if she didn't say so. When Annie did that, it meant she was seriously considering something but wasn't ready—yet—to discuss it. The fact Sam hadn't mentioned it meant he either didn't know or that Annie asked him not to talk about it.

That could explain why Sawyer would bring Mia to town right now—assuming he was responsible for her sudden appearance. But it didn't explain what happened to Annie. Sawyer was a bully and I trusted him no further than I could throw him. But I didn't see him actually assaulting Annie.

"We need to know when Mia got to town."

Quinn nodded. "Lucas is working on it. So far, there's nothing to show she was anywhere near when Annie was hurt."

I toyed with my glass of iced tea, tracing circles on the tabletop. "I know Annie didn't have their security system on. But did any of her neighbors see anything or catch anything on video?"

Quinn shook her head. "The best Lucas has found are a couple of kids down the block who thought they saw a dark car parked several houses up the street from Annie's. But they didn't see anyone, and they couldn't tell him anything more than it was a dark colored car and they didn't think they'd seen it there before."

In other words, a dead end. Damn it.

"And last night?"

"Even less." She stood and paced the length of the kitchen, as restless as I felt. "He has asked the neighbors and businesses on possible routes the car may have taken to turn over any video they might have. But you know how that is."

I didn't, but I could guess. It would take time to get the videos and then more time to go through them. And all with no guarantee any of a payoff.

"What the hell are we supposed to do now, Quinn?" I was so far out of my comfort zone, it wasn't funny.

"You rest tonight. Rafe is keeping an eye on Annie's place. Sam is at the hospital with her and the kids are with the Caldwells. Tomorrow, we'll all meet at Annie's and be there when she gets home."

Before she could say anything else, she tensed. Her head cocked to one side, as if listening. Whether it was to the house—which she swore talked to her at times—or something else, I couldn't tell. Then she relaxed. A moment later, we listened as Judith greeted someone at the front door. Before I could ask, Quinn stood and moved to the refrigerator. When she handed me a beer, I knew this was probably not going to be something I liked.

"What now?" Resignation and frustration filled me. Couldn't I get one day, just one fucking day, without either running into my parents, Sam's ex or whoever the fuck shot me?

"I don't think we need to be worried."

Unfortunately, she didn't look convinced.

"But?"

199

"Miss Serena and the others are here." She paused, listening. "And your Aunt Bitsy."

My eyes went wide enough I'm surprised they didn't pop out of my head. I could guess why the others were here but Bitsy? Maybe I was still unconscious, and this was all some sort of weird dream I'd soon wake up from.

A few minutes later, we sat around the kitchen table. Quinn tried slipping out of the room only to be stopped by Miss Serena. I bent my head, hiding my smile, as Quinn did an excellent imitation of a kid told they had to sit with the adults and behave. Then, when someone touched my uninjured hand where it rested on the tabletop, I looked up and cringed as Dr. Pat nodded to my beer bottle and arched one brow.

"Quinn gave it to me."

Okay, it was childish, but it was the truth.

"When did you last have a pain pill?"

"I haven't." I hated them and wouldn't take one unless the pain became unmanageable, which it hadn't.

"Then just the one beer."

"Yes, ma'am."

She chuckled and grasped my hand, giving it a quick squeeze. "It's just that I worry about you."

"We all do." Aunt Bitsy sat next to me, her expression concerned as she took in my appearance.

"I'm fine. But I'd really like to know why everyone's here so late."

"We'll let Bitsy tell you why she's here in a minute." Miss Serena sipped her hot tea and smiled slightly in appreciation. "Very nice, Judith." She sipped again and then turned her attention to me.

I swallowed hard. The last time she looked at me like that, she told me I was the new guardian.

Please don't let her have another surprise for me. I'm not sure I can survive it.

"Annie is being released tomorrow at noon. We've done everything we can to prepare the house for her and the security system both Lucas and Rafe wanted has been installed."

I nodded.

"The four of us, as well as Quinn and the others, need to be there when she gets home."

I didn't gape at her. I didn't run for the hills even though I didn't want to be there when Annie figured out what we'd done. But it was close.

"Why?" Maybe not the most intelligent question. I had a good idea why we needed to be there. I simply didn't want to admit it.

"The house and grounds are still keyed to us, especially to you," Miss Serena explained. "We need to make sure they are attuned to the family. We will always have a tie to it, since we activated the wards, especially you, but it will be a distant tie, something that will reside in the backs of our minds."

"Sure. But you need to understand one thing. I am not, absolutely not, going to be the one to tell Annie what we've done or why."

And God help all of us if the house started talking to her. We might think she's an *Other*, but she didn't. With my luck, she'd kick my ass, and probably Quinn's, before we finished explaining everything we'd done.

"Don't worry, that will fall to Mary Kate and me," Miss Serena assured me.

"Now, you're coming upstairs with me so I can check your wound." Dr. Pat stood and helped me to my feet. "We'll be back in a few minutes," she added to the others.

Twenty minutes later, I once again sat at the kitchen table. Dr. Pat had not given me a clean bill of health but she'd assured everyone I was healing nicely. Then she excused herself, saying she needed to get some rest. Between the events of the night before and then a long day today, she was exhausted.

I halfway expected the others to leave, but they didn't. And Bitsy was still here. Her presence at this meeting was probably the last thing I expected—well after being named a guardian and I was still more than half hoping I'd wake up and find that had all been a dream. For the life of me, I couldn't figure out why Bitsy was here.

"We know you need to rest, Jax, but there are a few things we need to discuss before morning," Judith said as she poured out hot tea for everyone.

"I'm almost afraid to ask."

Not just almost. I was terrified. In the last week, my life had turned upside down and inside out. Much more and the rogue would turn coward and run for the hills.

Judith chuckled softly and patted my shoulder as she walked behind me before taking her place at the table. "It's nothing serious. Just a reminder that we need to start working regularly with you, Quinn and Meg. It is especially important where you're concerned. We need to get used to working together as four instead of three."

Okay, that wasn't so bad. At least I hoped it wasn't.

Quinn, on the other hand, paled and swallowed hard. Part of me wanted to tease her but I wouldn't. I understood how she felt. Besides, until a little more than a year ago, she hadn't realized she was an *Other*. This had to be messing with her. It certainly was me.

"What else?" Better to get it over with. Then Quinn and I could decide if we were staying or running to save our sanity if not for our lives.

"I guess that means it's my turn." Bitsy reached into her oversized purse and pulled our several folders. "Are you serious about moving back here?"

This was it. My last chance to break free from the trap Annie and Quinn had warned me about. Except was it really a trap when it was something I wanted?

I nodded. "Yeah, I'm serious."

"Good." She nodded for emphasis. "Here are the latest financial reports and other documents pertaining to our family holdings and the company. It includes the purchase agreement signed by our agent when he bought the shares from your father and the agreement about how the shares were then dispersed between the two of us." She placed one folder in front of me. "You need to study them and, while I don't mind voting your proxy, it is time for you to start taking an interest in the company."

"Bitsy." I shook my head and wondered if I could take back my decision to move home. "I'm not giving up being a vet."

"And I'm not asking you to." She patted my hand. "But I am asking you to learn what you can about the company your grandfather built and help me protect it."

I nodded. That I could do.

I hoped.

"All right." I looked down at the thick folder and closed my eyes, praying this was the worst of it. "What else?"

"I recommend you hire Meg to represent you, at least where the business is concerned. Annie's my attorney and this way, the law firm continues to protect our interests but we can still have our own representation if necessary."

"I'll talk with her in the morning." Assuming Bitsy hadn't already.

"Then that brings us to the last thing we want to discuss with you tonight, Jax."

Oh-oh. Miss Serena sounded serious as she looked from Judith to Bitsy and then to me.

"About?" I drawled it out, not really wanting to hear the answer.

"When you first entered town, what happened?"

I looked at Judith, not sure I understood the question. Then, as understanding dawned, my eyes went wide and I sucked in a quick breath.

"I felt the land—at least I think it was the land—responding. Just like it always does when I come back."

Miss Serena nodded, a small smile on her lips. "Good. That will make it easier."

"I don't understand." And that was putting it mildly.

"Promise you won't go running for the hills." Bitsy grinned and I groaned. They were up to something and I was definitely the target. It didn't help to see Quinn grinning, clearly pleased she wasn't the one they were aiming for just then.

"What?"

"The fact you felt the land greet you, for lack of a better word, is important. It means it recognized you as one of the guardians before we asked you to join us." Miss Serena smiled and, for the first time since she first broached the possibility of me becoming a town guardian, she looked relaxed.

"Why do I feel there is a *but* coming?"

"Because there is." At least Judith didn't try to deny it.

"What we're trying to say is you need to decide where you are going to live, Jax," Miss Serena said. "You are more than welcome to remain at the caretaker's house as long as you want. However, you aren't truly connected to the land there and that is going to be necessary sooner or later. Necessary because you are an Earth elemental and necessary because you are a guardian."

"And you know you're more than welcome to stay with me," Bitsy put in, grinning. "But I'm afraid my social life might scar you."

I groaned and beat my head none-too-gently against the table, ignoring the pain in my shoulder as I did. Then I looked at her, torn between laughing and crying. "Aunt Bitsy, your social life scarred me years ago, at least that's why my folks say."

She laughed gaily. "Your parents wouldn't know a healthy social— or sex—life if it bit them on their asses. I've sworn for years they must have found you on the doorstep because neither one can relax enough to actually enjoy sex."

I choked. Quinn giggled and then turned red trying not to actually laugh.

"Don't pay any attention to her, Jax." Judith fought not to laugh. "What we're getting at is all those are temporary solutions. You are going to need your own home, some place where you can connect with the land. The question is if you want a house in town or one with some land."

"Why don't you ask me something difficult?" I made no attempt to hide the irony on my comment. Overwhelmed, I climbed to my feet. When Quinn started to follow, I shook my head. I needed a few minutes to clear my head. Too much had happened too quickly. Less than a week ago, I had no intention of returning to Mossy Creek for anything more than a day or two here and there. Now, without really thinking about it, I'd agreed to not only move home but to become one of the town's guardians. I was upending my life and I'd done so without thinking it through. That wasn't like me. I might jump in without thinking when my friends needed me, but I didn't do it where my own life was concerned.

What the hell had I done?

"Jax?"

I turned and smiled at Bitsy. She stood in the doorway to the den, watching me in concern. I held out my hand and waited for her to join me. When she did, she slid her arms around me, hugging me carefully. Then she stepped back and looked at me, searching my face as she tried to figure out what I was thinking.

"Are you okay?"

I nodded. "Overwhelmed, if you really want to know." I smiled slightly.

"That's why they asked me to be here." She ran a reassuring hand down my arm and linked fingers with me. "No one is going to push you into doing something you aren't ready for. But you do need to hear us out. Just remember, the decisions are yours and we will respect whatever you decide."

"Thanks." I let her lead me back to the kitchen. As I returned to my seat at the table, Judith pressed a cold beer into my hand. Before I could say anything, she told me Dr. Pat didn't need to know. Laughing, I leaned over and kissed her cheek, glad I had her and the others in my life. "I'm going to start by telling you what I just told Aunt Bitsy. I'm feeling overwhelmed right now."

"Jax, that is the last thing we want," Miss Serena said. "Please, forgive us. We are so very excited to finally be complete. And, to be honest, we are thrilled you—Jax—are coming home. We've missed you. Because of that, we forget to think about how this must feel to you."

I smiled and stopped her before she could apologize again. "Then I need to be honest with you. I never wanted to leave town. I simply couldn't stay here and face the prospect of running into my parents every time I left my apartment. I'm still not thrilled with the idea, but I'm not going to let it stop me. Mossy Creek is home and my family is here." I reached for Bitsy's hand. "That family is each of you as well as the others who opened your homes and your hearts to me when I was growing up and who continue to do so now that I'm an adult. I want to be here, with you and yours."

Miss Serena blinked back tears and Judith smiled happily. But it was the way Bitsy slid her chair closer to mine and rested her head against my uninjured shoulder for a moment that convinced me I'd made the right decision.

"To answer your question, Judith, my dream home is out in the country. Somewhere I can commune with the earth but also where I can shift and run without fear of an overzealous neighbor calling animal control on me." I stuck my tongue out at Quinn as she gave me a thoughtful—and very mischievous—look. "But I have a ton of student loan debt and that is outside the realm of possibility right now. So I guess I need to find something in town that won't cost too much.

"*Ow!*". I glared at Bitsy who didn't look at all contrite for having slapped the back of my head.

"Quit being so stubborn." The hint of anger in her voice told me I'd better pay attention. "You have the money. Well, to be accurate, your trust fund has it. All you need to do is find a place you like and submit the information to the trustee." Now her eyes sparkled, and I knew I'd been outmaneuvered. "Assuming you don't go completely off the rails, that trustee—me—will approve the purchase."

I swallowed hard as the feeling of being trapped intensified. It didn't matter I wanted to move back. I hated being manipulated. It would be simple to shift and run for the hills. Instead, I shook off the image of my coyote self disappearing into the trees and tried to consider the situation like the responsible adult they seemed to think I was.

"All right." I ran a hand over my face and inhaled. Please don't let this a huge mistake. "When I find someplace that fits my needs, I'll let you know. And, yes, it needs to be someplace with land. Someplace I can relax after work and where I can have a few horses."

"If you don't mind having some help, Serena and I know of a place not far from her hers that is about to come up on the market. We can take you to see it in the morning."

I didn't groan, but it was a close thing. "Please tell me you haven't done any of what Quinn calls the woo-woo stuff."

A glance at her told me Quinn didn't know whether to laugh or look insulted. I grinned and shrugged my good shoulder.

"No woo-woo stuff," Miss Serena assured me with a smile. "The previous owner passed away a year or so ago. The property has been tied up in probate. That's been settled now, and Marla was talking about it at Wanda's the other day."

That made sense. If there was any place in Mossy Creek that rivaled the café as gossip central, it was Wanda's Beauty Salon. It was the place to go if you wanted big hair along with your dose of everyone else's business. Add in Marla Whitaker, one of the local real-tors, and I had a feeling they had a list of places for me to look at.

"Before you ambush her with anything else, I promised Dr. Pat I'd make sure she got some rest."

I looked at Quinn and considered kissing her for coming to my rescue. She smiled and gave a slight nod. She knew what I felt. She'd been through her own version of it when she returned to Mossy Creek.

What was it about this town making sure its wayward children all came home?

"Why don't you meet me at my office before you head over to Annie's?" Bitsy suggested as she climbed to her feet. "And bring the information about the property if you like it."

Afraid of another head slap, I nodded.

I watched as Judith walked my aunt and Miss Serena out. Then I turned to Quinn. "What the hell just happened?"

"Mossy Creek." She grinned and linked arms with me. "C'mon. Let's get you upstairs. I have a feeling tomorrow's going to be longer than either of us anticipate."

18

Shortly before two, Rafe picked me up at Quinn's house. To say I felt like I'd been on a roller coaster is putting it mildly. My shoulder hurt, my head hurt, and it felt as if the world had been turned upside down. Possibly even inside out.

Hell, this might be an alternate universe. I certainly felt like it was.

"Well, how did the house hunt go?" he asked as he pulled away from the curb.

"Oh gawd. You wouldn't believe me if I told you."

"Try me."

"Don't say I didn't warn you."

He chuckled and rested a hand on my thigh. Well, he did ask for it.

The house hunt had been anything but a hunt. It quickly became apparent Miss Serena and Judith had been planning this for who knows how long. Oh, they hadn't done any "woo-woo". At least none that I could detect. But they made it clear they'd been on the lookout for homes for me should I decide to return to town. When I screwed up enough courage to ask about it, Miss Serena explained they had known the time was coming when those of us who left town would be coming back. Meg had been the wildcard. Quinn's situation was settled when the house accepted her. Annie was taken care of by her grandfather's bequest. That left me and Bitsy warned them I'd be the hardest to crack—because of my parents and my stubborn streak. Well, she had that much right. So the two of them, with help from Dr. Pat when she had time, kept their ears to the ground and knew whenever an appropriate place came on the market. Right now, the old Taggart place was, in their opinions, the best for me.

If I liked it and if the land talked to me.

I hadn't expected anything to happen. Hell, who am I kidding? I didn't really want anything to happen. The feeling of being maneuvered was growing and I didn't like it. Then Judith turned onto a private drive and everything changed. The land did more than talk to me. Its energies rose up, enveloping me, welcoming me. The trees lining the drive whispered how I was home, home, home. Birds took flight but, instead of winging away from us, they flew around the car, darting near and then veering off, following us as we drove further onto the property.

In the back of my mind, I kept hearing "Home, you're home, you're here," or variations of it. When I mentioned it to Judith and Miss Serena, I fully expecting them to pat me on the head and take me to Dr. Pat for a mental exam. Instead, they smiled and nodded. Apparently, this was what they hoped for. Miss Serena then explained that connection would make it easier to make my home there like what she had or what Quinn did. And that was important for the guardians because it was our first line of defense if anything endangered the town.

"It sounds perfect, Jax. So why are you acting like you're ready to run away without a backwards glance?"

"Because I finally understand what Annie meant when she kept grumbling about her grandfather reaching out from his grave to manipulate her." If I could have crossed my arms and slumped down like a sulky teen, I would have.

He glanced across the cab of his pickup, his expression worried.

"The property has been in the Taggart family for the last fifty years. A title search, something my busybody aunt already ran since she knew where Miss Serena and Judith were taking me, shows the original owners were one of the founding families." I shook still had a hard time accepting it. "Rafe, one of those who lived there was an original guardian."

She was also one of my ancestors.

And I was getting pretty damned tired of Fate hitting me over the head with a metaphorical two-by-four.

"Damn, no wonder you look like you're not sure which way is up." His hand lightly squeezed my thigh, a little thing but enough to let me know he was there for me.

"Oh, you haven't heard it all yet."

Hearing the mix of resignation, frustration and disbelief in my voice, he pulled over and turned on the truck's flashers. He turned in his seat and waited. I reached for the hand resting on my thigh, linking my fingers with his.

"Bitsy and Meg were waiting for us at Bitsy's office." I should have known something was up when I saw Meg. But I was still reeling from everything I'd felt at the property. It didn't dawn on me that I was about to get hit by that cosmic two-by-four again. "Let's put it this way, you are now looking at Mossy Creek's new large animal vet. Miss Serena and Meg, not to mention Bitsy and the trust, are my investors. The clinic will be built on land that borders the Taggart place." Maybe I should start calling it my place since Bitsy was already working on finalizing the sale, but I wasn't ready for that.

"Personally, I think it sounds wonderful." He grinned and lifted my hand to his lips. "But I can see why you're feeling overwhelmed. Are you sure about this?"

I nodded. "I am. I just didn't expect it to all be settled so quickly."

"If you don't mind me being a bit selfish, I'm glad it is." His smile sent shivers through me.

Maybe all this wasn't going to be so bad after all.

"Want to go see the place after we're done at Annie's?" I tried to sound sexy but instead sounded like a scared teen. There's a reason I don't do sexy.

"I'd love to." He checked the mirrors, turned off the flashers and pulled away from the curb. "Have you given any thought to who you're going to ask to build your clinic?"

I nodded, relaxing. That was the one decision that had been easy to make. "Yeah.." I glanced at him, grinning. "How busy are you and Sam?"

He flashed me a smile before turning his attention back to the road. "I think we'll be able to find time. Especially if you and I get a head start on it tonight."

"Really?" I all but purred it. Damn, there might be something good come out of me staying in town after all.

He didn't say anything, but I saw the satisfied look on his face. I bet myself I could make him even more satisfied once we were done at Annie's.

"Jax, be honest. Are you okay with all this? Everyone is expecting you to just upend your life and they really haven't given you a chance to think it through."

"Thank you." Now it was my time to reach for his hand and lift it to my lips. "I'll admit I feel manipulated. But what choice to I have?"

"You could say no and go back your life."

I shook my head. "Not really." I kissed his knuckles again. "You see, I figured something out over the couple of days. I want to do this. It feels right. This is what I'm supposed to do."

It went beyond being here and keeping Annie safe. It even went beyond completing whatever fate had in store for me. Of course, I'd really appreciate it if the storm I felt gathering didn't turn out to be as bad as I feared.

"Besides." I might as well put all my cards on the table. I only hoped I wasn't about to make a fool out of myself. "I'd like the chance to see what develops between the two of us." I ducked my head, a blush heating my cheeks.

"Me too." He grinned and once again pulled over. Looking around, I realized we were a block from Annie's house. "I want you to know two things. The first is you make me feel whole. It's like I was missing a part of me before we met. The second is I meant it when I said I had your back. I always will. It doesn't matter why you need me. Whether it is as part of your duties as guardian or to help you renovate your new house. I will be there with you."

"Rafe."

"Shh." He reached over and placed a finger against my lips. "I mean it. Besides." Now he grinned. "I know the Taggart place. It's a beautiful house and I envy you all that land. I've always wanted a place where I can have a bunch of dogs, a few horses and no neighbors close enough to worry about."

"That's what I love about it." Well, one of the things. "If you meant it earlier, I'd love to take you by after we finish. I still have the keys, so we can do a walkthrough. That would give us a chance to talk about some of the changes I already have in mind." And maybe the chance to do a few other things as well.

"Sounds good. But we'd better get to Annie's and Sam's before they send out a search party."

I nodded, part of me wishing we could postpone it. I wasn't sure I was ready to go over everything with Annie. Hell, I might not ever be ready to. She was absolutely going to blow a gasket when she realized what all we'd been up to.

Half an hour later, Ali and Robbie were sent upstairs to play. Annie narrowed her eyes at me and crooked one finger in a "come here" motion. I shook my head. I didn't know what I dreaded more: telling her what we'd done to her house and property or telling her I'd been shot.

"Jax."

She spoke softly, almost gently. But it didn't fool me. Not one bit.

I shook my head again and leaned against Rafe. Then I felt him chuckle. Traitor. Well, I could deflect as well as the anyone.

"Did Sam tell you about the new security measures?" I asked, smiling sweetly when Sam looked at me with something close to panic.

"N-no. I thought I'd let all of you do it."

Annie looked at him and then at the rest of us. Suspicion turned to concern. "Sam?"

"Honey, they need to explain."

"Grandma?" Now she looked at Mary Kate. Which was much better than looking at me.

"Annie." Miss Serena moved to sit on the sofa and reached for her hand. "While the men updated your security system, we added a layer of protection as well."

"We who?"

"Pat, Judith, Jax and me. Quinn, Meg, Amy and your grandmother helped."

Annie looked at each of us in turn. I could almost see her brain at work as she started putting it all together. Before Miss Serena could say anything else. Annie stopped her. We waited, not knowing if there would be a demand for an explanation or an explosion.

"What did you do?"

"We did only what we felt necessary to keep you and the rest of the family safe," Mary Kate said.

"Grandma." Annie drew out the word, sounding like a mix between an irritated mother and a sulky teen.

You're home. You're safe. Home. Safe.

Annie's eyes grew wide and she looked frantically around the room trying to locate the source of the voice. Quinn and I exchanged grins before bursting out laughing. Meg leaned against Drew and buried her face against his chest, her shoulders shaking as she tried not to laugh too loudly. But it was the sounds of Ali and Robbie racing downstairs that shut us all up.

"Mom! Did you hear it? Did you hear the house?" Robbie asked, excitement lighting his expression.

Miss Serena smiled serenely but it was Camille's reaction that surprised me. Pride shone on her face as she looked at her grandson. Interesting. Was there something about Annie's mother-in-law I hadn't realized?

"Oh my god, what the hell did you do?" Annie then did the one thing I hadn't expected. She looked to me for the answer instead of Miss Serena or Mary Kate.

Rafe's lips brushed the top of my head, reassuring me not only that I could do this but that he was there for me. I patted his hand at my waist and then stepped forward. As I did, I braced myself. This could very well be one of the most difficult things I've ever done.

"Annie, of all of us, Quinn's probably the only one who knows what you're feeling right now." I sat on the edge of the coffee table, my knees almost touching hers. "Before I answer your question, I need you to answer something for me and I need you to be completely honest. Did you hear the house just now?"

We waited, all eyes on her, as the implications of what I asked hit her. She paled and reached for Sam's hand. With her other hand, she pulled Robbie close. They anchored her, reminding her the world hadn't gone completely insane. The only question was if she'd still think that way by the time we were done.

Instead of saying anything, she nodded once.

"I heard it too, Dr. Jax." Robbie definitely thought it more exciting than his mother did.

"That's really cool, Robbie." I grinned and then turned my attention back to Annie. "Miss Serena can explain this better than I can, but the short version is that the four of us, with help from the others she named, activated certain wards around the house and land. They are keyed to you and your family." Or would be once we finished the binding. But she wasn't ready to hear that.

If possible, she paled even more.

"Are you saying my house is now like Quinn's?"

The look she turned on her twin brother spoke volumes. She wanted to know why he'd let this happen. Poor Drew simply held up a hand and shook his head, denying having anything to do with it all. Not that I blamed him. I'd deny it too if I could.

"Not exactly." I waited until she looked at me again. "Annie, we both know Quinn's house is unique. It has its own personality. So will this one. But I'm confident telling you it won't be as vocal or as much of a trickster as hers."

Quinn rolled her eyes. Until her talents began manifesting, the house had been a major thorn in her side. She never knew if it would slam the gate in her face, lock her out or actually let her in. Now it was most definitely her house and she still wasn't quite sure she could trust it.

"B-but I'm not an *Other*. I shouldn't be able to hear it." Then she all but grabbed Robbie to her and I knew she remembered him saying he'd heard the house. "Jax, what the hell did you do?"

"Me?" I tried to sound affronted. Instead, I sounded like I felt—worried she'd find some reason to blame all this on me.

"Don't you dare blame her, Julianna Grissom Caldwell," Mary Kate scolded.

Annie swallowed hard and ducked her head. We all knew when Mary Kate called her by her full name, she was in trouble.

"Grandma."

"Don't you grandma me, young lady."

If I could have slipped out of the room and out of the house, I would. Mary Kate was more than formidable in this mood. It was where Annie learned how to do it.

"Jax wasn't the only one involved in this. We all." She waved at everyone gathered in the room, most everyone looking like I felt. "We all had a hand in it. Some of them, like Rafe, Sam, Drew and Lucas saw to updating your mundane security system. There will be no more chances of someone getting into the house without you knowing it and without a camera catching their image.

"The rest of us did what we do best. We raised arcane protections that you wouldn't feel if you weren't an *Other*. You've spent your entire life denying your talents. It's time you grow up and embrace them. It's not like we're asking you to call Fire like Quinn."

"But I don't have a talent." She made air quotes around "talent".

"Don't give me that." Mary Kate actually snorted in disgust. "You have what your great-grandmother would have called the gift of the gab. It's a more empathetic talent that helps you say what people need to hear. Think of it as a healing talent, one of the spirit and soul instead of the body."

"Jax?"

"What she said." Okay, a bit childish, but I couldn't say it any better than Mary Kate did.

"And Robbie?"

"The house was welcoming all of you. I'm sure Sam heard it as well." Miss Serena glanced at him and he nodded.

"God, I feel like I've fallen down the rabbit hole." Annie ran her hands over her face. Then, when she looked up, her eyes narrowed, and she reached for my uninjured hand. "What happened?"

"Nothing important." I fought the urge to pin everyone else with a look warning them not to say anything else. "Are we okay?"

"Yeah." She started to say something and then stopped when Dr. Pat stepped forward.

"You need to rest for a bit, Annie."

"Dr. Pat," she pouted.

"She's right, love. I'm sure Jax and the others will answer all your questions later."

We nodded, our heads bobbing up and down. The others might not welcome the respite, but I sure did.

"Don't think this is over," Annie said as she climbed to her feet.

"I promise we will answer all your questions. But only after you get some rest." Mary Kate laid a gentle hand against Annie's cheek. "Shall I come up with you?"

"Please." She looked at the rest of us. "Thank you."

"We're family." I smiled and stood, cradling my injured arm in my good one. "Why don't we meet here for breakfast in the morning? I'm sure Miss Peggy will be more than happy to feed us, especially if we let her stay and listen in."

Annie laughed and nodded. Then she started up the stairs, Sam on one side and Mary Kate on the other. Robbie followed, wanting to make sure his mom really was all right.

"What now?" I asked once I heard the bedroom door close.

"You go home and get some rest," Dr. Pat said firmly. "I know you didn't get any this morning." Now she looked at Miss Serena. "No lessons for her until tomorrow."

"Agreed." Miss Serena stood and smiled at me. "You've done so well, Jax. I'm proud of you. But Pat is right. You need to rest and heal. Rafe, please make sure she does."

Quinn chuckled as I rolled my eyes. Rafe, on the other hand, simply nodded. "Yes, ma'am."

"We'll let you know what time to be here in the morning, Jax," Miss Serena said. "Now run before Annie thinks of a reason for you to stay."

That was all the encouragement I needed. I reached for Rafe's hand and led him outside. After everything that happened today, I needed time alone.

No, I needed time alone with him. He'd let me talk or just stare into space. But he would be there, ready whenever I was. that was what I needed.

"Where to?" he asked as he slid in behind the steering wheel.

"We've still got a couple of hours of daylight. Let's go to the Taggart place. You can tell me what you think. Why don't you let me buy you dinner afterwards?"

"Sounds good, but dinner will be on me."

"Rafe."

"Hush. I bought steaks and fixings this morning. I can grill them up and then we can relax. You look like you've been through the wringer today."

I'd argue, but I felt like I'd been through a wringer a couple of times. "Thanks. That sounds wonderful."

19

One week later, one very long week that included a run-n with my parents, meeting with Sam and Rafe about building my clinic, dealing with the paperwork on my new house (and boy was I still having trouble with that), working with Miss Serena and Judith on a daily basis and Dr. Pat when she could join us, I felt like I was meeting myself coming and going. The one constant, the one very welcome constant, was Rafe. Every evening, we had dinner together. Sometimes, we went to the café. One night we drove into Dallas. Other evenings we ate at his place or the caretaker's house where I was staying until I closed on the Taggart place. Some nights we spent together. Others, we'd talk, go for walks and then go our separate ways. He let me set the pace for our relationship, probably because he realized I'd run for the hills if much more happened.

Annie was recovering nicely. Her headaches were less frequent, and her strength was returning. So was her stubborn streak. Every day she called, wanting to know when I was coming over. Now that she knew I planned on staying in town, she pummeled me with questions about my future plans, the house and clinic, the lessons Miss Serena and Mary Kate had her doing, my role as a guardian and, all too often, Rafe. At least she no longer argued about having a house that talked to her. Between it and the security system the guys updated, she felt safe. And, when she left the house, she did so armed. For once, she wasn't taking any chances and everyone approved.

But that's where the good news ended. Lucas and his deputies had yet to make an arrest in the attack on Annie. They had no forensic evidence, at least none Lucas was talking about. The investigation was open but didn't seem to be going anywhere. Quinn assured us he wasn't giving up and that this wasn't that unusual. Intellectually, I knew she was right. But that didn't stop me from wanting to take matters in my own hands.

Especially since I couldn't shake the feeling that something bad was about to happen.

Part of that stemmed from the fact Mia hadn't left the area. She might not have violated the TRO, but it had been a close thing on a couple of occasions. She'd been seen parked down the street from Annie's office. On another occasion, she foolishly walked into the café, expecting to be served. Miss Peggy, Janny and half a dozen patrons formed a human wall just inside the door. Miss Peggy then told her in no uncertain terms she was not welcome. When Mia threatened to sue her for denying her service, Miss Peggy did exactly what anyone who knows her would have expected. She told Mia she'd rather close the café for good than serve the likes of her. From all accounts, Mia flounced—yes, flounced—out, threatening to talk to her attorney and take Miss Peggy for everything she had.

Lucas knew about the threat before Mia drove off, thanks to half a dozen people texting him. Janny even sent a video of the encounter. By the time Mia's car turned the corner two blocks up, an unmarked sheriff's car was on her tail. Unfortunately, the deputy lost her half an hour later when they got separated in traffic on the highway leading to Dallas. Since then, no one had seen her and that made me itchy as hell. I knew down in my bones she hadn't left town.

Then there was Sawyer. Friday afternoon, just before end of business, he officially filed for DA. The press was waiting as he walked out of the courthouse. Standing on the steps, he puffed up and talked about how he was the best for the future of the county. He may have made mistakes in the past, but he'd learned from them. He promised to be hard on crime and do all he could to help push the county into a future we could all be proud of.

I had no doubt his idea of what that might be was vastly different from mine.

"Are you ready to leave, Miss Serena?"

She looked up from the oversized picnic basket on the kitchen table. The house smelled of freshly baked pies: apple, peach and something I couldn't quite identify. The part of the table not covered by the basket held loaves of fresh bread. A smile touched her lips and she motioned me closer.

"Almost. If you would carry out the cooler, I'll finish packing all this up."

I looked at everything and wondered how in the world we'd fit it, not to mention her Belgium Malinois and the two of us, into my Camaro. As if reading my mind, Miss Serena pulled a set of keys from her pocket and tossed them to me. I reached out, catching them instinctively. Then, seeing the logo on the keyring, I groaned. Meg had warned me, but I didn't think I had anything to worry about. After all, I had my own car. Not to mention the Porsche Aunt Bitsy still refused to take back. So there was no reason for me to need to borrow a car from Miss Serena, much less the Land Rover. Yet here I stood with those keys in hand.

Maybe I'd get lucky and all I'd have to do is pull it around front. Surely, Miss Serena planned to drive into town.

I pulled the Land Rover around from the garage and started loading everything. By the time I finished, Miss Serena was there, Athena on a lead. We loaded her into the back where her travel cage was secured. Then, to my dismay, Miss Serena settled in the front passenger seat and waited for me to climb in behind the wheel. Like it or not, I was the designated driver, at least for now.

As we neared the house, I felt the wards reaching out, as if sensing our approach. There was a flare as we parked in front and stepped over the boundary. Then everything settled down and the sense of belonging I felt the night we set the wards returned. Miss Serena told me it would ease as the wards strengthened their ties with Annie and her family, but I would always feel them since I helped make them. That reassured me because the connection would let me know if there was trouble.

Of course, once Annie realized the guardians were tied into her early warning system, she might not appreciate it. Hell, I wasn't going to appreciate it if it warned me every time she and Sam had a fight or the kids started picking on one another.

"Relax, Jax," Miss Serena said softly as she lifted the picnic basket from the backseat. "Annie and the kids are safe and we're going to keep them that way."

"Damn straight we are."

I shook off my concerns and let Athena out, clipping her lead to her collar. Then I lifted the cooler out. By the time I turned, Rafe was there. He planted a light kiss on my lips and took the cooler from me.

"Everything okay?" he asked as we strolled down the driveway toward the backyard.

"Yeah." I bumped my hip against his and let myself relax. "Just tired and frustrated. But I promised Miss Serena I'd try to enjoy myself."

"Good." He looked at me and I knew he had something on his mind.

"What?"

"How about we get out of here as soon as we can?" I arched one brow even as I wanted nothing more than to say yes. He blushed slightly and I grinned broadly. He could be so cute when he realized how transparent he'd been. He quickly looked around, making sure no one could hear. "Yes, that's one reason I want to get out of here."

"Only one reason?" I teased.

He closed his eyes and shook his head before continuing. "The other reason is I have some preliminary plans for the reno on your house I'd like to go over with you. Bitsy said you'll be signing the final papers Monday. So there's no reason to delay."

I gulped as a flicker of fear raced through me. It was really happening. I was about to be a homeowner and business owner and—oh my god—an adult.

"Sure." I hoped he didn't see how uncertain all this made me.

"Buck up, Doc. You can do this."

With those two simple sentences, my fear receded. I slipped my arm through his and leaned my head against his shoulder. Over the past week, he'd begun calling me "Doc" more often, usually when we were alone. When I asked about it, he said Jax was the rogue. Doc was who I really was, the caring, responsible woman. The rogue was part of me, one he never wanted me to lose, but it was Doc who kept the rogue in check and who allowed me to be the woman I was.

And yes, my heart melted a little when he said it.

"Thanks." Another hip bump. Then Ali and Robbie raced around the corner of the house, telling us to hurry up. "We're coming," I laughed.

The afternoon proved to be exactly what we all needed. Ali and Robbie played with the dogs while the rest of us took turns looking after the twins. Annie lay on a chaise lounge, our appointed supervisor. She pouted some, telling us she could get her own drink and could most certainly change her babies' diapers. Then, when little Luke filled his diaper with what his father called "toxic waste", she laughed and reminded us we said her only job was to supervise. So one of us could clean up the little boy. The men looked on in panic as the rest of us, including Ali and Robbie, found other things to be very busy with. Finally, Rafe lifted Luke in his arms and took him inside.

"You're falling for him." Wonder and approval filled Annie's voice as she reached for my hand.

"Yeah, I am."

She grinned and I groaned. I didn't need her playing matchmaker. Not that I had much choice, judging by the look on her face.

"Don't worry." The mischief turned to understanding. "Been there, done that and didn't like it. Just remember I'm here for you."

I slipped an arm around her shoulders and hugged her. "I know and thanks." That was the opening I needed. "We're not going to talk business, but I need to tell you one thing. With you laid up, I hired Meg to take care of a few matters for me. Part of that is dealing with the legalities around me opening my clinic. But she is also going to deal with my parents if they keep trying to cause trouble. It's not that I don't trust you to do it, but you are also Bitsy's attorney and we thought it best to avoid the appearance of a conflict of interest."

She smiled and nodded. "I know. Meg and I talked about it. Don't worry. I agree with the decision."

"No business allowed," Quinn said with a grin as she joined us.

"Then you'd better tell that to those three." Meg nodded to where Rafe, Sam and Drew stood in the middle of the backyard, motioning here and there.

"What are they talking about?" Annie asked even though her tone said she had a pretty good idea.

"Whether or not you should put in a pool."

"Just what we need with three kids and a pack of dogs." She sighed and then smiled. "It would be nice, though."

"Dr. Jax!"

I looked to where Robbie and Ali stood near the men. Instead of looking at the ground, planning where a pool should go, the kids seemed to be studying the trees. Annie simply shrugged when I looked to see if she had any idea what they were up to. I set my beer bottle down on the nearest table and went to see what my godson wanted.

"Mr. Rafe, you too," Robbie added as I neared.

It was my turn to shrug as Rafe looked at me.

"What's up, Robbie?" I asked as Rafe joined us.

Robbie looked at Ali who nodded in encouragement.

"Dr. Jax, Mr. Rafe, do you think you could build me a treehouse up there?" He pointed at one of the large oak trees as Sam and Drew joined us.

"I didn't know you wanted a tree house," Sam commented. "I'd be happy to build you one, son."

I know, Daddy, but you need to take care of the twins and Mom." Robbie sounded so grown-up. "It's not that I don't want you to do it, but they are more important."

Sam dropped to a knee and pulled his son close. As he did, I reached for Rafe's hand. I had a feeling this was a conversation the two needed to have but that Sam might need our support.

"Robbie, they are important but so are you. I never want you to doubt that."

The little boy smiled and nodded. "I don't, Daddy. But I'm not a kid anymore. I can do stuff for myself. The twins can't. They need you and Mom a lot more than I do."

"You are my little man and always will be," Sam said softly as Annie and the others joined us. Tears glistened in Annie's eyes as she knelt next to Sam and reached for their son.

"I've got an idea," Rafe said and all eyes turned to him. "Why don't we all help build the treehouse? Your dad, Uncle Drew, Lucas and I can do all the heavy lifting. Doc and I can design it for you—with lots of help from you and Ali." He grinned as excitement lit the kids' expressions. "We can even start on the plans today."

"When can we build it?" Robbie wanted to know.

"Let's get the plans drawn up and then we can figure that out. Okay?"

"Daddy?"

"I think that's an awesome idea. Mom?" He looked at Annie who nodded in agreement.

"Can we start now?"

"Sure." I laughed as first Robbie and then Ali launched themselves at me, wrapping their arms around my waist. "How about we go find some paper and pencils and we can get started?" Why Robbie wanted my help designing the treehouse was beyond me. But I'd do just about anything to see that smile on his face.

Later, after eating, we sent the kids inside to watch a movie. The rest of us sat around the firepit Sam and Rafe built several months ago. Dogs rested at the feet of Quinn, Annie, Meg and Miss Serena. For several minutes, a companionable silence settled around us, interrupted only by the normal night sounds. I leaned back, Rafe's arm about my shoulders, and relaxed. This was my family.

And, like it or not, Mossy Creek was my home.

Now it was time to talk about the two hundred pound gorilla in the room.

"Annie, have you made a decision?" I asked.

Everyone looked at her, waiting for her answer. For a moment, she glared at me. Then she sighed. I'd put her on the spot, something she didn't like. Not that I blamed her. Even so, it was past time for her decide what her next step in town was going to be.

I'm not sure." She climbed to her feet and crossed the deck to the cooler. We watched as she pulled out a beer. A moment later, she twisted off the top and tossed it into the trash. Then, as if realizing we weren't going to let her off the hook, she sighed. "Seriously, I really don't know what to do."

"Annie," Sam chided.

Oops. Apparently, they'd had this discussion before.

"If you're worried about the practice, don't," Meg said. "As DA you can still have a civil practice. If I need help on the criminal side, we'll hire someone."

"It's not just that."

"Then what?" Quinn asked.

"Robbie and the twins, Sam, how our lives will be impacted by this. I don't want to put them through a campaign, especially not one against Sawyer."

I understood. Hell, I figured we all did.

"Sam, what do you think she should do?"

He moved to his wife's side and pulled her close. "I think she should do what she wants and not worry about the campaign. We stood up to Sawyer before an we will again. But only if this is what she wants."

"So, what do you want, Annie?" I asked.

"I don't want Sawyer to run unopposed."

"You're not answering the question," Quinn said. "What do you want to do?"

Annie blew out a breath. "Would you be satisfied if I said I don't want him to be DA?"

"No," Rafe said.

"Annie, let me put it to you this way." I patted Rafe's hand before standing. Then I lifted my now empty beer bottle in question. He nodded and I crossed to the cooler, using the time to gather my thoughts. "You just admitted you don't want that little prick to be DA. Have you heard about anyone else running against him?"

She shook her head.

"Neither have any of the rest of us, including Miss Olivia." And if she hadn't heard, that meant no one else planned on running. "I think the explanation why is pretty clear. Everyone knows Jason Alvarez will throw his support to you if you decide to run. It's clear everyone else is waiting to see what you do. Unfortunately, because of everything that's happened, you postponed making the decision and that gave Sawyer the chance to be the first to file."

"Don't remind me," she grumbled.

"Annie, I'm not criticizing. Far from it." I returned to Rafe's side and handed him one of the two beers I held. "But I am saying you can't put off making a decision any longer."

"Sam, are you sure?" She looked at him and I knew she halfway wanted him to say no.

"I told you, Annie. I'll support whatever decision you make."

"I'm not going to be able to do this on my own."

Meg grinned and high-fived Quinn. Then she sobered and looked at her law partner and sister-in-law. "Your grandmother already has everything ready to file. Well, she and Miss Olivia. Mary Kate said to tell you she worked enough political campaigns with your grandfather that she figures she can run yours with her eyes closed."

I laughed, thinking about how Sawyer would probably piss his pants to learn that not only was Mary Kate helping Annie but Miss Olivia as well. Both were good friends with his mother, and they wouldn't hesitate to let her know if he stepped out of line.

"I'll need a treasurer." Annie sounded almost triumphant, as if not having one just this moment meant she wouldn't have to run.

Now it was my turn to smile. One of the things I discussed with Bitsy just that morning was the possibility of Annie running for DA. "That's covered as well. Bitsy will meet you at the bank first thing

Monday morning to set up an account for the campaign. Said she thought being your finance manager would be fun."

Annie groaned, all too familiar with my aunt and her idea of fun.

"It is your decision, Annie," Miss Serena said. "But we all think you would be good for the office and for the town."

"I'm still not sure."

"Annie, Jason Alvarez has offered to not only endorse you but to campaign for you," Meg interrupted. "You know he wouldn't do either if he had any concerns. I know you've been approached by the county bar association to run and that the sheriff's department has asked as well." She winked at her husband and Drew grinned broadly, clearly enjoying his twin sister's discomfort. "So why are you really hesitating?"

The moment Meg asked, I knew the answer. A mental finger snap sounded as all the pieces fell into place. She was afraid of being manipulated. Since I knew that feeling all too well, especially since returning to town, I understood.

"Annie, this isn't like when you came back to defend your mother." I handed Rafe my beer and climbed to my feet. Annie watched as I approached. "This isn't Judge Caldwell springing his *little surprises* on you. Nor is it your grandfather trying to reach out from his grave to direct your life. But it is something that's in your blood. The only question is if you want to do it or not. Take Sawyer out of the equation and ask yourself if you want to be DA. But answer honestly."

We waited, the silence drawing out. Finally, Annie tipped up her beer bottle and took a long draw, as if bracing herself for what she was about to say.

"I won't be able to do it by myself."

I grinned, barely resisting the urge to pump my fist in the air. "I think we've made it pretty clear you won't have to."

"Then tell your aunt I'll take her up on her offer. Guess that means I need to call my grandmother as well." Before any of us could respond, she leveled a serious look in my direction. "Now, what about you? Care to share your plans for the future? I know you've been up to something but neither my law partner nor anyone else will tell me what."

"Oops?" I glanced around, considering shifting and running for the hills.

"Right, oops." Annie glared at me. "Why don't you start with why you were wearing a sling the first of the week?"

"Let's just say there was a complication when we were setting the wards here. Nothing serious and I'm well now." Or as close to it as possible, thanks to Dr. Pat's care and healing sessions with Miss Serena and Judith. "And you know the rest of it. I'm moving back. Hell, I've bought a house, hired your husband and Rafe here to design a clinic for me and do some renovations at the house. On top of that, I'm working for Miss Serena in the meantime."

"And?" she prompted, crossing her arms under her breasts.

I rolled my eyes. She was in a cross between stern mother and lawyer mode. That meant she wouldn't be put off. But it didn't mean I wouldn't try.

"And what?"

She actually stamped her foot in frustration. I grinned, wisely looking over my shoulder at Rafe so Annie couldn't see.

Before I could answer, the defenses we'd built into the land and house came to life. I felt like a train slammed into me. Even as I dropped to one knee, fighting to make sense of all the energies suddenly blazing to life around me, I heard Miss Serena gasp. Someone—Quinn?—asked if she was all right. Rafe appeared at my side, his hands carefully lifting me to my feet. Annie reacted on instinct. I *felt* her pulling on her ties to the defenses, trying to figure out what happened.

"Annie, Sam, get inside. Keep the kids there. Take the dogs with you," I rasped. "Miss Serena, Drew, go with them."

"No!" Annie pulled against Sam's hold on her.

"Don't argue," I snarled. "The wards will hold but you need to reassure the kids and keep the twins calm." I didn't wait to see if they obeyed. Instead I turned to the others. "Quinn, you're with me. You too, Rafe. Lucas, Meg, you're our backup." God, I wished Judith and

Dr. Pat were here. Between them, Miss Serena and me we'd be able to deal with whatever happened—I hoped.

With Annie still arguing, I took off at a dead run for the front of the house. As I did, my senses seemed to go on high alert. Nothing looked out of the ordinary. No fires, no explosions, no one trying to drive a tank through the front door. But something had caused the wards to come to life. The only question was what and if we'd be able to deal with it.

My feet slipped on the grass as I rounded the corner. Before I could stumble, Rafe righted me. With his hand on my arm, we ran side-by-side. A few moments later, we slid to a stop in front of the house. He might not be able to see the way the energies that created the wards rose high in the air before arcing over the house, but I could. Earth and Air, Fire and Water combined and formed a protective net, preventing anyone and anything from entering.

"Quinn?" I asked softly even though I had a feeling no sound could escape to the outside world.

She shook her head. For the first time, I realized she held a gun in one hand. It didn't surprise me to see Lucas armed but it was the sight of Rafe with a gun in his hand surprised me. Not that I minded. Until we knew what we were dealing with, the more weapons, arcane and mundane, the better.

"Quinn, with me." I reached for her free hand.

Reluctantly, she slid her gun under her belt at the small of her waist, where I assumed she had a holster of some sort. Then she took my hand. Instantly, the connection I'd first felt the night we set the defenses snapped into place. Interesting. I needed to talk to Miss Serena about it. Now, however, we had a job to do.

Still holding her hand, I dropped to one knee. As I touched the ground, my fingers digging into the soil, she lifted her free hand skyward. This would probably be better with all the elements represented, but I wanted to make sure we had backup if we needed it.

The dome flared as something hit it from outside. Quinn hissed. Her grip on my hand tightened and I felt her talents come to life. Her head turned, her eyes searching. Knowing she and Rafe watched the perimeter, I *looked* downward. The earth and plants could tell me more.

At least I hoped they could.

"East," I rasped.

The wards flared again and then dropped. The moment they did, I surged to my feet. Quinn and Rafe were already racing east, toward town. Quinn's Mals appeared, catching up with their mistress. She said something in Dutch and they ran ahead.

"Jax?" Sam called from the front porch.

"Stay there!"

Feet pounded the pavement and elbows pumped as we ran. The dogs barked as they disappeared around the corner. Quinn called out something in Dutch. Then she somehow managed to find another gear, running even faster, putting distance between us.

"Quinn, wait!"

She ignored me. Cursing, I told Rafe to follow her. He nodded once and sprinted past me. I was in good shape but the last week plus had taken its toll on me. Too little sleep. Too much energy expended. Being shot. It all worked to slow me down.

The sound of a car engine revving filled the night. Tires squealed. A dog yelped in pain. Quinn shouted something and somehow managed to run even faster.

"Damn it, Quinn, wait!"

I slowed, my feet suddenly dragging, as I turned the corner. Quinn knelt in the middle of the street. Rafe stood at her side, one hand on her shoulder. One of her Mals sat at her other side, whining softly. In front of them, not moving, lay the second mal.

No, dear God, no!

Quinn turned. Tears ran down her face. Before she could say anything, I rushed forward. I didn't need to see the pain and fear in her eyes. She'd lost a Mal in a drug bust gone bad not long before she and Ali moved back here. Rainier's death left a hole in her heart. That was part of why Judith gave her Zeus and Sasha, arranging for them to be delivered the day after Quinn and Ali arrived in Mossy Creek.

I dropped to my knees opposite Quinn and gently ran my hands over the dog's side. Quinn's breath caught as Sasha whined once. I smiled slightly, hoping my concern for the Mal didn't show. I could tell she'd been injured badly. I needed to get her to a clinic as quickly as possible.

"Call Dr. Oliver. Tell him to meet us at his clinic." I didn't look up. I was too busy trying to check Sasha for injuries.

Rafe cursed a few moments later and I glanced at him, worried. "Clinic's closed. Recording says if it's an emergency to go to the 24-hour clinic in Denton."

I bit back my curse. I wasn't sure Sasha could last long enough for us to drive her to Denton. That meant I had to do whatever I could at the limited setup at Miss Serena's. Any lingering doubts I had about opening a practice in town flew out the window. I wouldn't let anyone else suffer the way Quinn and Sasha did right now.

"Quinn, it's your call. I can try to stabilize Sasha and then we'll take her to the emergency clinic."

She shook her head, her gaze not leaving her injured dog. "You," she croaked. "You take care of her."

"Quinn, I don't have a full clinic."

She grabbed my hand, holding it over the dog. "You, Jax. I trust you to do whatever is best for her."

I nodded, praying I could save her dog. Then I blew out a breath, drawing on my training to push back my emotions.

"Rafe, go get your truck. I'm going to need blankets and towels. Tell Miss Serena what happened. We're going to take Sasha back to her place. I have what I need to treat her there." I hoped. If her injuries were as bad as I feared, there wasn't much I'd be able to do except ease her pain.

He nodded and sprinted off.

"Jax?" Quinn wanted me to reassure her and I couldn't.

"Do you have your cellphone?"

She nodded.

"Turn on the flashlight. Hold it here." I carefully positioned her hand where I wanted it. "I promise I'm going to do everything I can to help her, Quinn. Trust me."

"I do."

Several neighbors came out as we waited for Rafe's return. Someone brought out a blanket and draped it over the Mal. Someone else wrapped a light blanket around Quinn's shoulders. There were offers to drive us to the local vet's office or even the hospital ER. Then, as they recognized me, they asked where I wanted them to take us. I thanked them and said Rafe would be there soon. But if they had security cameras, would they please check to see if their cameras caught anything?

Minutes passed. Not long in the grand scheme of things but as I worked to identify what injuries I could and keep Sasha calm, it seemed much longer. Finally, Rafe's truck pulled to a stop next to us.

As he jumped out, other cars parked behind him. Ali climbed out of the first one and ran to her mother, tears rolling down her cheeks as she looked down at Sasha. When she turned fear-filled eyes on me, I swallowed hard. As much as I didn't want to have to tell her mother the Mal wouldn't make it, I wanted to tell Ali even less.

"What do you need me to do, Doc?"

I glanced around, relieved to see Drew and Lucas, as well as everyone else, waiting for instructions. The men were the muscle I needed to shift Sasha to the bed of the truck.

It didn't take long. Carefully, we moved the Mal onto one of the blankets. Meg lowered the tailgate. Rafe, Lucas, Drew and Quinn gently lifted Sasha, each at a corner. They moved slowly to the pickup bed. I climbed in and leaned forward. My hands slid under the dog and guided the others as they settled her in the bed of the truck. Someone had put down a thick layer of blankets before Rafe left the house. They would cushion her as we rode to Miss Serena's.

"Quinn, you stay back here with me," I said as Rafe closed and secured the tailgate.

"Can I stay with her, Auntie Jax?" Ali asked softly.

"No, sweetie. I need you to ride up front with Rafe. Keep him company for me and make sure he doesn't get lost on the way to Miss Serena's." I smiled at her, hoping she didn't argue. Every moment we delayed was a moment that made it harder to keep Sasha alive.

"Mama?"

"Do as she says, Ali," Quinn said. "Please."

"Okay, Mama." She looked at me, tears in her eyes. "Help her, Auntie Jax."

"I'm going to do my best."

"I'll take point," Drew said. I had no doubt that meant he'd be running with lights and sirens.

"We'll be right behind you," Lucas added. "Miss Serena is riding with me."

"I've called Jimmy Reardon, Jax. He'll meet us at the clinic."

I nodded, relieved. "Let's go." Everyone ran to their cars. As they did, I settled in the truck bed on one side of Sasha, watching as Quinn settled across from me. "We need to keep her as still as possible, Quinn. If she starts to wake, keep her calm. Can you do that?"

She nodded, her expression saying it all.

The drive to Miss Serena's was a nightmarish version of bumper cars. Even though Rafe managed to get both speed and a relatively smooth ride out of it, every turn, every curve had Quinn and me working to hold Sasha still. I didn't want her sliding around, potentially aggravating her injuries.

When we finally reached Miss Serena's and the small clinic I'd been working feverishly to bring up to my standards—and a week had not been long enough, especially not now—the wait, at least for the others, began. We carefully carried the Mal inside. Rafe and the others placed her on one end of the examining table. Okay, it was an old table from Miss Serena's I'd appropriated, but it would serve as examining table and surgical table right now. I'd been forced to make do with what was on hand before. That's part of being a large animal vet where emergencies usually happened in fields and not in the sanitary confines of a clinic.

Fortunately, Jimmy Reardon anticipated the problem and scrubbed down the table and covered it before we arrived. He expertly instructed the others on how to position Sasha while I scrubbed up. Then, assuring them we'd do everything possible for the Mal, I sent everyone up to Miss Serena's house. I didn't need them hovering while I worked and they certainly didn't need to be here during the surgery I felt sure was coming.

"Quinn." I drawled out her name to see both she and Rafe standing by the door when I turned away from the sink.

"I'm not leaving."

From the defiant stance to the pain in her eyes, I knew better than to argue.

"All right. But you're going to have to stay over there unless I tell you to come forward. Rafe, if you don't mind, scrub up. We might need and extra set of hands."

Four hours. Four very long hours later, I stripped off my gloves and tossed them into the trash. I rested a hand on the Mal's flank and said a quick prayer. She managed to come through the surgery to tie off several bleeders, but she wasn't out of the woods yet. If she pulled through, she had a long recovery time ahead of her. On top of internal bleeding and several broken ribs, one of her rear legs had been broken.

"Doc?" Rafe looked at me in concern as I turned away from the table. Quinn stood next to him, pale and drawn.

"We wait and see." I wouldn't lie to them, especially not to Quinn. "I'll clean her up now and then I need to get her settled where I can watch her."

The question was where. This clinic, and I used the term loosely, was nothing more than a converted office off the stables. It didn't have anywhere I could hold her long-term.

"Can you move her to the house, child?" I looked at Miss Serena in surprise. I'd not realized she was there. "We can set her up in the library. We've already set up Athena's pen for her. That way we can keep an eye on her and you can get some rest."

I smiled slightly, considering. I didn't like the idea of moving the Mal so soon after surgery, but I also didn't want to leave her here. "All right. We'll need something solid to move her on."

While Rafe and Reardon went searching for something to use, I moved to where Quinn and Miss Serena stood. Quinn looked at me, tears in her eyes. I smiled gently and ran a hand down her arm. Now my job was to reassure her the best I could. I only wish I had better news.

"Quinn, look at me." I waited as she tore her eyes from Sasha and focused on me. "I'm not going to lie to you. She's hurt badly. I'm pretty sure you figured out what her injuries were as I worked but I'll give you the short version. She had internal bleeding and her rear leg was broken. So were a couple of her ribs. The next few hours and then the next couple of days are our first goals. Do you understand?"

She nodded before reaching up to wipe away a tear tracking down her cheek.

"After I get her cleaned up and we get her settled at Miss Serena's, I'll write up a report for Lucas. He can add that to his investigation."

And I hoped to hell he or one of his deputies had answers. Better yet, that they had the bastard who hit Sasha. "But you need to get some rest. Sasha's going to need you when she comes out from under the anesthesia."

"Let's get her settled first."

I nodded, understanding. It took a while. I did my best to clean the mal up, not wanting Quinn, much less Ali, see all the blood. The road rash down her right side was bad enough. The cuts in the rash, half a dozen of which I'd stitched up, were worse. I couldn't tell Quinn her Mal would recover, not yet. At least I could make looking at her a little less traumatic.

An hour later, Rafe and I carefully settled Sasha on a stack of soft blankets in Miss Serena's library. He stepped back and watched as I checked the Mal's IV and vitals. She still slept under the effects of the anesthesia. It would be another hour or so before she began regaining consciousness. I wanted to be there when she did.

"Auntie Jax, is Sasha going to be all right?" Ali stood next to her mother, her arm around Quinn's waist, her face pale.

I wanted to tell her everything was going to be fine, but I wouldn't lie to her. Instead, I climbed to my feet and pulled off my disposable gloves, turning them inside out. I looked around for a moment and then nodded in appreciation as Miss Serena held out a paper bag. I tossed them inside and then moved to stand in front of my best friend and her daughter.

"Ali, I'm going to treat you like the big girl I know you are." God, let me do this right. "Sasha is hurt badly. I won't lie about that. I had to operate on her and she has a broken back leg. But she is young and she is strong. You and your mom have done everything right with her and the other dogs. So that gives her a fighting chance to recover. I'll know more after she wakes up and then over the next couple of days."

"She's going to be all right." Ali spoke with such conviction I almost believed her. "Can I stay with her?"

I looked at Quinn. When she didn't say anything, I knew she needed me to. She was at her breaking point. I understood. I wasn't far behind. The only thing holding me together just then was an anger boiling just below the surface. I was damned tired of being one step behind whoever was trying to hurt Annie and those she cared about. But I had to hold it together, at least for a little while longer.

"Sweetie, not right now. I'm going to let your mama stay and you know she'll send for you if Sasha needs you." I knelt on one knee in front of Ali and reached for her hands. "Both she and your mom are going to need you tomorrow though. So you need to try to get some sleep."

"I've already made a bed up for you, Ali, right next to my bedroom," Miss Serena said as she joined us. "Let's let Dr. Jax and your mom talk for a few minutes. Then your mom will come tuck you in."

My heart almost broke as the little girl nodded before bending down and gently kissing the dog's snout and telling her not to be afraid. She was going to be all right. I prayed nothing happened to break Ali's heart.

Miss Serena placed a hand on Ali's shoulder and urged her to her feet. As they left the library, I glanced at Rafe and indicated the door. Fortunately, he understood. He pressed his lips to my cheek, squeezed Quinn's shoulder and left, closing the door behind him.

The moment we were alone, Quinn turned to me. I opened my arms and she all but dove into them. I held her close, one hand stroking her back, as she cried. She understood how badly injured the dog was. She also knew it would break Ali's heart if anything happened to the Mal. But what she wouldn't admit, at least not to herself, was how much it would hurt her to lose another dog so soon.

She eased out of my grasp and scrubbed her face with her hands. "Thank you."

"Don't. Not yet."

Now she shook her head. Red eyed, hurting, and yet determined. "*Thank you*," she repeated. "You've done more than I had any right to ask. You sure as hell did more than Dr. Oliver would have." She looked down at our linked fingers. "If Sasha survives, it's because of you."

I sniffled, blinking back my own tears. "Quinn, I need you to listen to me. Even if she makes it, she might never be able to be a working dog again. A great deal is going to depend on how her leg heals and how she heals emotionally."

Quinn nodded, understanding. "I'm going to sleep with her, Jax."

"I know." I smiled in understanding. "I'm going to let you sit with her while I run back to the caretaker's house. I need to grab my bag." Well, my backpack. And I'd not be leaving it behind from now on. I could have used it when that bastard tried to run down Sasha. "I won't be long."

"You don't need to come back. I'll stay with her." She looked at her dog, still sleeping under the effects of the anesthesia.

"She's my patient and you're my best friend. Of course, I'm coming back." I gave her a reassuring smile. It was the best I could do.

Leaving her with Miss Serena, I stepped outside. Rafe stood on the porch, staring into the night. Then he looked over his shoulder at me. Smiling, he held out a hand. I took it and let him draw me close. I nestled against him, wishing I could turn back time.

"I need to go pick up a few things at the caretaker's house." I stared into the night, wondering how everything could seem so peaceful when someone wanted to hurt, maybe kill, people I loved.

"I'll drive you over."

"Thank you." I leaned my head against his shoulder. "Did they find the bastard?"

"No. But we have the make of the car and a partial plate according to Drew."

"Annie and the family?"

"Safe at their house. The ward calmed down but Judith says she feels them on alert. Said she was going to spend the night there but we're to call if we need her."

I turned, sliding in front of him. His arms went around me as I slid my hands inside his hip pockets. For several long moments, we stood there, letting the peace of the night wash over us.

"Thank you." I listened to his heart beating beneath my ear.

"I told you, Doc. I am here for you, no matter what."

I smiled and inhaled his scent. "Let's go get my things. I don't want to stay away too long."

He nodded and led me down the steps and across the lawn to where he'd parked. As he helped me into the pickup, he brushed his lips against mine.

"Doc—Jax, it's good you came home. For more reasons than you know."

I wanted to believe him but just then I couldn't. I had failed at keeping Annie and her family safe. Oh, the protections snapped into place when they were needed. But they shouldn't have been needed. We should have figured out who hurt Annie. We should know why Sam's ex suddenly showed up in a town she'd refused to step foot in when they were married. All of that should have happened before Sasha was almost killed.

"Let's get what you need and then maybe you can try to get some rest," Rafe said as he slowly drove toward the caretaker's house.

Rest would be good, but I knew it would be in short supply that night.

"Jax."

I buried my head in my pillow, praying whoever it was went away. I'd stayed up all night, keeping a close eye on Sasha and doing my best to reassure Quinn. A little after six, Ali crept downstairs, worried about the dog. By then, Sasha's condition had stabilized. She wasn't out of danger yet, but I felt a bit more encouraged.

At seven, much to my surprise, Reardon arrived to spell me. When I tried to argue, he simply shook his head and said Miss Serena asked him to take over so I could get a couple of hours rest. Then he assured me he'd already checked the two horses I'd been keeping an eye on. Finally, with encouragement from Rafe, who'd stayed with Quinn and me last night, and Miss Serena, I agreed to get some rest. Half an hour later, I fell into bed at the caretaker's house. I was asleep before my head hit the pillow.

Now someone wanted me to get up when all I wanted was to sleep some more.

"Doc, I hate to wake you."

My eyes snapped open. Rafe stood next to the bed, dressed in only a pair of jeans. In one hand, he held a cellphone. Worried Sasha had taken a turn for the worst, I tossed back the sheet and sat up. His appreciative gaze as I did set my cheeks burning. There is no better way to start the day than to know you could turn your man on even with bed hair and morning breath. Then reality intruded and I looked at him in question.

"What?" I croaked, my throat dry.

"Text from Annie." He handed me the cellphone. "And I talked with Miss Serena a few minutes ago. Sasha is doing well. She and Amy worked on her after we left. She hopes you don't mind."

I shook my head, relieved. Anything they could do arcanely to help the Mal, I welcomed. Then I glanced at the text. I read it once and then twice. Oh my, she was pissed and ready for blood. Good. It was past time for her to strike back at whoever was targeting her.

I handed the phone back him with a grin. "She texted you. I'll let you answer."

He chuckled and the look in his eyes said he'd pay me back—in a way I'd most definitely enjoy. "You okay with going right there?"

I didn't hesitate. "No. I need to check on Sasha first. And that comes after a shower and coffee." Lots and lots of coffee.

At least we didn't have to worry about food. The text assured us there was more than enough food for everyone for a week. That said Mary Kate, and quite possibly Judith, had been busy. Not that it surprised me. Both tended to bake when they were troubled.

An hour later, we pulled away from Miss Serena's house. Sasha's was doing better and Jimmy Reardon promised to have one of the hands sit with her until someone got home. They'd call me if there was any change in her condition. Relieved, I thanked him and promised to get back as soon as I could. As Rafe and I walked out to his truck, I made a mental note to send a bottle of good bourbon to the farm manager and find out from him what to send the hand. They both were going above and beyond.

"Rafe?" I looked across the cab at him in question.

"We need to stop by my place first." He glanced at me a gave a little shrug. "I want to pick something up."

A few minutes later, he unlocked the front door and stepped aside so I could enter. He placed his hand at the small of my back and led me through the den toward the back of the house. Off the kitchen was a room overlooking the backyard. A large desk rested in front of the window. A laptop sat on the desktop. Everything about the room screamed "male" and "comfortable".

"Your parents?" I nodded to a framed photo on the corner of his desk. An older man and woman stood in front of a ranch-style house, their arms about the other's waist. Their body language and expressions spoke of love and a comfort with one another that only a lifetime together could bring.

"Yeah. I took that last year when I went back for their anniversary." He ran a light finger over the frame, his expression softening with his love for the two. What I wouldn't give for that feeling where my own parents were concerned. Unfortunately, that wasn't going to happen.

He leaned against the edge of the desk, his expression suddenly serious. "Doc, I don't know what the hell is going on, but I'm tired of people I care for getting hurt. We've done everything we can to protect Annie and the kids. Quinn isn't going to take any risks with Ali or the dogs from now on. That leaves you." When I started to respond, he gave me a quick shake of his head. "Do you know how to use a gun?"

I blew out a breath and nodded. "I do, but I prefer using either teeth and claws or my Earth talents over using a mundane weapon."

"I get that, but you might not have time to shift or be in a position to use your talents." He hated saying it, I could tell, probably as much as I hated hearing it. "Do you own a gun?"

I shook my head.

"We're going to take care of that."

He opened the closet door to reveal a gun safe. With his back to me, he unlocked it. A moment later, he studied its contents. As he did, he muttered to himself. I could have stepped forward to listen but didn't. Part of me wanted to but part of me resented the fact he thought I couldn't take care of myself.

"This will do until I can take you shopping for your own gun." He handed me a Sig P365 and Kydex holster. A small duffel with four extra mags and two boxes of ammo followed. Then, when I said nothing, he looked at me, his brow knitted in concern. "Am I pushing too much?"

I gave him a little shrug. Then, realizing he was worried he'd overstepped, I reached for his hand and took a step closer.

"Rafe, I love that you're worried about me. It's been a long time since someone other than Aunt Bitsy and the girls have. You know what it's been like with my parents. That means I've been forced to learn to depend on myself. It's hard to admit I might need help or that I can't just rely on my talents if I get in trouble."

He nodded and pulled me so we stood toe to toe and I had to tilt my head back to look in his eyes. "I understand, Doc. I always had my folks growing up. In the Army, I had Sam and the rest of our squad. But I also saw things that scarred me and has made it very hard for me to trust anyone. That's why it took so long after I got out before I could accept Sam's suggestion I move here. You are the first person since before I enlisted I've felt an instant rapport with. I knew I could trust you and, even more surprisingly, I wanted you to trust me and let me protect you—even if you don't need it." He cupped my face and gently kissed me. I sighed against his lips and then rested my cheek against his chest.

"Rafe, what's happening here?" I leaned back and linked my fingers behind his neck. Then I went up on my tiptoes and kissed him much more thoroughly than he had me. "We've known each other only a couple of weeks. Yet I feel like I've known you my whole life."

"Doc." His thumb traced my lower lip. "I don't know, but I sure wish we didn't have to go to Annie's right now."

"Me too," I laughed. "I promise we won't stay long."

"And I'll hold you to it." He kissed me again, a promise of what would come later. Then he nodded to where the Sig and the small duffel rested on his desk. "I'll talk to Lucas and see if he can't push a carry permit through for you. Until you get one, don't brandish the Sig and you'll be fine. You know Lucas and the rest of the SD won't bother you about it."

Before I could respond, my phone buzzed. I pulled it from my pocket and rolled my eyes as I glanced at the display. "Quinn wanting to know where we are." I quickly replied we were on our way. Then I shoved the phone back into my pocket. "Let's go before they send a search party out for us."

He chuckled and, once we gathered everything up, escorted me back out to the pickup. Time to go find out why Annie wanted to see everyone.

"Thank God you're here." Meg pulled open my door and all but dragged me out of the pickup.

Worried, I grabbed for my backpack and slung it over my good shoulder. By the time I had, Rafe rounded the truck to join us. His hand found mine and gave it a slight squeeze, just enough to let me know he was there.

"What's wrong?" What else had happened?

She frowned and all but shook herself, as if shaking off the fear and frustration I'd sensed in her. "Sorry. She's pissed and wanting blood. We'd just managed to calm her down when Quinn arrived. That set her off all over again."

Shit. A pissed off Annie was never good. Of all of us who grew up together, she'd been the slowest to anger. Because of that, she was the one to talk Quinn and me down. The few times she finally lost it, she made the two of us look like pikers in the anger department. This was not good, not good at all.

"What set her off?"

I was stalling. I knew it and I didn't doubt Meg knew it as well. Not that she argued. She seemed glad to be outside and away from the potential explosion. Not that I blamed her. Besides, by stalling I'd find out everything I needed to deal with the situation. Right?

"Drew."

Meg's voice held frustration and anger I knew had nothing to do with Annie, at least not directly. No, she felt her husband had done or said something exceedingly stupid and now they—we—were paying the price.

"What did he do?"

"He didn't pay attention, is what he did." She ground out the words. As she did, the air turned electric. A quick glance at her hands explained why. Lightning danced around her hands. I arched a brow, caught her eye and glanced down. She growled much as I would in one of my animal forms. Then she closed her eyes. I watched as she seemed to relax, muscle by muscle. As the tension flowed from her, the lightning dissipated. Good. She might be angry and frustrated, but she'd maintained control.

Oh, God. Control!

I looked toward the house, eyes wide as the possible implications of Annie being pissed hit me. Until a week ago, she hadn't realized, much less admitted, she was an *Other*. She still wasn't convinced. But she had started taking lessons with Miss Serena and Mary Kate. So far, her talents had all be passive. That didn't mean there wasn't something that might decide to come to life while her emotions ran high.

"Shit!" Meg rasped as if she, too, suddenly realized the danger.

"Doc?" Rafe looked between us in question.

"You may want to stay out here." Hell, I wanted to stay out here. "Annie pissed is never good. Annie pissed now that she's starting to train her talents is a very bad thing. There's no telling what might happen."

He blanched. More, I think, at the thought of Annie being pissed than anything else. Before anything more could be said, the front door opened. I tensed, seriously considering grabbing the keys from Rafe and speeding off. Annie stepped outside. Her hair danced in the wind —except there was no wind. Our Air elemental stood next to me and she wasn't using her talents.

"Are you coming or are you going to keep hiding out here?"

Shit.

I drew a deep breath and looked at Rafe, turning so Annie could neither see nor hear what I said. "You don't have to stay." I reached for his hands. "Trust me, this isn't going to be pretty."

"Are you staying?"

I nodded. I had to stay. Annie was my friend, my sister by choice. She'd always been there for me and I wasn't about to walk out on her when she needed me.

"Then I'm staying." He leaned down, touching his forehead to mine. "I'm not going to leave you."

I brushed my lips against his and then turned. As I did, I smiled slightly when he kept hold of my right hand. Now to face the music. With a nod to Meg, I started up the walk, moving past Annie where she stood on the porch, arms folded and toe tapping.

I nodded to the others as I stepped inside. I'd expected to find Miss Serena, Judith and Mary Kate. Quinn and Meg, as well as their husbands, were no surprise either. Each of us represented the old guard and the new. When one of us was in trouble or needed help, the rest of us would respond.

What I hadn't expected was to find Beth and Miss Olivia there. They sat on one of the sofas, coffee cups in hand. Miss Olivia looked vaguely amused at the sight of a very agitated Annie pacing the room. Beth simply caught my eye and shook her head. That told me she'd been unable to calm Annie down any, another sure sign this was not going to be a fun meeting.

I glanced around and sighed when Miss Serena nodded in Annie's direction. Her intent was clear. It was up to me to try to break through to her. I squeezed Rafe's hand before releasing it. Then I took a step in Annie's direction. Time for the rogue to make an appearance.

I cocked my head to one side and made a show of looking Annie up and down. Hopefully, my expression was more amused than concerned because, just then, I was damned concerned. Her eyes flashed and were more amber than blue. My pulse beat a quick rhythm before I calmed it.

"Enough!"

I didn't yell, but it was damned close. A moment later, the sounds of both Ali and Robbie racing downstairs filled the air. I turned and jabbed a finger at them and then at the second floor landing. I'd explain later, but they did not need to be here for what happened next. I didn't wait to see if they obeyed.

"Rein it in, Annie, or by all that is holy, I'll knock you on your ass." As I spoke, I slid my right foot back a little and dropped my hands to my sides. I watched for any indication of how she planned to respond.

"Try it," she snarled.

"Think very carefully before you repeat that, Annie." I spoke almost softly. She, like the rest of them, knew that meant she'd better do as I said. "I don't know what the fuck set you off, but you need to chill the hell out. Look at yourself. I mean it. Go look in a mirror. Your eyes are more amber than blue. Your hair looks like it is blowing in the wind but there is no wind in here. Then look at your dog, who usually is glued to your side. Look where she is. She's staying by Sam, not you. Why? Ask yourself that. Once you have the answer, we will talk but not before then."

I turned and started out of the den, motioning for everyone to come with me. I kept my back straight, my shoulders squared and I hoped to hell I hadn't overplayed my hand.

"Wait."

I stopped and glanced over my shoulder. Annie stood where I left her. But instead of looking at me, she looked at her hands as she held them out before her. The house, which I just realized had been on alert, relaxed. It no longer felt like it might respond to whatever Annie had been thinking or feeling. When she looked up, her eyes were once again blue, no hint of amber to be seen. I blew out a relieved breath and turned back to her.

"Are you ready to talk now?" Still the rogue, still demanding my friend not do anything foolish when all I really wanted to do was pull her close and protect her.

She nodded. Then she straightened. "I'm sorry. I reacted badly and took it out on all of you. I'll understand if you want to leave."

"Don't be foolish," her grandmother said firmly. "We understand."

"I don't. What the hell set you off?"

Someone needed to explain and soon.

She glanced at Drew where he stood next to Meg.

"Drew?" I prompted when no one said anything else.

"She overheard me talking to Sam about Mia and Sawyer."

I groaned and rubbed my forehead with the fingers of my right hand. No wonder Annie was pissed. I would be to. She'd feel like the two men she trusted most were keeping secrets from her. Coming on the heels of the attempted attack, or whatever it was, last night, she reacted without thinking. I wondered if any of them realized how close she came to her losing control of her talents and possibly doing something she'd regret for the rest of her life.

Something I needed to talk with Miss Serena about as soon as possible.

"And?" I wasn't going to let her off the hook yet.

"She's been seen around town. Tried to rent a room at the B&B but the Okoros refused." She waved off approval of their actions. We didn't need local businesses giving Mia or Sawyer reason to sue them. "They were booked. But Mia still threatened to sue, and Sawyer actually stopped by to try to bully them into letting her stay there—for a discount, of course. Thomas simply gave him the name of their attorney and showed him the door."

I smiled, picturing the scene. Thomas Okoro and his wife, Mala, moved to Mossy Creek a decade or so ago. They immigrated to the United States as children and were proud naturalized citizens. Once here, they bought the old Zhan place, a three-story Tudor-style home that had fallen into disrepair. Two years later, they opened the bed and breakfast. If anyone ever gave Miss Peggy a run for the best breakfast in town, it was Mala. That woman could cook.

"And?" That wasn't enough to account for Annie's temper.

"Sawyer notified Meg yesterday." Now she turned to her law partner and sister-in-law and glared. "Said he would be filing a motion on Mia's behalf to void the termination of her parental rights and to void my adoption of Robbie."

That explained it. Obviously, Meg hadn't said anything about the notice, not that I blamed her. That's the sort of thing you did at work, with witnesses and something solid between you and Annie when you told her someone wanted to take her son away from her. A set—or three—of handcuffs wouldn't be a bad thing to have either because you'd have to find a way to keep her from going after both Mia and Sawyer.

"What do you plan to do about it?"

"Fight her," she snarled.

"And what about Sawyer?"

From the way she all but rocked back on her heels, I knew she hadn't expected that question. Now she narrowed her eyes at me. Even so, I knew she considered what I asked. Suddenly, she cursed and spun on her heel, taking a step toward the front door.

"Stop it!" I snapped. As I did, I heard the door lock. Oh goodie. The house was taking my side against her. She was so going to kill me. "Julianna Grissom Caldwell, you will stop and think for a moment." I looked at Quinn and Meg, wishing they'd say something, anything.

"Would you stop?" She whirled toward me. "Would you stand there and wait as someone threatened to take your son away from you?"

"I don't know." The admission stopped her more than anything else could have. "Annie, I don't know because I don't have a child. But I know how I feel about you and Sam and all three of your kids. You're family. The thought of anyone trying to take one of the kids from you makes me want to go to war. Knowing Sawyer is involved? You know me. I'd love to go straight to his place and pound him to sand. But that would play into his hands, both regarding Robbie and with regard to the election."

"She's right, Annie," Quinn said. I gave her a slight nod and held a hand out to her. "Sawyer is doing this because he knows it will hurt you and because he wants to keep you so distracted you won't think about running against him."

"Listen to them, Annie." Miss Olivia spoke for the first time since Rafe and I arrived. "They're right about Sawyer. He's been bragging about taking Mia on as a client because it will throw you off stride. He's counting on you focusing all your efforts on fighting Mia and letting him take office unopposed."

Annie seemed to wilt and Sam rushed to her. We watched as he led her to the sofa. They sat and he pulled her close. Then he looked first at Miss Olivia and then at me. Damn it, even he thought I needed to lead the charge.

"Annie." I knelt in front of her and took her hands, holding them between mine until she looked at me. "I don't blame you for being pissed and wanting Sawyer's hide. But you need to be smart about this. So let's start with the most pressing issue, the threat Mia is going to challenge the termination of her parental rights." I glanced at Meg and motioned for her to join us.

"Sam, who handled the petition when you originally filed it?" I realized I didn't know if it had been done here or elsewhere.

"Annie's grandfather."

"All right. I assume that means Meg would normally handle it since Annie is a party to the other potential motion. Am I right?"

"If he wanted to keep it with our office," Meg said. "Or he could get another attorney."

"No, you," Annie said.

"Then that means you need an attorney as well." I looked at her, daring her to say she'd represent herself.

"Depends on the outcome of the motion to vacate. If it's denied, Meg can represent me. We'll wait to see what happens." Annie waited until I nodded.

I didn't like it, but it made sense.

"And Sawyer?"

She didn't hesitate. "I'm going to beat his ass."

"Then you know what you need to do." I pinned her with a firm glance. "You finish the paperwork and file first thing in the morning. You meet my aunt at the bank and set up your campaign account. You let Miss Olivia here spread the word and make sure the media is present when you file. I guarantee you there will be more there than Sawyer had. And then you take this straight to him. You don't pull punches. You turn up the heat and you keep at it. But do this only if you want to be DA and not just because Sawyer is an ass and is doing his best—yet again—to hurt you."

I climbed to my feet and took a step back. "Talk to Sam, your grandmother, Miss Olivia and Beth. Even Miss Serena. The rest of us will be out back. Come get us when you've made your decision."

I didn't wait for her to reply. Instead, coward that I am, I made my way outside. It didn't surprise me the others followed. Now to face another issue, one I shouldn't have to.

"Thank you." Meg sighed in relief as the door closed behind the last of us. "She walked in on Drew and Sam and blew. I was afraid she'd do something foolish."

"Drew." I looked at the redhead as he stood behind his wife, his hands on her shoulders. "I'll rip you a new one some other day. You should have known better."

He hung his head, his forehead touching the back of Meg's head. "I know."

"But?" I prompted. I crossed my arms and waited. "Damn it, Drew, what else? What didn't you blab to your sister?"

"Jax." Meg's voice held an edge of warning in it.

"Don't. I've known your husband long enough to know when he's trying to hide something. He's already made one mistake today. He'd be smart not to try for an encore."

Drew stepped around his wife and moved to stand in front of me. "Nothing for you to be concerned with."

I narrowed my eyes at him. Then I glanced to where Quinn and Lucas stood. Seeing Lucas take sudden interest in the tops of his boots, I cursed.

"I am tired. I am pissed off and, in case none of you noticed it, Annie was damned close to losing control of at least one talent a few minutes ago and I guarantee you it wasn't a passive one. So either tell me what the hell is going on or I'm going back home to get some more sleep."

Quinn gasped and then took a long look at her husband. If I was mad, she was suddenly furious. She grabbed Lucas' upper arm and gave him a shake. Her eyes flashed when he didn't say anything. Undaunted, she turned to Drew and the years suddenly fell away and we were back in high school. Drew had foolishly bragged about how he'd slept with Quinn. She broke his nose in response. If the look on her face was any indication, she'd do worse now.

"Easy," I soothed and waited until she joined Rafe and me.

Once she had, I rested a hand on her shoulder for a moment. Then I turned my attention back to the others and realized Meg didn't know the answer any more than Quinn did. Interesting. My guess was it meant whatever it was had to do with the investigation either into the initial attack on Annie or into what happened last night.

"Stupid, foolish men." I put a bite in my voice, leaving them no doubt about how I felt. "You both should know better. We've all talked about how the rogue is back. But I've held her in check. You know that. If not, you need to have your memory checked. Tell me what is going on or I let the rogue out and what happens next will be on your heads."

To prove I wasn't kidding, I reached for Rafe's hand, praying he understood. He lifted my hand to his lips. Then, still hand-in-hand, we walked across the lawn to the gate. Rafe was reaching for it when Lucas called for us to stop.

"Well?" I asked as we looked back.

"Come sit down. I'll tell you what I can." He sounded resigned and not happy about it.

"You will tell me everything. I'm tired of being jacked around."

"Damn it, Jax. Don't fight me on this."

My upper lip curled and I shook my head. "Not gonna happen, Lucas. Especially not since your deputy was going to tell Sam." I nodded to Drew who flushed and glared at me.

When neither man said anything, I shook my head. Idiots. "C'mon. I want to check on Sasha and then get some more rest. Maybe go out and check the house. When these idiots decide what they want to do, they can come to us. Quinn, tell Annie I'll talk to her later." I shoved open the gate and stepped through, praying Rafe followed.

I climbed into the truck and watched as Rafe hurried to the driver's side. Once settled behind, he slid the key into the ignition. The engine came to life and we pulled away from the curb. As he turned at the corner, I blew out a breath, leaned my head against the seat and fought the urge to cry.

"Don't." He didn't snap but the order was clear. "They deserved it. I get that Lucas is trying to protect his case. But he knows he can trust every person there. Worse, his protests fell flat considering Drew was going to tell Sam everything. Besides, you handled the main crisis and forced Annie to accept what she already knew. You aren't responsible for everyone and everything, especially not when it comes to that group. They rely on you too much and you let them. It's time they finally learn you have your limits."

I looked at him in surprise. It had been a long time since someone had been this upset on my behalf. If the truck had a bench seat, I'd have released my seatbelt and slid to sit side-by-side, thigh-to-thigh with him. Instead, I reached out, slipping my hand around the back of his neck, my fingers lightly caressing the stiff muscles.

"Thank you."

My cellphone buzzed and I glanced at the display. Quinn making sure I was all right. A second text came in before I finished reading Quinn's, this one from Meg. She and Quinn were having a "discussion" with their husbands. I nodded once and put the phone away.

"Where are we going?" I looked around and frowned as he drove out of town.

"Just taking the long way in case they decide to go looking for you." He didn't sound quite so angry. "Then we'll stop at Miss Serena's to check on Sasha. If you think she's up to it, we'll take her to my place with us. That way, you won't worry about being away from her."

"Rafe." He glanced at me and I smiled. "Are you trying to make me fall in love with you?" I wasn't sure where the question came from and I didn't care.

"Is it working?" He gave me a cocky grin and I laughed before nodding.

"Yeah, it is."

And that didn't scare me nearly as much as it would have even a day ago.

I looked up from my laptop where I'd been inputting my latest notes on Sasha as the sounds of several cars pulling up the drive reached me. Rafe patted my thigh and stood. As he moved to the front of the house, I heard him stop in the dining room where we'd set up the pen for Sasha. He spoke softly to her, telling her he thought her mommy was there. I smiled slightly to hear her whine softly. Soon, she'd want to get up and go to Quinn. For now, however, I was happy just to hear her reacting.

When my phone buzzed a few moments later, I glanced at it, grinning. Rafe. Letting me know we had company. It seemed the "party" had moved here. Now to see if the guys were ready to talk.

I finished my notes and was closing my laptop when Rafe showed everyone in. As he did, I bit back a smile. If I'd played the rogue earlier, he played the protective and angry—what? Lover? Partner? Friend? All of the above?

That was something we'd have to figure out sooner or later.

Annie, Sam, Quinn, Lucas, Meg, Drew, Miss Serena and Mary Kate filed into the room. I stood and carried my laptop into the second bedroom I currently used as my office. By the time I returned, everyone had found seats, with Quinn and Meg sitting on the floor at

Miss Serena's and Mary Kate's feet respectively. Rafe leaned against the kitchen doorframe, arms crossed, expression closed.

"How's Sasha? Quinn asked before I could say anything.

I smiled and assured her Sasha was doing better than expected. I wanted to keep an eye on her for another day or two. Then she could take the Mal home, as long as they made provisions to keep her downstairs. She did not need to be climbing the stairs.

"Well?" I asked. I slid my arm around Rafe's waist and smile slightly as he mirrored the move. We stood, hip-to-hip, shoulder-to-shoulder. He told me he would be there for me and now he was proving it.

"I did as you said. I finished filling out the paperwork. I'll be filing first thing in the morning. Miss Olivia is pulling together a press conference for drive time. I'm meeting Bitsy at the bank as soon as we're done. And, before you ask, Miss Olivia and Beth are looking into Sawyer, documenting his public statements about filing the motions just to harass me." Annie smiled slightly. "And thank you. I needed someone to knock some sense into me. Hearing what those two were planning blindsided me and I reacted badly."

"Your son's involved. You're allowed." I smiled at her in reassurance. "But you can't lose control of your talents."

"About that." She paled slightly and swallowed hard once before continuing. "What the hell was all that about?"

"Miss Serena?" Hopefully, she had an answer because I sure didn't.

"We'll figure it out," she promised Annie.

"Is that all?" I glanced at Lucas.

Annie looked between the two of us. I couldn't believe it. They hadn't told her, letting her think I'd left the house because I was angry at her. Well, Lucas and Drew were about to find out just how foolish that was.

It took only a few steps to close the distance between us. Before the men could react, I reached out and grabbed each one by their collars. Even as their hands closed around my wrists, I dragged them toward the door. Rafe, anticipating what I had in mind, beat us there. He held it open and watched, a smile on his lips, as I pulled sheriff and deputy outside and then tossed them down the steps. Then he moved to my side, making it very clear where his loyalties lay.

"Goddammit, Jax. I ought to arrest you." Lucas climbed to his feet and dusted himself off.

"For tossing out a trespasser?" I wasn't about to let him off the hook. "You're the ones playing games, you and Drew. And I'll bet my last paycheck on the fact you didn't tell Annie why I left the house. That you let her think it was because of what she said and did."

Annie's eyes went wide. Then she hissed out a breath. That answered one question. They hadn't told her everything that happened.

"Lucas," Quinn drawled from where she stood behind me.

Interesting. There was more to this than I expected.

"You told me the two of you were going to talk to Annie."

"They did. They told me about Jax leaving. Said she was worried about Sasha and wanted to give me time to get over my *snit*." She made air quotes as she said the last word.

That was it! I took a step forward only to find my feet suddenly in the air and strong arms around my waist. Rafe turned and set me next to Annie. Then he stalked down the steps, stopping in front of Lucas. Before I could say anything, Sam was by his side. Once again, they were brothers-in-arms, ready to help one another, not matter what.

Any other time, I'd find it endearing, maybe even a little funny. But we couldn't risk dissention in our ranks. I moved to where they stood and stopped at Rafe's side. I gave his hand a quick squeeze before stepping forward.

"Lucas, I understand you want to protect your case. But you know each of us well enough to know we won't do anything to jeopardize it. You also know me well enough to know you're lucky I'm not separating your head from your shoulders right now. You should have told Annie everything.

"But you, Drew. I can't believe you let your sister think she is why I left the house. I ought to let Quinn take another shot at you. I thought you'd grown up." Now I did let derision into my voice. Meg opened her mouth to say something but snapped it shut. I had a feeling the response had been the automatic response of a wife not wanting her husband attacked. "Now, it is up to the two of you to first apologize to Annie and then tell us what we need to know to keep her safe. And, before you argue, remember that last night someone tried to gain access to the yard and, presumably, the house. That same person then did their best to run down Sasha and damned near killed her. I've been shot."

Annie gasped and turned to me, her eyes going wide before narrowing. Shit. I hadn't meant to say that. We'd managed to keep that from her. Well, I'd deal with her later.

"You were shot, and you didn't think I needed to know this?" she drawled as she reached for my arm.

"That's right. You were in the hospital and I was more worried about making sure no one else tried to hurt you." I met her gaze and held it. "We will discuss this later, after we find out who that bastard happened to be and after we deal with Mia and Sawyer."

She didn't like it and I had a feeling she'd let me know about it sooner, rather than later.

"Now, what haven't you told us?" I looked from Lucas to Drew. They, in turn looked at one another. I threw my hands up in the air in exasperation. "I'm going to check my patient and take care of a couple of things. Meg, Quinn, I suggest you have a talk with your husbands. I'm really tired of being behind the eight-ball. They either decide to trust us or not. Our friendship is strong enough to survive—as long as nothing else happens. But I don't particularly want to see either of them if they keep playing mute."

I turned and started inside. As I did, I slowly counted to ten. If I reached ten before someone said something, it meant only one thing: the day was going to be much longer than I'd like.

"Can we at least go inside and talk?" Lucas asked, resigned.

I nodded and continued on my way. I'd give them time to get settled before joining them. And it seemed I wasn't the only one with the same idea. I was carefully checking Sasha's incision when Quinn entered. The Mal lifted her head and whined softly to see her. Quinn dropped to her knees and cradled the dog's head in her lap, one hand gently stroking Sasha's neck.

"Well?" I looked up and Quinn sighed. "Lucas didn't mean to be an ass and thanks for tossing him on his ass. He needed it."

I didn't say anything. Instead, I rebandaged Sasha's wound. Then I bent and kissed her snout, taking time to reassure her. My heart melted when she licked the back of my hand, her way of thanking me for helping her.

"It's still early days, Quinn, but I think she's going to recover." I squeezed her hand, understanding the tears that suddenly pooled in her eyes. "You're going to have to be careful with her for a long time and I don't know how well the leg will heal. I want you to be prepared for the possibility she will never be able to return to duty."

"That doesn't matter. I just want her to be all right." She smiled slightly and reached up with one hand to dash away her tears when Sasha whined softly and nosed her for attention.

"Did Lucas tell you what he's been holding back?"

She nodded. "On the way over."

"Then stay here with Sasha. You're good for her and I think you need it too." I climbed to my feet. "If she keeps responding like she has, you'll be able to take her home in a couple of days."

I rested my hand on her shoulder for a moment and then made my way to the den. As I entered, Rafe pressed a beer into my hand. Then, once I settled in the one free chair, he sat on its arm, his arm going over the chair back. I took a sip and waited.

"Doc, I'm going to toss them out in a minute if they don't start talking," Rafe said softly, his displeasure obvious.

"All right," Lucas growled. "But if one word of this gets out, I'll bring whoever talked out of turn up on charges."

"Oh, get the hell over yourself, Lucas," Sam snapped. "This isn't the first time we've all worked together to protect one—or more—of our own and not once have we done anything to impact your cases."

"Easy enough for you to say," he grumbled.

I tilted my head back and looked at the ceiling as the pieces began falling into place. This wasn't a case where he wanted to keep us out of the investigation for fear we'd say something we shouldn't. Far from it. This went back to what happened to Quinn when she and Ali returned to town. More specifically to what he and Ciara, Quinn's sister, had done. They'd killed Quinn's ex-husband. It was a righteous shoot. He'd kidnapped, drugged, beaten and was in the process of attempting to rape her when Lucas and Ciara found them. Zeus, Quinn's other Mal, rushed him and was stabbed in the attempt to get him off Quinn. He recovered, as did Quinn. But her ex hadn't gotten up after Lucas and Ciara shot him.

And Lucas didn't want to put any of us in that position. Interesting. I needed to talk with Meg and Annie to see if he'd tried the same when Meg came to town or if this was just him being extra cautious since Annie was involved. After all, each of us wanted blood because of the attacks against her.

"Lucas, it's okay." Annie and Meg looked at me in disbelief. Drew's eyes narrowed as if he didn't trust his ears. I ignored them. This was between Lucas and me. "We would do better knowing what you can tell us but if you think it best to keep it to yourself, we will respect that. But I want you to think about this before you make your decision. You aren't protecting any of us by keeping us in the dark. That decision could put not only Annie but the rest of us in more danger. That isn't said to pressure you. At least not too much. I give you my word, we will respect your choice and, believe it or not, I understand the need to protect."

He held my gaze for a moment and then nodded. A slight smile, one that relayed appreciation and a touch of wry humor, lifted the corners of his mouth. "Thanks. I handled this badly. Guess I owe each of you an apology. Jax is right. I've been trying to protect you instead of remembering you can be valuable assets in the investigation."

He nodded and I leaned back, wondering if the pieces of what had been going on would finally fall into place.

An hour later, Rafe dropped onto the sofa and pulled me close. I pulled my feet up and leaned against him. His lips brushed the top of my head. Then he eased me down until my head rested on his thigh.

Gently, he caressed my cheek. I smiled, feeling safe and cared for, something rare for me.

"Rafe."

"Shh." He rested a finger against my lips. "You are so tired."

"Yeah. I don't think I've gotten a good night's sleep since coming home." I yawned and then apologized.

"Don't. All I want you to do is relax. Close your eyes and try to nap."

"You?" It didn't seem fair he wasn't going to rest as well.

"Don't worry about me, Doc."

I struggled to sit up. Before he could protest, I stood. Then I took his hand and pulled him up. For a moment, we stood there, arms around one another. When I stepped back, I linked fingers with him and led him down the hall to the bedroom.

"Please stay." I paused as I pulled my tee shirt over my head. "You're right. I'm exhausted. But I don't want to be alone."

He nodded. While I finished undressing, he turned back the covers. Then he watched as I slid into bed. I bunched the pillow behind me and let the sheet pool around my waist. Tired as I was, I still enjoyed the sight of him quickly stripping out of his shirt. He undid his jeans and then sat on the edge of the bed. His movements were quick and efficient as he removed his boots. I blew out an appreciative breath when he stepped out of his jeans. Damn, but he had a fine ass.

He slid into bed and smiled at me. "Come here."

I moved closer, resting my head on his shoulder, one hand on his chest. He stroked a hand down my bare back. Softly, he soothed me. I fell asleep to the sound of his voice telling me everything was going to be all right. He'd make sure of it.

- 2 3 -

T he next several days were a blur. Annie walked inside the courthouse at exactly eight thirty Monday morning. Reporters followed her as she went through security and then up the old marble stairs to the second floor where the clerk's office was housed. With Bitsy and her grandmother at her side, she filed all the necessary paperwork and paid the filing fee. She was now officially in the race for DA.

Outside, she stood on the top step and addressed the press. From where I stood at the back of the gathering, I smiled proudly. I saw her nerves, but I doubted anyone else did. She thanked everyone for turning out. Then she said why she felt it important that she join the race. This was more than following in her grandfather's footprints. This was about honesty and integrity, about doing what was best not only for Mossy Creek but for Harkin County.

Even though she didn't mention Sawyer by name, one of the reporters asked why she thought she would be a better DA than Sawyer. Annie seemed to consider for a moment before answer. Then she did exactly as I told her she needed to: she went for Sawyer's political heart. Without referring to a single note, she detailed not only how he violated his oaths as an ADA with his prosecution of her mother but other cases where verdicts were overturned due to prosecutorial misconduct or negligence. Each of those cases cost the county money and made a mockery out of the justice system. As someone who values that system, she knows she would be a better DA than he would.

Then Bitsy stepped up to the mic. This wasn't the ditzy Bitsy so many folks knew. This was the Bitsy who set seasoned corporate executives shaking in their boots. Dressed in black slacks and a red blouse, both of which had been tailored for her, she announced Annie's campaign staff. They had rented a storefront across the street from the courthouse as their campaign headquarters. She promised everyone it would be open and operational by end of day. Since Miss Olivia was in charge of that part of the operation, I had no doubt she was right.

Later, I met with Bitsy at her office. Somehow, she'd worked a miracle. The purchase papers for the house and surrounding property were ready for my signature. Because she pulled off another miracle, as soon as I signed, the house was mine. No drawn out closing periods, no waiting for inspections. The latter had already been taken care of, thanks to Rafe and his contacts. The former was unnecessary, and I wasn't going to press for why. An hour later, I walked out of Bitsy's with the keys to my house—My house!—in hand.

From there, it was a short walk to the law office and my appointment with Meg. By the time I left, my head pounded and I once again seriously considered running for the hills. Between a demand from my parents, my father in particular, for Bitsy and I to return the shares he sold to paperwork formalizing the offer Bitsy, Meg and Miss Serena to help fund my clinic, I felt overwhelmed. Everything was moving too fast.

So I did what any self-respecting walker would do. I drove out to my house—damn, but it was going to take time to get used to that— and shifted. I spent the afternoon as a coyote, running the land I just bought, getting to know it and, hopefully, running some of my doubts off at the same time.

That night, Rafe and I shared pizza and beer and then laid our sleeping bags on the floor in the den in front of the fireplace. We spent the night, listening to the rain beat on the roof, talking and making out like a couple of horny teens. At least here we didn't have to worry about anyone walking in on us.

Just before falling asleep, I swore to have a bed, or at least a mattress, delivered before spending another night there.

Tuesday saw me at Miss Serena's as the sun came up. I spent several hours checking her stock. Then, satisfied with Sasha's continued recovery, I carefully loaded her into my new Dodge Ram. The drive to Quinn's house took longer than usual because I did my best to avoid every bump and dip in the road. When I finally parked in the driveway, Judith appeared to help carry Sasha inside. Then, once we had Sasha settled, I left after promising to stop by later to check on the dog.

Back in the truck, I considered what to do next. I needed to make arrangements to have my belongings brought to the house from storage. Not that the furnishings of my apartment in New Braunfels would come close to filling the house. I needed to do some furniture shopping. Before that, however, I wanted coffee and food.

First stop, Miss Peggy's.

"What the hell?"

Walking down Main Street in the direction of the café was the one person I hadn't expected to see. Sam's ex, dressed to the nines and looking like she owned the town, strolled down the sidewalk, ignoring those around her. Cursing inventively, I pulled into the first parking spot I found, one halfway down the block. I was out of the truck, pocketing the keys, almost before the engine cut off.

Mia in town, on way to café, I texted Lucas. When I glanced up a moment later, I cursed loudly enough old Mrs. Custer looked out the door of her florist shop and frowned. I apologized and turned my attention back to my phone as I picked up my pace. *Annie's there. Send deputy. This isn't going to be pretty.*

I shoved the phone back into my pocket and broke into a trot. No way was I going to let that bitch bother Annie.

The café was stone silent as I entered. It didn't take a genius to know why. All eyes were focused on the back booth where Annie sat with Robbie and Camille. Robbie had burrowed into his mother's lap —and there was no doubt Annie was his mother even if she hadn't given birth to him—his arms around her neck. Camille slid out of the booth and stood between the two and the woman who had hurt her son and grandson so badly.

"Come here, Robert. It's time you and I got to know one another." Mia held a hand out to Robbie and the little boy shook his head before burying his face against Annie's check.

"I told you before you weren't welcome here." Miss Peggy appeared from the kitchen, chef's knife in hand. Behind her, Janny stood, a large iron skillet held at the ready. "I've called the Sheriff."

"This is my son and I am not leaving without him."

And that was my cue.

Almost silently, I closed the distance between Mia and me. As if sensing my presence, Robbie turned his head, I saw him relax a little. But it was the way Annie's arms remained wrapped around him, the way her eyes burned brightly with anger, that worried me. The energies swirled around her. The few stray strands of hair that escaped her French braid seemed to dance on a breeze no one else felt. If I didn't get the situation under control and soon, her talents might just burst forth full-force. I'd pay good money to see the look on Mia's face when it happened. But neither Annie nor Robbie needed that and Miss Peggy wouldn't thank me for the subsequent damage to her café.

"She bothering you?" I asked as I nudged Mia none-too-gently to the side, placing myself between her and the others.

"How dare you!"

Her hand caught me in a surprisingly strong slap. For a moment, stars filled my vision. Then I shook off the pain, waving back those patrons who surged to their feet, ready to intervene. I touched my stinging cheek. Feeling the dampness, I snarled and glanced at Mia's hand. She smirked and made a show of turning her ring around so it faced the right way on her finger. Bitch!

I stepped closer to her, forcing her to back up. Several of those gathered barked out a laugh as she slipped and barely managed to stay on her feet. Holding her gaze, I smiled, showing my teeth. My eyes glowed as they always did when my walker talents were close to the surface. Mia stumbled back another step as I growled deep in my throat, the warning clear.

"I believe Miss Peggy told you to leave."

I spoke softly, almost lightly. No menace roughened my voice and nothing about my posture could be interpreted as threatening. Unless you looked at my eyes. When Mia did, she paled and swallowed hard, looking around almost frantically for someone, anyone to come to her aid.

"Not without my son." She once again held out a hand, as if expecting him to take it. "Come here, Robert!" she snapped when he didn't so much as look at her.

The silence was broken as the door swung open. I nodded in greeting as Lucas and Drew moved toward us. Expressions grim, Lucas rested one hand on his sidearm while Drew pulled his handcuffs from his belt.

"I do believe we have a TRO violation, Sheriff." Drew opened one of the cuffs, ready to slap it on Mia.

"Damned small town and its politics," Mia cursed. "No court can tell me I don't have a right to my son."

Lucas smiled and I shivered. There was nothing humorous in his expression. "Mia Caldwell, you are in violation of the TRO granted by Judge Washington. You were present at the time of the hearing and the judge's ruling and you acknowledged understanding the order."

"I told you. No judge can tell me I can't see my son."

"Miss Peggy, did you agree to let her come into the café?" he asked, ignoring Mia's protests.

"I most certainly did not." She drew herself up to her full five foot nothing and glared at Mia. "And, before you ask, I did tell her to leave. She refused. I want her arrested for criminal trespass."

I smiled slightly and then winced as pain lanced my cheek.

"Dr. Powell, what happened to you?" If anything, Lucas' voice turned even colder.

"This lady—and I use that term loosely—took exception to me

stepping between her and my friends here. When she slapped me, her ring caught my cheek."

"So we can add assault with bodily harm to the charges." Lucas nodded in undisguised satisfaction. "Deputy, cuff her and read her her rights."

"What?" Mia looked between the two uniformed me. She obviously didn't think Lucas was serious. Then, when Drew began reciting her Miranda rights, she stepped back, jerking her arm away from him.

"Resisting arrest?" he asked.

Oh, this kept getting better. But we all needed to remember Robbie was looking on and he didn't need to see this.

"Sheriff, might I suggest this be taken outside?" I jerked my head to where Robbie, Annie and Camille sat.

Lucas nodded. Before he could say anything, Drew grabbed Mia by the arm and escorted her out. The moment the door closed, I blew out a breath. Then I turned to Annie, worried about her and, most of all, Robbie.

"Drew's already called Meg, Annie. She's drafting a contempt motion as we speak," Lucas said as he pulled a chair up to their booth. "Are you guys all right?"

She nodded. The energies swirling around her stilled, but fury shone in her eyes. It wouldn't take much to set her off again.

"Thanks for giving me the head's up, Jax." He stood and turned to me, reaching over and tilting my head so he could examine my cheek. "It doesn't look too bad, but you might have Dr. Pat take a look."

"Already called her," Janny said from the kitchen entrance. "She said to come straight to her office."

"I'll make sure she gets there," Annie promised. She slid out of the booth, Robbie still wrapped around her. "Will you make sure Mom gets home all right?"

Camille rolled her eyes as she climbed to her feet. "I am perfectly capable of getting myself home all right," she told her daughter-in-law.

"Are you, each of you, all right?" I reached over and tilted Robbie's face up so I could look in his eyes.

I barely had time to brace myself before Robbie all but launched himself out of Annie's arms and into mine. I held him close, softly telling him everything was all right. He didn't need to be afraid. Neither his mom, his grandma, me or anyone else was going to let Mia near him. Annie ran a hand down his back, her eyes stricken. She blamed herself for not being able to protect him.

Damn Mia!

"Jax, thank you." Annie spoke softly, one hand on her son's back, the other on mine.

"Nothing to thank me for." There wasn't. Friends took care of friends. You stood with and for your friends. "Robbie?" I shifted him slightly and smiled as his legs tightened around my waist, making it nearly impossible for me to put him down. "You're safe now. I promise."

"W-why did she come back?"

"I don't know, sweetie, but I promise your mom and I are going to find out." Gently, I disentangled myself from him and handed him to Annie. "I will be right back. Promise."

He nodded and once again buried his face against his mother's neck. I smiled, affection for them both filling me. Then I drew a deep breath and turned to rest of those gathered in the café.

"We have a favor to ask." Miss Peggy and Janny stepped out from behind the counter as everyone looked at me, waiting for me to continue. "If any of you managed to get a video or audio recording of what just happened, I'd appreciate it if you'd email it to Meg Grissom and to the sheriff. If you ever see that woman again, let Mrs. Grissom know. It's important."

"You don't be worrying about her, Doc," old man Derry said from his table near the door. "We don't take kindly to anyone bothering our own."

"Thanks."

Others chimed in, a few even offering to do more than simply turning over videos. I thanked them again and told them we'd let the law take care of Mia. Not that it wasn't tempting to let her taste a bit of old-fashioned Texas justice.

"Miss Peggy, everyone's tab is on me," Annie said. Before anyone could protest, including Miss Peggy, she smiled and shifted Robbie to her hip so he could look at everyone as well. "Please. I knew each of you would stand up for Robbie, Camille and me. Let me do this to thank you for caring enough to get involved."

"You get Jax to Dr. Pat. I'll total it all up and let you know the damage." Miss Peggy looked at Robbie and smiled, transforming from scary old woman ready to go toe-to-toe with Mia to loving family member even if they didn't share your blood. "You have your mama bring you back here later today. I'll have a very special treat for you."

He looked at her shyly and then grinned, mischief lighting his expression. "Ali too?"

"Robbie," Annie scolded.

"Of course, Ali too," Miss Peggy answered with a smile.

"Thank you."

He reached over and gave her a hug. Then he wiggled out of Annie's arms, no longer the little boy needing reassurance. Still, he took Annie's hand when she held it out to him. A moment later, I felt his fingers wrapping around mine. I smiled down at him, thanking all that was holy I'd been able to help keep Mia from upsetting him any more than she had.

And damn it, I didn't get my coffee.

- 24 -

I pulled the cork from a bottle of Sterling Vintner's Cabernet. For a moment, I considered lifting it to my lips and downing it. Although, to be honest, a bottle of whiskey better suited my mood. The day had started out so well, only to go completely to hell. I was seriously considering locking my cellphone in my truck and leaving it there until morning. All I wanted was to shut out the world and hibernate for a week or two, preferably seeing no one but Rafe during that time.

Not that it was going to happen. In less than two hours, everyone was meeting here to discuss not only what happened today but to figure out how to deal with both Mia and Sawyer.

For now, however, I did my best to put it all out of my head. On the stove, a pot of meat sauce simmered, filling the air with the smells of herbs and garlic and other forms of Italian goodness. Potato gnocchi rested on two cookie sheets, ready to go into the water. Raviolo al'Uovo waited to be dropped into another pot of water. Garlic bread was ready to pop into the oven to heat.

I reached for two wine glasses as the garage door opened. By the time Rafe stepped inside, I'd wiped most of the flour off me and stood there, a wine glass in each hand. He stopped and lifted his face, sniffing the air. Then he grinned and reached for the wine glasses. After placing them on the drainboard, he pulled me close.

"Something smells good," he murmured after kissing me so thoroughly my knees threatened to buckle.

"I thought you might like a home-cooked meal for a change." I blushed and hoped I hadn't overplayed my hand.

"I like." He grinned again and then frowned, tilting my head to the side. The sounds of him sucking in a breath through his teeth explained his sudden change in mood. He'd seen the cut and two butterfly bandages Dr. Pat placed over it. "Is this why Sam had to leave work without warning?" He spoke softly but only a fool would think he was anything but furious.

I nodded and reached behind me for my wine. I sipped and then smiled, wincing slightly as a flash of pain reminded me of the cut.

"I'll tell you about it over dinner. Go clean up. It will be ready by the time you're back."

"Doc?" He cocked his head, looking at me in concern. "You okay?"

I shook my head. Even though my initial impulse was to lie, I wouldn't. Not to him. Not when he'd been there for me from my first day back.

"I hurt. I'm mad. And I'm worried." I leaned up and lightly kissed him. "Go clean up or we won't be done by the time everyone else gets here."

"Jax, talk to me."

"After you shower. Promise."

He nodded, gently cupped my cheek and then left the kitchen. As he did, I sagged against the counter. When the hell had my life gotten so complicated?

"Jax." He paused in the doorway and turned back to me. "Thank you. I like coming home to you."

I laughed and threw the dishtowel at him. "You just love coming home to dinner ready to eat."

He grinned, mischief dancing in his dark eyes. "That too."

He tossed the towel back to me and left. A few moments later, I heard the shower running. A smile lifted one corner of my mouth and, for a few moments at least, all my concerns seemed to disappear. It wouldn't last, not until we finally figured out what was going on and why. But I'd accept it.

I was home, like it or not.

I was putting down roots, and this particular root I liked a lot.

An hour and a half later, anyone looking out Rafe's driveway and the street in front of his house would think he was having a party. Our pickups were parked side-by-side in the drive. Behind them were Sam's pickup and Amy's Toyota. Meg's Discovery and Quinn's SUV were parked in front of the house. Across the street was a second black SUV, one I now recognized as Lucas' unmarked unit.

This was not a party by any stretch of the imagination. It was, however, a war council. The incident with Mia and getting verification from Sawyer, by way of his defense of her at the contempt hearing, that he would stoop even lower than any of us expected in his campaign against Annie, proved we couldn't wait for the next shoe to drop. It was time to take the offensive and I, for one, was more than ready.

"Grandma wants you to call her," Amy said softly as she entered the kitchen where I was grabbing beers for those who wanted them. I looked at her, arching one brow in unasked question. "Dr. Pat called her and told her what happened. Grandma wants to make sure you're all right."

Affection for the old woman filled me, easing my anger for the moment. "I'll call tonight if it's not too late when we finish up here. Otherwise, I'll call her in the morning."

Amy nodded but she didn't leave. Instead, she reached out. Her fingers stopped short of touching my injured cheek and she looked at me in question. I dipped my chin. A moment later, her fingers gently traced the wound, seemingly unbothered by the butterfly bandages. Warmth, deep and soothing followed her touch. I sighed in relief, realizing for the first time how much the cut still hurt.

"Thank you."

"I could tell you were hurting. This way you'll be able to think more clearly."

Something I had a feeling would be needed before the night was over.

It didn't take long for everyone to get settled. We ranged around the living room, some of us on chairs and sofas, others on pillows on the floor. Drinks were handed around and desserts, sent by both Miss Serena and Judith, were being enjoyed. But that didn't fool me. I saw how everyone watched Annie in concern, worried about what had been going on.

"I'm not going to beat around the bush." When the hell had I become the leader of this group? I really preferred being the rogue, doing what I thought needed to be done and not worrying about making sure everyone else was onboard. "Things went south today and could have been a hell of a lot worse on a number of levels."

"I'm sorry." Sam slipped an arm about Annie's shoulders and drew her close. "I never thought Mia would come back into our lives."

"Don't." Annie turned to him, her eyes blazing. "This isn't your fault."

"She's right." I waited until he looked at me. "I know Meg asked this at the hearing, but I have to ask it again. When's the last time you saw or heard from Mia?"

"When she walked out on us." He ran a hand over his face and a shudder ran through him. "Hell, she didn't even have the decency to tell me face-to-face. She left a note for me." Now his eyes blazed as brightly and as angrily as his wife's. "She'd left Robbie in his crib. No one was in the house and he'd been alone for at least a couple of hours when I got home."

Annie's eyes widened in shock and then narrowed as anger took over. I watched in concern as her blue eyes took on an amber color, much as they had at the café. A quick glance showed Quinn, Meg and Amy watching her. Quinn and Meg looked worried, but it was the speculation reflected on Amy's expression that caught me off-guard.

"Annie!" I snapped as the air inside the house began to pick up.

"What?"

She looked at me, concerned. Then she cursed softly before closing her eyes. I watched as she visibly relaxed. If we didn't get to the bottom of what was happening and soon, things were going to get *interesting*.

"Annie, you've got to start working more with not only your grandmother but mine, even with Jax here," Amy said, her voice gentle. "I think it's clear that while your main talent is passive, not all of them are."

Annie blanched and clutched Sam's hand so hard, I expected to hear bones breaking at any moment. Then she nodded, little more than a quick jerk of her head. Before I could say anything, not that I knew what to say, Quinn moved to sit on the sofa next to her. She reached for Annie's free hand and held it, waiting until Annie looked at her.

"I know it's hard to accept. Hell, it's terrifying to suddenly realize you aren't what you've thought all your life. Right?"

Another nod.

"Remember what a basket case I was?" Quinn shot a look at Drew as he snorted in amusement. "I'd always felt like my family thought me a failure because I wasn't an *Other*. Then, suddenly, the house not only was talking to me, but it accepted me. I could throw fireballs and make feathers dance in the air. But Lucas and Ciara made me realize something. I'd always been an *Other*. I'd even been using one of my minor talents, a passive one, for years. I have a feeling it's the same with you."

Annie didn't say anything, but she began to relax.

"It is going to be very important over the next few months for you to work with Miss Serena and the others. You need to not only learn what you can do but learn control." Now Quinn gave a lopsided smile. "Something I'm still working on," she admitted and Lucas nodded most emphatically from behind her back.

"But that can wait until tomorrow."

"She's right, Annie." I smiled at her from where I sat on the arm of Rafe's chair. His hand rested on my thigh, reminding me he was there for me. "I hate to ask this, but had you heard from Mia before she showed up at the school?"

"No." She shook her head.

"Any threats from anyone, even anonymous ones?"

"Not since I left the Travis County DA's Office."

I glanced at Lucas. "We're running those down with the help of Austin PD. So far, nothing of any promise."

"So we don't have anything solid yet." Damn it. Wasn't it about time we caught a break?

"Not exactly." Lucas sounded hesitant and all eyes turned to him.

Quinn dropped Annie's hand. A moment later, she stood in front of her husband, hands on his hips, her eyes flashing.

"What do you mean?" She bit out each word and I hunched my shoulders in sympathy. Unless I missed my guess, Lucas was in a load of trouble.

"One of Annie's neighbors updated their security system after Annie was attacked. They emailed a copy of their security camera feed yesterday. We've checked it against other video we have from the night Sasha was hurt and managed to get a clear shot of the car's license plate. That's given us a name."

"And why aren't you out there grabbing up that son-of-a-bitch?"

Lucas' eyes flashed angrily. "Back off, Quinn."

"Actually, she asks a very good question." Meg angled in her chair to look at her husband.

Drew held his hands up and shook his head. "I didn't know."

"You couldn't!" Lucas snapped. "I can't let the brother of our victim be involved in the investigation. You know that." Now he turned his attention to Quinn. "And I sure as hell wasn't going to tell you because I know you. You'd grab up Meg and Jax and go out to have a *chat* with the registered owner. We don't even know if he was the driver or if it was someone else. I can't risk you doing something to muck up my case."

I hissed out a breath as the three women turned angry gazes on him. Sam muttered something that sounded suspiciously like, "you poor bastard". But he sat there, smart enough not to intervene in what happened next.

"Let me get this straight, *Sheriff*." Quinn bit out the words, poking him in the chest with each word. "You believe that I would do something to interfere with your case. Me, a trained DEA agent. Oh, wait, I am also one of your Reserve deputies. But I'm not capable of hearing about a lead in the investigation without running off and compromising the case."

Poke, poke, poke.

"Damn it, Quinn, you know what I mean." He rubbed at the point in his chest where she'd done her best to drive her finger through his breastbone.

"Stop it, both of you!" I snapped. I massaged my left temple where a headache was forming. "He has a point. As sheriff, he has to worry about the integrity of the investigation. But." I flashed a warning look before anyone could say anything. "Quinn has a point as well, Lucas."

He blew out a breath and nodded once. "To answer the question of why I'm not out talking to the registered owner, Denton County SD is looking for him. His last known address is in an unincorporated area of the county just northwest of Denton. He's in his sixties and doesn't have so much as a traffic ticket on his record."

Quinn shook her head, her expression reflecting her frustration. "So there's little chance he's our perp."

"Yeah." He looked across the room to where Annie and Sam sat side-by-side on the sofa. "I swear I am doing everything I can to find Mia and to find out who hurt you."

"I know, Lucas. Just don't keep things from us," Annie said.

"Are the Denton authorities going to let you know when they find the guy?" I asked.

Lucas nodded.

"Then let's worry about things we can control." I turned my attention to Annie. "You aren't going to like this, but I really don't give a damn. From now until we find the bastard who hurt you, you aren't to go anywhere on your own. You are to carry your gun and you are to have Brigid with you."

To my surprise, she nodded. Obviously, the run-in with Mia, on top of everything else, had been the last straw. "Agreed. I'm also withdrawing from the DA's race."

I rolled my eyes and waved everyone to silence. "Not only no but hell no," I said firmly. "Annie, think for a moment. All this could have been to keep you from running in the first place. I'll admit, it seems a bit much for Sawyer but the man's unhinged where you're concerned and always have been. The fact he's representing Mia only proves how far he's willing to go just to throw you off."

She closed her eyes and nodded.

"You pull out and you play directly into his hands, love." Sam once again slid his arm around her shoulders and pulled her close. "You can do this. We will do this together."

"The twins and Robbie."

Now I smiled, knowing she would think I lost my mind. "You let their grandmothers and yours alternate caring for them." Her eyes grew wide and I chuckled softly. "Annie, no one is going to try to get to them if they are with Camille or Mary Kate. Frankly, if they are foolish enough to try it when they're with your mother, they deserve whatever she does to them."

Catherine was self-centered and more of a ditz then Aunt Bitsy ever could be, but she loved those babies and Robbie more than anything. She'd fight to her last breath and then come back from the dead to protect them.

Quinn and Meg chuckled almost evilly at my suggestion, but Drew looked almost as horrified as his twin sister.

"As for Robbie, Judith will pick him up after school at the same time she picks up Ali. They'll either go home with her or she will take them to Miss Serena's. So they're safe."

Annie nodded, relaxing a little. Even so, I knew she'd argue about leaving the twins with her mother. But that was a bridge we'd cross later. Who knows? Maybe we'd get lucky and the Denton cops would find the driver of the car that hit Sasha before that happened and the case could be closed.

Except that only dealt with the immediate danger. I still couldn't shake the feeling something else, something much worse, was coming for us and we weren't ready for it.

"There's something else." I patted Rafe's hand where it rested on my thigh and stood. How to tell them this without them thinking I'd lost my mind?

"Jax?" Quinn looked at me in concern.

"Annie and the kids aren't the only ones we need to protect." I lifted a hand, motioning everyone to hold their questions. "I need all of you to listen and not interrupt."

"Jax, you're worrying me." Annie looked at me in concern.

"Hell, you're worrying all of us," Drew said as he pulled Meg close, wrapping his arms around her as if to protect her from some unseen threat.

"Good. Because there's more going on than any of us have been willing to admit." Well, most of us.

I took a long draw of my beer and then stood. This was something I needed to be on my feet for. I thought better that way and by moving around, I gave them a moving target to focus on. Hopefully, I'd get it all out before they decided to call the men in white jackets on me.

For the next half hour, I spoke. When my mouth turned dry and my beer bottle was empty, Rafe silently slipped out of the room and returned a few moments later with another beer for me. I smiled, squeezed his hand and continued. Their expressions turned from disbelief to dawning understanding to anger and concern. Good. Now they could share my nightmares.

"Mossy Creek is like any other town. It has its problems. But you have to admit the last couple of years have been unusual, to say the least. More than that, much of the trouble has surrounded each of you." I nodded first to Annie, then Quinn and finally Meg. "And, before you begin objecting, Annie, Drew, think about something. What is the one sure way of getting Annie home, short of doing something to Drew or Mary Kate, both of whom can more than take care of themselves?"

Drew cursed softly but it was Annie who answered. "Put our mother into a situation she can't get out of on her own."

"Exactly." I waited half a beat. "Have you never asked yourself why she suddenly took up with Spud Buchanan? For years she hated him. Not only because of the way he egged your father on with his

drinking and gambling but because of how he tried to swindle her—
and you and Drew—out of what your father owed you. Her suddenly
deciding he'd changed and was the man of her dreams was out of
character. It didn't matter that he was single and rich, two things she
is always on the look out for. She wouldn't have done it because of the
two of you. At least not without something else coming into play."

Annie paled and swallowed hard. Then she looked at me, her
expression all but begging me to say this was all some sort of bad joke.
Quinn, however, looked at me through narrowed eyes and I could
almost see her putting all the pieces together. But it was Meg who
surprised me. She nodded, looking like everything was finally starting
to make sense.

Interesting.

"Go on," Quinn said.

"I'm not the only one who's been wondering and worrying about
this. So have Miss Serena, Judith and Dr. Pat." There would be time
later—I hoped—to go into detail. "Why do you think they've been
working so closely with Quinn and Meg? Or me for that matter? Have
any of you asked why, after each of us were gone from here for so
long, we've been finding our way back and then not leaving? We had
lives away from here, lives we loved and jobs we enjoyed. Yet, one by
one, we've returned and we stayed."

Even me, and I was still trying to work my head around that one,
but for more reasons than I was willing to go into right now.

"I think I see where you're going with this, but finish it out," Meg
said.

"Jax, may I?" Amy asked.

I nodded, glad she was there. Not only did she know about her
grandmother's concerns, she shared them.

"Grandma and the others have been worried for some time about
what's been happening. The situation with Catherine wasn't the
beginning of their concerns but it did bring them to the forefront.
Mary Kate kept telling them Catherine would never fall for Spud,
not matter how charming he might have been. But she didn't see
anything other than this change in behavior to worry her. Until

Drew called to tell her Catherine had been arrested for Spud's murder.

"Then you came home, Quinn. Your mother was kidnapped before you arrived. The pharmacy burglary, the attempt to break into your house and then your kidnapping."

I swallowed hard as Quinn paled at the memory. Everyone assumed her ex found out about Ali's newly emerged talents as an *Other* and wanted to take advantage of them. But, with him dead, no one asked the next question: how had he found out?

"And Meg?" Annie asked.

"Her mother sent her here to learn who she really is. We all know that."

Amy waited as everyone nodded. We knew the story by now. Meg's maternal family didn't tolerate *Others*. There was anecdotal evidence that, in the past, those family members met with untimely ends if they didn't run far and never return. Her mother had chosen the latter after suffering years of abuse at her family's hands. Not that it saved her, at least initially. Her family found her and her brothers and one of their friends tracked her down. When she refused to return home with them—unknown to Faith at the time, they wanted her back only so they could get their hands on the trust left to Faith by her great-grandmother—they beat her and the friend raped her. Her brothers did nothing to stop him.

Meg was the product of that rape. Her mother never held what happened against Meg. Instead, Faith did her best to be a good mother and to protect her from the evil that was her family. Not once did she mention Mossy Creek to her daughter. The first Meg heard of it was after Faith's death. In a letter to her daughter, Faith asked her to come here and meet Miss Serena. That set off a chain of events that came close to costing Meg her life before Lucas was finally able to build cases strong enough to keep all the players in jail for a very long time.

"But they acted as one would expect, given what they did to Faith," Sam said.

I shook my head and Amy let me answer. "Think about it, Sam. When Faith still lived here, she never called out her parents for what they did. In fact, it was only when Miss Serena stepped in that the abuse started coming to light. Sure, she'd show up at school with bruises, but her parents were smart. They never lifted a hand to her in public. They acted the victim when Miss Serena helped Faith file for emancipation from them. Not once that I know of, whether it was with Faith or with any of the *Others* living here, did they publicly do more than hold their religious fanaticism close. Yes, they condemned *Others* for being ungodly, but they didn't take overt action against our kind in public."

"Until I showed up." Meg's eyes grew wide and I could almost hear the mental finger snap.

"Yeah. It is as if someone or something is manipulating events here in town."

"And that has my grandmother and the others worried," Amy put in.

"Yes, and that brings me back to where I was going initially. Each of you have come under attack. Annie is, unfortunately, still under attack. But we need to be realistic. If there really is someone or something trying to cause trouble here, sooner or later they will take direct aim at those protecting the town: Miss Serena, Judith, Dr. Pat, even Mary Kate and—heaven help me—Miss Peggy and Aunt Bitsy. We have to keep them safe as well."

"Don't worry about Grandma," Amy said. "I'll be keeping an eye on her and Lexie will help. I've already talked to her about it. And I'll make sure the wards around the house are fully charged."

I nodded, knowing she meant to add her own layer of protections to the property. Good.

"I'm calling Ciara and Ciaran," Quinn said, referring to her older brother and sister. "We'll make sure Mom is safe."

The fact Judith was much more careful after all that happened to her and to Quinn helped. Then there was the small fact their house would literally eat anyone who tried to break in if they refused to turn back. . . .

"We've got Gran," Drew said and Meg nodded. "Our place is more than big enough for her to come stay with us for a while."

I didn't laugh, but it was close. I had no doubt Mary Kate would refuse. But they might surprise me and find a way to convince her to stay.

"Annie will be safe with me," Sam added.

"With all of us," I corrected. "But that does leave Dr. Pat."

"Maddy needs to know," Annie said and the others agreed.

I waited until I realized they expected me to make the call. Then I rolled my eyes and pulled out my cellphone. We really were going to have to talk about this decision they seemed to have made that I was the leader of our little cadre.

"Hey, Jax, what's up?" Maddy asked a few moments later.

I put the call on speaker. "Hey, Mads. You're on speaker. Annie, Quinn, Meg, Amy and the guys are all here with me. You got a minute?"

"That's about all I have. What's up?"

"Your mom's been keeping you up-to-date with what's going on with Annie."

"Yeah, and like I told her, I can't get free for another couple of days at least. Work's a bitch right now."

I frowned. Something in her voice worried me. But I couldn't put my finger on it.

"Mads, there's more to what's happening than we realized. I need you to be honest with me. How long until you can get here?"

She muttered something I couldn't quite catch. My worry ratcheted up a half dozen notches to see Quinn and Annie frown.

"Maddy, what's going on? Are you all right?"

Dear God, let her be all right.

"I'm trying to deal with the client from Hell and not lose my cool or my job. I'll get home when I get home. That's the best I can tell you."

I closed my eyes and counted to ten. There was much more to whatever was bothering her, but I'd known her all my life. She wasn't going to say anything else. Not without me flying to London to kick her ass. Since that wasn't going to happen any time soon, all I could do was try to get through to her.

"Maddy, listen to me. There are things going on here that worry not just me but your mom, Miss Serena and Quinn's mom. We're doing our best to deal with it, but we could use your help. I get that you have a job. But get here as soon as you can. We'll hold down the fort." I hoped. "But promise me something. If you need us, any or all of us, you will call. We're here for you."

She blew out a breath and fell silent for so long I worried the call had dropped.

"I know. I'm sorry. I'm not where I can discuss it right now." She paused and I listened as she muffled the phone against her and said something to someone. "Jax, I've got to go. But tell me this. Is my mom all right? Do I need to be worried?"

Now it was my turn to blow out a breath. Part of me wanted to lie but I couldn't. Not about something this important.

"Mads, I don't know. We're still trying to find the bastard who attacked Annie, but it is obvious there's more going on here than any of us first realized. And yes, I'm worried about your mom as well as Miss Serena and Judith, not to mention Annie's grandma. If someone really wants to hurt this town, the best way to do it is to go after them."

Silence. I pictured her sitting there, eyes closed, mouth firmed, as she considered what I said. "All right. But I really can't leave. Keep me in the loop. And keep my mom safe until I get home."

"We will." I made a quick decision and hoped it wouldn't bite me in the ass later. "Maddy, do you need me to come out? The others can hold the fort down here until I get back."

She hesitated just long enough for me to catch it. "No. At least not yet. I'll let you know if I change my mind."

We said goodbye and I rang off. As I put my phone away, I looked at the others. They looked as troubled by the call as I felt. Frustrated, I sipped my beer and thought, wondering if this was yet another result of whatever had been troubling Mossy Creek.

"Well, that means we need to keep eyes on Dr. Pat as well."

"Leave that to me," Amy said, and I gladly agreed. She had contacts at the hospital I didn't. "And, whether she likes it or not, I'm flying to

London once things are under control here. Something's going on. Otherwise, she'd already be here."

"I'll make a few inquiries," Quinn said, her expression thoughtful. "Let me see what I can find out."

"Thanks." I turned to Annie, knowing what she was about to say. "Don't. I'm not leaving here until I know you are safe. So don't even suggest I leave now."

"Thank you."

The fact Annie didn't press the issue convinced me she was more worried about what was going on than she'd admitted. Not that it surprised me. I had a feeling we were all more worried than we wanted to admit.

"Starting now, none of us goes anywhere alone. If you're licensed to carry, you do so, no exceptions. If you aren't, you need to get your license and, until it comes through, let Quinn set you up with a dog or two. We aren't going to take chances with ourselves or our loved ones. Agreed?" I looked at each of them, waiting as they agreed.

"I'll call Ciara and Ciaran on our way home," Quinn said as the group began to break up. "Lucas and I will make sure Annie and Sam get home okay," she added softly from my side. "But you need to take your own advice."

I laughed, knowing where she was going with this. "Quinn, I don't need a dog. Remember, I have my own teeth and claws."

"You can never have too many." She grinned and I had a feeling she was up to something. "Talk to Lucas. He'll push your carry permit through."

A few minutes later, I rinsed the first of the dessert plates and loaded them into the dishwasher. I smiled as Rafe came up behind me. He slipped an arm around my waist and pressed his lips to the nape of my neck.

"You don't have to do this. It will wait until morning."

I shook my head and turned to face him. "I know, but I hate waking up to a dirty kitchen." The fact I assumed I'd spend the night rocked me for a moment. Then I smiled and cupped his cheek. "I don't mind. After all, it's my fault there's a mess. I invited everyone over."

"No, *we* invited them," he corrected. "You need to accept that you're not alone anymore, Doc. I'm in this with you."

"I know and I really do appreciate it."

I turned back to the sink and made quick work of the dishes. As I did, he dealt with the trash and recycling. It was a domestic scene and one that helped settle me. But something was bothering Rafe. I saw it in the tension in his shoulders and the tightness in his face. Worried, I took his hand and led him to the kitchen table.

"Rafe, what's wrong?" I covered his hand with mine and waited.

"Nothing."

I looked at our hands where they rested on the tabletop. Then I glanced back at him. "I know better than that. Something's bothering you. So let me say this before you say anything else." I licked my lips, searching for the right words.

"Rafe, you've been wonderful. You've had my back since I returned home. You've done all you can to help protect not just Annie and the kids but me. But you didn't sign on for all this. I'll understand if you need to step back. This isn't your fight." I chuckled softly. "Hell, Rafe, I didn't sign on for this. But, apparently, it's my destiny or something." And I still needed to figure out how I felt about that.

"Stop." To my surprise, he leaned over. His hands closed around my waist and a moment later I found myself sitting on his lap, his arms around me. "You need to understand a few things about me. I wasn't lying when I told you I fell in love with this town long before I stepped foot in it. Sam used to tell me stories about Mossy Creek and everyone here when we were in the Army. We never knew one day to the next if it would be our last. I made up my mind then that if I made it out of there alive, I'd come here and see if it was home. It took me longer than I expected because I needed to learn to deal with what I saw and did while still on active duty. But I have never regretted coming here. This is my home and I will do whatever I can to protect it and those who live here."

I smiled and rested my head against his shoulder.

"I think I even fell a little bit in love with you then." He smiled shyly and a blush heated my face. "Sam talked about all of you. But you, you were the one I wanted to hear more about. You were someone I could identify with, someone who valued friendship and loyalty as much as I do, someone who didn't shy away from doing what is right."

"You make me sound like a much better person than I am."

"Now that is something we're just going to have to disagree about." He smiled and his arms tightened around me. Then he eased his hold, leaning back so he could look at me. "What I don't like is not knowing who the enemy is and not being able to take direct action against them. More than that, I hate seeing you so worried and so exhausted."

I tilted my head enough to brush my lips against the line of his jaw. Then I smiled and cupped his cheek with my right hand. "I am tired and I'm just as frustrated as you are. Add in having this whole guardian thing dropped on me and there's a part of me that wants to run for the hills. But most of all, I want to stop whatever happens and then spend the rest of my life just being Jax. Not the protector. Not the guardian. Not the rogue. Just me."

He laughed softly. "Those are you just as much as the gentle, loving woman I know."

"Rafe." I swallowed hard, searching for the right words. "The only thing that matters right now is knowing you're here, with me." Or maybe I should have said I'm there with him. After all, we were in his house. "You are the best thing to happen to me in, well, just about ever."

I didn't know what the future held, but I didn't want to do any of it without him.

He lifted my hand and pressed his lips to it. Then he carefully stood, cradling me in his arms. I rested my head against his chest, listening the slow beat of his heart. I turned off the lights as he carried me out of the kitchen and to his bedroom. For now, for however long it lasted, I'd let myself relax and enjoy being where I was.

The ringing of my cellphone woke us. Rafe's arm tightened around my waist, I considered ignoring the annoying sound. But I learned long ago, a call this early never meant anything good. Eyes still closed, I reached out and fumbled for the phone where it rested on the bedside table. Then, I rolled onto my back and slid my finger over the sensor, unlocking the phone. As I did, I smiled slightly as Rafe's hand found my breast and his fingers lightly traced over my nipple.

This had better be good or someone would get an earful.

"What?"

Quinn chuckled and I growled in response.

"Sorry to wake you two." She paused and I knew she was grinning. Damn her. "I did wake the two of you, didn't I?"

"I won't dignify that with an answer." Of course, that was an answer and I cursed silently. "What's up?"

"We've got him!"

It took me a moment. I'm never my best in the morning, especially not before coffee and a shower. Then the possible meaning of her statement hit. I tossed back the sheet and sat up, swinging my legs over the side of the bed. Rafe leaned up on one elbow. He watched as I gathered up my clothes.

"I'm putting you on speaker, Quinn." I tossed the phone onto the foot of the mattress. "Talk to me."

"Denton County called a few minutes ago. They found the suspect and have taken him into custody. Lucas is on his way to interview him."

Relief weakened my knees. I dropped onto the mattress, smiling as Rafe scooted down to sit next to me. As we waited for Quinn to continue, I prayed Lucas could finally close out the investigation.

"Did they tell Lucas anything else?"

"Not that he told me." Her frustration came through and Rafe chuckled softly. "He'll touch base after he's seen the perp."

I frowned slightly. Knowing the suspect was in custody should have been good news. So why did Quinn sound worried?

There was only one way to find out.

"What else?"

She didn't answer right away. Rafe looked at me, concerned. I shrugged. I didn't have any more of an idea of what was bothering her than he did. All we could do was wait until she decided to explain. Well, that and start getting dressed. I had a feeling one or both of us would be heading out before long.

"I don't know."

The admission worried me almost as much as the fact she was still troubled.

"All right. Where are you?"

I glanced at the clock. Almost six. Still too early but Rafe and I managed to get almost six hours of sleep. That's more than I'd gotten at a single time since returning home.

"Home. I'm meeting Meg at the café in half an hour."

"I'll meet you there." Maybe by then we'd know a little more.

"What do you want me to do, Quinn?" Rafe asked as he climbed to his feet.

He padded across the room to his closet. As we waited for Quinn to answer, he reached inside. A moment later, he tossed two tee shirts and a black cotton button down onto the bed.

"Will you head over to Annie's and Sam's? Drew is on his way, but I'll feel better with two sets of eyes on them this morning. He'll stick with Annie. You'd be doing me a big favor if you stayed with Sam."

He glanced at me and I nodded. We needed to cover as many bases as possible until this was over. Just because Sam hadn't been targeted yet didn't mean he wouldn't be.

"I'll head over as soon as I'm dressed."

"Thanks." She paused. "Jax, I know it doesn't make any sense. Maybe my imagination is playing games on me after everything we talked about last night. But I can't help feeling this isn't over yet."

I didn't curse, but I wanted to.

"We'll talk about it soon. I'll meet you at the café."

"Don't forget your gun. Your rules, so you have to follow them too."

I rolled my eyes. "Yes, mom."

"Bitch," she laughed. "Later."

"Well?" Rafe asked as I retrieved my phone.

"I'm worried," I admitted. "Quinn's not one for flight of fancy. Not over something like this."

"I want you to be careful, Doc."

"We both need to be careful." I moved to where he stood and reached up to lightly kiss him. "I need a shower."

He grinned and grabbed my hand. Laughing, I let him lead me to the bathroom.

Forty-five minutes later, I parked in front of the café. As I did, I smiled slightly. Almost as if we'd rehearsed it, Quinn pulled in to my right and Meg to my left. Their SUVs made my pickup look small. Even so, I'd put the Ram up against theirs any day of the week. Then, as they climbed out, I chuckled softly. Anyone looking at us would think we'd coordinated our looks. Black jeans or, in Quinn's case, cargo pants. Black tees. Quinn's gun was in plain sight on her hip. I saw the slight bulge of Meg's under the shirt she wore over her tee shirt.

But it was the sight of the woman who climbed out of the passenger side of Quinn's SUV that brought me up short. Ciara O'Donnell, Quinn's big sister, bad ass Texas Ranger and Fire elemental. Smiling, glad to see her not only because I knew she'd stand shoulder to shoulder with her sister if trouble came but also because she was a good friend. I waited at the front of the truck for her to join us. Then I hugged her, thanking her for coming.

"No ink today?" Ciara asked as we walked into the café.

I shook my head. I'd considered wearing a tank top and letting my ink show. No, letting everyone see the rogue was still in town. But, as I dressed, I'd changed my mind. My tats gave away too much this morning. Several of them seemed almost alive as I studied my reflection in the bathroom mirror. No need to remind everyone just how easy it was for me to slip into one of my animal personas.

"Back booth," Miss Peggy said and nodded to the booth Annie usually occupied every weekday morning.

By the time we slid into the booth, Miss Peggy had coffee poured. Janny appeared as her mother stepped back, ready to take our orders. Then, seeing Miss Peggy still hovering nearby, I smiled, shook my head and motioned her closer.

"What's going on?" she asked. "You all look like you're ready to go to war and Ciara here wasn't due home until the holiday."

The look she gave us, not to mention the way the half dozen other patrons watched and waited, spoke volumes. We weren't to try to avoid the issue, much less lie. Not that there was any sense in either. They'd find out soon enough. Besides, I had a feeling we might need their help.

"Not to leave here. Promise." I waited until everyone agreed. Fortunately, I knew everyone and had no doubt they'd keep their word. "Lucas has a suspect in what happened the other night. He's gone to Denton County now to interview him. In the meantime, we're not going to let our guard down. Too many things have been happening to relax just yet."

"How's Annie?" Janny asked.

"And how's your dog, Quinn?" Mr. Miller asked from his table near the door.

"Annie's fine. Pissed off." I ducked the head slap Miss Peggy aimed at me. When I grinned unrepentantly, she shook her head. We both knew she hadn't really tried to hit me. She wouldn't have missed if she had. Still, she made her point.

"And Sasha is recovering, thanks to Jax here." Quinn gave me a cocky grin. "In case you haven't heard, she's moved back and is opening a vet clinic in a couple of months. But she's working out of Miss Serena's right now."

That started everyone talking. I sighed, knowing exactly Quinn was up to. Yes, it diverted the conversation from Annie and other things best left to somewhere private. But it also made sure the grapevine knew my plans, ensuring the trap that was Mossy Creek was now impossible to escape.

"What can we do?" Miss Peggy asked more softly.

"The same as usual," Ciara answered. "Keep an eye and an ear open. Let us know if anything seems out of the ordinary."

I reached for Miss Peggy's hand before she could leave. "We mean anything, ma'am. And not just something that might be aimed at Annie or her family."

Miss Peggy's eyes narrowed. Shrewd enough not to ask any of the questions I saw reflected in her eyes, she nodded once. Then she made a show of wiping up a drop of coffee I'd inadvertently spilled. A moment later, she shuffled toward the kitchen, motioning for Janny to come with her. As they disappeared from sight, I had no doubt Miss Peggy was issuing her own orders and making sure the grapevine was put on alert.

For the next hour, we listened more than we talked. The café quickly filled with regulars, folks we trusted to have our backs. There were offers of help. A few even commented they'd already been in contact with Lucas about helping patrol Annie's neighborhood. I didn't know whether to laugh or cringe because some of those were older than dirt. The thought of them going around armed terrified me. But the idea they wanted to help also reassured me we could do this. We could keep Annie and everyone else safe until we got to the bottom of this.

Whatever the hell *this* is.

Things got interesting when some of those gathered started talking about Sawyer. Anyone wandering in would assume this was normal. The patrons bantered about the upcoming election. They talked about the strengths and weaknesses of each candidate—of course, they had very little in the way of weaknesses when it came to Annie. It mainly came down to her youth and the fact she'd only been back a couple of years. But Sawyer? Oh my, did they have a lot to say and it was difficult not to ask Janny or Miss Peggy for pen and paper to take notes. Then I saw Ciara place her cellphone on the table. No doubt about it. She was recording everything so we could go over it later.

"Hey, did you hear the really interesting bit about all this?" Bubba Smithson asked from where he sat at the counter.

He turned so he looked at us. As he did, I glanced at Quinn and arched one brow in question. Her shrug was all I needed to know she was as nonplussed by not only his presence but his appearance. Bubba was Lexie's older brother and one of the three banes of her existence growing up. The other two were her sister "Perfect" Patty and their mother. Last I heard, Bubba had finally gotten tired of his mother's machinations—not to mention the family's dearly departed returning to the homestead—and moved to Denton. But here he was sitting in the middle of the café, for all the world as if he started every day like this. More than that, he wore work pants and shirt and looked more like he was going to work in his father's garage than in an office.

"Hey, Bubba. I didn't know you were back in town." I moved to the open stool at his side.

"Could say the same about you, Jax." He grinned over the top of his coffee mug. "There are some folks in town not real happy the rogue's back."

I chuckled, knowing exactly who he meant. His mother and I had a hate-hate relationship that rivaled the one I had with my parents.

"That's their problem." I thanked Janny as she handed me a mug of coffee and lifted it in a salute to Bubba. "What's this about Sawyer?"

Bubba set his cup down on the counter next to his plate of half-eaten eggs and pancakes. Then he swiveled so we sat almost knee to knee.

"I moved back to town about six months ago when my boy started suddenly setting stuff on fire without the aid of matches. Seems he takes after his Aunt Lexie." He grinned and took a bite of pancakes. "Pissed Mama off something bad, but Lexie's been great working with him. And Mama, well, she can learn to live with it or not. That's up to her."

Wow, Bubba had grown up in the years I'd been gone.

"So you moved home and gave up your job and everything?"

He nodded and swallowed another mouthful of pancakes. "Never liked that job but I needed to get away from Mama."

That I understood. I'd done much the same.

"Now that I'm back, I'm helping Dad and he's let me take over the business end of the shop. That lets him focus on the mechanic end of things, so we're both happy."

Since Jacob Smithson was an *Other* with a special talent for all things mechanical, I had no doubt he was glad to hand the rest of the business over to his son.

"So, are you still Bubba or what?"

"Mama still calls me Bubba--when she's talking to me. But most everyone else calls me Jake now."

I smiled, approving of the change. "So, Sawyer?"

He nodded and drained his coffee, holding the mug up to signal he wanted a refill. Then he wiped his mouth. "You remember Dad's shop is out in the old industrial park off of North Main?"

"I do." In fact, I needed to drop the pickup by there to have Jacob take a look and make sure Aunt Bitsy didn't get taken to the cleaners when she bought it.

"Well, when Sawyer could finally practice law again, the only place he could afford was out there. Seems his mama wouldn't open her checkbook up for him anymore. Said he needed to prove he'd learned his lesson and could walk the straight and narrow as an attorney and as a man before she gave him another dime."

Interesting but not unexpected. Mrs. Sawyer was a stickler for propriety. Annie told me how refused to hire her son an attorney or do anything to help him when he had to answer charges before the State Bar.

"And?"

"Last night I was working late. Dad and I have decided it's time to expand the garage and update equipment, so I was running down cost estimates." He thanked Janny as she refilled his mug. "As I drove by, I saw Sawyer leaving. It must have been close to midnight. He wasn't alone. It was dark, but I'm pretty sure he was with the woman you and Miss Peggy threw out the other day."

My heart beat a quick staccato and I snarled softly. Mia. I should have known. But was I jumping to conclusions?

"And?" I prompted.

"They got into a car and drove off together. Headed out of town."

"All right," I stood. Then I extended my hand. I liked Jake a lot more than I did Bubba. "Thanks."

"You let me know what Dad and I can do. Annie's good people and I remember Sawyer from school. He made even me look good."

I chuckled and lightly punched his arm before returning to the booth where Quinn, Ciara and Meg waited. They listened closely as I filled them in.

"Quinn, why don't you let me drop the SUV off at Jacob's this morning.? You were telling me on the drive in that the engine's been making a strange knocking sound." Ciara climbed to her feet with a grin. "I don't think it will take him long to figure out the problem, so I'll hang around. Maybe take a stroll through the area, seeing what sort of gossip I can turn up."

"And I need to get to the office. Annie's meeting with the Rotary Club this morning, so I get to cover the docket call." Meg dropped several bills on the table. "Quinn, can I drop you somewhere?"

"No thanks. I think I'll hang for a bit with Jax." She smiled, leaving me little say in the matter.

I grinned, figuring she had something in mind, and finished my coffee.

An hour later, I sat on the floor in the middle of Judith's workroom in the basement of the house she shared with Quinn, Lucas and Ali. Quinn was somewhere upstairs, seeing what she could find out about Mia. Judith sat across from me, relaxed and looking entirely too wide awake this morning.

"Serena had an appointment in Dallas this morning with her investment advisor," she said. "She asked me to work with you."

"Cool." I grinned. I'd always enjoyed learning from Judith.

To my surprise, my "lessons" that morning weren't focused so much around honing my powers or figuring out how to blend my elemental powers with my walker abilities. Instead, I got a lesson in what made her house so alive. She took me all the way down through its various layers of protections and energies. As an earth elemental, I could see how they all tied into the earth and the ley lines running through town. Then I saw how the other elements were tied in as well.

But more surprising was the way the energies tied back to Judith. I had no doubt, now that I knew what to look for, that I'd see the same with Quinn. It wasn't so much an anchor. They weren't tied to the house or the land. Instead, it reminded me of a direct line, something that would activate if the house—or if they—were in danger. Something Quinn confirmed happened when her ex kidnapped her. The front gate slammed shut and locked, keeping Ali safe from her father.

"This is why you and Miss Serena said the house reflects the personality of the one it recognizes as the owner, isn't it?" I pushed a lock of sweat dampened hair off my forehead.

"It is. There will always be resonances from previous owners. But if there is a solid connection with the current owner, that will be the strongest resonance."

I looked at her for a moment and then started chuckling. I remembered how the house would treat Quinn, sometimes locking her out. Other times, the front gate would slam in her face or close quickly enough to catch her clothes. She never knew what was going to happen. But, in the end, it always let her in and, when she and Ali moved home, it welcomed her with open—if metaphorical—arms.

But it was the memory of how the house reacted whenever Drew came over when we were younger that set me off. I couldn't recall even once when the gate opened for him or when he could simply walk through the front door. Instead, no matter where he fell in a line of us, the gate would slam shut, leaving him outside. Everyone else could pass through but not Drew. At least not without a lot of pleading and cursing from Quinn or her mother or Ciara telling the house to behave.

"The house knew," I said softly.

Judith nodded, not needing me to explain what I meant. "It recognized her talents even when the rest of us figured they'd never manifest. I always knew she was an *Other* but I worried she was going to be one of the rare ones where their talents remained dormant. I should have paid more attention to what the house was doing. It was trying to tell me, tell all of us, and we ignored it."

"You can't blame yourself. She was so busy denying she was an *Other*, no one saw the signs." Me included.

She nodded. I knew she wasn't ready to let herself off the hook and I understood. But that was a conversation for another day. Especially since I had a feeling my "lesson" wasn't yet finished.

"What next?"

"Do you think you can recognize the energies that bind the land to someone?"

"I do." I should. Between the wards we raised at Annie's and today, I'd gotten a very thorough lesson in what to look for.

"Then it's time for the next part of your lesson." She stood and helped me to my feet.

Less than half an hour later, we stood in the middle of a field near Miss Serena's house. It wasn't part of her property. I knew that without asking. It didn't *feel* like hers. In fact, something about the feel of the land worried me. Something was wrong. But what?

And why could I sense it?

"We need to cast a circle. Then we'll get to work," Judith said.

I watched as she scratched a line in the dirt, marking the edge of our circle. As she did, she chanted softly. The energies within the circle rose as she closed the two ends of the line she'd drawn. Until the circle was broken or dismissed, we were safe.

"What do you see?" She sat on the ground facing me.

I knelt, sitting back on my heels. Closing my eyes, I let my awareness flow outward. All around me, the air and earth were alive with sounds. Birds flying overhead. Tree leaves rustling in the slight breeze. Smaller animals scurrying in the shadows. In the distance, a horse neighed and a dog barked.

Everything sounded normal but something was wrong. The energies within the circle danced over and around me. It felt wrong, as if the energies were unbalanced. Worried, I opened my eyes and leaned forward on my knees, resting my hands, palms down, on the grass.

Instantly, the world seemed to pitch. My stomach did a roll and I swallowed hard. Energies flowed upward into me, as if grasping me like a lifeline. Part of me wanted to pull back and break the contact. Another side wanted to sink my hands into the soil and do whatever I could to heal the land. Somehow, it had been damaged, almost wounded and was crying out for healing.

"Jax, stop." Judith's hand closed over my shoulder. "Break off, Jax, now!"

I shook my head. Every instinct told me I needed to help. My Earth magic responded to the need, pouring my own energy into the soil even as I reached for the nearest ley line to pull energy from it.

"Damn it, Jax, break it off!"

Her fingers tightened around my shoulder and she shook me hard enough that I needed to brace myself or fall over. That was enough to break my connection to the land. Gasping, I fell back on my ass, the world swirling around me. Instantly, Judith knelt beside me, her hands taking mine and I felt her healing energies flowing into me.

"Breathe, sweetheart. Slow and deep," she soothed. "I'm sorry. I didn't think you'd react this strongly."

"W-what happened?" I ran my hands over my face, fighting the urge to bury my hands in the soil and reestablish my connection with the earth.

"You confirmed what we were afraid of." She stood and moved to the pack she'd brought with us. When she returned, she handed me a bottle of water. I twisted off the top and drank my fill. "Serena told you how we've been worried for some time now because we've been unbalanced without the fourth guardian."

I nodded.

"We've all felt a subtle change in the land the town sits on. But it wasn't until you came home and we felt the guardian connection snap into place that we began to worry things are worse than we thought."

"But why haven't I felt this sort of need from the land before?"

"Because this strip of land doesn't have anyone living on it. So there is no one caring for it."

I nodded again. In Mossy Creek at least, people cared for their land and spent time and energy in seeing to it. That lent the land at least some of their energy, even if they were normals. Because of that, it would be harder to know the trouble the land was in if they weren't Earth elementals.

"I need to heal it." It pulled at me, demanding, almost pleading.

"And you will, we will, but not now. We need to do our research to make sure we do it right. We also need others here to not only assist but to witness. Serena is already looking into what must be done."

"Then why bring me here?"

"Because we needed to know how serious the problem is and, judging from how you reacted, it is worse than we expected."

I didn't like it, any of it. But I had a feeling if I tried to do this without knowing exactly what I was doing, it could consume me. So I nodded and slowly stood. Then I knelt and, before Judith could stop me, placed the palm of my right hand against the grass.

I will be back. I will help and heal. Rest until then. Rest.

The energies swelled for a moment and then receded. I felt them sinking deep into the Earth. I climbed to my feet and brushed my hand on my jeans. Then I turned to Judith and nodded once. As I did,

I made a decision. Whether she agreed or not, we had one more stop to make before heading back to her house.

"I know I said I'd be the fourth guardian," I began as we drove off. "But I never really accepted it personally. It didn't make sense. I've been away from here for so long. I'm young and relatively untrained— or at least out of practice for what I'd expect for a guardian. And, to be honest, the whole idea scares the shit out of me."

"But?" she prompted.

"I can't deny it now. Not after what I just felt and *saw*." Heaven help me.

Hell, heaven help Mossy Creek.

"I guess what I'm saying is I'm not going to resist the idea any longer. I can't. Something is happening to this town we all love." Even me. "I want to stop it and will do whatever is necessary to do so."

She smiled and rested a hand briefly on my upper arm. Then she glanced out the windshield before turning her attention back to me. "Jax?"

"I need to do this. Don't ask me why. I'm not sure why. But I need to do this."

A few minutes later, I turned up the drive to my new house. As I did, it dawned on me the house was in the exact middle of the property. That made it the perfect focal point for what I wanted to do. I parked in front of the house and got out.

I stood at the front of the pickup and tilted my face skyward. Eyes closed, palms out, I inhaled deeply. Then I knelt and placed my palms on the ground. This time when the energies reached out to me, there was no desperate clinging. Instead, it was as though a welcoming hug surrounded me. I smiled and dug my fingers into the soil through the thick sod. I needed that connection.

Following the energies, my consciousness sank deep into the earth. The energy flowed strong and healthy throughout the land, all the way to the property line. Then it rounded upward, much like the wards we placed around Annie's house. All that needed to be done was to recharge the shielding and bind it to me. The connection of energy to energy was already there. All it needed was a tie to my life force.

I didn't hesitate. I pulled my pocketknife from the front pocket of my jeans. Before Judith could stop me, I opened one of the blades and sliced the pad of my right thumb. Pain caused me to hiss out a breath. Using the knife, I cut a small hole in the sod. After dropping the knife at my side, I held my thumb over the dirt and squeezed it with the thumb and forefinger of the other hand. Half a dozen drops of blood fell onto the dirt. I placed that hand, palm down over the dirt and opened myself to the energies again, welcoming them, binding myself to the land in a way I'd never done before.

Home, home, home.

The voice, for lack of a better word, was stronger, more vibrant than what I'd heard my first visit here. A sense of belonging stronger than anything I'd ever felt filled me. I owned the land but it was a part of me. I wondered if the others felt the link with their homes as strongly as I did or if being an Earth elemental might be at play here.

"Jax?" Judith stood at the front of the pickup, watching me in concern.

"I needed to be sure."

She tilted her head to one side, studying me. Then she closed her eyes. I felt her reaching out, calling on her own gifts. A moment later she gasped softly. The corners of my mouth curled up in a smile. And I waited, wondering what she'd say.

"How did you know what to do?"

"I didn't. It just felt like the right thing to do." Suddenly, I wondered if I'd done something wrong. "How bad did I fuck up?"

Judith suddenly smiled and hurried to where I stood. She took my hands and pulled me close, hugging much like I used to dream my mother would. Then she kissed my cheek before stepped back.

"You didn't screw up, Jax." Pride and something else shone in her eyes. "You did what none of the rest of us can do without your help. You instinctively knew how to strengthen the ties with your home and land on a level that will rival Serena's. Her mother did the binding for her not long before the old woman died. She did the same with me. But Pat hasn't had that sort of binding done because she became a guardian not long before then and Serena's mother died before she could do the binding. Then we didn't have an Earth elemental to complete the ritual."

"We'll take care of that first thing." I didn't wait for her to respond. "Do we need to bind the house to Quinn?"

Judith smiled and shook her head. "Not yet. I'm afraid my youngest would run to the hills if you suggested it right now."

I chuckled and nodded. She was right. Quinn still wasn't convinced she liked being an *Other*.

"One last question. I've accepted—truly accepted—my place as the fourth guardian. But do we need to do anything to formalize it?"

Please don't let there be some sort of ceremony out in the middle of town where I have to dance naked under the full moon.

"We'll discuss it tonight. Serena wants all of us to meet at her house for dinner." She glanced at her cellphone as it buzzed. Then she smiled. "Quinn. She said the two of you need to take care of a couple of things."

I frowned, wondering what she had in mind. "Then let's head back." Once again, I dropped to a knee and touched the ground. I promised I'd be back soon. Then I stood and returned to the pickup.

Time to see what Quinn had up her sleeve. Then I needed to check in on Annie. Somewhere along the line, I'd really like to talk with Rafe and see if he'd caught wind of anything yet. Most of all, I needed time to think about everything that happened this morning.

"No." Quinn crossed her arms under her breasts and shook her head, her expression mulish. "Not only no but hell no."

I didn't laugh, at least not much. It helped that I understood. Even though Miss Serena and the others had talked around the topic of guardians with all of us before tonight, this was the first time she'd come right out and not only named me as the fourth but stated her plans for the others. Only Annie looked relieved, mainly because she hadn't been tapped as potentially joining us when an opening occurred. Quinn looked like she might run for the hills. Meg had actually taken a large step away from us and Ciara looked like she'd been hit by a two-by-four.

"It's not something you need to worry about, Quinn. Not for a long time," I told her, praying I was right. But the feeling of coming danger had only grown the last few days and that worried me more than I wanted to admit. "Besides, we have other things to deal with right now."

"Jax is right." Lucas shot his wife a look and she snapped her mouth shut before saying anything else. "Let's start with what I found out."

That shut everyone up. He'd spent most of the day in Denton and had said nothing about how the interrogation went.

"Denton SD interviewed the registered owner of the car that hit Sasha. He didn't know anything about what happened. When asked where the car was, he finally admitted he'd given it to his son six months or so ago. The SD found an address for the son and brought him in on outstanding warrants. That's when they called me.

"There's no doubt the son's the SOB who tried to run down Sasha. The car was in his garage and has substantial front-end damage and some scorching on the rear bumper and trunk."

He glanced at his wife. Quinn returned his gaze without flinching. She hadn't said anything at the time, but I knew what that scorching meant. She'd flung at least a couple of fireballs at the retreating car. Good. That meant it would be easier to tie the car to what happened.

"He's still claiming it was an accident. That he was afraid Sasha was going to attack him and he got in his car and drove off without knowing he'd hit her."

"What about trying to get onto our property?" Sam asked.

"He denied it and I didn't let him know we have video of it. I'll spring that when I need to. Today wasn't the time."

"So we don't know if he's responsible for the attack on Annie or not," Mary Kate said softly.

"Actually, we do." Lucas' smile was as predatory as any of my animal forms could be. "The perp isn't nearly as smart as he thinks he is. While I didn't get a confession, he did finally admit he'd been in town the day Annie was attacked. The car is equipped with GPS. I've already asked the DA's Office to get us a search warrant. I could have gone straight to a judge but I'm covering all my bases here. This way, no one can claim we cut any corners when this goes to trial. As soon as we have the data off the unit, we'll know where he was at the time of the attack."

"Until then?" Ciara asked as Sam pulled his wife close.

"He's sitting in the Denton County Jail. Like I said, they picked him up on outstanding warrants. But don't worry. I've placed a hold on him for animal cruelty and fleeing the scene of a crime. He won't be going anywhere except straight to our jail."

"Other than knowing he was in town, did you find anything connecting him to anyone who might have a grudge against Annie?" Quinn asked.

"Yep. He has one outstanding charge here in town for DWI. He's out on bail for it right now. On top of that, he shouldn't be driving. His license was suspended more than a year ago. He's set to go to trial next month on the DWI charge. His attorney of record on it and on a couple of other charges in Denton County is a certain Joe Bob Sawyer."

Could it be that simple?

Hell, was Sawyer that dumb?

"I'll kill the bastard," Sam growled.

"No, you won't." Annie held his hand tightly between hers and looked at him, waiting until he nodded. "We need to be sure." He frowned but nodded again. "Lucas?"

"I'm doing everything I can to get answers, but I don't want to tip our hand."

"Did he ask for an attorney during your interview?" Ciara asked.

Lucas shook his head. "No, and that bothers me. He's been around the system long enough to know better. So he is either confident we can't connect him to what happened or he thinks the fix is in."

I knew where my money lay.

"Then let's give Sawyer a push, something to distract him just like he's been trying to distract Annie."

"What do you have in mind?" Miss Serena asked, a hint of suspicion in her voice. She knew me well enough to understand I would do just about anything to protect my friends.

"Give me a minute. I need to make a call."

I stood and pulled my phone from my hip pocket. As I started out of the room, I looked back. Seeing Rafe watching me, questions reflected in his eyes, I gave a small jerk of my head. If I was going to do this, I wanted him to know what I had planned because it could wash back on him and, eventually, on Sam and the company.

"Hello?"

"Hey, Aunt Bitsy. I've got a quick question for you. Are my parents still hassling you about the stocks Dad sold?"

"They are. I received another demand via email from your father today. I've already forwarded it to Annie as well as to corporate counsel."

"By any chance, would Joe Bob Sawyer be my father's attorney?"

I knew my father. He loved money and spending it but not on things like attorneys who could actually win a case for him. He'd rather hire an ambulance chaser with questionable ethics and morals like Sawyer than pay for quality. Still, my plan wouldn't work unless he'd stayed true to form.

"He is. Why?" A hint of something colored my aunt's voice as she tried to figure out what I was up to.

"How much would you enjoy seeing my father finally get cut off at the knees where the business and Granddad's estate is concerned?"

"About as much as I'd like to spend a long weekend alone in bed with a good book, a better bottle of wine and a really fine man."

I sputtered out a laugh. "Never change, Aunt Bitsy." I chuckled again and then sobered. "How long until you can get me installed on the Board?"

"I may regret asking this—I doubt it, but there is that possibility—but what are you up to?"

"I think it's time to kill several birds with the proverbial stone."

I quickly outlined my plan. Bitsy listened, never interrupting until I finished. Then she asked a couple of questions. A few minutes later, we agreed to meet for breakfast and finalize the details. Grinning, I slid my phone into my pocket and turned to Rafe.

"Are you sure about this?"

"Yeah." I slid my hand into his and smiled up at him. "This should do two things, if we play it right. It will keep Sawyer focused on Bitsy and me—and my parents. They are not going to like being challenged and will want his full attention. It will also, if we're lucky, show whether or not he's really involved in what happened to Annie."

"You understand this means I'm not letting you out of my sight."

I stepped closer and wrapped my arms around his waist, resting my cheek against his chest. Then I looked up at him and smiled.

"Rafe, I want you with me—and for more than just this." I pressed my lips to his. "But we can talk about that later, when we're alone. For now, let's tell the others what I have in mind and then I'd better take Fenris for a walk." I glanced down at the young German shepherd that had been my constant companion since shortly after noon. I still wasn't sure how Quinn had convinced me to buy the solid black shepherd.

"You know you are going to have to explain how you wound up with him." Amusement twinkled in Rafe's eyes.

"You know exactly how. Be glad you weren't with us. You'd probably have a dog as well."

"Let's fill the others in and then get out of here."

I nodded and let him lead me back to the den, Fenris at my side.

"Well?" Miss Serena asked, clearly concerned.

"I'll fill everyone in tomorrow morning after I see if this can be pulled off." I lifted a hand before anyone could interrupt. "If this works, it's going to be something that will keep Sawyer focused on Bitsy and me and not on what Annie or the rest of you are doing."

"What are you planning?" Quinn looked ready to beat some sense into me if she didn't like my answer.

I didn't answer. Instead, I turned to look at Meg where she and Drew sat on the far end of the sofa. "Are you in court in the morning?"

She shook her head, her eyes narrowing as she tried to figure out what I was up to.

"If you don't have anything, I'd like to meet with you around nine."

She pulled her phone and made a quick entry in her calendar. "About?"

"Let's say the rogue is going rogue and a few folks are going to get a rude awakening." I grinned and looked at Miss Serena in surprise as she chuckled almost evilly.

"I think I see what you plan." She stood and moved to me. After scratching Fenris behind his right ear, she studied me. "Are you sure?"

"I am." I rested a hand on her arm. "If I am going to be the fourth guardian, that means taking the position seriously. It means doing what I can to protect this town and those living here, even if it means doing something that will be difficult. Besides, this is something I should have done long ago but didn't."

"I'm lost." Quinn looked at her sister and Ciara shrugged.

"I'll explain tomorrow. Promise." Hopefully, they'd agree this was our best alternative. Even if they didn't, I'd move forward for Aunt Bitsy and the company. "Now, we—" I indicated Miss Serena, Judith and Dr. Pat.--"Need to talk to the rest of you. Rafe already knows most of this, but you need to as well."

"Nope." Quinn shook her head much as she had earlier and, imitating her older sister, took a big step back. This time, she wasn't the only one. Meg and Ciara joined her. All three looked ready to run.

"Cool it, Quinn!" I jabbed a finger in their direction and then to the sofa. "Sit." Unlike my recalcitrant friends, Fenris obeyed. I chuckled and rested my hand on his head, my fingers caressing his ears. "It's a sad day when a dog I've had less than twelve hours minds me better than my best friends."

Before I could say anything else, the sounds of someone hurrying downstairs reached us. I looked up and smiled to see Ali skipping down the stairs. Misty, her black lab was on her heels. Ali raced into the den and pulled up short. Eyes wide, her mouth an "O" of surprise, she stared at me. Then she looked at her grandmother.

"Auntie Jax, you're glowing! That's so cool. Can you teach me how to glow?" She ran to me and wrapped her arms around my waist.

"Ali, you're supposed to be upstairs doing your homework," Lucas reminded her as Quinn, Meg and Ciara stared at me.

"All done." She broke her embrace and held a hand out to Fenris, letting him sniff her. "Can you, Auntie Jax? I want to glow."

"Someone want to tell me what she's talking about?" Sam asked softly.

"I'd like to know the same thing," Lucas admitted.

"Jax made a decision today, one that impacts all of us," Judith said before I could answer. "Ali is simply seeing the results of it—and it is something Jax will learn to control."

"Mom?" Ciara looked between Judith and me, her brow creased as she tried to figure it out.

"Serena?" Judith looked to the eldest of the guardians and I was more than happy to let her be the one to explain.

"This is something we'll be discussing at greater length later, especially with Quinn, Meg, Ciara, Amy and Lexie. But the short version is something they already know, even if they've done their best to ignore it." She smiled at them, letting them know she was fully aware of their concern—and their denial of their part in what needed to be done going forward. "For the rest of you, there have always been four *Others* who have acted as protectors or guardians for the town. It is their duty to keep the town safe and help normals and *Others* to coexist. Each guardian represents one of the elements. It gives a balance and strength to the ties they hold with one another and with the town."

"Judith?" Lucas asked as Quinn dropped back onto the arm of his chair.

"This generation's guardians are Serena, Pat and me. Meg's mother would have been the fourth but we all know what happened. So the town has been without a guardian all these years."

"Until now." This was my story and I should be the one to tell it. Although, it was very tempting to leave it to the others. "You know I'd already decided to stay and had made the commitment to do whatever I could to not only find the person who hurt Annie but make sure they never hurt anyone again." Heads nodded. "I'd even told the others I'd be the fourth guardian. But it wasn't until this morning that I fully embraced it."

"And what does that have to do with the rest of us?" Ciara took another step toward the door.

I grinned and motioned for her to stop. "It means we are going to be relying on you, each of you, to help us—especially me. You are my friends and you won't hesitate to tell me if I'm about to do something stupid."

"Now that's something I can happily agree to." Quinn grinned and waggled a finger at me.

I let her have her moment. There would be time later to tell her that she would very likely take over when her mother no longer felt able to handle her duties as guardian.

"What Ali sees right now is a little harder to explain." I paused for a moment, thinking. "Let's call it an energy boost. Judith and I worked together this morning and things all seemed to come together for me. I'm sure she, Dr. Pat and Miss Serena can help me dampen the effect."

"No," Ali drawled. "I like it. You're all shiny."

I grinned and ruffled her hair. "Yeah, but it might scare some folks, kiddo. Tell you what, though. I'll shine for you anytime."

"Cool!" She hugged me again. Then she looked from me to her mother. "Can I take Fenris outside and let him and Misty play?"

"Not today, Ali." I knelt in front of her, one hand on Fenris' head. "He needs to get used to all of us and all the dogs. This is all a little much for him right now."

She cocked her head to one side and studied the shepherd. Then she nodded, her expression very grown up. "Okay, Auntie Jax. Can I come play with him tomorrow?"

"I'm sure something can be arranged." I smiled and ruffled her hair.

"Hey, Ali, why don't the two of us go to Grandma's workroom and practice using our talents?" Amy suggested.

"Can I, Mama?"

Quinn checked her watch and then looked at Miss Serena. Something about the way Miss Serena looked back at her answered her unasked question. "Not tonight, sweetie. It's time we get you home so you can get to bed. Tomorrow's a school day."

"And we need to pick up Robbie and the twins from Sam's folks," Annie said as she stood.

"Cowards," I muttered, earning a chuckle from Meg who was close enough to hear.

"I don't know about everyone else, but I'm glad you're home and that you've decided to do all you have, Jax." Drew held a hand out to his wife.

I watched, my eyes narrowing as Meg took his hand and let him pull her to her feet. There was something I couldn't quite put my finger on. . . .

"Auntie Meg!" Ali gasped and then giggled before launching herself at the Meg. "When's your baby due?"

"She's your daughter," Lucas said when Quinn looked at him in surprise.

"Ali, how did you know?" Quinn asked, sounding very much like she really didn't want to know.

"She's got a really pretty new aura layer, Mama. This one's sort of soft and looks almost like a cloud."

Miss Serena hid her laugh behind her hand as Meg stared wide-eyed at Ali. Then Drew gave a shout. His hands went around his wife's waist and he spun her around. The moment Meg's feet touched the floor again, Amy was there. She placed a gentle hand on Meg's still flat abdomen. Her gaze seemed to unfocus for a moment. Then she grinned and nodded her head.

"You'll want to take a test to confirm it, but Ali's right. You're pregnant."

"Congratulations, you two." Quinn hugged Meg and then grinned at Drew, punching his shoulder. "I think I'm going to take my daughter home now before she reveals any more secrets."

"Mama?" Ali looked at her mother, worried. "Did I do something wrong?"

"No, baby, you didn't do anything wrong." Quinn hugged her and then lifted her and settled her on her hip.

As she did, I smiled slightly. Ali was growing up. Soon Quinn wouldn't be able to carry her like that. "Ali, your mom's right. You didn't do anything wrong. In fact, you did everything right. You are being observant. More than the rest of us." I ran my hand over her hair.

"Really?"

"Really." I looked at Quinn and grinned. "We'll talk some more tomorrow."

"We most certainly will." The look she gave me left no doubt about it.

"We will all talk tomorrow." Annie pinned me with a look that promised something other than a calm discussion. "Miss Serena, thanks for dinner."

"My pleasure, Annie."

Over the next few minutes, everyone else said their goodbyes and left. Rafe took Fenris out back and I carried the last of the dishes from the dining room. Amy stood at the sink, loading the dishwasher. Miss Serena, Judith and Mary Kate busied themselves putting away the leftovers.

"You okay?" Amy asked.

"Yeah." I grinned suddenly and gave her a hip bump. "I don't know who looked more surprised: Quinn or Meg."

She chuckled, her eyes sparkling. "Quinn is so going to have her hands full with that little girl."

"Serves her right for everything she put me through growing up," Judith said, smiling, as she looked up from the pie she was putting away. "But it does mean we're going to have to talk with Ali and with Quinn."

"Which we will do soon," Miss Serena commented. "Jackie, are you all right? Judith told us about this morning."

"I am." In fact, I felt better than all right. I felt whole, something I hadn't realized was missing until today. I looked at the door as Rafe entered, Fenris on his heels. "I know we have a lot to discuss, but I'm exhausted. If it's all right, I'd like to wait until tomorrow to finish. I'm going to need to get an early start in the morning."

"Go, child. Call me after you finish with your aunt and let me know your plans." Miss Serena kissed my cheek before reaching down to scratch Fenris' ears. "You take good care of her, Rafe."

"I will, ma'am."

"And don't worry, Jax. You did everything right today. This is right for you and for us and, more importantly, for the town," Dr. Pat said.

I hoped so. God, I sincerely hoped so. But, for the moment, all I really wanted was to go home and crawl into bed. Maybe even hide from the world for a while.

" **A** re you ready?"

Annie stopped and looked at us, her expression serious. She wore what I called one of her power suits, this one red, with a white silk blouse and matching red heels that made my feet hurt just looking at them. Meg stood next to her. Instead of red, she wore black with a light grey blouse. The final member of the "legal team" was Clayton Nelms, the head of the company's legal team.

I glanced at Bitsy as she stood next to me. Gone was the ditsy woman so many thought her to be. This as the woman I knew determined, focused and ready to do whatever it took to protect family and the family business. She smiled and squeezed my hand.

Show time!

"Let's do this."

Annie nodded and pushed open the doors. As we walked outside onto the courthouse steps, I smiled slightly. This had Miss Olivia's touch all over it. Several microphones had been set up in front of the courthouse entrance. Members of the press, not just the local paper but the Dallas/Fort Worth stations as well, waited on the sidewalk. Beyond them, folks started to gather, alerted no doubt by the town's grapevine.

I reached out and lightly touched Meg's arm. When she glanced back at me, I nodded toward the back of the crowd. Standing there, doing his best to blend in, was Sawyer. Good. Now to put the plan into motion.

"Good morning, ladies and gentlemen. Thank you for coming at such short notice," Nelms began. It had been decided to let him start things off. Annie would be front and center soon enough and, heaven help me, so would I.

Unless I got lucky and the earth opened up and swallowed me.

"My name is Clayton Nelms and I am chief corporate counsel for Powell Properties. The company, originally known as Powell Real Estate, was founded shortly after Mossy Creek was first settled. Its former CEO, Thomas Powell, prior to his death executed a will laying out not only how he wanted his estate handled upon his death but also laying out provisions for the continued health of the company. Not just for the family but for Mossy Creek and all of Harkin County.

"Today, motions were filed with the court to not only honor Mr. Powell's wishes but to prevent one of his heirs from taking any further action that might harm the company and those working for it." He looked to his right and nodded. When he did, several people, including Carli Sanderson, began handing out copies of the motions we filed. "Because we believe in being transparent, you now have copies of what we filed. We won't be commenting on the specifics of the motion beyond what is outlined in the paperwork. However, we will take questions at this time."

For a moment, silence seemed to fall over the crowd. Then, as the pleadings were read, a murmur began. Less than a minute later, the questions started. Annie nodded to Nelms and stepped up to his side.

"One question at a time." She waited for everyone to settle down. "Most of you know me. For those who don't, my name is Julianna Grissom Caldwell. This is my law partner, Meg Sheridan Grissom. We represent Elizabeth Powell-Gunnerson and Dr. Jaqueline Powell, the daughter and granddaughter of Thomas Powell."

"Mrs. Caldwell, does this action have anything to do with you running for DA?" one of the reporters asked.

"No, it does not. It does, however, have everything to do with protecting the interests of my client, Mrs. Powell-Gunnerson, and Mrs. Grissom's client, Dr. Powell."

"But isn't the timing of this something your opponent could say is very convenient?" the same reporter asked.

I stepped forward. Even though I knew Annie could handle the question, I wanted the attention on me, not her. That was the entire point of this spectacle.

"I'll answer that," I said as I took Annie's place at the mic. "As Mrs. Caldwell said, my name is Dr. Jacqueline Powell. As Mr. Nelms and Mrs. Caldwell said, I am one of the petitioners in the motions you now have copies of. I want to begin by saying this is not something either my aunt nor I wanted to do. In fact, we have done everything reasonably possible to avoid having to bring the matter to court. However, my grandfather was a wise man and he made his final wishes concerning the family, our inheritance and Powell Properties very clear. As stewards for his legacy, we are honor bound to do our best to carry out his wishes.

"For those of you not familiar with Mossy Creek or its history, my grandfather's family was one of the first to settle here. From the beginning, they were determined to do whatever they could to not only protect the town but to see it grow and prosper. Over the course of time, the family has owned a number of different businesses, bringing jobs and opportunities to the town.

"Under my grandfather's leadership, Powell Properties became one of the most successful in the industry. Its success is rooted in a handful of foundation beliefs the company was built upon and that my grandfather held dear. The first is that it would always have a sales and development force located in Harkin County and the company headquarters would never be far from Mossy Creek. The second was that the family would maintain control of the company and act as stewards for all who have worked for us, all who do work for us and all who will in the future. The third is related to the first. Because of his commitment to our community, he included in his will a provision that required any family member wishing to sell his or her interest in the company to offer it first to the other members of the family holding shares. If they wished to purchase the shares, they would do so at fair market value. Each member of the family receiving shares under my grandfather's will signed documents at the time acknowledging not only that we knew and understood the provisions and what they required but that we also agreed to follow those provisions.

"As you will see in the filings, the members of the family who received shares when my grandfather died were my aunt, my father and myself. Because I was away at college and then vet school, I gave my aunt my proxy to deal with anything concerning the business. And, before you ask, she did so but she also consulted with me every step along the way. We are all fortunate because she takes her role as caretaker for her father's, my grandfather's, legacy seriously. Because she does, she knew when shares of the company were put up for sale in violation of my grandfather's will."

"Dr. Powell, are you saying your father violated the terms of his father's will?" Tony Forsythe, a reporter for the local paper, asked.

"That is exactly what I'm saying."

A murmur of disbelief ran through the crowd. A number of those gathered, those from Mossy Creek, turned to look at Sawyer. He ignored them as he lifted his cellphone to his ear and began talking to someone. I might not be able to hear him, but my money was on him trying to contact my parents. We'd blindsided him and he would need to do something soon to try to refocus the spotlight off of him and his clients and back on Annie and her "shortcomings".

"My father, in violation of the terms of my grandfather's will and in direct contravention of the agreement he signed after learning of the contents of the will, tried to sell his shares without first offering them to either my aunt or myself. In order to protect the company and follow their father's wishes, my aunt purchased those shares through an intermediary. She then sold half to me, thereby keeping the company in family hands."

"So why bring the suit now?" a female reporter I didn't recognize asked.

"For several reasons. First, my father has been demanding we return the shares to him, without repayment, and place him on the board of directors. While we might be willing to consider the former, he has done nothing to reassure us he won't try to circumvent the will's provisions again."

I lifted my hand and ticked off another point on my fingers. "Second, he has been threatening to sue both my aunt and me if we don't give in to his blackmail." Another finger ticked off. "Third, it has come to our attention that he has overextended himself financially and is deeply in debt due to some bad decisions at the track."

One last finger tick and it was time to go off-script. "Finally, our attorneys and corporate counsel learned that my father's attorney, Joe Bob Sawyer." I pointed to where Sawyer stood at the back of the crowd. He looked up at me, his eyes going wide, before he said something and then shoved the phone into his pants pocket. "Yes, that's him right there, looking like a deer caught in the headlights." I grinned, enjoying this game of cat and mouse probably more than I should.

"As I was saying, it came to their attention that Mr. Sawyer planned to file suit against us and against the company for a number of spurious complaints, all aimed at forcing us to return the stock without recompense. It would be a frivolous lawsuit and Mr. Sawyer knows it. However, he would rather risk being sanctioned by the court in an attempt to keep Mrs. Caldwell's attention on doing her job representing my aunt than on running against him for DA."

"Lies!" he countered angrily as he took a step forward.

I grinned, the cat that just cornered the mouse.

"Since he's stepped forward, why don't you ask him why he took on my father's case when his field of expertise is most definitely not probate or corporate law? While you're at it, ask him why he has also taken on the case of Mia Caldwell, the ex-wife of Mrs. Caldwell's husband. A woman who abandoned Mr. Caldwell after he'd been seriously wounded in the service of our country. A woman who walked out on their infant son and who has not had any contact with either of them since the day she deserted them. A woman who dared attempt to remove the little boy, who Mrs. Caldwell has legally adopted, from school without authority.

"Now, I'm not saying there's any connection, but the timing of this is all a bit more coincidental than I like. Both of these cases came to light just days after someone attacked Mrs. Caldwell in her home. Perhaps someone should be asking Mr. Sawyer some very hard questions. I know my attorney." I motioned to where Meg stood a few feet away, doing her best not to look like she wanted to kill me. "Has more than a few questions for Mr. Sawyer concerning the sale of the company stock. My father is many things but careless he isn't. He would have discussed the matter with an attorney. It would be interesting to know when Mr. Sawyer accepted the case, wouldn't it?"

Sawyer turned an interesting shade of purple as I looked straight at him, all but daring him to say anything else. He opened his mouth and then snapped it shut. For a moment, I wondered if he was going to stroke out. Not that I wanted him to. I'd much rather watch him dance in court as he answered to charges against him.

And I knew if we dug deeply enough, we'd find something to use to go after him.

"I make this pledge to you and to everyone in Mossy Creek and Harkin County. My aunt and I will do everything possible to ensure my grandfather's wishes are honored. Powell Properties will be here for years to come. We will not bend to threats or blackmail. If my father and Mr. Sawyer want a fight, they've got one. In fact, we look forward to meeting them in court. Thank you."

I stepped back. As I did, Bitsy nodded, pride shining in her eyes. Together, we walked down the steps, occasionally stopping to answer a question. By the time we made our way through the reporters and the others who gathered, Rafe was at my side. He took my hand and gave it a quick squeeze. Together, we walked to the café where Janny stood by the door. She let us in and then locked the door behind us. As she did, she flipped the sign to "closed", telling everyone trying to get in that the café would reopen in an hour or so.

"Sit. Mom's getting your drinks now," she said as she waved us to the back booth.

"Thanks." I followed Bitsy, knowing the others were on our heels. "Well?" I asked once everyone had settled in the booth and around the nearest table.

"Have you lost your fucking mind?" Meg demanded. Seated next to her, Annie nodded and glared at me.

"Not at all."

Before I could say anything else, Nelms chuckled and everyone looked at him in question. "Dr. Powell played that perfectly. I couldn't have wished for a better performance. Tell me, doctor, did you know Sawyer would be there?"

I shook my head. "No, but I figured if he was anywhere near the courthouse when we got started, he'd come see what was going on."

"So all that was ad lib?" He shook his head, a smile on his lips. "Damn, but you are good."

"I wouldn't say ad lib. I'd given a lot of thought to what to say if he showed up." Annie opened her mouth and shut it at my warning look. "My friends here aren't considering everything yet. They're only worried I put a target on my back—which I did. But I did so know-ingly. For several reasons, we need Sawyer focused on me right now and not Annie. It will throw him off stride when it comes to trying to invalidate our purchase of my father's stocks. It will also throw him off stride when it comes to the election. After all, I've planted a lot of seeds for the media to follow. Then there's the jab I took at Mia. If she's still in the area, you know she's going to respond. It will be inter-esting to see if it is through Sawyer or some other way."

"Robbie," Annie whispered, fear for her son clear.

"Will be protected," I assured her. "For now, we wait and see."

"And prepare to go forward with our suit against your father," Nelms said and I nodded. He stood and extended his hand. "I've long enjoyed working with your aunt, Dr. Powell. I look forward to working with you as well." He bent and kissed Bitsy's cheek and left, promising to be in contact as soon as he heard from Sawyer—which he expected to be sooner rather than later.

"You did good, Jax," Miss Peggy said as she stopped next to the booth. She quickly handed out Irish coffees to everyone but Meg who got a cup of herbal tea. Seeing the mutinous look on her face, I pressed my lips together to keep from laughing. "And don't any of you be worrying. I'm keeping my ear to the ground and so is everyone else. We'll let you know if we hear anything."

"Thanks, Miss Peggy." I lifted my cup and saluted my friends, my real family. "Here's hoping this will soon be over."

Now all we had to do was wait to see what happened next.

28

For the next week, we all stayed on our guards. Lucas now had the man responsible for hurting Sasha in the Harkin County Jail. As promised, Kerwin Jones wouldn't be going anywhere anytime soon. Between the outstanding warrants and the additional charges Lucas filed—including possession with intent to distribute—after locating an almost derelict trailer Jones had been staying in, he was looking at a high bail, something he'd been unable to post yet.

Unfortunately, he continued to refuse to tell Lucas anything beyond his name and demand an attorney. He had tried calling Sawyer once back in Mossy Creek but without success. Now he had a court appointed attorney and was cooling his heels in a cell. I was fine with that because it meant he couldn't do anything to hurt Annie or anyone else I cared for.

The press conference, on the other hand, yielded much of what I'd hoped for. Bright and early the next morning, Sawyer appeared in the District Clerk's Office. He filed half a dozen motions and a counter suit. Unlike the day before, his press conference was poorly attended by both the media and local residents. Those who did attend were more interested in what I'd said than in anything he wanted to talk about.

Nelms, Annie and Meg didn't wait to be served copies of his paperwork. They appeared at the clerk's office less than an hour later and picked up their copies. Meg told me later they met for a couple of hours, going over everything, and then they drafted motions to dismiss on each one.

Two days later, they were in court. Bitsy and I watched from the gallery as Annie, acting as lead counsel, totally demolished each and every one of Sawyer's motions. Judge Aaron Zimmer dismissed each motion and then turned his attention to Sawyer's counter suit. In very short order, he let Annie prove up that my grandfather's will had been properly executed and probated. Before Sawyer had a chance to object, Judge Zimmer dismissed the counter suit, citing a lack of time-liness in filing. Then he set a trial date six months down the road to hear our case. Before anyone could say "boo!", Zimmer adjourned the hearing and left the bench. As he did, my parents turned to Sawyer, demanding he do something. Knowing what would happen next, Bitsy and I beat a hasty retreat to avoid having to say anything to them.

We won round one, but it wouldn't stop my parents for long. Nor was it stopping Bitsy. She called a special meeting of the Board of Directors and I formally took the seat that had been held for me. Then she dropped a thumb drive on the table in front of me, telling me it had our financials and other information I needed to look at. Before I could protest, she said the one thing I had no counter for. The best way to convince a judge that I was a good caretaker was to actually be a caretaker for the business.

So what little free time I had was shortened even more. I didn't need to sleep, did I?

At least Rafe was there to help as much as he could. Those nights when I shifted and ran my property, he watched my back. He was with me when we kept an eye on Annie's house. He was in my bed or I was in his most nights.

Friday dawned bright and early. I lay in bed in my new house and stretched. Then I tossed back the sheet and padded across the room to the window. I stood there, staring outside. I loved the isolation, especially since I knew town was only a few minutes away. A smile touched my lips as I watched Rafe and Fenris returning to the house after their morning run.

"You've been very quiet this morning, Doc. Is everything all right?" Rafe asked as we dressed.

I nodded and then smiled. "Yeah. Sorry. Just thinking."

"About?"

"My life and how much it's changed this past month or so." I stepped into my jeans and reached for a tee shirt.

"Changed for the better, I hope."

"Much." Tee shirt in hand, jeans still unzipped, I moved to stand in front of him. "And you are a big reason for it being better. I'm not sure I'd have been able to keep it all together without you. So thank you." I leaned up and lightly kissed him.

"Doc, you've been good for me too." He rested his hands on my waist and pulled me close. "You've shown I can let myself feel again. You've reminded me there's more to life than the pain I saw overseas. Sam kept telling me there was and that I'd realize it sooner or later, but I didn't really believe him. Because of that, I existed but didn't live. You've shown me how to live again."

I pulled his head down and kissed him again, this time doing my best to let him know how much he meant to me. We hadn't really talked about the future, but it was becoming almost impossible to think about not having him in my life.

"Rafe." I rested my head against his bare chest. "Are you sure about this?"

Whatever *this* was.

He framed my face with his hands and looked at me for a long moment before gently kissing me. "I am more sure about this than I have been about anything in a very long time." Another kiss, this one deep and with enough feeling to curl my toes.

"Good." I grinned and nipped his lower lip. "Because I feel the same way. But, if I don't get dressed, you aren't going to get to work before noon."

He laughed, his eyes sparkling. Before I knew what he meant to do, he had me in his arms. He crossed the bedroom and tossed me onto the bed. I landed with a surprised "oof!". Then he launched himself at me, catching himself on hands and knees so he didn't crush me. His head dipped and his teeth scraped the side of my neck.

"Work can wait." He shoved one hand inside my panties, cupping me as I moaned lowly.

"Rafe," I moaned.

"Shh." He covered my mouth with his. "Just enjoy it." He stroked me and I moved my hands between us, struggling with his zipper. "No." He shook his head and reached for my hands with his free hand. "Let me do this for you. Think of it as a hint of what we'll do tonight." He grinned and I moaned again, my eyes glazing over with lust.

"You? What about you?" I panted as he expertly brought me close to climax before slowing, teasing me with the promise of a release to come.

"This is enough for now." He brushed his lips against mine.

"No." I shook my head and arched my back, trying to free my legs from where he had them pinned beneath him.

"Behave, Doc, or I'll have to make sure you do." He grinned, as if daring me to try him.

I lay back, chest heaving, heart racing. He held my hands above my head with one hand. His other still played with me, teasing but not bringing me to release. Well, two could play. I lifted my head. My lips traced a gentle line down his neck to his shoulder. I used my nose to push aside his collar and kissed him. Then, as he relaxed, I bit down. He gasped. Then he thrust his finger in me, distracting me as he pumped in and out.

"I told you to behave," he chided, humor lacing his voice.

He released my hands long enough to slip his belt from his jeans. Before I could react, he looped the belt around my hands and secured them to the headboard. Then he bent and kissed me, gently, lovingly.

"Trust me?" he asked.

I nodded even though my heart beat a quick staccato.

"You can stop this whenever you want." He gently cupped my

cheek, his thumb stroking back and forth. "Do you want me to stop and let you go?"

I tugged against the belt and shook my head. I wasn't normally one who liked this sort of game. Hell, I hated giving up control for any reason. But I could with Rafe.

He smiled and gently kissed me. Then he sat up. His hand cupped my breasts, thumbs and forefingers gently rolling and tugging my nipples. I gasped and arched into him as he kissed his way down my throat to my chest. I would have held his head where it was as his teeth scraped my right breast before he took that nipple into his mouth. Moaning, my body alive with need, I writhed beneath him and he chuckled, pleased with himself and his effect on me.

"Like that?" He looked into my eyes and I nodded, trying to find my voice. "Then I think you'll love what happens next."

He shuffled on his knees to the foot of the bed. I lifted my head, watching as he slowly pulled down my jeans and then my panties. Once he had, he nudged my legs open wider. He knelt between them, his hands running up my calves to my thighs. His lips followed. By the time he reached my clit, I was panting with need. He chuckled softly and blew across my clit, almost making me come.

"Leave your legs open, Doc. If you don't, I'll tie them open."

"Need you," I rasped.

God, I needed him so badly right then.

"And I need you." He shimmied out of his jeans without ever leaving the bed. "Let me show you how much I need you."

Half an hour later, he wrapped a towel around me as I stepped out of the shower. As he did, I lifted my face to his kiss. I wouldn't argue if I had to start every morning like this. Of course, I might have to return the favor and tie him to the bed. I wonder if he'd beg for release as much as I did. I'd certainly like to see.

"Thank you."

I paused toweling my hair and looked at him. "I think I should be the one thanking you."

He shook his head. Then he reached for my hand and pulled me into the bedroom, seating me on the edge of the mattress. A moment later he sat back on his heels in front of me. He looked so serious, I swallowed hard.

"Rafe?"

"Jax—Doc, you just gave me a gift I didn't deserve." He reached for my hand and cradled it between his. "You trusted me. At a time when I could have taken advantage of you, when I could have hurt you, you trusted me not to. You didn't see my shadows. You weren't afraid of me. Why?"

"Because I knew I could." I drew him onto the mattress at my side. "Rafe, I don't know who hurt you and, to be honest, it's best that I don't. I'd probably go looking for them to have a little *chat*."

He laughed and pulled me onto his lap. His arms wrapped around me and he buried his face in the crook of my neck.

"Rafe, I trusted you because you are a good man, a man of his word. You told me I could trust you and that I could stop it any time I wanted to. I knew all it would take was a word."

He nodded, his face still pressed against my neck. I felt the tension in him and that worried me.

"Rafe, what is it?" I stroked his hair, giving him the time he needed to answer.

He sighed, and then smiled slightly. So many emotions crossed his face. Then he kissed me so gently and tenderly I almost wept.

"I know what a gift you gave me, Doc." He ran his fingers through my damp hair. "You gave up control."

I touched my forehead to his. Then I looked him in the eye. I wanted him to see I was serious. He needed to hear this and I had a feeling he needed to hear it badly. He had scars that ran as deep as my own—if not deeper.

"Rafe, I didn't give up control. You gave me control over everything. I'll admit I rarely play like we did because I don't like giving up control. I haven't dated anyone I trusted enough to do what you did and not take advantage of the situation. But I know you." I rested my hand on his chest over his heart. "*I know you*. I knew you wouldn't do anything I didn't want you to."

I brushed my lips over his again, willing him to listen and believe.

Then I grinned, letting devilment dance in my eyes. "Of course, the question is if you'll trust me in a similar situation."

He laughed and hugged me, his arms holding me tight against him. "What are we doing here, Doc?"

Wasn't that the million dollar question? And didn't it deserve and answer?

Hoping I didn't scare him away, I decided it was time to be honest with both of us.

"I don't know about you, but I think I'm falling in love." I held my breath, waiting for his response.

"Oh thank God." He blew out a long breath and kissed me. Then he nuzzled my neck and I tilted my head to give him better access, all but humming in response. "I told you once that I think I started falling in love with you back when Sam would tell me stories about Mossy Creek. That night when I figured out what you are and realized how much you were risking to look after Annie, you stole my heart."

"Annie's special, Rafe. That's something you have to understand. She and Quinn are like my sisters. I'll do anything for them. Same for Maddy."

Which reminded me I wanted to call and check on her. I still felt uneasy by her decision not to come home.

"And I love you for it. Annie and Sam are my family."

"I know. And that's another reason I fell for you." I slid off his lap. A moment later I pulled him to his feet. "Where do we go from here?"

I couldn't believe I'd asked that. This wasn't me. I was always the one to resist getting involved with someone. I valued my freedom, my independence. But this was different. He didn't try to make me into someone I wasn't. He embraced the fact I was different, even for an *Other*. I wanted to see if I had a future with him.

God, what was it about Mossy Creek that made everyone want to settle down?

"I don't want to overplay my hand here, Doc, but I want to be part of your life and I want you to be part of mine. I want you watching my back as I watch yours. I want to share your bed and your life." He looked at our joined hands.

"Me too."

It scared the shit out of me, but I wanted it more than I realized. Telling him to stay where he was, I hurried out of the room. It didn't matter I wore only a towel. There was no one else in the house or nearby to see. I needed him to know I was serious.

"Here," I said when I returned to the bedroom. I handed him a set of keys and a remote. "I want you to have these."

He looked at them and then at me. "Doc." He cleared his throat. "Are you sure?"

I nodded. "More sure than I have been of anything else I've done since coming home."

"Thank you." He held me close for a moment. "God, I wish I didn't have to go to work."

"Me too." I wished we could stay home and hide from the world. "And I need to check Miss Serena's stock and then I need to meet with Meg. There's more legal wrangling than I expected where the new clinic's concerned."

"It won't last much longer. Sam said the plans are almost ready. Once you've okayed them, we can file them with the city and county and start pulling permits. "

I grinned, excited. I looked forward to this new chapter of my life, especially if Rafe was there to share it with me.

"How about meeting back here after work? I'll pick up some steaks while I'm out and we can throw them on the grill."

"Sounds good. Do you want me to pick up anything?" He reached for his shirt and pulled it on.

"No." I changed my mind. "Yes. Pick up a nice bottle of red wine. I haven't had a chance to stock up on liquor yet and we're almost out of everything after the other night. Just get enough for the two of us. I want you to myself tonight."

"That sounds like a most excellent idea." His grin sent shivers of lust down me. "I'll touch base later." He stepped into his work boots and straightened. "I need to say this and I hope to hell you don't go running for the hills."

I frowned, wondering why he suddenly seemed so serious.

"I love you, Jax Powell." His expression softened and he looked strangely vulnerable. "I never thought I'd say that again. One day I'll explain why. But know you have my heart."

Tears pooled in my eyes and I dashed at them. Smiling, I held a hand out to him. "Rafe, that is the most wonderful gift I've ever received. You need to know you hold my heart as well." I sniffled and then grinned. "Now get out of here before I decide we both need to take the day off."

He kissed me and was halfway across the room when my cellphone rang. His went off at almost the same time. Worried, I reached for my phone where it rested on the bedside table. I mouthed "Annie" when I saw the readout. Then, as my stomach did a slow roll when he whispered "Sam", I answered the call.

"What's wrong?" I asked without preamble. As I did, I struggled to get into my jeans using only one hand. "Annie, what is it?"

"He's gone." She didn't sob, but it was a near thing. Her voice strained, her breathing labored, I prayed she hadn't been hurt again.

"Who's gone and are you all right?" I grabbed my tee shirt and carried it and the phone into the bathroom where I could put the call on speaker and not disturb Rafe.

"Robbie."

I reached for the counter, gripping it so hard I'm surprised it didn't break. While Rafe and I had been having fun and games, something happened to Robbie.

Damn it!

"What happened?" I pulled on my tee shirt and grabbed my phone, carrying it back into the bedroom.

"The school called. He's disappeared. They can't find him."

I inhaled, held it for a count of five and then exhaled. Calm. I needed to be calm and I needed to think. But first, I needed to reassure Annie.

"Where are you?"

"Home. I came home to see if he'd come back here for some reason."

"Stay there. I'm on my way." I thought for a moment. "Have you called Lucas?"

"Y-yes. Sam did."

"Good. You stay there and don't worry. We're going to find him. I'll be at your place in a few minutes. Promise."

"Hurry," she begged before I hung up.

As I turned to Rafe, he slid his phone into his pocket. He looked about like I felt: stunned, worried and furious. "Finish dressing. I'll get Fenris' lead and our guns. Don't argue with me on this, Doc."

"Not going to." Not if having a gun helped tip the odds in our favor.

"Once you're ready, head to Annie's. I'm going to meet Sam at the school, see what they can tell us."

I nodded, pulling on my boots. I was heading downstairs before he had the lead attached to Fenris' halter. "Let me know what you find out," I said as I reached up to kiss him. "And stay safe."

"You do the same." He reached under his shirt and pulled out his dog tags. I watched as he removed one from the chain, slipping the single tag into his front pocket. Then he slid the chain over my head. "To remind you that I'm always with you."

"Be safe, love." I gripped the dog tag in my right hand as I kissed him. Then, I hurried outside, Fenris at my heels.

Trouble had once again come to us and, by all that was holy, we would win.

29

The moment I parked out front of Annie's house, I felt the wards around the property. They were on full alert. If possible, the house and land were angry and worried. Exactly what I felt from Annie when she called.

I raced up the walk to the front porch, Fenris at my side. The front door opened as one booted foot hit the bottom step. Quinn and Ciara appeared. To my surprise, they grabbed me and spun me away from the door. As they all but frog walked me to the far end of the porch, I demanded an explanation. What the hell was going on and why wouldn't they let me inside?

"Calm down!" Quinn snapped. "We need to talk."

"Let. Me. Go." I bit off each word.

"Stop fighting and listen to us." Ciara grabbed my chin and forced me to look at her. "I mean it. We need to talk."

"Then talk."

"Lucas called after you talked to Annie. There's video of Robbie leaving the school with someone. They climbed into the same car Mia was seen climbing into the day she tried to take him out of school. An APB has gone out and he's getting things rolling on issuing an Amber Alert."

I jerked my head free and stalked off the porch. I didn't wait to see if they followed. I made my way around the house and opened the gate to the dog run. At my signal, Fenris went in. I bent and rubbed his ears, telling him I'd be back soon. Then I straightened and turned to the others. There were questions I needed answered before I went inside.

"How long ago?"

"Almost an hour," Quinn answered.

My hands fisted at my sides and I looked heavenward, trying to rein in my temper. "Why did it take so long to let Annie know?"

"From what they told Lucas, they wanted to make sure Robbie wasn't hiding somewhere on campus." Ciara's tone told me she was no happier about what was going on than I was.

"By then, Ali had called me," Quinn added, explaining how her daughter called to tell her Robbie had gone to the bathroom and hadn't come back to class.

"Have you let the others know?"

Quinn nodded. "Everyone is here or on their way."

"Everyone?" God, the last thing Annie needed was her mother making everything worse.

"Don't worry. You aunt picked up Catherine and is going to keep close to her," Ciara assured me. "Mary Kate called her and asked."

That much, at least, was good. "Annie?"

"Barely hanging on right now. She's inside with Meg, Mary Kate, mom and Miss Serena. Dr. Pat is at the hospital and will get here as soon as she can, but it will be at least another few hours. Lexie and Amy are on their way. Sam called as you pulled up. He is on his way back and said to tell you Rafe is heading this way. Drew's on his way as well."

"Ali?" Lucas will be bringing her when he heads over in a few minutes.

We paused, listening as several cars approached and stopping out front. Ciara looked at her sister and something seemed to pass between them. Then Ciara turned and trotted around the corner, calling out to the newcomers, identifying them even as the protections reared up before lowering so they could come in. Both told me they were family and not seen as a threat.

"How is she, really?"

"How do you think?" Quinn looked down at her hands and shook them when she saw the flames flickering around them. "Sorry." She tried to smile. "She's terrified. She is also convinced this is Mia, possibly with help from Sawyer."

I nodded, in full agreement.

"Has anyone decided on a course of action?"

She shook her head.

Well, that was about to change. No way was I going to just sit there as we waited for someone to contact us. I'd promised Annie I'd keep her family safe. I wasn't about to let her be separated from her son any longer than possible.

Inside, I found Annie and Sam in the den with the others already gathered. As I entered from the kitchen, Lucas and Rafe came through the front door. Lucas looked around the room, nodding slightly. Drew, his expression stone cold, talked softly on his phone to someone. Bitsy—bless her—was there and keeping Catherine under control. Meg was on her cellphone, coordinating with Beth and Miss Olivia about their court schedule for the day and updating them on what little she knew. Judge Caldwell was on his cellphone, probably talking to the governor, calling in favors to help as well.

But it was the sight of Camille, always the calm one, pacing back and forth, anger fairly radiating off of her, that brought me up short. When Mary Kate placed a hand on her arm, she shook it off. Then she stopped and apologized. Mary Kate told her it was all right, that she understood. But I saw the worry in her eyes. Worry for more than just Robbie. Camille was always the calm one. Now she looked ready to strike out on her own to find her grandson. I couldn't let her do that any more than I could let Annie or Sam go hunting for their son. No, it was up to us—the current and future guardians—to find the boy and deal with whoever took him.

"Where's Ali?" I asked as Rafe hurried to my side.

"Out back with the dogs," Lucas said. "We need to talk before she comes in."

"What?" Quinn stopped near me, suddenly the protective mother.

"She's feeling responsible for what happened." He reached out and stopped her before Quinn could go to her daughter.

"Lucas!"

"Listen to me. You need to hear this." He waited until she nodded, her expression thunderous. "Robbie told her he was going to the bathroom when they were on their way back inside from a fire drill. When he didn't come back, she asked their teacher to check on him. She knew something was wrong. The teacher couldn't find him and notified the office. They asked Ali if Robbie said anything about leaving school. They didn't blame her but she's blaming herself. She thinks if she'd told Robbie to go to class instead of watching him go to the bathroom, he wouldn't be missing now."

"Go," I told Quinn, understanding her need to reassure her daughter. As she turned to leave the house, I looked at Judith where she stood across the room and motioned for her to go with her youngest daughter. Then I turned my attention back to Lucas. "Video?"

"I'm sure Quinn told you, Robbie was caught on video getting into a vehicle similar to the one we know Mia has been using."

Sam cursed and then shushed the twin he cradled in his arms, apologizing for upsetting him. "Find him, Lucas, and then throw that bitch in the deepest darkest cell you have. Then give me the keys. Let me have five minutes alone with her."

Annie put a calming hand on his thigh and shook her head. "Lucas?"

"I've notified every agency in the state. The airports have been notified. So have car rental agencies, etc. We'll find them. I promise."

I moved to kneel in front of Annie. I rested a hand on little Maggie's head, silently promising that I'd bring her big brother home. Then I smiled up at Annie and Sam, my heart breaking for them both.

"I want the two of you to stay here. You'll be safe here and this way you are with the twins. They need you right now." I shook my head slightly when Sam started to say something. "Rafe and I are going to check something out. We won't be long and it might help find your son."

"You be careful." Annie grabbed for my hand, looking at me so intently I felt like she was seeing into my very soul.

"Always."

I leaned over and kissed her cheek. Then I squeezed Sam's hand. As I stood and turned, Lucas frowned and opened his mouth to say something. Before he could, Miss Serena stepped forward. She rested a hand on my shoulder, reassuring me and letting Lucas know she backed me with whatever I had in mind.

"Go. Let us know what you find out."

"You and the others keep them safe."

"We will." She patted my shoulder and then put my hand in Rafe's. "You watch her back, young man."

"Always, ma'am."

Ciara followed us outside. As we crossed the lawn to where I'd parked, she stopped us. "Here. Take the SUV." She handed Rafe the keys. "You'll find everything you need in the back in a lock box. Key's on the ring."

"Thank you." I gave her a quick hug. "Tell your sister we'll have something in half an hour if everything goes as planned."

"Just don't do anything that will land you in jail. Neither she nor Annie will thank you for it."

I nodded, thinking for a moment. "Is there any way the two of you can have a chat," I made air quotes around the word, "with the bastard Lucas has in jail?"

She shook her head. "I wish, but no."

"Then how about coming for a ride with us?" Rafe chuckled almost wickedly and I grinned, glad he not only knew what I had in mind but approved. "In fact, let's see if your sister won't come as well."

Ciara laughed softly and rubbed her hands together. "You are an evil woman, Jax Powell, and I love you for it. You two get the car started. I'll grab Quinn."

"She's wrong," Rafe said as Ciara disappeared around the back of the house. "You aren't evil. You are loyalty and determination personified. And, like her, I love you for it."

I wasn't sure either of them was right, but I wasn't going to argue. Today, I would do whatever it take, play whatever role was needed, to bring Robbie home to his parents.

"Care telling me what you have in mind?" Quinn asked as we pulled away from the curb. She and Ciara sat in the back and I listened as they checked their weapons and slid them back into holsters and sheathes.

"We're going to go pay a visit to Sawyer." Of course, that meant making sure we knew where he was. I doubted he'd answer the phone if any of us called. Same thing if I asked Beth or Miss Olivia to. As much as I loved modern technology, this time I wished we didn't have the convenience of caller ID. Then inspiration hit and I dialed a number I still knew by memory.

"Smithson Garage," a familiar voice said after the third ring.

"Hey, Jake." I almost stumbled over the name. It was going to take time to get used to him no longer being Bubba. "It's Jax. I'm wondering if you could do me a solid."

"Sure, Jax. What'd you need?"

"Any chance you can tell if Sawyer is in his office?"

"Hang on. Let me walk outside."

He put the phone down and I listened to the sounds of his father at work. Almost two minutes later, Jake was back. "Sorry it took so long. All I can tell you for sure is his car's in the lot. No one else seems to be there."

"Great. Thanks." I got ready to hang up and then stopped. "Jake, do me a favor. If you see him leave in the next ten or fifteen minutes, let me know. It's important."

"Anything Dad or I can help with?"

"Not right now, but maybe later."

"Just let me know." Now he paused before saying anything else. "Is this anything to do with why Lexie tore out of here instead of leaving her car like she planned? She got a call, said she had to leave and burned rubber as she drove off."

"It does. I'll explain later." Or Lexie would. "Thanks again."

I dropped the phone onto the console between my seat and Rafe's and thought hard for a moment. Then I swiveled around some so I could see Quinn and Ciara.

"Sawyer appears to be at his office. Bubba—sorry, Jake—says his car is there. So that's our first stop. I think it's time I had a discussion with that little bastard. The two of you don't have to go in. In fact, it would probably be best if you don't. I don't guarantee I won't step over the line."

The sisters looked at one another and then back at me. "We're going in," Quinn said. "He'll probably shit his pants to see the three of us and Rafe."

Rafe didn't say anything, but one corner of his mouth lifted in a grin.

"How do you want to play this?" Rafe asked as he pulled over half a block from Sawyer's office. "My bet is he has cameras and will see us pull up and lock the door."

Now I grinned, looking forward to confronting a childhood nemesis. "Trust me, a locked door isn't going to keep me out."

He nodded, apparently satisfied, and continued to the office. As he parked, I studied the area. This was more of a fall from grace for Sawyer than I thought. The office sat in the middle of what looked like it had originally been built as a small strip mall. Instead, as warehouses began to spring up, it had been converted into cheap office space. The parking lot was pitted and in need of resurfacing. I doubted any of the lights worked. Paint on the building itself was peeling and most of the storefronts were boarded up. In fact, at the moment it looked as if Sawyer's was the only office that was actually open.

I climbed out of the SUV and stretched. I rotated my head, hearing my neck crack. Then I knelt on one knee. As I placed a hand on a spot where the pavement had broken away to reveal the dirt beneath, I pulled on my Earth magic. I sensed small creatures, probably rats and mice, maybe a feral cat or two, in the immediate area. Then there was Sawyer. Even from here, out of sight and with the walls of the building between us, his aura screamed of anger and frustration but overriding that was desperation.

Well, he ain't seen nothing yet.

I stood and quickly closed the distance to the office door. Like most commercial doors, it was a combination of metal and glass. And, as Rafe predicted, locked. I shook my head, amusement filling me. So many forgot that being an Earth elemental meant I could manipulate metals, even composites and manmade metals because they all originated in the Earth.

I placed my right hand over the lock and focused. My palm grew warm and the metal beneath my hand began singing to me. A moment later, the lock *snicked* open. Grinning, I pulled the door open and stepped into what could euphemistically be called a waiting room. At least it had a couple of battered, discolored plastic chairs and a coffee table that looked like it had been dragged out of a dumpster.

A security door on the far wall prevented entry to the private area of the office. Not that it kept us from hearing the sounds of someone hastily gathering things together. Rafe bent and whispered in my ear that he was going to take a stroll around back in case Sawyer decided to do a bolt. I nodded and waited, giving him time to get in place. Then I moved to stand in front of the security door, a smile on my lips.

"Sawyer, we can do this the easy way or the fun way," I called out. "Open the door or I will open it for you."

The only answer was the sound of more things being moved around from the other side of the door.

I motioned the others back. Then I closed my eyes and opened my senses. I reached for the source of all my power: the Earth. Every cell came to life as energy filled me. When I opened my eyes, I knew they glowed a bright green. I could open this door the same way I had the front door but I wanted to go for effect. It was past time to remind Sawyer just who and what he was dealing with.

My fingers flew through a complicated series of motions as I drew sigils in the air. Quinn gasped as she watched them hang there before me. The I slid my right foot back. I drew my hands toward my chest. Focusing on the sigils and on the energies I'd called, I shoved my hands forward, sending the sigils flying at the door. It blew open with a bang and then hung by a single hinge. I stepped through and looked around.

"Going somewhere?"

I waved a hand as Sawyer turned and raced toward the back door. He went sprawling across the yellowed tile, stopping at Rafe's feet as he stepped inside the rear door. Before I could say anything else, Rafe grabbed Sawyer by the collar and dragged him to a chair where he unceremoniously dumped the man.

"I'll have you all arrested!" Sawyer tried to stand only to be shoved back by Rafe.

"Please, call the sheriff. Then explain to him why you have failed to return his calls. Explain to the media why you have been in a conspiracy with Mia Caldwell to not only prevent Annie Caldwell from being elected DA but to kidnap her son. Explain to your mother why you are going to prison where I guarantee you will make some con very happy."

He paled and looked around, as if hoping for some avenue of escape to miraculously appear.

"Here's how it's going to go," I continued. "You're going to sit there and answer our questions without hesitation and without leaving anything out. Then you're going to write it all down and wait for the sheriff or one of his deputies to arrive. You will cooperate fully with him. If you don't, I promise you will not like what comes next."

"Threatening me? I'll have you in prison and your father installed in your place with the company."

"Oh, Joe Bob, you really must get your memory checked. Have you forgotten how foolish it was to force my hand when we were younger? Do you really want to do so now, when I am so much stronger and can do so much more than I did then?"

He paled some more and swallowed hard. Before he could say anything, Quinn stepped forward. She looked bored and began juggling fireballs, something I knew she'd never normally do. But she was adding her bit to the scene I'd been setting and I loved her for it.

"I really wouldn't try to argue with her, Sawyer." Ciara joined her sister. As she did, she focused on a stack of papers on the corner of the man's desk. A moment later, they lifted and began to swirl around, as if caught in a small tornado.

"And don't mind me." Rafe rested a heavy hand on Sawyer's shoulder. "I'm just the muscle, not that these ladies need it."

"Question number one." I held up a finger, waiting until he focused on me. "Did you search out Mia and tell her to come to town, that you could help her get Robbie back or did she search you out?"

"Remember, we can verify the information by checking your files, not to mention your phone and bank records," Quinn said.

For several long moments, he didn't say anything. Then Ciara took a step toward a single battered file cabinet in the corner of the office.

"All right!" His hands rested on the arms of the chair and I wondered if he was going to try to stand. Part of me wanted to just to watch Rafe shove him back. But that would only take time we didn't have. "I searched her out. I knew if I convinced her to come to town, she'd be enough of a distraction that bitch might not run against me."

"Now, now, it isn't nice to call names," I chided. I was definitely enjoying this too much. "Does she really want Robbie or is she just out to hurt Sam and Annie?"

"Or is going after Robbie your idea?" Ciara put in.

"M-my idea but she agreed."

"When did you first contact her?"

"Six-eight weeks ago. Does it matter?"

It mattered a great deal, but I wasn't going to tell him. Not yet at any rate. But it did lead to my next question.

"When did she actually get here?"

"Not long after that. Maybe a week, if that, after I called her."

It fit. God damn it, it fit.

Anger rising, I forced it down. Much as I wanted to beat some sense into him, I couldn't. I still needed information from him.

"Where is she now?"

"Don't know. Don't care. She's caused more trouble than good since getting here."

Well, that's something we could agree on.

"When did you last talk to her?"

"This morning. Told her to find herself another attorney. I have bigger fish to fry right now." He grinned at me.

Poor sod, he really thought he had a chance of winning against me and Bitsy.

"Why did she call?"

He didn't answer. Rafe arched one brow at me over Sawyer's head and I nodded.

"I suggest you answer her. Otherwise, the two of us are going to have a chat while the ladies take a walk. Trust me, they are the nice ones. I'm a vet with PTSD. No jury will convict me." He rested his hands on Sawyer's shoulders and dug in with his fingers.

"All right!"

"See, that wasn't too hard, was it?" I crossed my arms and waited until Sawyer nodded. "But let's talk about something else for a moment. Tell me about Kerwin Jones."

Sawyer blinked, surprised by the question. "Don't know him."

Before I could respond, Ciara did. Before I could tell her no, she sent a gust of wind at him strong enough to throw him from the chair. Yet she maintained enough control of it that it didn't so much as ruffle Rafe's hair.

"She warned you what would happen if you lied," she said coldly. "Now answer her question."

"Okay!" He rubbed his hands over his face before looking at me. "He's a client."

"Really? Then why did you refuse his call from the jail after his latest arrest?"

"I-I figured it would be bad optics to represent him since he was accused of trying to run over a dog."

Quinn growled and I bit back a smile.

"Really? It had nothing to do with the fact he'd been seen trying to make entry onto the Caldwell's property or that he is a suspect in the attack on Annie?"

He paled and swallowed hard. "I don't know that he did any of that."

"Don't know or don't want to know?" Ciara asked.

He hung his head.

"Look at me!" I snapped. "Did he attack Annie in her house?"

"I don't know!"

"Did you introduce him to Mia or put them in contact in any way?"

He nodded.

Well, that answered one question.

"Final question. Where is Mia right now?"

"Don't know. Don't care. She said she was leaving town as soon as she finished some business here."

My heart skipped a beat. That little bastard knew what she planned and did nothing to stop her. "Where's she staying?"

"Again, don't know and don't care."

I thought for a moment, considering my option. As much as I wanted to be the truth out of him, I didn't dare. I wanted him to stand trial for what he'd done. But he held the key to locating Mia. I simply didn't know how.

"Give me his phone." Ciara held out her hand and waited as Rafe searched Sawyer before tossing her a cellphone that looked as if it had seen better days. She took it and activated it, muttering about how she loved it when the bad guys were stupid enough not to lock their home screens. A moment later, she pulled out her own phone and placed a call to someone, giving them Sawyer's number and another number I assumed must be Mia's. "I need the second number pinged for location. It's related to the Amber Alert out of Harkin County. . . Thanks. . . Yes, call me back on this number. I'm in the field."

"I told you what you wanted. Now get the hell out of my office."

"Not yet," Rafe said, patting Sawyer's shoulder like they were old friends. "You have one more thing to do. Write everything down, every detail. Don't leave anything out."

Quinn tossed a legal pad to Sawyer and chuckled as he fumbled to catch it. "Write."

It took longer than I wanted, but he finally finished. I read it over and then passed it to Quinn. With Ciara looking over her shoulder, they read the five pages and then nodded. Quinn handed the tablet back to me and stepped toward Sawyer, pulling a pair of handcuffs as she did.

"On your feet," she ordered.

Rafe expedited matters by grabbing Sawyer's collar and hauling him to his feet.

"Joe Bob Sawyer, you are under arrest for charges including but not limited to harassment, stalking, conspiracy and anything else the sheriff can think of." She pulled his arms behind him and cuffed him. Then she finished reading him his Miranda rights.

"And I will make sure the state investigates as well. There may even be federal charges since you used the internet and phones to bring Mia in from out-of-state," Ciara added.

As she did, Quinn checked out the rest of the office. When she turned back to us, she grinned and nodded to the door she stood next to.

"Filing room. The door locks."

That was all the encouragement Rafe need. He marched Sawyer into the small room and tossed him inside. Telling him to relax and enjoy having some alone time, he closed and locked the door. As he did, Quinn pulled her phone and quickly called her husband. Without going into detail—or giving Lucas time to say anything—she told him to get to Sawyer's office. She had a gift for him. Two, actually. The first was on the man's desk and the second was in the file room. Then she ended the call and grinned.

"We have probably five minutes max before he gets here. I suggest we get the hell out before he arrives."

I nodded and followed everyone to the outer office. Once there, I had Rafe help me lift the door leading to the back offices into place. I focused, picturing the door as it had been before I blasted it open. Sweat poured off me as I manipulated the energies and then the door itself. When I finally stepped back, it was back in place and nothing showed it had ever been knocked off its hinges.

"Let's go."

Hopefully, Ciara's contact would get back to her soon. Every moment that passed as a moment that put Robbie further out of our reach.

"Where the hell are you?" Meg demanded.

I chuckled, picturing her look of frustration, and put the call on speaker.

"Damn it, Jax, where are the four of you? And why the hell did Lucas race out of here a few minutes ago, muttering something about how he better not have to arrest all of you?"

"Let's say we left him a present, all wrapped up." Quinn hit the back of my head even as Ciara laughed softly. "Meg, can you talk?" I didn't want Sam and Annie overhearing.

"Yeah. I felt the need to stretch my legs."

"All right. We have a location—well, a general location—for Mia."

"Where?" I heard the sound of keys and knew she was heading for her car.

I gave her the location Ciara's contact had sent. "Meg, I don't know what we're going to be walking into. So don't tell Sam and Annie. Not yet. But contact Dr. Pat and ask her to meet us." I paused. I didn't want her getting there before we did. Before I could figure out a good meeting point, Quinn broke in and gave Meg the name of what sounded like a convenience store of some sort.

"Got it. I should be there in twenty, thirty minutes."

"Bring Amy and her grandmother as well."

"And Mom," Ciara said. "We might need all the guardians for this."

I nodded, not liking the idea of them being in what could be a fire zone. But she was right. We didn't know what we might find.

"How do we do this?" Rafe asked as he pulled off the highway onto a two lane road.

I'd been thinking about that since leaving Sawyer's office. "You need to find some place out of sight of the cabin to park. Then I'm going to shift and take a closer look. We're far enough in the country, a coyote roaming through won't be anything out of the ordinary."

"There are other ways. We can keep an eye on the cabin until backup arrives," Quinn said, repeating what Lucas had said in his last call.

I shook my head. "She doesn't give a damn for Robbie. If she gets spooked, she will use him as a shield--or—worse."

"You just don't take any chances," Rafe said, glancing across at me.

I didn't say anything because that was a promise I couldn't keep, not if Robbie was in danger.

Fifteen minutes later, Rafe pulled off the dirt road he'd taken after we entered the camping area. Wayman Park had been established a decade or so earlier and sat in both Denton and Harkin Counties. That meant this could turn into a jurisdiction nightmare, another reason none of us wanted to wait. Now, sitting in the idling SUV, we studied the map of the area Rafe picked up at the park entrance. The attendant on duty told us, after checking both Quinn's and Ciara's badges, that one of the six cabins on this side of the park was occupied. We were parked a mere five-hundred yards or so from there.

Everyone else climbed out of the SUV and checked the perimeter. As they did, I climbed into back. It didn't take long for me to strip. Then I pictured my coyote self. Pain overtook me and I curled on the leather seat, hoping I didn't damage it too badly. Then I chuckled, at least I think I did. I hurt too badly to be sure. If Quinn thought her dogs would be pissed when she let me in while shifted before, what would this do to them?

Panting, I stood and shook, getting used to four legs and paws.

Then I barked, hoping someone let me out. A moment later, the back door opened. I scented Rafe and jumped down. I pushed my head against his hand. He scratched my ears. Then he apologized. If I could have frowned I would. Then I saw Quinn approaching, something in her hands.

"Can I put this on you?" She knelt in front of me and held out a wide leather collar, probably one she used on one of the Mals.

I bobbed my head up and then down, the closest I could come to saying yes. Then I sat on my rear haunches and let her fasten the collar in place. As she did, I hoped no one looked too closely, especially Mia. If she saw it, she'd know I wasn't a wild coyote and that could blow our plan to pieces.

"Jax." Quinn touched the side of my head and I looked at her. She held something else, something I didn't recognize right away. "It's a camera. We'll be able to see what you do. It fits on the collar. Okay?"

I did the strange up and down nod of my head.

As Quinn secured the camera, Ciara did something with her phone. Probably checking the image. Quinn glanced up at her and she nodded.

"All set. No risks, remember."

I let my tongue loll out the side of my mouth. Then I reached up and licked her cheek. Quinn scrubbed at the wet mark I left as the others laughed. Without giving her a chance to stand, I butted her with my head, sending her onto her backside.

"Okay, okay," she laughed as she tried to fend me off. "You win. Just quit licking me. It's like kissing my sister."

I chuffed once and then trotted off, picturing the map and our current location in relation to the cabin as I did.

Before rounding the curve leading to the cabin, I veered off the road. Keeping low to the ground, the tall grass hopefully camouflaging my movements, I emerged from the trees. I paused, sitting up enough for the camera to have a good view of the cabin. The same car seen at the school when Robbie went missing was parked out front. The cabin door was shut, the drapes pulled across the windows. From where I sat, I couldn't tell if anyone was inside, but my money was on both Mia and Robbie being there.

"I wanna go home!"

My ears flattened against my skull and I growled softly. Robbie sounded scared and mad. But he was all right. At least relatively speaking. Now to figure out how to get him away from the bitch who gave birth to him and then abandoned him.

"Shut up!"

I ran forward half a dozen steps and stopped as the sounds of skin striking skin filled the early afternoon air. It was followed by a cry of pain. Every piece of fur stood on end and I growled again. I could only imagine how the others were reacting as they watched and listened to the video feed.

Keeping low, I made my way back to the trees then I broke into a run.

"Get this fucking thing off of me," I growled ten minutes later when I finished shifting back to human. Quinn dropped to her knees next to me and quickly removed the collar and camera. Then she handed me my clothes, watching as I quickly dressed. "How long before the others get here?"

Even as I asked, the sounds of approaching cars reached up. Moments later, Meg and Amy parked their cars behind the SUV. People piled out. While Ciara and Rafe caught them up on what we knew, Quinn led me a short distance away.

"What else can you tell me?" she asked.

I shook my head. "They're inside the cabin but I couldn't see them. Robbie's alive. She's hurt him and terrorized him. I'm worried about what she'll do if we don't make our move soon."

"Mundane or arcane?" she asked simply.

"Arcane. It's our best way of keeping Robbie safe."

I hoped.

She nodded and called her sister and Meg over. As she did, I smiled slightly. All four elements were represented. Good. That settled how I wanted to handle at least the first part of our attempt to free Robbie and deal with Mia once and for all.

With Lexie and Amy, along with Rafe, watching our backs, we moved closer to the cabin. Each of us took a compass point. Earth to the north, Fire to the south. Air to the east and Water to the west. We formed a circle that came alive with power as our magic flowed together. I knelt, my right palm against the ground. My energies mixed and melded with the Earth's and I studied the energies flowing around and through the house.

Meg, standing to the east, held her hands high above her head. The wind began to pick up and lightning danced between her fingers. Quinn stood opposite me. Her hands were extended in front of her, palms up. Fire danced from her fingers, growing as it reached toward the sky. Ciara, our jack-of-all trades stood opposite Meg. Like me, she knelt on one knee and her palm rested on the bare earth. I saw the water in the earth as well as in the air begin to respond to her call. Our energies joined and began to bind together. It was as if a protective shell formed, starting below the earth and then towering above us and closing over the house.

I stood and tied my energies to the others. As I stepped forward, Amy took my place. Rafe followed as I ran, keeping as low to the ground as I could, toward the cabin. Power built inside me, flowing through me and down my arms to my hands. I leapt, my boots sliding on the porch as I landed. Without pausing, I blasted the front door.

It exploded in a shower of splinters. I enclosed them in a bubble, making sure they couldn't hurt Robbie, wherever he was. A second later, I broke the energy bubble and the debris fell harmlessly to the floor. Riding my fury, I stepped through the door, my magic close to hand, my animal side closer.

"You!" Mia spun toward me.

"Dr. Jax!" Robbie tried to run to me but she stopped him.

"Let him go," I snarled as she wrapped an arm around his neck and held him against her. Too small to be a shield, he would be a weapon she'd gladly use against me. . . if I let her.

"Not a chance in hell. His father's going to learn what it's like to lose everything he loves. He took that from me when he refused to leave the Army. He came back a near cripple and expected me to take care of him. Then, when he healed and started making money, he refused to give me my fair share."

"You don't care about Robbie. Let him go. We'll work out everything else."

I needed the boy away from her. She was too close to the emotional ledge. If she went over, I knew she'd hurt him simply because it would hurt Sam. At least I didn't see a weapon of any sort.

Yet.

"Dr. Jax." Tears ran down his cheeks as he tried to break free.

"It's okay, Robbie." I smiled and hoped I wasn't lying. Then I turned my attention back to Mia. "You need to pay very close attention to what I say right now. If you want to walk out of here, you do it now, without the boy." I cocked my head to one side, listening. "Hear that?" In the distance, sirens sounded. I knew Lucas and probably half of the Sheriff's Department was on the way. "That's the cops. They get here and all bets are off."

"I don't like the odds." She held Robbie closer.

Anger rising, I tried to figure out the best way to get us all out of this alive. Then I heard a step behind me. Every instinct screamed for me to turn, to see who was there. But I trusted the others. I knew they had my back. More than that, I doubted anyone save Miss Serena and possibly Judith would be able to get through our workings. Still, a bead of sweat ran down my spine and I felt my powers gathering.

"Robbie, look at me." I kept my eyes on Mia as I spoke. "In ten seconds, she's going to let you go. When she does, I want you to run outside. Don't look back. Don't slow down. Not until you're with Rafe, Quinn and the others. Do you understand?"

He nodded, sniffling.

"You're not going anywhere, boy." Mia glared at me, daring me to contradict her.

I smiled confidently. I felt more alive than I had in a very long time as I pulled power from the earth. The energy pulsed inside of me, the arcane version of the beat of war drums. At my side, the fingers of my right hand drew sigil after sigil in the air, focusing the power, narrowing the target. Mia, being a normal, couldn't see them but it surprised me she couldn't feel the change in the atmosphere inside the cabin.

Suddenly, from behind her, a glass flew off the table, smashing against the wall. A picture fell off the wall. A door slammed. The cabin began to shake as tremors woke the earth below our feet.

I drew more power and then fed it into the ground beneath the cabin. The walls creaked and groaned as the tremors grew stronger. Mia looked around frantically as a window in the rear of the cabin shattered. The cabin gave a lurch as the ground rolled. My gaze never left Mia as I waited, feet braced, ready to act.

"What are you doing, you bitch?" She cried out and staggered when the cabin seemed to rise in the air before dropping back down to earth.

Her grip on Robbie loosened as she fought to maintain her balance. I darted forward. My hand closed around Robbie's arm and I pulled him free. Mia grabbed for him, her fingers brushing against the thin material of his tee shirt. He cried out and launched himself in my direction. I spun, pushing him toward the door, all but throwing him into Rafe's arms.

"Run!"

I didn't wait to see if they obeyed. Instead, I pivoted again. Mia regained her footing. Without Robbie as a shield, she darted toward the back of the cabin. I snarled, wishing there was time to shift. No way was I letting her get away.

One step. Two. I dove for her. My shoulder hit her in the small of the back. My arms wrapped around her and I rode her down. She cried out, a mixture of pain and fury, as we hit the floor. I *oofed* in pain when her head slammed back, striking me in the face. Well, two can play that game.

Elbows flew, feet kicked as she fought against me, trying to roll onto her back. Idiot. I grabbed a fistful of hair and slammed her head against the floor. I got an elbow in the kidney as a reward.

We tumbled along the floor as the cabin stopped trembling. Hands and fists flew. She fought light a girl, pulling my hair and trying to bite anywhere she could. Her nails raked my face, bringing tears to my eyes. I shoved her off and rolled away. When I touched my cheek, my fingers came away bloody.

Bitch. She'd pay for that.

Mia cursed, tears running down her cheeks, as she climbed stiffly to her feet. For a moment, we circled one another like two fighters from a bad B movie. Okay, more like a C or D, maybe even an F movie. Her eyes darted around the room, looking for a weapon or an avenue of escape or who knows what. I waited, breathing deeply, trying to ignore the aches and pains that ate away at my focus. It would be so easy to give in to the urge to use my gifts to level her, to wipe her from the Earth. But I couldn't. I wouldn't. This needed to be done right and, as much as I wanted to hurt her, I wouldn't do it. I wouldn't abuse my talents that way.

I would not walk down that dark path.

Mia lunged, but not where I expected. Instead of trying to flee to the rear of the cabin where she could lock herself in the bathroom or climb out a window, she all but leapt across the kitchen to the drainboard. Plates and utensils clattered together as she plunged her hand into the sink. Light glinted off of metal as she turned, butcher knife in hand.

Damn it!

Well, I wasn't exactly without weapons of my own.

"I'll teach you to interfere in my business, bitch!"

Mia feinted with her left hand and then slashed out with the right. A sharp kiss of pain burned my side. The sound of material ripping filled the air, drowned out a moment later as I gasped. Instinctively, I lifted my left hand, trying to block her next blow. I hissed as pain radiated from from hand to elbow. All control lost, I dropped to my knees as my walker side fought for dominance.

"You're gonna die, bitch."

Mia's foot caught me in the ribs and I fell to all fours. Bile rose in my throat. I curled in on myself as she kicked me again. Consciousness receded and I shook it off.

No!

I wasn't going to let this bitch win!

I couldn't.

"Stop!"

Air blasted through the cabin, sending me tumbling along the floor. Mia cried out. I lifted my head and watched as she flew through the air. Her head hit the far wall with a sickening thud. For a moment, she stood there. Then her eyes rolled back and she crumpled to the floor.

It was over.

Robbie was safe.

Now if I could just find enough strength to get out of the cabin. I didn't care if I had to crawl. I just wanted out.

"Easy, baby." I opened my eyes and saw Rafe kneeling next to me. "Let's get you out of here."

"Mia?"

He nodded and I turned my head, watching as Ciara rolled an unconscious Mia onto her stomach and cuffed her.

"Now let's get you out of here."

He gently gathered me in his arms and carried me outside. The moment he stepped off the porch, Robbie raced forward.

"Let me down."

Fortunately, Rafe kept an arm around my waist because I would have fallen on my ass when Robbie all but wrapped himself around me. Carefully, doing my best not to let him know how badly I hurt, I hugged him. Then I tilted his face up to look at me. As I did, a fresh wave of anger washed over me to see the bruise on his cheek where Mia hit him.

"You okay, kiddo?"

He nodded, still clinging to me.

"Want to talk to your mom and dad?"

Another nod.

Moving carefully, I pulled my phone out of my pocket. After unlocking it, I programmed in Annie's number. She answered before the first ring ended and I had no doubt everyone still at the house listened in.

"Jax?" Tears roughened her voice. She was so scared, not that I blamed her.

"Hey, I've got a really brave young man here who wants to say hi." Annie sobbed in relief as I handed Robbie the phone. As I did, Quinn appeared and led him away from the cabin. Rafe once again swung me up in his arms and I hissed in pain.

"Sorry, love."

"Don't. Just get me to the SUV. I'm sure they've got a medical kit there." Besides, Lucas and others from the SD had arrived. I'd prefer not having to deal with them until I didn't hurt so badly.

"How about a hospital instead?" he suggested.

"Dr. Pat."

We discussed it all the way back to the SUV. Then he settled me in the backseat. Amy slid in, kneeling on the floorboard as she helped me lie back. Rafe closed the door and, a moment later, slid in behind the steering wheel. By the time he started the engine, Amy had me settled and was lifting my shirt to see where I'd been injured.

"Hospital," she said simply.

"No." I shook my head. There was still too much to do for me to go to the hospital where they'd just poke and probe and not let me rest.

"Yes. My grandmother and Dr. Pat have given us our orders. If you don't like it, you can argue with them when we get there."

Before I could say anything else, she lay her right hand on my forehead. Warmth spread out from her palm and my eyes grew heavy. By the time we pulled out of the park, I gave up fighting and went under.

One week later, I stepped outside and paused. A smile touched my lips and I lifted a hand as Ali and Robbie greeted me before racing off, their dogs and Fenris on their heels. A light breeze rustled the leaves of the trees. Birds sang overhead and insects rustled in the grass beyond the deck.

Home.

It still felt strange to know I was a homeowner. Every night this week, Rafe worked at the house, doing all he could to help get it ready for me to "officially" move in. Each day, Sam sent over crews to paint, replace the carpet and linoleum with hardwood floors and make sure the plumbing and electrical were up to code. He even had plans drawn up for a pool out back. Construction on that would begin in the next week or two.

Last night was my last in the caretaker's house where I'd been staying while the crews worked. As he had every night since we rescued Robbie, Rafe stayed with me. Life was good, at least for now.

A little before six this morning, Rafe woke me. The only reason he still lived was because he handed me a large mug of coffee before I realized how early it was. Then he told me to get dressed. The others would be there soon to start moving me the rest of my belongings into the house. My only job was to supervise. When I opened my mouth to argue, he reminded me Dr. Pat had yet to release me to do anything strenuous.

Besides, wouldn't I enjoy telling Quinn and the others what to do?

An hour later, the "crew" arrived. Rafe, Sam, Lucas and Drew unlocked the storage container that had been taking up part of the front drive for the last two weeks. Then they carried in the last of my furniture from New Braunfels. A delivery truck arrived mid-morning with furniture I ordered after signing the purchase papers on the house.

What I hadn't expected was the pickup truck and trailer that arrived shortly before noon. Jimmy Reardon and one of the hands got out and began unloading. With Quinn on one side and Ciara on the other, I stood there, shaking my head. From the shine of the wood to the obvious quality of construction, I knew without asking each piece was expensive and probably antique.

"Where do you want these, Doc?" Reardon asked as Drew and Lucas carried a roll top desk out of the trailer.

Before I could answer, Miss Serena drove up. She parked behind the trailer, giving the men enough room to work. Then she climbed out of her Lincoln and moved in my direction.

"Close your mouth," Quinn whispered.

I did, but it took effort. "Miss Serena?" I motioned to the furniture.

"My housewarming gift," she said with a smile. "It isn't much."

Isn't much?

It looked like enough to furnish and office for me as well as a bedroom and then there were the smaller pieces: lamps, coffee tables, even a box labeled fragile/china.

"I-I can't." Although I really liked the look of the desk.

"Jax, you'll be doing me a favor accepting it." When I looked at her in question, she continued. "These were in storage, along with enough furniture to furnish several houses. They'll do better here than locked away where they aren't being cared for."

I walked across the lawn and stopped at the desk, running a hand over the smooth wood. It felt warm to the touch, a warmth that had nothing to do with the morning sun. Someone had loved this desk and cared for it and the wood still resonated with it.

"Whose was this?" I asked as I turned to face her.

Her expression softened and she smiled slightly as memories returned. I could tell they were good memories and hoped she'd share them with me one day.

"My father's. It sat in his office downtown until he retired. Then he put it in storage because he had a full office already set up at the house."

"This should go to Amy then," I protested.

"She doesn't want it. She prefers my desk, which happens to also have been my father's."

"Thank you." I hurried to her side and hugged her. Somehow, I'd find a way to repay her for all this.

"Welcome home, Jax." She patted my cheek and then looked around. "Drew, Rafe, there are two trays and a cooler in the backseat. Will you take them inside?"

"Yes, ma'am." Rafe trotted down the front steps in the direction of the Lincoln where Drew joined him.

"I brought lunch for everyone," she explained. "Don't overdo, Jax, and don't forget dinner at my house tomorrow." She kissed my cheek and returned to her car. A few moments later, she drove off, Reardon and the hand following behind in the pickup with its trailer.

Six hours later, my home was furnished and I could officially "move in".

Now everyone lounged on the back deck. Rafe and Sam manned one of the largest grills I'd ever seen. Drew hauled a cooler filled with beer, water and soft drinks out from the kitchen. Ali and Robbie ran around the backyard, their dogs and Fenris barking happily as they chased the kids, fetched tennis balls and played tag.

"We needed this, Jax. Thanks," Annie said as she slipped an arm around my waist.

"I should be thanking all of you." I gave her a light hip bump. "You've gone above and beyond the call of friendship."

She shook her head as she watched the kids play. Then she glanced at the travel crib a few feet away. The twins slept inside, oblivious to everything going on around them.

"Jax, when are you going to believe that we love you and want to do for you the way you do for us?"

Watching my friends—my family—I smiled slightly. "I've always known you felt that way, Annie. It's just hard sometimes to believe I deserve it."

"You deserve it and so much more," she said firmly. "Now, how are you feeling?"

"Fine." I smiled in reassurance before she could protest. "Really, I am feeling much better. I still have to be careful how I move. But I was lucky. Mia didn't do any serious damage and Amy got the bleeding stopped pretty quickly. Dr. Pat's checked on me every day. Judith and Miss Serena have done several healing sessions with me. You don't have to worry."

"We're always going to worry," Quinn said as she joined us. "Mainly because we love you. Then there's the fact you do tend rush headlong into danger if you think it will keep one of us safe."

"It's my job. I'm the rogue." I grinned, wondering if they had yet to figure out just how true my words were.

"Let's go into the kitchen for a minute," Quinn suggested as she motioned to Meg and Ciara. "They guys are happy playing with the grill and they kids are having fun with the dogs. Besides, we need to talk."

Curious, wondering what they had in mind, I followed her inside, Annie on my heels. As we waited for Ciara and Meg to join us, I walked to the large, stainless steel fridge that came with the house. It was much more fridge than I needed but it fit the kitchen. I hoped the day would come—and soon—when I wasn't the only one living here. For now, it was filled with beer, wine, soft drinks and more food than I knew what to do with. I grabbed a beer and turned to face my friends who now stood shoulder-to-shoulder like a united front.

"What?"

"You're still worried about something. What?" Annie asked.

I shrugged. I was still worried, but I really didn't want to get into it today. We all needed an evening to relax and enjoy ourselves. More than that, Robbie needed to see us acting normally. It was one of the last things necessary for him to realize life went on and he'd never have to worry about Mia again.

"C'mon, Jax. What's bothering you?" Quinn looked at me in concern and I knew they weren't going to let the subject drop.

"Have any of you heard from Maddy?" While it didn't exactly answer Annie's question, it also wasn't an evasion. I was worried about our friend, very worried.

"I love her, you all know that," I said when they only looked at one another. "But I'm worried. You were there when I called her. That's been what? Two weeks ago? More?"

They nodded.

"Have any of you heard from her since then?"

No one said anything for a moment. Then Quinn cursed softly. One by one, they admitted they hadn't heard from her either.

"Dr. Pat hasn't heard from her either."

I gave them a moment for that to sink in. "Yeah." I nodded grimly. "Despite knowing what's been going on, she hasn't contacted her mother once since my call."

"Could whatever is happening here be affecting her?" Meg asked.

"I don't know." I tipped up my beer bottle and took a long draw. "As I said, I don't know, but I plan to find out. If one of us hasn't heard from her by end of week, I'm flying to London a week from Monday. Dr. Pat and Amy are coming with me."

"Should you be gone right now?" Annie asked in concern.

I shrugged. "I don't know but I can't just sit here if she's in trouble." They knew it and, fortunately, didn't argue. "But it means each of you will have to work closely with Miss Serena and Judith, not to mention Dr. Pat and me, until then. While Dr. Pat, Amy and I are gone, you'll continue working with the others."

And that brought me to the last bit of business before we could rejoin our men and the kids.

"Annie, tomorrow night, we're going to finish the wards around your house. That will complete tying them to you. Then we'll show you how to renew them. Something you'll have to do from time to time. We'll head to your place next, Meg, to do the same thing."

And after that, Miss Serena, Judith, Dr. Pat and I would begin renewing the wards around the town.

"You're really worried, aren't you?" Ciara moved to where I stood and reached for one of my hands, her expression concerned.

I nodded.

"I can't explain it any better than saying I know something is coming. Something bad. Something that wants to destroy the town and all we love. I plan to do everything I can to prevent it." I glanced at each of them, knowing what I was about to ask of them would forever change their lives. "If we're going to have any hope of coming out of this, we need your help. Will you each step up and join us?"

They didn't hesitate. Just like when we were kids, they nodded. I held out my right hand, palm down. Annie's hand covered it. Meg reached over and placed her hand on Annie's. Quinn's came next and then Ciara's. I smiled, relief filling me, and turned my hand over. As my palm met Annie's, power built between us, surrounding us, confirming and strengthening our ties.

"We'd better join the others before they decide to come looking for us."

As if on cue, Ali and Robbie appeared at the wide glass doors leading to the deck.

"C'mon." Quinn draped an arm around my shoulders and grinned. "You and Rafe can tell us when you're getting married."

I spluttered and choked. Without thinking, I reached up and touched the chain under my tee shirt. Rafe's dog tag hung from it. This morning, he added something else, telling me that way it would stay safe until later. Then he'd kissed me and the doorbell rang, signaling the arrival of the first of our friends.

What would Quinn say if she knew about the ring secured on the chain? It might be worth the fuss my friends would cause over not being told sooner to have Rafe remove it from the chain and put it on my hand when we finished dinner.

But I might let it stay where it was. For tonight at least. I wanted to celebrate privately with Rafe, let him know how much I looked forward to spending the rest of my life with him. Quinn and her interference could wait.

I looked at my friends, my sisters, and smiled. I might be the protector, the rogue always out to champion those unable to champion themselves, but Quinn was the one who kept me grounded. Annie was my conscience, Meg my counselor and Ciara my partner in crime.

Heaven help Mossy Creek.

And Hell had best be ready to welcome anyone who dared stand against us.

AUTHOR'S NOTE

When I first started writing about Mossy Creek and its denizens, I had no idea it would turn into a series. But there is something about the town that keeps pulling me back in. I hope you've enjoyed this latest installment as much as I enjoyed writing it.

Here's where I ask for your help. If you enjoyed the book, please let your friends and family know. Take a few moments and leave a review. The best advertisement an author can get are recommendations from our readers.

Going forward, Jax, Quinn, Annie and the rest are in for a rough ride. There will be a price to pay for letting the town's protections weaken. Who will walk out on the other side has yet to be determined. But you know our determined cast of characters are going to do all they can to protect those they care for and the town they love.

Look for *Magic Rising*, book 5 in the Eerie Side of the Tracks series, January 2021 (or sooner, if my muse doesn't do something unexpected like throw another book at me).